P9-CFO-800

BLUEPRINTS OF THE AFTERLIFE

Also by Ryan Boudinot

The Littlest Hitler

Misconception

BLUEPRINTS OF THE AFTERLIFE

RYAN BOUDINOT

Black Cat

a paperback original imprint of Grove/Atlantic, Inc.

New York

Published simultaneously in Canada
Printed in the United States of America

FIRST EDITION

ISBN: 978-0-8021-7091-0

Black Cat
a paperback original imprint of Grove/Atlantic, Inc.
841 Broadway
New York, NY 10003

Distributed by Publishers Group West

www.groveatlantic.com

12 13 14 15 10 9 8 7 6 5 4 3 2 1

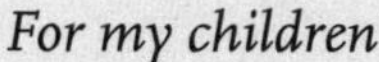

For my children

BLUEPRINTS OF THE AFTERLIFE

WOO-JIN

The world was full of precious garbage. Woo-jin passed through it on his way home from work, scanning the field at the end of the runway for aluminum cans, bits of copper wire, rare earth elements scavenged from junked computers. He found a beer box, but whoever'd left it hadn't put the empties back in their cardboard cubicles. He kicked the box and swung a plastic bag of rescued leftovers from his finger. As a professional dishwasher he only rescued food from the trash when he was certain none of his coworkers would catch him. If they spotted the clamshell box on top of the Hobart washer they'd think it was an order somebody never picked up from the takeout window, and if they happened to see that the burger inside had a bite out of it, they'd think it was Woo-jin who had bitten the bite rather than it being a burger that had already had a bite taken out of it. He'd scraped this particular burger out of a plastic basket along with congealed gravy fries. Patsy, his foster sister, was going to want that burger,

Woo-jin knew. He could either eat the burger and gravy fries now, in the field, and go home stuffed but not have to share with Patsy, or he could show up with the food and have Patsy yell at him about who needed the three-quarters of a burger the most. Patsy was always talking at him about how lucky he was with his job because of all the free food. If he showed up empty-handed she accused him of not bringing food home on purpose. The only times she was really grateful was when he'd bring home a whole pie. Usually the pie was apple, or rather rhubarb. Sometimes, when he had to decide between taking something home that both he and Patsy liked or something that only he liked, he went with what only he liked so he didn't have to share. And if he didn't bring anything home he had to start right in and cook something for her anyway because usually she forgot to eat and was in a mood and yelled at him like he was a dick. Even though it was she who was growing penises out of her tits.

A UPS plane came down low like an earthquake riveted to the sky.

Glory hallelujah here was a can of Bud Light! He shook the remaining pissdroplets of beer out of it and slipped it into another white plastic bag, the one that wasn't holding the food.

Did he even like his foster sister? Patsy? He never really asked himself that question, considering her as unremarkable as the clothes he schlupped to his body or the route he walked to work. Patsy simply was. What was she anyway? What did she do? While he was at work? It was like she was part house, part TV, and part something to give the plumbing to do, a way to collect money from the government in exchange for growing drugs and tissues in her plus-sized body. She was a pharmer. How it worked was this—she'd eaten herself to a size that meant she couldn't move too good, and not moving too good meant one time she hurt herself in a bad fall and permanently messed up her back, and because her back was messed up she couldn't get a regular job, and because she couldn't get a regular job she was perfect for the job of pharming, which involved lying in bed most hours and watching inspirational videos. So she got money every month that let her eat enough to stay as plus-sized as she was and not have to get a job that asked her to move around, not like Woo-jin's where the word *hustle* came routinely sputtering from the lips of the manager. As in *hustle you bastards, we got the whole Elks Lodge to feed.* Patsy plugged her face with food and her eyes with TV. She wobbled with anger if Woo-jin didn't feed her the food they got from the money from the checks and the extra trash-saved food items from the restaurant where Woo-jin put in double shifts to pay for her to eat.

Woo-jin kicked a car muffler that was, for some reason, there. A plane took off, looked like a private jet, blowing his hair all over the place as it passed overhead.

Woo-jin didn't feel particularly hungry. If he saved the three-quarters of a burger for later, Patsy would definitely want some and might even try to eat the whole thing. If he ate it now he'd at least get it to himself but then might get really hungry later and have something not as cool to eat, like ramen noodles with no flavor packet (Patsy liked to double up on the flavor packets, so by the end of the month the only ramens left—the ones she'd taken the extra flavor packet from—tasted like packing material). There was also the issue of the fries to deal with. Even fifteen minutes after they're out of the deep fryer they start making the eater depressed on account of the coldness. Once the fat starts to congeal, well, forget you ever lived, pal. So it was because of the threat of congealing fries and the possibility he'd never get to eat the whole three-quarters of a burger that Woo-jin popped open the clamshell container and sat on a piece of airplane equipment. It was like a big refrigerator lying on its side, painted green with some sticky-outy parts.

Far down the tarmac a two-seater rose wobbling into the sky. The sky was looking purply and airbrushed like a druggie band album cover. Patsy knew a lot about druggie bands and their secret messages. She'd showed him some of the album covers in books she got at Good News Bookstore. What kind of good news was that supposed to be? News that guys in studded codpieces were controlling his mind to make him hail Satan and abuse cocaine like a goatfucker?

Woo-jin squirted ketchup from a packet he'd stashed in his jacket. He'd only taken one because technically it was stealing, so he had to make it go a long way. No fry could get more than a droplet of ketchup. It was a rationing decision. It bothered him that he'd dishonestly taken the packet, but what was he going to do? Eat congealed fries without the ketchup, like a mentally ill person? No thanks, guys. When the fries and burger were gone he put the clamshell back in its white plastic bag and proudly declared silently that he was not a litterer. In fact, he was the opposite of a litterer. Remembering the reason he'd taken a detour through this field in the first place, he looked around to see if there were maybe any redeemable cans lying around. When he looked behind the big metal piece of forgotten machinery he saw the dead girl.

Woo-jin was first all like *There go the bugs—oh no there go the bugs!* because three guesses as to what was crawling on the girl's face. She was an Asianish-looking human wearing a dirty white button-up fancy-style shirt, black pants, and one black leather boot with the other foot just bare, hanging out there. Woo-jin's three-quarters of a burger and fries rose up through his trunk and horizontally departed his face. He fell to his knees on the opposite side of the refrigerator-like machine and wheezed, then slowly rose and looked at the dead girl again, thinking, *Please no bugs this time*, but again there were the bugs! Bugs all over!

Woo-jin stumbled west toward the frontage road feeling—what's the best word—probably *bad*. Not because some girl was dead with earwig accompaniment, but because now there'd be complex questions someone was going to ask him. Most likely a cop. He didn't want to talk to any of those social people. He'd grown up talking to social people, sitting in waiting areas with complimentary brochures with titles like *Suicide's a Huge Bummer for Everyone* while the smart smiling lawyers made decisions about him in closed rooms. His ears hurt from coldness, paradoxically throbbing and hot. Patsy would have all sorts of opinions about the dead girl and would probably get him in trouble for not doing something differently. What could he possibly do? He had no phone and couldn't see the benefit of sticking around. He wished he hadn't eaten that burger. No wonder the much-appreciated guest had sent it back.

Woo-jin was twenty-five and Korean. At least in his skin he was; he'd never been to Korea. He lived in the Pacific Northwest. More specifically, he lived in a shithole. The shithole in question was some subsidized housing between the freeway and a construction storage area where backhoes and skid steers and cement trucks and cranes shoved raw material into piles at obscene hours. The trailer looked like it had been shat out of a mansion. When he showed up, shaking in his body at the door, he found Patsy where he'd last seen her, hogging the whole couch in the front room lit by TV, eating melted cookie-dough ice cream out of a gallon bucket with a wooden spoon. How much did she weigh? North of four hundred. She had a pink bow in her thin hair and was missing a front tooth. The TV was showing some action, some lady in tight, butt-complimenting leather pants firing machine pistols with both hands as she exploded backward out a skyscraper window pursued by guys in suits with semiautomatics mouthing the slow-motion words, *Tell us where the messiah is or you'll pay with your* [bleep]*ing life*. Though he'd never seen the episode before, Woo-jin recognized this to be *Stella Artaud: Newman Assassin*, from all her billboards.

"What did you bring, bitch?" Patsy said.

"I brang nothing."

"Then what's in that plastic bag?"

Woo-jin was surprised to find the takeout bag with the empty ex-burger box still inside, dangling from his finger. "It was a burger."

"You ate my burger?"

"It was a bad one. I threw it up."

"You are so so not fair. All you get to do is eat free food and drink free soda while I grow tissues all day."

"I wash dishes, too, you know," Woo-jin said.

"You look like you saw a phantom of the opera."

Woo-jin confronted the kitchen-like area and found a glass that he filled with water. Then, he drank it. "I saw a dead body," he said, and started feeling the ennui. That's the misnomer a caseworker had used for it one time. A hellish onrushing of fanged empathy.

"I need you to lance my boils," Patsy said. Woo-jin slunk back to the living room, meaning he turned around and walked two steps. Patsy sat sweating under three flickering fluorescent tubes, her head small compared to her neck. Bandages covered her left shoulder where they'd last extracted tissues.

"I'm sorry, Patsy. I feel it coming."

"What did you say about a dead body?"

"I said I saw it in a field. It was a girl, a nicely dressed girl. Bugs crawling on her." Woo-jin picked his mouth guard out of his shirt pocket and slipped it between his teeth. He tried not to look at Patsy's thick and sweating face because that would make it worse, but he couldn't help it and now he started thinking about how mean he had been to eat her burger. How selfish. This meant it was building, the flying, multitentacled, and fire-breathing ennui attack. He took off his shoes, making it as far as shoe #1, aka the left one.

On TV Stella Artaud landed on the moon roof of a limo, climbed inside, and received a drink from Dr. Uri Borden, as played by Neethan F. Jordan. Who. Woulda. Thought.

"My boils!" Patsy said. "I need my boils lanced before my caseworker comes."

Woo-jin pushed back the ennui by turning his thoughts to that old standby, puppies in party hats, and fetched the boil-lancing kit from the bathroom. Actually there was no room separately called the bathroom, only Patsy's room where the toilet was. For convenience. Patsy's walls were decorated with some of the finest unicorn posters in all the land. There was one of a unicorn being ridden by Chewbacca that Woo-jin appreciated. Sometimes while taking a dump he'd wish he could ask Chewbacca for advice. Like: where can I get one of them fly utility belts? Patsy's boil-lancing kit: where was it? Here it was sitting on top of a Harlequin paperback. It looked sorta like a gun. Except instead of shooting slow-motion bullets this gun poked and sucked boils.

Back in the living room Patsy had rotated on the sofa so the ass was up and the panties pulled down to show the butt with the boils on it. No one had ever measured the butt but Woo-jin guessed it to be nine miles wide.

"Hurry and get it over with," Patsy said. "The workers will be here soon and I don't want to get penalized again for hygiene, lack thereof."

"You're talking like a TV person," Woo-jin said, "with the lack thereofs." He pressed the gun to the first boil and squeezed the trigger; the hiss and wheeze of puncture and extraction.

"What was this dead person thing about?" Patsy said.

"This dead person thing was about me sitting there wishing I still had a burger."

"You were such a liar about that burger."

"I was not a liar."

"You'll have to go to the mart later for pork rinds and chipotle ranch. What more about the girl? The dead one."

"She had face bugs. She looked like a nice person. I should call the cops, right?"

"I can't understand you with the mouth guard."

"But I don't wanna eat my tongue." Woo-jin dropped the boil gun and dug his fingers into his chest. Hyperventilating, he fell to his knees then clawed around on the carpet as if underneath it were some fancy-pants answer to his problems. Gravity appeared to be shifting to the left, wanting to suck everything in that direction. Woo-jin crawled against the leftward pull to his hammock. Shivering, sputtering, blinking, he pulled himself into the netting and attempted to unwad the thin gray blanket.

One time on TV there was a show about historic animation guys who made the cartoons way back in the day. They'd draw their pictures on sheets of clear plastic and layer them like a sandwich, making the action go with the background. The ennui was kind of like that, with the world of real shit serving as the background layer, going about its real shit business while on top of it, layer upon layer, were sheets of dread, planes of condensed suffering, a thickening wall between Woo-jin's regular ole self and the black hell of emotions. It was almost worse that he didn't pass out when he had an attack. Instead, he had to watch people looking at him, hopefully someone like Patsy who'd gotten used to these attacks, but sometimes, when the ennui hit in public, some stranger bending down low gawking at him clinging to a newspaper box, or commuters ignoring him as he writhed on the concourse of a bus station, their eyes saying, *This freak's on something nasty.* Sometimes cops picked him up and were pricks about it until they could prick his finger and get a whole history from the sesame-seed-sized droplet of blood they fed to their vampiric Bionet monitors. *Oh. This guy's got an actual condition. He ain't an embodiment.* After which they'd maybe toss a blanket at him and make sure he was as far as possible from respectable citizens. And all the while he couldn't make his body move through space like it was supposed to, only vibrate shivering regardless of the temperature.

Now, in the relative safety of his hammock, through his eye slits, he watched Patsy pull up her drawers and mumble curses about burgers. Predictably her suffering was the primary tributary to the ennui. He saw her for the prisoner of her own body that she was, sensed acutely the tragedy of her not understanding her own enslavement. Then deeper. The chorus of shrieks!!! He'd seen in a magazine that one painting by that one guy, *Study after Velázquez's Portrait of Pope Innocent X*. The sound generated by that painting was what he was dealing with here. Like wind whistling in your ear, except multiplied, skull-rattling, sourceless. Here's where the mouth guard came in handy. Woo-jin bit down so hard his jaw began to ache. A couple times he'd come out of the ennui unable to open his mouth for over an hour. Now he rode that clattering thrill ride of skeleton bones down, down, down, fingers grinding like machines in the gray blanket, gurning his face around the mouth guard, trying to bring into his mind the calming presence of Chewbacca on that unicorn with his fly utility belt, snot jetting out of his nose, a real winner of an ennui attack here, folks, and then, most horrible of all, he found himself wearing the dead girl's face. He couldn't see it, wouldn't dare seek a mirror, but he trembled, convinced that the face was superimposed on his own, its mucousy underside squirming to find purchase on his own contorted visage.

Woo-jin whispered, "Patsy? Is my face my own face?" but she didn't seem to hear, and if she could she couldn't hear words, just squashy sounds of a choking variety muffled by the rubber half-circle stuffed into his mouth. Besides, she was primping for her case worker Hattie's visit, rearranging the bow on her head, bored by now with this kind of activity from her trailer mate/foster brother, still smarting from her unbegotten burger. Patsy pressed her thick thumb to the remote control and changed the TV from sequences of slo-mo artillery to *Fashion Tips for the Beautifully Obese*, on Discovery. Onscreen a naked woman was being prepared for her fitting, rolls of fat obliterating any view of adult content regions. Like a rivulet of suffering feeding into the tributary, this new source of sad humanity bled from the TV into the empathetic response portion of Patsy's brain then amplified into Woo-jin's ennui attack, which had previously begun to level off in terms of the intensity. As it picked up again, *Fashion Tips for the Beautifully Obese*'s host measured and marked the TV woman's arms with a felt-tip marker. Chewie, where were you when you were needed most?

Woo-jin fell out of the hammock, which was no surprise. This happened all the time. Which was why underneath the hammock there were throw pillows and gold shag carpet into which had been ground bits of bark, hair, a gum wrapper, toothpicks, the bitey plastic clip from a bread bag. The peak of the attack had definitely passed and he slid into a numb, thrumming part, quiet and immobilized. The door seemed to knock itself then Hattie let herself in. She was a mom-looking woman with glasses and frizzed hair, wearing a brown artificial-fiber pantsuit, encumbered by a gaudy purse overflowing with notes, nicotine gum, and half-drunk bottles of water. Her assistants, two younger guys in white jumpsuits and latex gloves whom she referred to as Thing One and Thing Two, trailed her burdened by equipment in sturdy metal cases, which they began to unload.

"Patsy! You look fabulous!" Hattie said, hugging part of the woman. Patsy got kind of quiet and blushed. It amazed Woo-jin every time that the same Patsy who gave him such ball-busting moments for cutting her toast wrong turned into this meek mouse of a gal once the extractions went down. Hattie spread her belongings out on the kitchenette dinette table, pulling out a stethoscope, cramming a VHS tape into the mouth of their

VCR. "You're really going to love this week's installment," she said, pressing PLAY. As the tape started, she took Patsy's hand in her own and rubbed the dimples of her knuckles.

On the TV appeared the boilerplate intro, the same thing they saw week after week. There was a beach with silhouetted lovers hand in hand, a waterfall, a rainbow over a field where a tractor tilled in the distance. The music was solo acoustic guitar, plaintive yet uplifting. A title materialized over an image of a grainy sunset: YOUR GENEROSITY AT WORK and beneath that the Bionetics logo. After which the music picked up tempo, into a we're-getting-things-done kind of deal. Shots of busy streets, a race car driver flashing a thumbs-up, a human pyramid of enthused cheerleaders. Then into the meat of the program, the part that had been changed from the month previous. There was a dark-skinned kid playing trucks in a preschool with other kids, making the usual truck noises. Over this came recorded narration from a confident-sounding man. "Juan was born without thumbs. Many of the activities we take for granted he just couldn't do. Now, thanks to your generosity, he can open jars, climb the rope in gym class, and even high-five his friends. No more high-fours for Juan. Thank you so very much—" Here the audio cut out for a second. Hattie's voice came on and said "*Patsy.*" Then it returned to the man's voice, saying, "The reconstructive surgery we were able to perform with tissues you provided made all the difference. Thank you!" Then followed three or four more segments such as this, each showcasing a person who owed their new livelihood to Patsy. There was a blind guy who could now make out shapes, a quadriplegic who'd begun taking baby steps. Patsy sniffled through the reel, moved. Woo-jin had never watched one of these reels during an ennui attack before. He felt no empathetic response to this sequence of vignettes. Where he should have been soaking up these folks' suffering he felt a blankness. Different from nothing, blankness had a border around it, edges where he felt something. He circled around the feeling as Hattie rubbed one of Patsy's shoulders and offered her a tissue and Things Two and One plugged all manner of instruments and monitors into sockets and laid a tarp on the living room floor. This was all prep before the part with the blood and freaky noises, the part Woo-jin hated most. Hattie helped Patsy disrobe and sit on a fold-out carbon microtube chair. The assistants orbited her, swabbing, lifting curtains of flesh, pressing various equipment against unidentifiable parts of her anatomy. Hattie slipped in another tape for Patsy's enjoyment, a live music concert by the singer Michael Bolton.

Here goes, Woo-jin thought. Went it did. He turned to the wall, making himself not see, but his hands couldn't block the high-pitched dental whine of the saw and the vacuum's irregular sputtering. Worst was when it smelled like burning hair. As they removed kidney tissue from her knee, Patsy quietly sang along to Michael Bolton's ballad about a man loving a woman so much that he'd sleep out in the rain if that's the way she said things oughta be.

Woo-jin woke in his hammock. There were talking people in the next room. He was killer hungry. Always happened this way after the ennui attack, the ravenousness, and this time it was worse because he'd projectiled his burger at the sight of the dead girl's buggy face. Woo-jin crawled out of his hammock and peeked around the doorframe into the living room, where the Things were finishing their cleanup, rolling the tarp, stuffing bloodied paper towels into a garbage bag. Hattie sat with Patsy on the couch, petting her hair. Patsy was covered with bandages and doing her usual postextraction crying bit, while on TV once-thumbless Juan was playing Wii with the best of 'em.

"It hurts," Patsy said. "It hurts worse every time."

"Oh, you dear, sweet girl," Hattie said. "You just take your medicine and think of Pegasus, riding free through the clouds."

"A winged unicorn is *not* a pegasus," Patsy sniffed.

Woo-jin crawled to the fridge as though his stomach was propelling him across the floor. Nobody seemed to notice him even though the trailer was hardly eight feet wide. One Thing was saying to the other, "Yeah so like I heard this one guy down in Argentina or whatever grew a whole human head in his abdominal cavity."

Woo-jin at last arrived at the fridge and upon opening it to the jangle of condiment jars everyone's head turned and considered him in silence while on the screen commenced a racquetball tournament for recent transplant recipients. Inside the fridge were red-bagged specimens of biological valuables, a picked-over turkey carcass, some Pabst Blue Ribbon, celery, a jar of Tom & Jerry's hot-buttered-rum mix, fake sausage oddly enough made out of meat, one dead banana, ketchup, muffins, a lone pizza roll, and what Woo-jin was really looking for, peanut butter from Trader Joe's. Barely able to stand, he leaned against the counter and found a spoon, then retired to his corner.

He heard Patsy say, "My foster brother never does nice things for me. He just has his attacks and eats the last of the cheese. I always tell him to bring me things from the store and restaurant but does he? All I ask for is a free hamburger or maybe a slice of pie? Something to show he cares?"

Hattie said, "It's hard to have a no-good foster brother. You hang in there and recover, lance your boils. And guess what? Next time you get to see someone special. Santa Claus!"

The medicines were kicking in and Patsy started to say something but slurred the words like a demoralized tape recorder. Woo-jin hastily ate his peanut butter, sticking his mouth up with it. Hattie said, "Let's get out of this cesspool," then left with Things One and Two, who carted away ice chests packed with harvested tissues. The VCR still played images of happy people engaged in healthy outdoor recreation, breathing the salty ocean breezes on a catamaran or taking in the foliage on a misty mountain trail. Woo-jin slipped in another spoonful of peanut butter and this seemed to represent the tipping point of his mouth's mobility. He might as well have eaten cement. He could no longer move it at all. A line of buttery drool trickled down his chin. Patsy, for her part, had become more debilitated on the couch, her sagging and bruised form occasionally hiccuping as she settled, asleep, to dream of sea turtles and Neptune, who called to the sea nymphs with his conch-shell megaphone. Hattie and co. peeled out from the dirt driveway in their van. Woo-jin stood in the living room, his mouth immobilized. He knew he had to return to the dead girl.

The steady clang of machines hypnotized Woo-jin as he left the trailer that morning, jar of peanut butter in one hand, spoon in the other, his mind still carbonated from the ennui attack, feet taking him around the crumbling brick buildings of Georgetown to the edge of Boeing Field, where planes roared and dipped like immense predatory birds. Oh, if only some action hero of yore were to give Woo-jin a pep talk and reinforce his nerves as he walked through the grasses, retracing his path to where a police helicopter now sat, its blades spinning lazy-like, slower and slower as if the thing was nodding off to sleep. Three or four cops were gathered around the fridge-like contraption, taking pictures, spitting profanities into walkie-talkies, drinking coffee, a clump of vaguely authoritative-looking humans in nonetheless shabby police uniforms. This was like a TV version of something that was actually happening, an instantaneous reenactment in which the original experiencers of an event immediately reexperience their experiences for the cameras and fake their initial reactions. Woo-jin stuffed another goopy wad of peanut butter nervously into his mouth. He came to the congregation of officers—two men, one woman, a helicopter pilot smoking a cigarette—and raised his spoon-holding hand as if wishing to be called upon to speak.

"Who the hell's this guy?" said an officer with a wide head topped with a flattop. Another, a skinny tall man drinking a short coffee, nodded at Woo-jin. "You know anything about this?"

"Wooolmph mmmr," Woo-jin said. "Wwrrmmth hmmph."

"What are we waiting for?" said the skinny tall one. "Get this fellow a glass of milk!"

"I've got some milk in the bird," the pilot said, and quickly located some two-percent and a glass, which he filled with a steady hand. The glass was translucent brown and pebbly and would not have looked out of place neglected behind a sectional in the Midwest. Woo-jin nodded his appreciation, consumed the refreshing glass of milk, smacked his lips a few times, and said, "I saw the body last night. Coming through the field."

"That's nice," the wide-head cop said.

"I saw her when I came through looking for cans and eating my three-quarters of a burger. She had face bugs!"

Woo-jin couldn't see the body from where he was standing. It was hidden behind that big green thing. The officers frowned like they suddenly remembered they had work to do. The woman cop rolled her eyes. Her hair was pulled back in a ponytail that yanked up her eyebrows.

The skinny tall one said, "Well, thanks, but we have it covered here."

"But I saw her. It made me puke. Who is she? Am I under arrest?"

"You're not under arrest," said the chopper pilot. "Can I have my glass back, please?"

Woo-jin handed back the glass, now frosted with milk film.

"We've got lots of work to do here, so you best be on yer way," the woman cop said.

"So you don't think I killed her?"

Laffs all around. "Hoo boy. No, we're pretty certain you didn't kill her," wide-head snorted.

"We could book you anyway, if it would make you feel better," skinny cop said, to his colleagues' guffaws.

"Who is she?" Woo-jin asked.

"You mean the body?" skinny tall said. "We haven't gotten that far yet. We just got here."

Woo-jin said, "I want to help find the killer."

More laughter, louder this time.

"The killer!" the chopper pilot snorted.

"Find him!" the woman cop laughed.

Nervously, Woo-jin started in again with the peanut butter, goops and goops of it shoved at the tooth-ringed hole in his head. "Woolf," he said.

"Get the guy more milk," wide-head said. The chopper pilot refilled the glass and handed it over. Woo-jin drank as enthusiastically as before.

"Thank you. I really could help you guys find the killer."

"Get the hell out of here," skinny tall said.

Woo-jin, upset but not really understanding why, decided to push his way through space by walking. Time to go to work anyway. The ground scrolled beneath him with its broken pieces of crud, rodent carcasses, pebbles, fibers, the granularity of byproducts. He crossed the oily Duwamish into the ruins of South Park, ghosts of Mexican restaurants and a store where cell phones once were sold, Sunday circular advertisements pushed along by an underperforming wind. This was the shortcut he took to the staging area in West Seattle. A cat trotted in front of him with something purple in its mouth that didn't look like food, and Woo-jin realized the thing hanging out of its mouth was part of its mouth, and the cat looked at him as if it rightly understood Woo-jin had nothing at all to offer it. Woo-jin wondered briefly about the people who used to live in this neighborhood and their broken empathies. Their absence struck him like the musty sweet odor from a discarded cola bottle. Why, by the way, hadn't the cops taken him up on his offer to assist with the dead body? They'd seemed more interested in standing around looking cool than investigating the appearance of a dead girl in a field above which airplanes screamed. Time and again Woo-jin butted up against the intelligence of other people, the walls of confusion from which they peered down on him and leered. In times of fresh panic he wondered if he might be even stupider than he suspected he was, and maybe these smiling case workers and librarians and such noticed deficiencies in his brain that he himself could not begin to appreciate due to the fact of his being somehow fundamentally flawed in that department. Maybe their occasional kindnesses were a way of humoring him. Maybe he wasn't even smart enough to see their secret cruelties.

There were dilapidated houses and something that used to be a gas station, structures absent of human life, remnants of foundations, charred heaps of cracked wood and bricks, as Woo-jin came to the parts of the neighborhood reclaimed by the trees. Trees pushed up through the concrete in what was once the middle of the street, birds clinging to branches, watching. The road became a path, and the path disappeared into weeds and thicket, but Woo-jin knew the way. He emerged onto a sidewalk and spotted the revolving sign of his employer, Il Italian Joint, a hundred paces away.

Il Italian Joint mostly served the workers going to and from the New York Alki staging area and it was Woo-jin's job to make sure the pots were clean. Great quantities of soups and sauces bubbled in these pots and, once emptied, they needed to be scrubbed. The heat baked a thin, nearly impenetrable layer of food to the bottoms of the pots, which Woo-jin attacked with a number of scrapers, wools, soaps, and picks, chiseling the solidified minestrone or marinara until the pots gleamed silver. He wondered on occasion if it was possible for the food to chemically fuse into a new sort of compound with the steel. Maybe the cooking process became so intense that it negated the difference between the organic food material and the ore-based material that constituted the pot and the only way to truly clean a pot would be to actually scrape away layers of metal at the bottom. His implements seemed inadequate for the task. He scraped and sweated over the pots and never really got one to the clean state of his satisfaction. Each pot it seemed he polished to a level of just-adequate cleanliness. He fantasized about sandblasting them.

Woo-jin's boss was this guy by the name of Sandford Deane whose eyes always looked closed. And yet he still managed to not often bump into things. He was supposed to be the guy who greeted valued guests at the door, but often ended up out back behind the grease bin smoking the cigarettes he called fags. He was supposed to be the owner of this place, or pretend to be, but everyone knew he was just some actor in a stained tuxedo going table to table complimenting the guests on their fashion decisions and asking if they'd care for a glass of port on the house. The real owner of Il Italian Joint was a company in Shanghai. Sandford Deane stood in as a representation of what the owner might have looked like had he been a human being instead of a collection of codes and spreadsheets, meetings, and quarterly reports in sexy buildings. He was standing in the doorway next to the Dumpsters when Woo-jin tumbled through some shrubbery into the near-empty parking lot.

"I'm early I think," Woo-jin said.

"You're early every day. You could at least use the time to do something useful, like masturbate," Sandford said.

"But I'm a dishwasher," Woo-jin said, slipping past his boss, snatching his apron off a hook by the back door. "I figured out the ultimate pot scrubbing device."

"What's that."

"Diamond-coated steel wool."

Sandford nodded. "That, or we could start scrubbing the pots with lasers."

"Lasers." Woo-jin clenched his eyebrows at the thought, pushing his way into the kitchen's greasy yelling and clanking. "Lasers."

The wash station looked like it had been hit by a car bomb. Three guys from the previous shift were standing basically gaping at the pile of dishes, spraying a bowl here and there, overwhelmed by the madness of it all. The three dishwashers were Pontoon, Ben O'Winn, and Bahn Kan, fellows comprised of scraps of ethnicities, doused in food particles, and enduring some kind of experiment in sleep deprivation. Waitresses screamed at cooks, something burned on a stove, and a couple sauciers were trying to rescue one of their kind who'd gotten trapped in the walk-in freezer. Pontoon held out a spatula with something black stuck to it. Ben O'Winn trembled and whimpered from the stress. Bahn Kan scratched one sideburn, the only one he had, and said something in a language that sounded like Vietnamese but with a lot more sighing.

"Sometimes maybe you guys could do a better job with the dishes," Woo-jin said sadly then started telling them what to do. Pontoon hauled a pile of clean dishes back to the prep area. Ben O'Winn snuck to the edge of the dining room and commandeered the bus carts. Bahn Kan fetched Woo-jin an orange soda. Woo-jin roughly counted the dishes in their precarious stacks, assessed the number of pallets on the dishwasher, considered the time of day, anticipated the rate of new dirty dishes arriving, then let the part of his brain that washed dishes for a living kick in and do its shit. He almost felt like he was sitting back and watching a robot do the job. He was the best dishwasher in the world and he had the gold medal to prove it, from the previous year's Restaurant and Hotel Management Olympics. The medal hung spattered with grease and soap on the wall behind the washer. Often, when feeling discouraged by the rate of dirty dishes coming in, Woo-jin glanced at the medal, smiled, and recalled how he'd defeated the Red Lobster regional champion in pot scrubbing by point-nine seconds. Sometimes dishwashers from out of town showed up at the back door of Il Italian Joint, hoping to watch Woo-jin work. Tonight the champion's arms wheeled over the mass of forks and coffee cups, fruit rinds and disintegrating napkins, smears of Bolognese, ramekins, cigarette butts, hardened macaroni and cheese, the fossils of burgers and fries, and steadily the pile shrank in the curling steam. By midshift the pile was obliterated and the three ineffectual dishwashers skulked home to their television sets and prescription medications, with sitcom theme songs stuck in their heads, falling asleep into the routines of hideous dreams. For a while, work had pulled Woo-jin's thoughts from the previous night's morbid discovery, but as the dinner rush thinned out her face came to him again, floating phantom-like in the steam.

"Yo, Mike." It was a waitress named Sally who commuted a hundred miles both ways. An older woman, she was always showing pictures of her grandson to her coworkers, who would smile and say he was cute despite the ghastly facial deformity that nobody wanted to acknowledge. Sally held Woo-jin's shoulder and repeated, "Yo, Mike." He looked at her. She had thought his name was Mike since she started here two years ago and no one had gotten around to correcting her, including Woo-jin. "Are you okay, Mike?"

Woo-jin glanced around at the spotless dish-washing station and the dormant kitchen beyond. Everyone had gone home, it looked like.

"I am definitely not okay."

"Walk me to my car. I'll give you a cigarette."

Sally was on who knew how many painkillers and her body seemed to generate little bursts of static electricity as she walked. Woo-jin hauled the last of the trash bags and Sally locked up. From the parking lot they witnessed the erratically lit-up skyline of New York Alki peeking over some nearby houses and businesses. Sounds: distant construction banging, two guys yelling in the near distance, a piece of cellophane scraped along the asphalt by the wind. Sally took his arm and hugged it close under her own and, choked up, said, "Sometimes I think you're the only person who knows I exist."

Woo-jin's guts fluttered as this old waitress's manifold sufferings bled a path into his nervous system. She was going to tell him again about her grandson and all the cruel things the neighborhood boys did to him, how they taunted him about his facial challenge, murdered his cat, knocked his special-ed books out of his hands onto the ground. Woo-jin really would have rather avoided her by slipping out the back door at the end of his shift but nightmare visions of the dead girl had mesmerized him at his station long after the last cup had been dried and shelved.

"I don't know what to do with those boys they're so cruel. What would their parents think if they knew they were giving wedgies to my poor Donald? Well, they'd probably laugh, being cruel and unthinking themselves. That's where those boys got their cruelties, I'm sure."

Woo-jin said, "They don't know what to do with their suffering, so they give it to your Donald."

Sally sighed. They'd made it to her car, a North Korean something banished from a factory. "Even though you're a retard, Mike, you have a gift. A gift for understanding all the ways people feel like crap."

Woo-jin wanted to tell Sally about the dead body but knew she'd only nod and let the horror of it slide off the protective surface of her own woes. He found her tragic this way, stewing in the nasty things that happened to her immediate family but incapable of feeling anyone else's pain. Sally's eyes were glossed over almost like she was sleepwalking, maybe to prepare for her commute. But then Woo-jin understood she was looking over his shoulder at the construction rising behind them into the night.

"Doesn't it blow your mind," she said, "that of all the places they could have picked to rebuild New York City they picked Puget Sound?"

That night Woo-jin passed again through the grass and trash near Boeing Field. The chopper, corpse, cops, etc. had of course disappeared. The sky reeked of jet fuel. He found the big dead machine and the spot where the dead girl had been, now a dead-grass outline, a snow angel without snow. The ennui attack came fresh and out of nowhere, so fast he didn't have time to slip in his mouth guard. Woo-jin crumpled as overhead a cargo plane came ripping down with a belly full of parcels. The air took on the appearance of a multitude of rippling threads. He was on the ground, nose bleeding, jaw clenched, jerking his torso. He spotted a Coors can through the slit of one eye and there flooded a choking series of sadnesses for its crumpled and abandoned form. An unloved, forgotten object hoping only for swift disintegration to its original elements. Wait a minute, he was feeling sorry for a beer can? The ennui attacks used to feel like they were at least showing him something; this one was like riding the tip of a thrashing bullwhip. Here then came the hallucination: a night world seen through the thermal ripples of a campfire. No longer in the soggy bosom of the Pacific Northwest, he was surrounded by desert, atop a mesa of sorts. Blood rode the breaths out of his nostrils as his twitching self in the field receded behind a curtain of perception. He peered more fully into this seizure dream and saw the campfire ringed with carefully placed objects—a refrigerator, a tire, three stuffed animals, a pile of books, a full-length mirror. He crawled toward the latter, which was tilted up to reflect trillions of deceased stars back into the cosmos. An unforgiving wind ravaged the mesa, stretching the flames like curls of taffy. His hands, cracked and covered in layers of dirt and dust, clawed across the rocks. When at last he pulled the mirror down he found it a window into the face of an impossibly old man, toothless, skin beset by sores, lips peeling, eyes cloudy and almost blind. A gust of wind came across the mesa again and seemed to push Woo-jin back into his own body, convulsing on the ground outside Boeing Field. He smelled shit. Before he passed out he reached over and touched the beer can and drew it to his chest as if he were comforting an abandoned kitten.

Noon. Consciousness and a punishing sun. Woo-jin coughed and spit blood and snot. Was it—gawd, he'd bitten his tongue.

A small charter plane rattled across his vision, departing and entering peripheries. He made it up on one elbow. An ant crawled up a nearby stalk of grass and this occupied Woo-jin's attention for several minutes. His body unpersuasively argued against gravity. He rubbed his eyes and turned around.

There was the dead girl again, lying in the grass exactly as he'd found her the first time. Woo-jin nodded and sat on the big machine.

"This isn't real," he said. "I'm just remembering you." He tossed his Coors can at the body, striking it in the chest. Maybe if he looked away then looked back, she would disappear. Didn't happen. "Oh well," he said.

Woo-jin headed homeward, stinking, bloody, incapable of walking a straight line. Semi trucks blasted past, inches away, on the road. One step to the right and he could've put an end to this BS. But he wanted something to eat; the café smells of Georgetown tormented him. A couple tourists veered out of his way as he passed them on the sidewalk and in the window of a music store that only sold vinyl he witnessed this haggard, face-fucked-up vision that he thought must be a Halloween mask.

Woo-jin heard the helicopter as he approached his home but couldn't formulate the thought that it might have anything to do with him. This one wasn't a cop 'copter. It was a big lifter, like the kind they used for construction on New York Alki. It hovered over the spot of land where the trailer stood, with cables attached to the mobile home's four corners and a man in a helmet and flight suit standing on the roof. This guy gave a thumbs-up and slowly the trailer creaked and broke free from its moorings.

"Patsy!" Woo-jin cried. He saw parts of her through the various windows, fleshy mounds of arm or back, it was hard to tell. Her face appeared in the window above the kitchen sink. She was not happy.

"You never came back to feed me!" Patsy yelled. "What the Jesus were you doing all night?"

"Patsy, where are they taking you?"

The helicopter rose, the cables strained. Woo-jin sprinted, leaped, and grabbed a dangling portion of the porch.

"You left me to starve to death!" Patsy yelled, her face red, popping out cartoon stress droplets.

Flight suit guy bent down and hollered, "You're gonna want to let go, son! We're only going up from here!"

"Where are you taking my sister?" Woo-jin yelled as the two-by-four he had been holding on to groaned with slippy nails and he tumbled ten or so feet to the ground. A flower pot with a dead flower in it thunked him on the head, inducing a swirl of stars and chirping birds. Flight suit guy and Patsy both yelled at him, maybe revealing Patsy's destination, but over the chopper's blades and head bonk confusion there was no hearing for Woo-jin. In a great whirl of dust he shut his eyes tight and did his best to cover his mouth. The helicopter headed east, toward the Cascades, trailing the trailer from which Patsy did her best to wave good-bye.

"I shouldn't have eaten her hamburger," said Woo-jin. He lay for some time in the dirt, wondering when he'd need to head back to Il Italian Joint for another round of dishwashing. After a time he came to feel he was being watched. Sounded like wind chimes. He opened an eye. Standing nearby was the man from the neighborhood who demanded to be addressed as the Ambassador. None who knew his real name felt compelled to share it. He was just the Ambassador, nearly seven feet tall, hair in tight dreads, wearing the primary colors of an African wardrobe, big dangly cubist earrings, and a fat ring on every finger. His scepter was crafted from a toilet brush duct-taped to the shaft of a plumber's helper, decorated with pipe cleaners and words of positive reinforcement written in tiny script circumnavigating the handle. He also sported a great white beard and a pair of sunglasses he'd discovered in a ditch.

"Ambassador," Woo-jin said, "I could use some help."

"You certainly could," the Ambassador said, leaving the thought hanging.

"Maybe you can find a helicopter and convince them to follow the guys who just kidnapped my sister and have them yell out their window at the other helicopter to have Patsy throw down some extra pairs of my pants and shirts and stuff."

"Or I could let you borrow a deluxe sweatpant-and-shirt ensemble," the Ambassador grinned.

The Ambassador helped Woo-jin to his feet. They stood a moment inside the foundation where the trailer used to be. Sun baked the dusty afternoon air. The Ambassador invited Woo-jin to join him in a constitutional, and as they walked he bore his scepter across his chest. They passed the Denny's and a do-it-yourself car wash place. A few people bowed as they proceeded, paying the man his respect and casting a wary eye at Woo-jin, whose hairdo looked like it had been barfed up by a cat. They traversed the parking lot of a metal prefabricator and came to the Ambassador's three-story, mid-twentieth-century home. A freshly painted white fence restrained a postage stamp of a yard resplendent with gerbera daisies, nasturtiums, and great purple gouts of lilacs. The Ambassador unhooked the gate and led the way up the cobbles to the porch, where a gallon jar of sun tea absorbed UV rays. Inside, the Ambassador pointed Woo-jin in the direction of the mud room and adjoining bathroom, and provided a plastic garbage bag for his soiled clothing. This was the fanciest shower Woo-jin had ever seen; to use it he felt he might need an engraved invitation. He stripped down and groaned disgustedly at what he'd done to his undershorts, then climbed into the hot shower and puzzled over the abundance of scented soaps, selecting a bar of artisanal lemongrass-oatmeal soap after some deliberation. As the caked-on dirt slid off his body he recalled the previous night's vision, the man in the desert with his refrigerator and stuffed animals and full-length mirror. Who was that character? An insane dude somehow invading Woo-jin's freaked-out mind space on an astral plane? Yeah, probably. Or he could have been something manufactured by Woo-jin's imagination, though he doubted that, having little confidence in his brain to make up cool things out of the blue.

Then there was the dead girl. Again? She'd showed up again? He wondered if he should get in touch with one of the police officers who'd so kindly given him a glass of milk and told him to get the hell out of there. Or maybe they'd just dumped the body back where they'd found it. Unlikely. They had big storage units for that kind of thing. Or cemeteries.

Woo-jin, clean, found a tracksuit getup outside the bathroom door and slipped into it. The sweatshirt was a zip-up, and both it and the matching pants were a blazing red with white piping. On the left breast of the sweatshirt were embroidered the words "Official Delegate." At the sink he located a jar of his favorite brand of hair gel and pulled his hair into its usual spikes. With an electric razor he shaved what little stubble he'd generated in the last twenty-four hours. He admired himself in the mirror. He looked like a sex machine. Whatever sex was.

Woo-jin found the Ambassador in his front room, sitting in a ornate, baroque-looking gold and vermilion chair next to a matching love seat. The walls were done up with tastefully muted pinstriped brown wallpaper. The whole place looked official, like it was just waiting for big-time state business to go down. Like some guys in suits would show up and shake hands amid stuttery camera flashes. The Ambassador motioned for Woo-jin to sit. In rolled a room-service cart with two of those silver round tray thingies, pushed by a gaunt waiter-type. As Woo-jin took his seat, the waiter revealed a meal of artichoke and feta lasagna, green salad with sliced pears and an herbed kumquat vinaigrette, garlic-lime mashed potatoes, asparagus, an assortment of rolls, mineral water, a dish of sorbet, and a slice of raspberry cheesecake. Woo-jin about passed out.

"I thought you'd be hungry," the Ambassador said as his famished guest attacked the food. "Any day now," the Ambassador continued, "the delegation will arrive. I have prepared thirteen years for the delegation, studying the lifeworks of the world's great diplomats. I am uniquely positioned to represent the interests of humanity to our otherworldly visitors."

Woo-jin had heard the Ambassador's spiel before, mostly on the corner of 12th and Vale Street, but he nodded politely, with asparagus hanging from his mouth, as though hearing it for the first time. He'd used the guy's soap and was eating his food, after all. Pretending interest was the least he could do.

"At one time I was without direction, without purpose, see? Convinced the universe was a mad game of entropy and meaninglessness. I looked upon the pursuits of office workers and engineers as trivial or worse. I saw them as despicable drones manufacturing the methods of their own suffering. Oh, I was among them, making my money, driving my fancy car, with season tickets to all the sports teams and bar tabs at the finest brasseries, what have you. I was going crazy in the stew of my own success and self-loathing, drowning in another man's vision, rewarded beyond my imaginings. I was hollowed out and no matter how much money I threw into the void of my sadness I couldn't fill it. I treated women like disposable Bic lighters. I failed to communicate my emotional life in any way. And then one night I took too much cold medication and went out onto the balcony of my condominium. I looked upon the Seattle skyline, brilliant and glittering like a jewelry box beneath a full moon."

"Here comes the good part," Woo-jin said to the camera, raising his glass of sparkling water.

"Indeed. For when I looked up into the sky above Queen Anne Hill I discovered a gigantic celestial head gazing down upon me. The next day I would call the customer-service line of the cold medication company and ask whether giant celestial heads were a known side effect of their medicine. As it turns out, they were not. The celestial head had a large forehead, brown hair, a square jaw, and intense eyes. Some blackheads on the nose. Caucasian fellow. He looked down upon me and affirmed his reality by asking me to get a pen and paper. Numb, I did as I was instructed. 'Okay,' the celestial head said, 'I want you to write down a couple things. First, the Mariners will lose tomorrow to the Oakland A's, 3–2, with closing pitcher Cody Montero walking in the winning run. Shortstop Vic Garbler will get a hammie in the sixth with runners on first and third and two outs. Once these two events are confirmed, you will have the confidence to know that I speak the truth, and that you really need to do what I say. You will resign from your job, effective immediately, and submit to the purposes I design for you. From now on you will be known as the Ambassador. You will take all your money out of your 401(k) and invest it in a company called Argus Industries. They'll announce their IPO next quarter. Pour as much money as possible into this company. Wait a year. After the stock splits three ways and hits $179 a share, sell. With your profits, buy a house in Georgetown on Orcas Street and make sure it is immaculately maintained and staffed. There you will live and wait for further word on how you should fulfill your duties. You have been assigned the incredible responsibility of greeting a special interplanetary delegation. Don't fuck this up.' And with that, the celestial head disappeared behind some cumulus clouds. The next day, the celestial head's prophecies came true. The Mariners lost in the manner described. I was in a bar when it happened, staring up at the TV, confirming what I had written down."

"So did you quit your job on the spot?"

"No, I did not. The following night as I was watching a rerun of *Stella Artaud* I heard a voice coming from the direction of my balcony, calling my name. I went out to find the celestial head frowning at me. 'How come you didn't quit your job like I said?' it scowled. I replied, 'How do I know you're real?' The head rolled its gigantic eyes and said, 'Look, you need more proof? Adventronics' stock is going to go through the roof tomorrow. Call your broker first thing and buy as many shares as you can, then sell in the afternoon for an over 200 percent profit. I'm not yanking your chain. And once this occurs I expect you to devote yourself to your duties as my ambassador.'

"So the following morning I did as instructed, and made a killing that day trading the stock of a company that made electronic Advent calendars. I do believe I made over $90,000. And yet I still didn't have the heart to quit my job. That night as I lay in bed, drifting to sleep, I was jolted awake by the celestial head screaming my name. I hurried to the balcony in my pajamas and gazed up to find the face red with rage. 'So you take my advice when you can pocket a fortune, but you still don't have the balls to devote yourself to the responsibilities of an ambassador. I'm starting to wonder if I picked the wrong guy altogether.' And with that, the head spat at me, a gigantic volume of garlic-scented saliva that coated me completely and took over an hour to shower off.

"That night I drafted my resignation letter and began getting my finances in order. I also settled upon the design of my scepter, constructed of a toilet brush symbolizing cleanliness through abrasive methods, and a plunger handle to symbolize getting situations unstuck and moving.

"I looked in amazement at all I had written down. The next day I purchased and staffed this embassy. And now I await further instructions."

Woo-jin said, "Do you know where I could catch a bus to get to Il Italian Joint? My shift starts soon."

The Ambassador rose grunting from his chair. "I'll have my driver transport you. Pierre!"

Pierre appeared: short guy, pasty complexion, snappy outfit. He looked like someone who'd been convinced erroneously that he was a chauffeur when he was actually hired to kind of pretend to be one. He bowed deeply and waved his gloved hand in the direction of the front door. Woo-jin thanked his host for the shower and the new clothes and the food. He ached to get back to the steam and suds of his wash station.

After a short ride in a comedian's idea of a limousine, Woo-jin was dumped in front of Il Italian Joint. The place was packed with drunken idiots and their significant others spilling food all over the floor, screaming at the waitstaff, sending entrées back to the kitchen, and selecting the most cloying, earwormy tunes from the juke. Sandford Deane wore a tux with tie askew, disheveled hair, eyes looking like they'd recently shed tears. Woo-jin was early and Sandford accepted this turn of events with biblical-quality gratitude. "Oh thank you dear God, we need you in the kitchen asap, Woo-jin. Our savior!" Sandford clung to the champion dishwasher's shoulders for a moment like he was hanging on to a piece of buoyant jetsam in the midst of a hurricane. "By the way, I have a special treat for you." Sandford reached into his tux jacket and withdrew something fuzzy and shiny. "It's the diamond-encrusted steel wool you requested. I had it flown in from Berlin."

"Excellent!" Woo-jin said, bursting into the kitchen where the dishes were piled literally to the ceiling. Pontoon, Bahn Kan, and Ben O'Winn has started removing ceiling tiles to make room for the growing mound. Upon entering the kitchen the harried sauciers and waitresses paused a moment then erupted in cheers. Sally called out, "Mike! You're just in time!" The three dishwashers who'd so thoroughly proved their incompetence hugged one another and buried their heads in each other's shoulders with relieved weeping. Woo-jin cartwheeled past the fry station, popped into a midair somersault, and landed with scissoring double splits in front of the wash station. It pretty much helped the whole look of the performance that he was wearing a tracksuit embroidered with the words "Official Delegate."

The busboys kept bringing more dirty plates, coffee cups, lipstick-imprinted stemware, napkins smeared with remnants of dessert. The Hobart hissed and trembled, pumping out clean dishes to the point of exhaustion. It struck Woo-jin that this situation might be one of those mathematical "story" problems. The machine could do a pallet of dishes in a minute and a half. But how many pallets' worth of dishes arrived every minute and a half? If it was any number over one, it would be impossible to ever clean the dishes at a rate that would completely diminish the pile. In fact the pile would keep growing until it engulfed and overwhelmed Woo-jin and the wash station. Then again, there was a finite number of dishes in Il Italian Joint, wasn't there? But what if there were trucks pulling up to the loading dock, delivering shipments of new clean dishes every minute and a half? Then it would be mathematically impossible to clean all the dishes there were to clean. Well, that would be true if the dishes kept getting dirty and the stream of valued guests remained constant. Maybe there was a line of tour buses outside filled with valued guests, ensuring that dishes would continue to get dirtied. But after a while the food would run out. Unless, of course, there were constant shipments of new produce, pasta, cheese, etc. The dishwasher, Woo-jin came to understand, was the center of the restaurant universe. Without the dishwasher nothing could happen, and yet he knew he was the lowest-paid person working here. On the plus side, that diamond-encrusted steel wool was doing a bang-up job on the soup pots.

Over the course of the evening the pile of dirty dishes did shrink, but too much was troubling Woo-jin for him to take much pleasure in the achievement. Even at the end of the shift when all the dishes were stashed and the wash station sparkled he wasn't settled and knew he was about due for another ennui attack. Absentmindedly he slipped in his mouth guard in preparation. He looked forward to going home, collapsing in his hammock—oh, that's right. Where was he going to sleep tonight? He three-pointered his apron into the laundry on the way out and exited through the back door, where he was met by a plainclothes police officer. Tall guy with a mustache, smelled like peanuts. Under a flickering, bug-fouled light he introduced himself as Officer Wiggins.

"You're Woo-jin, am I correct? Woo-jin Kan?"

"No one says my last name usually. They think 'jin' is my last name."

The officer put his hands on his hips and swiveled a bit, subconsciously stretching. "I understand you came across a body last night just north of Boeing Field."

"I did. I already talked to some cops about it who gave me a glass of milk."

"I heard. And I also understand you came across this body again around noon today."

Three thoughts piled up in Woo-jin's head, three thoughts too many. It took him a while to get them unjammed. He stood there, drooling around the mouth guard, nodding to himself as he began to understand. There really had been another body that looked like the first. Or—second thought here—maybe the cops dumped the same old body where they'd found it. Third thought: how did they know he'd seen the body again if he hadn't told anyone?

"You need a ride?" Officer Wiggins said. "I'd like to bring you by the station to see something. Don't worry, you're not under arrest or anything. I was just hoping you might be able to help us sort this thing out."

It was true, Woo-jin did need a ride. Wiggins cocked his head at his police mini-chopper. Soon they were levitating above the Il Italian Joint parking lot, rising above the tree line into the cloudy night. Woo-jin craned to catch sight of New York Alki growing on what had once been Bainbridge Island. A concrete seawall circled the island, keeping the waves from eroding the new contours of the shoreline. Huge, blocks-long banks of halogen lights lit acres of scaffolding as hundreds of cranes swung their loads to re-create the greatest city the world had ever known. The new Chrysler Building stood alone in a five-block radius, waiting for its neighbors. On the north end of the island, crews felled trees and demolished abandoned houses, carving and reshaping the land with bulldozers. Harlem looked to be pretty much empty at this point, except for a tiny Apollo Theater glowing in the woods.

"What do you make of this?" Wiggins said, jerking a thumb toward the construction. It was so rare that Woo-jin was asked for his opinion on matters that didn't involve dishwashing that he didn't know what to say, or whether he actually had an opinion. Wiggins continued, "If you ask me, it's a huge waste. Rebuilding Manhattan when Seattle can't even get its act together to build a monorail? And the congestion it's going to bring to the region, don't get me started."

The chopper veered east, over the dome of Pioneer Square. This was the kind of night perfect for the appearance of a gigantic, celestial head, though Woo-jin couldn't imagine coping with the demands of such an apparition. The chopper landed atop the city administration building and they hustled to an elevator. Heading underground, Woo-jin said, "Hey, you fly a helicopter. Do you know anything about when houses, or really trailers, get yanked up and moved to another place by a helicopter?"

"Like what happened to your foster sister," Wiggins said. "That I can't talk about. But I can tell you she's safe and will be taken care of."

"What about my stuff? My clothes and posters?"

"I'm sure you'll come across some more clothes and posters before long," Wiggins said as the elevator doors opened on the morgue. Overhead speakers softly floated the idea of an instrumental version of "Do the Hustle." The walls, floor, and ceiling were painted a painfully bright white. There was a reception area where a thick woman murmured into a headset. A vase of lilies. Wiggins clipped a visitor's badge to Woo-jin's collar and offered him a clipboard filled with legalese. "Just sign here," he said. Woo-jin did as instructed. Through double doors they entered the stainless steel sanctum of corpses, an echoing hallway the size of an underground bus station, walls of cabinet doors behind which rested bodies in various stages of investigation. A gloved, balding, middle-aged guy with a Muppet Babies tie poking out from under his lab coat met them and nodded a quiet hello.

Wiggins said, "This is Dr. Farmer, our forensics director. Dr. Farmer, I'd like you to meet Woo-jin Kan."

Dr. Farmer's hand, covered in latex, squished and squealed as Woo-jin shook it.

"This is the fellow who happened upon the deceased?" Dr. Farmer asked.

"Indeed," said Wiggins.

Dr. Farmer directed them to a portion of the wall. He took hold of a handle and pulled out the slab. Woo-jin steadied himself against the wall as the coroner lifted the sheet. The young woman's clothes had been removed and thank God there were no more face bugs. Still Woo-jin reeled. Wiggins steadied him and Dr. Farmer began talking a string of words that Woo-jin knew nothing about. Anterior, posterior, medial, cranial. Woo-jin looked for the cameras to see if he was in fact on a highly rated medical drama. No dice. He was really here, in a morgue.

"Now," Dr. Farmer said, "here's where we come to the curious part of the case." He pulled out another slab and yanked back the sheet. It was the second body, identical to the first. "Our tests indicate these are not twins. Their profiles are 100 percent identical. By all appearances, these two bodies are *exactly the same person.*"

"They're not clones?" Wiggins said.

"They don't bear the watermarks of clones," Dr. Farmer said. "And their profiles are unregistered. I considered the possibility that they were born off the grid but that wouldn't explain the precise similarities in scarring. See here above the lip—tiny identical scars. And here on the left ring finger—you can still see the markings of three stitches from a cut she once received. Identical abrasions above the left knee, on the right buttock, and here, just a couple centimeters from the clavicle. Remarkable. In addition, the contents of their stomachs were identical. And the cherry on top, so to speak, are the identical stab wounds to the heart, made with an identical instrument—likely a flat-head screwdriver—to precisely the same depth. I've never seen anything like this in thirty years of forensic science."

"And the state of decay?" Wiggins said.

"Even though they were discovered a day apart, tissues indicate both bodies expired three days ago."

"And the only link between the two that we're aware of is that this guy happened to discover them," Wiggins said.

"I'm not a murderer," Woo-jin said. "I'm a dishwasher."

"We know," Wiggins said. "We're just trying to find out how someone managed to kill the same woman twice and leave two bodies."

"We've got our theories," Dr. Farmer said.

"But unfortunately our theories are lousy," Wiggins said.

"Something something qputers, something something *time,*" Dr. Farmer might as well have said.

"What?" Woo-jin said.

Wiggins spoke slower. "We think," he said, "that her *self-hood* has gone into *superposition.*"

"Can I be excused?" Woo-jin asked.

"I suppose so," Wiggins said.

"I was about ready to head out," Dr. Farmer said. "You need a lift?"

Woo-jin nodded. "I would appreciate a ride back to my foundation."

Wiggins gave Woo-jin a business card and a pat on the back. "Don't worry about your sister, Woo-jin. She's going to be a-okay."

In a parking garage that smelled of desperate cigarettes, Woo-jin got into Dr. Farmer's black sedan then spiraled up and out onto the street.

"You're a doctor, right?" Woo-jin said.

"That's correct."

"Maybe you can tell me what's wrong with my brain?"

Dr. Farmer nodded. "I have some passing, layman's familiarity with your condition but I'm a doctor of dead bodies, not live brains."

"If I was dead, would you be able to tell what was wrong with me?"

"Certainly, but I don't advise that you die just to find out."

"I keep having ennui attacks."

"That's the layman's term for it. Though ennui really means 'boredom.' From what I understand your attacks are related to the part of your brain that manages your empathetic response. Are you familiar with Abraham Lincoln?"

"The guy from the penny."

"A great American president. He grew up in Illinois, very poor. His family had nothing and lived in a little log house. But young Abe learned to read and taught himself about literature and law and became one of the greatest leaders the world has ever known. One day when Abe was a boy he was walking down a dirt road and passed a turtle that had rolled over onto its back and was helpless. It troubled him to see the creature suffering but he walked on anyway. The farther he walked, though, the more troubled he became, until the thought of that turtle lying helpless was more than he could bear. So he walked back nearly two miles just to flip the turtle over."

"Lucky turtle," Woo-jin said.

"I'm telling you this because Abe Lincoln was born with a cognitive tendency similar to your own, an abundance of empathy. And this tendency to feel the suffering of others was one of the reasons he became such a great leader."

"I'm not a leader. Just an official delegate."

At this they arrived at the lot of Woo-jin's former home, now nothing but a ring of cinder blocks. Dr. Farmer yanked the parking brake and leaned over. "Say, I couldn't trouble you to suck my wiener, could I?"

"That would trouble me a lot," Woo-jin said.

Dr. Farmer shrugged. "To each his own."

With Woo-jin deposited at the dusty trailer site, the coroner departed in a cloud of sedan-generated dust. Woo-jin walked to the place where the front door used to be and stepped over a cinder block. Here's where the living room would have been, overflowing with Patsy screaming for takeout. The TV would have been over here, broadcasting competitive defecation championships. Woo-jin turned in a circle and imagined what used to be in his line of vision, the bric-a-brac that had ascended to the heavens. Around this time he would have typically gone to sleep, pulling down the shades and curling fetally in his hammock. But there were no shades to pull or hammock to swing from so Woo-jin found the place where his hammock would have been and lay down in the dirt next to a newspaper advertisement that had blown under the double-wide long ago.

The ad was for women's hosiery, specifically the kinds that reduce varicose veins and provide a more shapely figure. An old ad, from when people used to care about those kinds of things. All the models pictured were probably dead now, maybe even in Dr. Farmer's morgue, waiting for someone to slice them open and formulate an opinion about them. Look at them, yearning to be thought attractive. The gutters of Woo-jin's eyelids filled with tears. Oh, so this was going to be the trigger. He bit down on his mouth guard and closed his eyes, letting the attack fuck him over. He twitched on the bare ground like a fish about to get clubbed. The steady drumbeat. It smelled like mushrooms and old socks down here, dryer lint and cobwebs. The ground took on the appearance of being illuminated by the moon. He turned over and got blasted with the vibrant rippling flames of the campfire. It was the mesa again, the high windy desolation. The ring of objects around the flame: a refrigerator, a tire, three stuffed animals, a pile of books, a full-length mirror. Woo-jin pulled himself up on his elbows. The wood smoke burned his eyes and may not have been wood smoke at all; it smelled of petroleum and dead creatures. He rose and looked around. The world below the mesa was nothing but bluish desert darkness in every direction. In the distance he made out something constructed, a gigantic letter T formed from white rocks lying on the desert floor. He approached the mirror and held out his hand, which appeared to be his own, and in the mirror confirmed the dumb reality of his own face. Next he considered the refrigerator. It was a model with a combo ice and water dispenser, one door for the freezer, the other for the fridge. He pulled open the fridge door and found it fully stocked with food. It hummed a bit as the fan got going. He located a pile of wrapped sandwiches, an apple, a bag of cookies, some bottled water, and took these over to the tire, where he sat and began to eat. Was that refrigerator even plugged in? It didn't appear to be. The power cord snaked behind it like a tail.

Woo-jin ate. The sandwiches were a perfect harmonization of condiments, cheeses, vegetables, and meats. One of them had this incredible pesto aioli. After finishing three sandwiches Woo-jin bit into the snappy apple. Dang! That was one fine piece of fruit. Finally, the cookies. Just the right chewiness, with chunks of chocolate, raisins, and cashews. At the end of his meal, Woo-jin stuffed his trash into the cookie bag and tossed it on the fire. While he'd been eating he'd forgotten about his troubles but now, under the cosmos, on what seemed like a vast soundstage, he wondered about the dead girl and if he was somehow responsible for her turning up dead twice. He was beginning to miss Patsy. And where was he supposed to live?

Woo-jin turned to the pile of books. He knew how to read well enough, how to get trapped in sentences and scratch out some words when needed, thanks to the various foster parents who'd made sure he didn't die and made him learn to read so they could keep collecting the foster-care checks. From time to time an older kid, somebody smarter, had read him a book and he recalled the reassuring process of blobs of ink turning into flapping lips and tongues. The book on top of the stack was a paperback without a cover, its pages yellow and blunted at the corners, eroded by sandy wind. He kicked it aside and looked at the book beneath it. He read the title once and read it again.

HOW TO LOVE PEOPLE
by Woo-jin Kan

Funny there'd be a book by another Woo-jin Kan. He picked it up and turned it over and looked at the picture of the author, a guy who looked kind of like himself but older, spiky hair gray-flecked, slightly smiling, a peaceful expression. He looked like the kind of guy who had his shit together, clue number one that this was a different Woo-jin.

He turned the book back over and opened it to the first page.

Dear Woo-jin,

This is your future brain sending a message to your past brain. For serious. Here's what you have to do to get Patsy back. You have to write this book you're now holding. It's one of the only books the Last Dude has to read, so make it really good. He needs to read your book so that he can make the messages about why we got extinct. He's writing them out in the rocks down there in the desert. You have to quit your dishwashing job and write this book. What's the book supposed to be about? Who knows, you haven't written it yet, but at least you have a title ha ha ha.

You think I'm joking? Since I'm your future brain I know what's about to happen to you. You're going to find that dead girl again. What I say is true and you really have to follow these directions. Seriously, bro.

Signed,
Your (Woo-jin's) Future Brain

P.S.: For serious. You have to quit Il Italian Joint and become a full-time writer.

As Woo-jin's eyes turned from the page to the sky, his mind got sucked back through some sorta tube, flailing, a squeal of astral velocity, as if he were recoiling from the strange fact of reading something yet to be. His head went smack against the ground as the day began anew in Georgetown, Seattle. There was the women's hosiery advertisement again, now drained of emotional oomph. Woo-jin's tracksuit was filthy. He stood, twisting the kinks from his joints, mouth painfully dry, hair flat on one side of his head and cantilevered in perpendicular spikes on the other and sort of fuzzed-up on top. He stepped over the cinder block where the door used to be and shuffled in a direction that seemed to have been chosen for him. His legs snapped back and forth and walked him through a playground nestled between an off-ramp and some train tracks. A cargo plane scraped the wind.

Woo-jin spoke a sentence through streams of spittle. "I want to figure out what's going on here." Speaking aloud surprised him. Like a thought had escaped his brain through a hole in a fence, scampering out into the open where ears could pick it up. If he had a celestial head like the Ambassador, that certainly would have been convenient. He would just ask his celestial head, "Hey, fill me in on what the deal is with the dead girl and this dusty place with the campfire with the refrigerator, books, stuffed animals, and a mirror. Oh, and the tire. And Patsy being yanked up into the sky. And my future brain, who says I'm supposed to be an author." His celestial head—he imagined him as a gap-toothed black man with an afro—would say, "Thanks for asking. Here's exactly what those things mean, my brother," and proceed to untangle the knot in Woo-jin's brain that seemed only to grow tighter the more he picked at it.

Now beyond the playground and its ghost children frolicking on dirty equipment, Woo-jin came to a concentration of warehouses, inside of which were squirts and clanks and whatnot, noises supposedly connected to purposes. Coming to the corner of 12th and Vale he found the Ambassador sitting on a milk crate with his toilet brush scepter.

Woo-jin said, "You ever heard of a book called *How to Love People,* by Woo-jin Kan?"

"I don't have time for books like that when I'm always consuming economics and political science texts," said the Ambassador. "Unless this love book of yours is an economics book. In that case, yes, yes, I've most definitely read it."

"Maybe it is about economics."

"I thought you said you wrote it."

"Another Woo-jin Kan wrote it. Or maybe it isn't a real book at all."

"In that case," said the Ambassador, "you might try getting it published."

"That's a really good idea."

Was it afternoon already? Looked like it. Soon it would be time for work again, the nightly river of flatware and crockery. A metro bus pulled up smelling of french fries, biodiesel. The Ambassador gently touched Woo-jin's shoulder with his toilet brush scepter and said, "Someday soon you'll witness the most epic peace talks in human history," then boarded the bus and asked the driver if it stopped near Rite Aid.

Woo-jin walked to the lot just north of Boeing Field where the body had appeared and appeared again. His legs carried him beyond the field, through South Park and up the road to Il Italian Joint. When he came to the back entrance he found piles of dishes literally spilling out the doorway into the parking lot. Thousands of them, encrusted from lunch rush. At first he stepped over them but the closer he got to the kitchen the harder it became to not break anything. He quickly found that the best way to navigate the dishes was to get prone and sort of swim through them. In the kitchen, the dishes reached a little higher than head level. With a modified breaststroke Woo-jin was able to keep his head above the line and edge closer to where the wash station was supposed to be.

"Bahn Kan? Ben O'Winn? Pontoon?" he called. "Sandford?"

Apart from some indeterminate hydraulic hissing, the kitchen was empty of noise. Sandford Deane's head popped up beside him from under a platter, wearing a colander for a hat.

"Thank God you're here, Woo-jin. Pontoon, Bahn Kan, and Ben O'Winn didn't show up. It's up to you to turn this place around," Sandford said, wiping a soggy crust of bread off his forehead. "I even got you some diamond-encrusted *platinum* wool."

Woo-jin paddled over to the Hobart and got down to business. As he shoved dishes through the machine the dish level slowly began to drop. Midway through his shift the dishes were only up to his calves. Tirelessly, he converted dirty dishes into clean ones, an act of prestidigitation as much as sanitization. Dinner rush came and went and by the end of the night the wash station was empty. Woo-jin dunked his apron into the laundry and grabbed his card to punch out. Sandford clapped him on the back, congratulating him on another evening for the record books.

"Thanks, Sandford. But I won't be back tomorrow. I'm quitting right now."

Woo-jin's boss looked aghast. "But you're the best dishwasher in Seattle. In the world, even. What will you do instead?"

"I'm going to write a book," said Woo-jin. "A book about how to love people."

Sandford shook his head and retrieved the gold medal from the Restaurant and Hotel Management Olympics then solemnly placed it around Woo-jin's neck. It looked good with the tracksuit even though the tracksuit looked like shit. Woo-jin stood a moment imagining a national anthem, not the new one, but the old one, the one with the terrorists getting castrated in front of their weeping children. How many hours had he spent in this kitchen, blasting caked-on food off porcelain surfaces? It had been his first and only job, started almost two-thirds of his life ago. He imagined a montage to go along with the national anthem, a series of slow-motion shots of him scouring pots and scraping baking sheets, drinking soda, punching his time card. All those good times seemed a prelude to this, the decision to write a book, which apparently he was going to have to figure out how to do. On the way out past the Dumpsters, Sally the waitress hugged him and said, "Good luck, Mike. We'll say we knew you when."

Woo-jin had no idea what she was talking about but he didn't let on. He walked into the backdrop of New York Alki rising amid northwestern cedars, helicopters swooping and jets crisscrossing the clouds, past trembling warehouses, across the sludgy Duwamish, into the only neighborhood he had ever loved, Georgetown, coming to the field where he had twice discovered a girl's body. He was going to write a book! He almost skipped at the thought.

Up ahead was the big unknown machine's silhouette in the dark waves of grasses, like a sea-tossed dinghy weathering a storm. Woo-jin came to the indeterminate and abandoned technology and looked to the place where he'd found the body.

There she was again.

The same girl, in the same place, in the same position. Same black hair, white shirt, black pants. Woo-jin leaned over and puked, witnessing the remnants of the sandwiches, apple, and cookies he had devoured on the wind-battered mesa the night before, introduced into this particular plane of reality. He wiped his mouth on his sleeve and looked again.

The girl grabbed his arm and screamed, "Help me! Help me! *Help me!*"

Q&A WITH LUKE PIPER, PART 1

the tape roll a bit here before we get . . . Luke? You need anything, Luke?

No, I'm fine.

I thought we could first talk about Nick Fedderly. About when he was a kid.

Sure. I first met Nick in kindergarten. Everyone knew he was poor. When he came to birthday parties nobody expected him to bring a present. When he came to one of mine he gave me a used *Mad* magazine, which was a big deal. The money he saved up to buy it. He lived with his mom—her name was Star—in what was basically a shack out in the woods on Bainbridge, in a place we all called Hippie Hill. This was before the real estate boom of the eighties and nineties. The island was back-to-the-landers, some berry farmers, very simple living. You got to Nick's house on a narrow road through the trees. It was almost like there was no ditch, just enough room for one car. And no gravel, just rutted mud. Steep. If it was raining, forget it. But at the top of the hill the drive opened into a little meadow with the shack. Smoke coming out of a stovepipe. At the edge of the property was the frame of a house that Nick's father had started building but died before finishing. In the shack they didn't have any electricity or gas heat and they cooked all their meals on a woodstove. His mom always looked exhausted. She would have been in her twenties but looked twenty years older. She wore stained housedresses and Holly Hobbie bonnets, her hair in thick, flower-child braid pigtails. It was just the two of them.

How did Nick's father die?

He died trying to build that house. Apparently he was working on it one day and fell. There's a right way and a wrong way to land. Apparently he landed in precisely the wrong way. This tragedy was pretty fresh when I first met Nick. I think I sat behind him the first day of class.

Did you two become friends immediately, or . . . ?

Not really. Friendships are fickle at that age, or at least they were for me. Part of it I think is that I wasn't ready for him yet. I hadn't grown in the ways I needed to in order to really get to know him.

Star. What did she do exactly?

Odds and ends. She sometimes sold chicks and ducklings at the feed store. Split lumber. Janitorial stuff. Nothing too noteworthy or dignified. Poor Star. I think she tried to get jobs at restaurants as a waitress but she was always so wrecked-looking. I remember grown-ups talking in low voices about her fitness as a parent. They'd see Nick show up at school without shoes. I think they mostly lived off the insurance payout they got after Nick's dad died. They kept living that same life up there in the woods in the shack with no electricity, an honest-to-god outhouse out back, the rain coming down hard turning everything to mud. Naturally everyone thought she was completely insane.

Did you ever go over to Nick's house?

Sure, once we started playing together. This would be second grade. I rode my bike to school and one morning my chain blew out, so I had to walk it the last half mile. When some of the bigger kids saw me they laughed and made fun of me and I guess Nick heard about it. I parked my bike in the rack behind the gym thinking I'd have to have my mom come pick me up. But that afternoon I found that my bike had been fixed. Another kid told me he'd seen Nick messing with it at recess. The next day I confronted him about it, asked if he'd been the one who fixed the bike. He wouldn't look me in the eyes, just sort of sank down into himself and stared at hopscotch markings. I finally got him to admit that he'd repaired it and I gave him a Superman trading card as thanks. He just pocketed it and ran away.

A while later I was assigned to be his reading buddy. We were supposed to read the same book and talk about it together in front of the class. We read some kind of science fiction story, I don't remember what it was, but I remember he started to open up a bit. He didn't get to see many movies, so I'd tell him the plots and highlights of the ones I'd seen. He didn't have a TV or a telephone at home, which amazed me. Not having a phone, more than not having clothes, equaled abject poverty to me.

What about your family? Tell me about your parents.

[sighs] My folks were college professors. They jokingly referred to themselves as the Doctors Piper. My dad, Gordon, taught English, and my mom, Gail, taught Library Science. Her dad had owned a shipping company and died when she was in her twenties, leaving her a sizable inheritance. Our house was on the north end of the island with a view of Seattle, a hundred feet of beachfront all to ourselves, right up against a steep embankment. We had a boat. A dog. The house was full of books and had big bay windows looking out on Puget Sound. My younger sister and I spent a lot of time exploring the beach and the woods, making up stories and games, on our own for hours at a time. My mom bolted a big ship bell to the side of the house that she rang when it was time for dinner. We took lots of vacations, to Canada and the San Juans mostly, but a couple times to Costa Rica, the Caribbean, Hawaii. My parents had lots of friends, brilliant colleagues from the university. One thing I noticed right away was how being smart usually meant also having a unique sense of humor. We stayed up late watching *Monty Python*, eating homemade ice cream, or we'd drive out to Suquamish to see a movie at the drive-in. You could say my childhood was an embarrassment of riches. I had toys, sure, but never an obscene amount. Mostly we amused ourselves with our own minds, the last generation to really do so, in my opinion. Nothing scheduled, no overload of after-school activities, just constant conversations with our parents about anything and everything. Their interests were all over the map. At dinner we'd talk about politics, economics, art, sex, history, war, astronomy. You could throw any obscure topic at my mother and she'd tell

you the three seminal works in that particular field, what the best editions were, and who published them. My dad liked to recite what he called his "Poem of the Week," something he'd committed to memory. My parents and Nick's mom were like two evolutionary branches from a common ancestor. My folks had grown outward, embracing the world, while Star had grown inward, into places the rest of us couldn't fathom.

What do you mean by "places"?

Well let me back up. You can understand how our community considered her a pathetic creature, someone who'd started off weird, probably fried her mind on acid then suffered the horrible loss of her husband. You could be forgiven for making that kind of judgment. That's how I felt about her when Nick started inviting me to his house. I kept on making up excuses as to why I couldn't go, then finally one day I came home from school and my mother told me I'd received a birthday party invitation in the mail. That Nick had wrangled up enough money for a card, envelope, and stamp was a small miracle. I tried to get out of it but my mom was adamant that I attend. So I bought him a *Star Wars* pop-up book and one spring afternoon my mother drove me to his house, bottoming out the Saab on that hellish driveway. She must have known about Star's reputation but she was an open-minded, Marxist liberal intent on exposing me to different social strata. Even so, I think she was a little shocked by the condition of their house. There was all this crap surrounding the shack, rusted and moldy junk that looked puked out of a garbage truck. I got out of the car wearing my ridiculous khaki slacks and polo shirt, the wrapped present under my arm, and walked up the muddy path to their front door. Star greeted us there, with Nick standing behind her. She reached out and took my mother's hand and said some things that made me want to cry. She said, "Thank you so much, Mrs. Piper. Luke is the only kid at school who is nice to Nick. It means so much to us that you came." She invited us in and we ducked into this little space almost entirely devoid of anything you could call a creature comfort. Table, two chairs, two beds in an adjoining room. Outside the shack was a disaster but inside was clean and well-kept. And it smelled nice, too, like incense. We sat on pillows in what would have been the living room but it could very well have been considered the dining room. Star served tea, and cake made from scratch. It was a chocolate cake with frosting, all made to look like E.T. The movie alien, remember? It took me a minute to realize this was the party. Star was relaxed and comfortable in her own house and made pleasant conversation with my mom. Questions like, "I understand you teach librarians?" It struck me that Nick had gleaned all these little pieces of information from me and formulated a comprehensive portrait of who my family was. Now, hearing about all the things Nick and I had talked about, I could tell that he admired me. His admiration didn't ever come out when it was just the two of us together, but hearing his mom talk about what he'd told her about me confirmed our friendship. When we finished the cake, Nick opened the present. I'd never seen such gratitude. It was as though I was witnessing the first act of altruism in human history, a pivotal moment in the development of the species. Nick's mother actually got teary-eyed. Nick was beside himself with happiness. We played with that pop-up book for over an hour, acting out scenes from the movies I'd seen a half dozen times and Nick hadn't seen at all. Nick added little addendums and characters, which at first bugged me because I wanted to stay true to the original version but then I kind of gave up and went with it. I remember his favorite character was Chewbacca, he kept wanting to be Chewbacca, while I, of course, was Luke, when really I should have been Han Solo. Anyway, while our moms talked we took our game outside, into the woods, and it was then that I noticed there was another building on the property. A small shed. I think maybe I tried to take a look inside but Nick stopped me, real serious, and told me it was off-limits. After a while our moms came outside, standing there chatting like they'd been friends forever, and it was time to go. No birthday party I ever attended ever matched what I felt that day.

What was in the shed?

Nick's dad's shop. They hadn't opened it since he died.

What did your peers make of your friendship with Nick?

My answer to that is going to sound like a lot of bragging but the fact is, my primary talent in life has always been my likability. When you're someone everybody likes you can get away with befriending people who aren't liked. My peers always looked to me as a leader, came to me for my approval or blessing, wanted my opinions on stuff. Kids questioned my friendship with Nick. "Why are you hanging out with that freak?" they'd ask me, and I'd tell them they were idiots who didn't realize Nick was a genius. The things that should have marked Nick as an outcast became, thanks to my psychological campaign, examples of his edginess. His clothes, the piercings he got before anyone else in high school. In a way I think I achieved the impossible by making poverty *cool*.

You mentioned his fixing your bike. Were there other times when Nick's mechanical inclinations became apparent?

He was always taking things apart to see how they worked, putting them back together about half the time. My parents, the most technologically inept people I knew, were amazed by this. My dad could barely get the lawn mower to turn over. Sometimes Nick came over and helped my dad in the garage, or fixed things around our house, like our water heater.

He fixed your water heater?

Yeah, when he must have been about twelve years old. He was coming over to our house a lot around that age. Our home was one of the rare places where Nick could find praise. He certainly wasn't getting any at school. School bored the hell out of him. And even though I had succeeded in making him sort of acceptable to our classmates, he really didn't take much initiative to make any friends other than me. He didn't like to play with me when I was with other kids. He'd wait to get me alone and then we'd enter our world of codes and secret passageways, our games of trap doors and monsters. He bonded with my parents and asked them lots of questions about history and science. Sometimes my sister and I would just end up playing together by default when Nick was over, since he was so wrapped up in learning about the Luddite movement and the invention of radio with my mom and dad.

Your sister. Tell me about her.

Man. She was incredible. She would have grown up to become a beautiful and talented woman. Claudine. I miss her every day.

She loved music. Always twisting my arm to sing songs with her. She considered all the heavy thinking in our household sort of comical. She could defuse a deep conversation with a perfectly timed joke. If my family was the Beatles, she would have been Ringo.

And you would have been—

Paul.

Let's talk about high school.

Sure. I was your typical debate nerd, specializing in Lincoln–Douglas, also did a pretty decent job as a fullback on the football team, elected to student council, founder and president of the Photography Club, never at a loss for a girlfriend. Again, I floated by on charm and all the things I learned through osmosis from my parents. Kept a 4.0 GPA, volunteered at a retirement home teaching senior citizens how to use computers. My high school career was an unmitigated success from start to finish. I was miserable. [Laughs].

And Nick?

He started smoking. Hanging out with the poorer kids, making out in public with these skanky chicks. Spent a lot of time in the vocational-tech departments. Those teachers, the wood-shop, metal-shop guys, sports coaches mostly, they loved him. He did really well in math and science, lousy in Spanish and English. Hated art.

And you guys remained friends?

Strangely enough, yeah. We had a real Goofus and Gallant thing going on. We orbited each other, admired each other as opposites.

Nick started smoking pot as a freshman and one night convinced me to try it. We stayed up watching Pink Floyd's *The Wall* and talking about philosophy. He told me he looked up to me for how I could get anyone to do anything I wanted them to. I told him I admired him for his genius. But there were whole weeks that went by when we didn't talk to each other. Just pass in the hallway with not so much as a nod. I still defended him when friends of mine talked shit about him but we started to have a lot less contact than we used to. Then the science fair happened.

The science fair at Bainbridge High was kind of a big deal. Sometime in the late eighties scouts from tech companies started coming over to check out the budding talent. The idea was to identify the innovators really young and give them scholarships. Of course this poisoned the spirit of the thing and after a while everyone was writing unoriginal programs in DOS. It turned into more of a computer fair than a science fair. So junior year, the first year Nick qualified, he shows up with these boxes of crap. Gears and wires and hammered-out panels and screws and stuff. Little pieces of wood and coils of string. It looked like the contents of a junk drawer. I sat there with my display on Puget Sound pollution watching Nick set up his project. He refused to say anything about it. The pieces appeared to fit together in random configurations but Nick worked on it with such a sense of purpose that I had to believe the machine he was building actually *did* something. Kids and parents wandered around, smirking about the bizarre contraption Nick was building. If Nick heard them he didn't show it. He was absorbed. After about an hour, his project was built. It was a battered metal cube, about a foot and a half square. He put up a sign that said, "The Machine" and sat behind his table, stone-faced, his black hair hanging in front of his eyes. I was convinced he was putting everyone on. Then the judges stopped by with their clipboards and frowns and asked Nick what the machine did.

Nick took a key from his pocket, like the kind used to wind up an antique toy. He inserted it into a hole in the top of the box and twisted it a few times. We waited. At first nothing happened. By now a crowd had gathered, curious to see what the hell this thing did. Then a panel popped off and landed on the floor. Inside were gears and screws, little pistons, whirling things. The machine shuddered and then appeared to dismantle itself. Screws and rivets shot out in all these directions. People stepped back. Somebody made a crack that it was a bomb. No one could take their eyes off the thing. Within a minute the entire machine was dismantled, lying in pieces all over the table and floor. There was a moment of quiet. Then, one by one, everyone realized this was the end of the show, and started to laugh. Nick didn't move. Just sat in the same position he'd been sitting in, quiet, while everyone roared. Once the crowd was tired of this they moved on to look at someone's model of a double helix.

One man lingered. He wore slacks and a black sport coat over a white shirt. Young guy, maybe twenty-five years old. Handsome, short haircut. He slowly bent down and picked up a gear from the floor and turned it over in his hand. He cleared his throat and told Nick he liked his invention. At this, Nick looked up, sort of wary and angry, prepared for a punch line. But there was no punch line. The man handed Nick a business card. The card just had a name and phone number on it. Dirk Bickle. He said he was a scout for an organization that was always on the lookout for innovative young minds, then nodded and said good-bye.

I helped Nick pick up the pieces of his machine. As I was putting the pieces back in their boxes I realized that Nick's machine hadn't just fallen apart. It had dismantled itself so thoroughly that every moving part had been detached from every other part. Not a single screw or gear was connected to anything else. When I pointed this out to Nick, he smiled for the first time that afternoon and said, "You figured it out."

What about this Dirk Bickle character?

Nick stashed the card. They didn't speak until a year or so later.

You guys weren't curious about why Dirk expressed interest in the machine?

Sure, I guess we were for a day or so, but other stuff came up, or we got distracted by the day-to-day bullshit of being kids. Nick got busted for smoking pot behind the art building. The principal pulled me aside and basically told me to stop hanging out with him. Said I would sully my reputation by associating with a kid like Nick. I told him that Nick was brilliant and if he couldn't see that it meant he wasn't doing that great a job as an education administrator. [Laughs]. That didn't fly so well.

You mentioned girls. I'm wondering if you could talk about your and Nick's girlfriends at this time.

So we're on to sex, okay. I went through quite a few girlfriends. I can't remember a lot of their names. I know that's bad. It was typical high school stuff. Leaving notes in lockers, slow dancing, finding remote places to make out. It's the make-out sessions I remember most. Spending literally an hour with your face pressed up against a girl's, that warm delta in her jeans. Her hair. They wore it long in those days, my God, I'd live in those ringlets and strands. The girls I was most attracted to weren't the designated popular girls but the smart ones who should have known better. They wore thick woolly sweaters you could just slide your hand under. Whenever I rode in the car with my dad, he'd try to start conversations by asking what I was thinking, and invariably I was thinking about sex. The way you think about sex before you've even had it, the unanswered hormonal question of it.

And Nick's sexual activities in high school?

Like I said, he trolled the lower echelons of the socioeconomic strata. Had girlfriends in Poulsbo, off the island. None of the rich, pretty girls wanted anything to do with him. He attracted girls who had self-esteem issues. He obsessed over them and despised them. Treated them really poorly. I got on him about this a couple times. While I worshipped female pulchritude, I think he found the whole act of sex degrading. There was this one girl Laura who he fucked with psychologically, over and over. Just ground her down emotionally, backing her into these arguments about the nature of reality while she was high. Fucked-up stuff. We argued about girls a lot. I'm tired of talking about this. Let's move on to something else.

Do you want to talk about the mud slide?

Okay.

Go ahead.

All right. Our house, I think I mentioned, was built against a pretty steep embankment. During the winter of my junior year of high school, we got twenty straight days of rain. Being hardy Pacific Northwesterners, we didn't think anything of it. One Friday night I was in my folks' VW van with a girl named Carrie Powers. I'd been seeing her for a month or so. We had gone out to a movie in Poulsbo and were driving home. She, or I, I can't remember, suggested that we find a remote road and pull over. We found a place and lay down a blanket in the back of the van and fucked hard for what must have been about two hours. That incredible, young fucking when you've finally figured out how to really fuck and no one's preventing you from fucking. The rain was coming down on the windows in sheets. It was beautiful. At some point one of us looked at a watch and realized we were way past our curfews. But it was totally worth it. I dropped her off a block from her house and drove home in the rain, my dick sore. I remember I was listening to an R.E.M. album, a song about being Superman. I sang along with the music on full blast, just elated after an epic screw. Then I came to my road and saw a lot of flashing lights. My first thought was that it would be strange for there to be a fire with so much rain. I pulled over and looked for my house but couldn't see it and for a second I thought maybe I was turned around. I kept looking for my house in the flashing lights but there was just this empty spot where it used to be. Then I noticed the mud. A big slick of it running down the embankment, across the road, across the beach, into Puget Sound. The mud slide had completely wiped out my house. And with it my family. I stood in the rain with the firemen and the cops, calling out for my mom and dad, my sister. Their bodies were recovered from the sound two days later.

What happened in the days immediately after that event?

I don't remember. I assume the whole social services side of things went into motion. There were counselors and the Child Protective Services. I met with people. Police. Lawyers. The thing I hated most was the way people wanted to be a part of my mourning. Moms of other kids came up to me in downtown Winslow, asked how I was doing, whether I needed anything, tried to buy me lunch. I suspected they were getting off on my tragedy. They were elated at the opportunity to show their concern. The reaction of the adult world to my circumstances appeared overly scripted to me. They spoke of "healing" and "closure" and used all this other bullshit terminology. For a while I stayed in a motel on the island and had these visitors constantly coming by to bring me fucking casseroles. I couldn't stand it.

After the motel where did you stay?

I had only a year until I was supposed to go to college so it didn't make much sense for me to go live with aunts and uncles I barely knew in Chicago. Everyone agreed it would be best if I stayed and graduated from Bainbridge High. So what I needed was a sort of foster home situation. That's where the limits of the island's generosity became apparent. No one came forward to offer me a place to live. Except Nick's mom, Star.

You moved in with them.

Well the beauty of it was that I had the VW van. I parked it on their lawn. Or the muddy patch that was supposed to be their lawn. They'd covered parts of the yard with slabs of plywood so you could walk from the shack to the outhouse without sinking. I slept in the van, ate in the shack, and used the outhouse. I got into a bunch of colleges but decided to go to UW. I was really worried about money even though my inheritance was in the seven figures, plus the life insurance payments. I was a parentless millionaire living in a VW van, shitting in an outhouse, and meditating with my best friend's mom in their shack, burning Nag Champa incense. I cried all the time, as you can imagine. But I learned to control the valves of my grief, making conscious decisions as to when I'd let myself cry. And Nick took care of me, too. He had been through this kind of grief before and had endured the disingenuous condolences of strangers. He helped just by keeping me to my routines, banging on the van in the morning so I'd get ready for school. He must have been grieving pretty hard, too, since he'd been so close to my family. The mud slide changed the game. Nick started to clean up his act, quit smoking pot and took a sort of vow of celibacy for a while. We started listening to these bands from Washington, D.C., called . . . I'm trying to remember the genre.

Punk?

It was an offshoot of punk. Straight edge. Yeah. It was this movement that evolved in the eighties, a sort of monastic offspring of punk rock that swore off drugs and alcohol. The real hard-core adherents swore off sex. The idea was that punk up to that time had railed against control and authority, especially governmental authority. By being straight edge, you attempted to cut out all the external forces that might control you. The band we got into in a big way was Minor Threat. Nick and I spent a lot of time in the woods talking about this philosophy, reading the fanzines. We realized that to break free of societal control you had to control yourself and exercise extreme discipline. I looked ahead to UW and started to get this dull ache in my gut. I had sort of arbitrarily decided to go into premed. But every night I spent under the spell of Star's Kwakiutl folk tales and herbal remedies, the more I began to see the whole university system as a sham. I started to hate my own conformity. How I'd learned to play the game of school without actually learning anything. How I could charm anyone. In retrospect I think I decided to withdraw my application because college reminded me too much of my parents. I decided I'd travel instead. Then, one afternoon while Nick and Star were away, in town or something, I don't know where, I did something I'd been wanting to do ever since that first birthday party visit. I broke into Nick's dad's shed.

Ah . . .

It didn't take me long to find the key to the padlock. It was where you'd expect it, in a random drawer in the kitchen. I pushed the key into the rusty lock and pulled open the door. Lots of cobwebs. Light coming through translucent windows. The place was about fifteen feet square. Along one wall were carefully arranged tools: saws, hammers, nothing that required electricity. The deal with Nick's dad was he had intended to build them a house using only tools that existed in the nineteenth century, or some such hippie shit like that. There was still a half-finished chair sitting there just as Nick's dad had left it the day before he died. A coffee cup with the coffee long evaporated. On the other side of the room stretched a bench, piled with papers. Some of them had become moldy and illegible. There were big sheets of paper tacked up all over the walls and tucked into cardboard tubes, too. Blueprints. Pictures of buildings. Cross sections of sewers and electrical systems and subways. Yellow legal pads filled with tiny, uniform engineering scrawl, three-ring binders with all sorts of tabs separating the sections. What was this even about? I looked closer, at the names of streets and parks and monuments. It was New York City. I became so enrapt in the schematics that I didn't hear Star and Nick until they were standing in the doorway. Their shadows fell on me. I asked them what this was, what it meant. Nick was silent, sort of frozen. Then Star spoke, calmly but with her voice carrying a weight that terrified me. She said, "Lock up when you're done." Then she walked away. What the hell was I supposed to think of that?

What did Nick do?

He joined me and started looking over the blueprints and notes. None of it made any sense to either of us. Especially when we started noticing there were maps of Bainbridge in there as well, with street names we didn't recognize. Lexington Avenue. Bleecker Street. In the notes we found several references to the "New York Alki" project. I'd taken Washington state history and knew what this meant. When the first white settlers came to the region in the nineteenth century, they debated what to call their settlement. They had big aspirations for their little frontier outpost but were really bummed out by all the mud and rain. To cheer themselves up they considered naming the place "New York Alki." Alki was a Chinook word for "by and by." Meaning, "someday." "New York Alki" meant that someday this place would be as big and vibrant as New York City. But cooler heads prevailed and decided that naming their city after New York, itself named after old York, was retarded. So they named the city after Chief Sealth and called it a day.

We figured that Nick's dad had latched on to this little piece of history, too, and had decided to create a game out of it.

A hobby. We convinced ourselves of this even though the notes seemed more intense than what a hobbyist would have come up with. Who would have dreamed up such a crazy idea in the first place, anyway? Who would have thought it possible to create a life-size replica of Manhattan in Puget Sound?

ABBY FOGG

Ever since childhood, Abby Fogg had wondered why she was herself instead of somebody else. She'd lie on her bedroom floor staring at the circle within a circle within a circle of the ceiling light fixture, freaking herself out with the fact that she was *Abby Fogg*. And while this Abby Fogg accumulated thoughts and memories, went to college, fell in love with archival films and a man named Rocco Petrone, the suspicion persisted that there'd been some mistake, that somehow Abby Fogg had been dropped into the wrong body. Since the age of five or six, Abby had suspected she'd been born in the wrong era, aching as she watched the grain of early-twentieth-century footage. But the previous century wouldn't have her, with its artists' salons and movie palaces and celebrity sex tapes. Nope. Abby'd been born into this era yet to be named, in the years that followed that dark period known as the Age of Fucked Up Shit.

Nowadays Abby rose early to make breakfast and spy on her neighbours from the Vancouver condo she shared with Rocco. Even though the place had a view of Granville Island, she preferred to sit in her undies in the dining nook, where she could read the news and glance through horizontal blinds angled at the precise diagonality to allow her a view into a condo across the courtyard and three stories down. The occupants of this condo were about the same age as Abby and Rocco, maybe a little older, not yet sinking into their thirties. The couple bore the same demographic characteristics as Abby's parents: she Asian, him sorta Latinoish Caucasian. The woman usually rose first, around 6:30 a.m., mounted a green fit ball in her panties and tank top, drank coffee from an ugly brown mug, caught up on email. The guy rose about half an hour later, shirtless, a landing strip of chest hair marking his sternum. He shuffled into the living/work space scratching himself through plaid pajama bottoms, planted a kiss on his girlfriend's neck, and performed a few push-ups and stomach crunches on the rug. The woman worked at home, doing something design-related. The man left around 8:30 for a job that didn't require him to wear a tie but sometimes he wore a collared shirt and a sport coat with jeans. Abby suspected these were days in which the man met with clients, whoever they might be.

This morning Abby watched the couple while periodically glancing at job listings on her laptop. An English muffin sat half-eaten on a Fiestaware saucer beside a glass residued with grapefruit juice. She punched "archivist" and "data retrieval" and "digital forensics" into the engine.

Across the alley three stories down the young woman sprang from her fit ball to answer the phone. She retrieved the phone from a kitchen counter Abby couldn't see, then walked back to the computer desk, inspecting the fronds of a nonnative perennial while she spoke. She was still in her underwear. Abby squinted to read her lips but the woman was too far away. The lips looked like a little pulsating blob of ochre in a milky female face.

At no point in their three years together had Abby confided to Rocco that she suspected she was supposed to be somebody else, mostly because he appeared to love her as she was. She doubted he ever woke up with the odd feeling that he lived in the wrong body and wrong time. He appeared devoid of insecurities, particularly when expressing ostensible insecurities, as if he knew he was supposed to have them and felt compelled to share fake ones lest he appear as confident and well-adjusted as he truly was.

The woman had a snazzier computer than Abby's. She collected expensive art books. Sometimes the couple used chopsticks to eat things that weren't Japanese.

Rocco entered the living space. Like the man across the alley, he tended to be lax about shaving. His broad face went through several test expressions.

"You forgot to make coffee again?" Rocco said.

"Sorry."

"That's okay, I wanted tea."

"You have a test today?"

"I have a test today."

Behind her Rocco assembled the apparatus for turning dried leaves into flavored water. Three stories down, the young woman was off the phone, leaning over her fit ball to finish another email before she darted to the bedroom to presumably shower and get dressed. Abby wished the couple's bedroom blinds were open. She wanted to see them doin' it. Or at least *nekkid*. Every time she looked away, to her computer or to the clock on the wall, she wondered if this might be the moment the woman was surreptitiously flashing a breast, or the man was taking his penis out of his pj's to pluck an irritating bit of lint from the tip. She wanted to break into their apartment, run her hands over the surfaces they took for granted, smell their disgusting toothbrushes. It terrified her, this voyeurism, but it was a candy-coated feeling, something she could sneak when Rocco wasn't looking.

Watching people.

Watching people who might not even be people at all.

Rocco said, "Some guy called for you last night when you were out. I got his name and number." He thumbed the Post-it note to Abby's forehead.

Abby peeled it off. "I don't know anyone named Dirk Bickle," she said, "Pickle?"

"He said it was about a job. You want tea, right?"

"What kind of job?"

"Okay, let me tell you how the conversation went. Me: Hello? Guy on phone: Is Abby Fogg available? Me: No, may I ask who's calling? Guy on phone: My name is Dirk Bickle. I'm calling with regard to a job opening. Me: Sure, let me get your number. Guy on phone: My number is, etc., etc. Thanks, good-bye."

"You're making Darjeeling, right?"

"I'm making the kind with the frog on the box."

"I hate that kind."

Gently mocking: "Who do you think you are, Ms. Fogg? Telling me what kind of tea to make?"

"I hate the frog tea."

"That's why I made the Darjeeling." He set the cup before her. "I know your likes and dislikes better than you do."

"Like that's an accomplishment."

"You hate olives, you dream in black and white. I'm the world's most esteemed authority on *Abby Fogg*."

"I know you, too."

"You have no idea who I am."

"Is this Rocco Petrone guy not a Bionet dork? Does he not obsess over cycling and artisanal lagers?"

"You could be describing anyone."

"Does he not like it when I put my finger up his—"

"I really wanted coffee."

"Aren't you late for school?"

"It's Thursday, right?"

"It's Friday."

"*Merde.*"

Rocco stumbled through the condo slapping on clothing, quickly kissed Abby half on the lips and grabbed his bike helmet on the way out. Somehow this was the same dude who knew his way around the human brain like a motherfucker.

"You're right," Abby said when he was gone. "I have no idea who you are."

Abby poked digits into a keypad. Dirk Bickle answered on the first ring. A dog's bark echoed in the background. They arranged to meet on Granville Island later that morning.

She passed through the steeled angles of Vancouver, clouds of falafel smoke and deep-fried exhaust. Near the pier a couple bike cops knelt on the sidewalk getting a Bionet reading from a passed-out homeless guy. He'd soon find himself in a detox center downtown where he would get wrung out like a dishcloth, be given a vitamin-rich meal, and suffer through some boilerplate therapyish remonstrations delivered by a bored staffer. The next day he'd get dumped back onto the concrete grid where he'd hit up a dealer for a decryption code to illegally download painkillers. A newman nanny maneuvered a double-wide stroller around the prone addict. A billboard featured a man's head, his hair all Einsteined-out, word-bubbling the message, "Holy Shit! Telepathy! For Real!" A seagull bashed its beak into some spilled popcorn. At the pier Abby hopped onto a water taxi and five minutes later stepped onto Granville Island, a maze of art galleries and fruit stands. Café Lumiere was at the end of a twisty walkway between a toy store and an herbalist. Abby ordered her usual and pulled a chair up next to a framed photograph of a smug-looking Georges Méliès.

An old man sat down across from her. Black jacket, white dress shirt, no tie, hair spiky white, tanned face drooping down at the corners a bit. He removed his sunglasses and placed them in his pocket. An old guy. Obviously a FUS survivor.

"Hi, Abby. I'm Dirk. Thanks for meeting me. This is one of your haunts?"

"My early-films club meets here."

"Before my time, even. I read your paper on the restoration of Edison kinetoscopes. I won't even attempt an intelligent comment. It went right over my head. I'm curious why you're not working in Hollywood."

"I'm staying in Vancouver until my boyfriend finishes grad school."

"Rocco, is it? Guy I talked to? Studying to be a Bionet engineer?"

"Yes."

"You want to know why I've contacted you. Here it is. I represent a client, another FUS survivor who lives in Victoria in this grand old hotel. Kylee Asparagus. She's been holed up there for over a century and has accumulated a big old archive. Books, periodicals, digital content going back to the late twentieth century. A lot of it beyond repair."

"You'd be surprised," Abby said.

"Well, so right, that's why I wanted to get in touch with you, Abby. The organization I represent has been interested in these archives for some time but Ms. Asparagus keeps turning down our offers for a full audit. Until last week, when a water pipe burst and destroyed a lot of her records. Her people cleaned it up as best they could but there are certain pieces of digital content in states that may or may not be salvageable. USB drives, DVDs, diskettes, videocassette tape. We need you to assess the damage, write a report, and take the steps necessary to save what can be saved."

"I'm going to need a team. I know some people—"

Bickle shook his head. "You're going to have to fly solo. Kylee Asparagus won't have a team crawling over her property."

"Why are you interested in these archives? How will I know what kinds of content to prioritize?"

"Before the FUS I worked for an organization called the Kirkpatrick Academy of Human Potential. We thought of ourselves as an incubator for geniuses. I was one of the scouts who travelled around the country looking for youngsters who fit our profile, who exhibited potential to become innovative business leaders, artists, scientists. In the early 1990s I identified a boy living outside Seattle named Nick Fedderly. I recruited him and he joined the academy. His best friend was this guy named Luke Piper. At some point Luke was interviewed and we have reason to believe there's a copy of it in Ms. Asparagus's archives."

"You want me to find the interview while I'm sorting through the mess."

"We're prepared to pay off your student loans."

"Why is this interview so important?"

"That doesn't matter."

"Who conducted the interview?"

"We honestly don't know."

"Who's 'we'?"

"I still represent Mr. Kirkpatrick."

"What if I don't find the interview?"

"We'll pay you the same amount for trying. Oh, and by the way, their names are Steve and Winnie. He's twenty-nine, she's twenty-seven. He's a consultant for a company that specializes in stealth-brand penetration. She's a designer, as you've probably guessed from the kind of work she does on the computer. They've been together three years, moved in just before you and Rocco moved to the apartment across the street. She's half-Japanese, half-Korean. He's Russian, British, French, Spanish. They met at a professional event, a conference. They both love sushi and Cajun food. His favorite author is Peter Ng, hers is Yasutaka Tsutsui. At home they listen to late-twentieth-century jazz and world music. They typically make love about three times a week. She's on a Bionet fertility plan. He's color-blind, wears contact lenses to correct it. When they go to movies they prefer lighter comedies. They're saving up for a trip to Italy. I can go on like this for a long time if you want."

"You've been spying on me."

"How is this information about your neighbours about *you*?" Bickle said. "I understand people like you, Abby. I know what it means to desire another person's life. Don't be embarrassed. Your interests are why we approached you. I think you've got enough information to make a decision. Call me when you've thought it over."

Bickle stood and stretched, then disappeared into a Native art shop. Abby checked her wrist for her pulse. Seemed high and what the Chinese doctor she consulted would have called "slippery." She left her coffee unfinished and let her body go through its routine of visiting her favourite shop, the one that sold old music and movies on formats only geeks like her bothered with anymore.

All her student loans, paid off!

That night Abby watched an episode of *Stella Artaud: Newman Assassin*. She hated herself for liking it, and prided herself on recognizing that she hated it. This was the opening episode to the second season, the establishing sequences padded with expository dialogue. A quick flash of credits then a fade-in to reveal two women reviewing a contract in the back of a limousine. One woman wore a powder-blue pantsuit and matching lipstick, blonde hair a hive held aloft with chopsticks, permanent eyeliner tattooed onto the ridges of her eyelids. This was Henrietta Stoner, agent for Third Eye Communications. (Nobody on the show ever explained what Third Eye actually did. Some minor character in season two, episode three, opined that the organization "made stuff happen metaphysically," whatever that was supposed to mean.) Henrietta penned an X next to each line Stella was to sign. Stella Artaud wore a tiredly sexist anime getup: dog collar, black push-up bra, latex skirt, stiletto boots. Both of her arms up to the elbows were covered in tattooed reproductions of Gustave Doré's woodcuts from the illustrated *Inferno,* souls in torment in the inner ring of the seventh circle. A close-up of Stella's pen leaving her signature on the contract, ink seeping from glossy to matte black.

Henrietta. "When you arrive there will likely be some rough suffocation play. Just pretend you can't breathe. The client may knock you around a bit. You need to make sure to react appropriately, crying out, gasping. It's important that you approximate, as closely as you can, a typical human response to consensual sadism."

"I'm a professional."

"Intercourse may occur at this point. You should do what you can to prevent him from ejaculating. He will want to ejaculate later, into your dead body or dismembered head or neck cavity."

Stella initialed the line.

Henrietta. "At this point he may want to start dismembering you. Most likely this will begin with the fingers and toes, and move on up the extremities. You are expected to react with appropriate terror and beg for your life."

Stella. "I can do that."

Henrietta. "Then he will likely decapitate you. Please, at this point, if you could, feign death. As I mentioned, it may occur to him to copulate with the orifices of your dismembered head. You are encouraged to reduce your body temperature and remain still, human-like, while this occurs."

"Not a problem." Stella stared out the window. The art director had done a pretty decent job re-creating Central Park. The limo pulled up to an apartment building across the street from a CGI Guggenheim. It was raining, a cinematic drizzle originating from sprinklers above. Stella stood for a moment in the rain, staring up at the penthouse as the doorman opened the door. The camera followed her gaze to a shadow of a man who was watching her from one of the high windows.

The elevator doors opened into the penthouse. Stella emerged in slo-mo, stilettos Foleying hardwood. Three of the client's assistants appeared, each of indeterminate gender and with a shaved head, monk-like in loose-fitting garments. Eunuchs. Quickly they towelled Stella off and took her handbag and vinyl jacket. One clasped her hand and led her to a sitting room. The penthouse was done up as one might imagine the digs of a 1970s porn magazine publisher. A lot of neo-Classical faux Greek shit, ornate tapestries, chandeliers, marble columns, fountains.

Abby pulled her knees up to her chin. This next part chilled her every time.

The client appeared from behind a shoji screen. A young white guy, boringly handsome, wearing a white cotton bathrobe, tan, confident. "You're the new one," he said.

"I am here to fulfill your pleasures," Stella said.

"My name is Quinn Hunt. You've no doubt heard of Hunt Investments, owner of practically all the world's energy sources?"

Stella was silent.

Hunt continued. "Of course you haven't. You never do. The last time you were here I asked you the same question. I got the same blank look. Tell me, Stella, how many times have you been here?"

"This is my first time."

"Well, good. I'm glad they've got you thinking that. I want to show you something."

Hunt waved his hand and a screen descended from the ceiling. With a couple more motions images appeared. Here was Hunt mounting Stella, or a previous version of Stella, on a plush canopied bed.

"We had fun the last time you were here. See?"

More pornographic images. A close-up of the in-the-present Stella's expressionless face as the reflections swam over her corneas. The camera remained on her as, off-screen, the recording of her previous self cried out, the sound of a cane striking artificial flesh, begging, more beating. A close-up of Quinn Hunt's cold face. "Here comes the fun part." The buzz of an electric blade, screams at a higher pitch. A close-up again of Stella's face, unbudged from its blankness.

Hunt. "You wonder why I'm like this. Why I keep bringing you out here to abuse you. I was designed this way. I was an experiment. They isolated the serial-killer profile and engineered me in utero in the lab. But they also engineered incredible health and an astounding mathematical mind. Someone who could swim freely in the world of high finance. Someone with real earning potential. But my pleasure centers are wired to light up in the presence of others' suffering. And they get really lit up when I'm inflicting that suffering. And when I'm lucky enough to kill someone, why, then it's a state of pure nirvana. Do I wish it were another way? Certainly. I curse these pleasures! I pass people on the street and observe their uncomplicated motivations, their children and possessions. I wish I could be one of them. My life would be so much less *demanding* if I could get off on what everybody else gets off on. It's a hassle bringing you out here every week. It's expensive. It's become a chore. But it's something I've been designed to do. And since killing flesh-humans involves breaking laws, I have to make do with the likes of you."

The eunuchs rushed to disrobe Hunt and Stella. Soon the two stood naked before one another, Hunt's cock erect. The camera lingered on their bodies. Hunt took a step forward. Then a quickly edited series of shots. Stella reached to her crotch. An outburst of brass on the soundtrack. The eyes of a eunuch going wide with shock. Stella whipping out a short dagger she'd smuggled inside herself. Hunt, startled. The dagger flashing, then buried in one of Hunt's eye sockets. Screaming. The eunuchs opening their robes to reveal machine pistols and—why not?—samurai swords. Stella whirling naked through the air, landing roundhouse kicks. Hunt screaming, twitching on the floor. Stella having some difficulty retrieving the dagger, as it appeared to be stuck in Hunt's eye, having to brace her foot on his neck to get the proper leverage while one-handedly jiujitsuing the shit out of those sword-wielding eunuch guys. The knife slurped out. Stella swiped it like a debit card across Hunt's throat. A blood puddle spread across the floor. Close-up of a eunuch lifting his machine pistol, getting off a smattering of shots, a round ripping through Stella's bicep, revealing the machinery and circuitry within. Stella backflipping, snagging one of the eunuch's swords while midair and upside down, then decapitating all three with a single swipe of the blade. An alarm. Stella snagging a couple machine pistols just in time to blast the security guards appearing in a nearby doorway, globules of flesh spattering oil paintings of landed gentry.

Stella turned to the camera. "The newman uprising is *on.*"

Then, firing both machine pistols and running backward, Stella propelled herself out the nearest window and some twenty stories down, still firing, the angry faces above screaming their threats to her bodily self, a body she didn't necessarily need because they could just give her a new one anyway. These questions getting somewhat obscured by the muzzle-lit ejaculations of fist-held firepower. Then through the sunroof of a waiting limousine, landing naked, covered in blood and glass, next to Dr. Uri Borden, played by supernaturally handsome Neethan F. Jordan.

Commercials.

Rocco returned after midnight smelling like his bike commute. After his shower he crawled into bed alongside Abby, who slept and dreamed of horses. He woke her by touching a nipple. She clambered into semiconsciousness and asked how studying had gone. He mumbled something and kissed her. They were supposed to make love now, this is what this meant. She spooned her back into him. He slid his hand over her belly, letting his pinkie rest in her belly button.

"I got offered a job," Abby said, then sleepily doled out the details, except for the part about Bickle knowing that she spied on their neighbours. Rocco gave her shoulder a little shake. "No more student loans. Wow. You're going to take it, right?"

"I think so."

"What is there to think about?"

Did Rocco have some secret reason for wanting her to leave for a few months? Some chick in the Bionetics department at UBC she didn't know about? He kissed her again, and the brevity of the kiss communicated there'd be no lovemaking. She listened to his breathing as he entered sleep, precipitously, plunging into REM in under five minutes. Down there, in his dreams, he would continue studying, reviewing lecture notes and sometimes mumbling aloud about the amygdala or basolateral complex.

Rocco liked to say that cerebral Bionetic enhancement was the scalpel edge of the next stage of human evolution. Putting it in terms Abby could understand, he explained that the fuck-or-fight, R-complex reptilian brain had evolved first, then the limbic system with its anxieties and need for hugs, then the rational neocortex, which was now working to develop the next stage of cognition—the Bionetic neural extension. Each component of the triune model had reached a point when it started to understand what the species needed next and so invented its own neural progeny. Instinct demanded emotion, emotion demanded rationality, and rationality demanded . . . what, exactly? This was what Bionet engineers debated after hours while downing Labatts. Some speculated that the brain was in the process of internalizing the Internet. A fringe faction asserted that this new stage would answer philosophical and spiritual questions that had haunted humanity since at least the Greek dudes. His was a brain, Rocco liked to say, that thought about how to build a better brain. But brains could forget and, by extension, cultures could forget. Abby's brain struggled to locate artifacts that had been lost by the collective brain of civilization, archaeologically scrambling into the washed-out past, while Rocco's brain clawed its way into some sort of future. From this nexus of memory and yearning and logic sprang their attraction to one another. They totally made each other cognitively and biologically horny. Usually.

Abby cursed herself for not telling Rocco about what Bickle had said about the neighbours but now it was too late. If she brought it up now she'd be admitting that she was ashamed of her voyeuristic streak. She'd missed her chance to drop that bomb in an offhand way.

"No more student loans," Abby whispered in the night. That was her excuse for taking the job. The real reason, the one she dared not articulate even to herself, was curiosity.

The city of Victoria appeared to have regressed in age, its green-built skyscrapers brought to heel, malls and parking garages and condominiums razed, all replaced by roiling wilds. What remained standing were the buildings worthy of the city's heritage—the Parliament, some Tudor-style B&Bs, a replica of Shakespeare's house. This was a city that had once aspired to London's botanical gardens and double-decker buses but had negotiated with the tribal culture that preceded it, arriving at an aesthetic truce, a fusion of potlatch and high tea. Here and there totem poles and longhouses materialized from the Emily Carr mists rolling off the harbour, monuments of extinctions far more distant than the end times of recent memory.

Abby disembarked, suitcase in one hand, a duffel containing her tools in the other. Up ahead was the Empress Hotel, a stately, ivy-clad structure that smugly lorded over the geography as if glaciers had sculpted the harbour for its benefit alone. It used to be a hotel, anyway. In recent centuries it had survived fires, vandalism, drug-addicted architects who'd added wings and bunkers. A scorched tower stood proudly unbowed. Abby ascended to the lobby entrance, skipping every other step.

Once inside, a fit, middle-aged man with gouts of grey chest hair frothing under his chin, wearing a silver tracksuit with the words "Official Delegate" stitched upon the breast, wearily took her bags. "So the entertainment has finally arrived," he said, sounding disappointed as he led her down the hall. "The lady of the house has been waiting impatiently. Federico #37? Costume, please?"

Abby scrambled to get her bearings. A floor of river rock, walls paneled in extinct woods, scents of imitation campfires, dried flowers, decaying leather chesterfields. The man led her through the lobby of distressed furniture, down a hall, and into a dressing room disheveled with clothing. Another man wearing an identical tracksuit—actually this looked to be a twin of the man currently pointing her in the direction of a changing screen—stumbled into the claustrophobia-inducing room wheeling a creaking rack laden with costumes.

"The bunny? I think it's supposed to be the bunny," the first man said. Federico #37 rifled through the clothes and pulled out a pink fake-fur bunny costume with a grinning head-piece.

"I think this is a mistake," Abby said.

"The bunny costume usually is," Federico #37 said.

"Oh, by the way, I'm Federico #18," the first man said. "This is #37."

"There are other Federicos?"

"Don't get us started," #37 said. "You're going to want to get down to panties and bra. It gets hot inside these suckers."

Abby ducked behind a screen and changed into the bunny costume. She took this for some kind of initiatory protocol, a little good-natured hazing. When she emerged she turned and held out her arms. "How does it look?"

"Could use some filling out in the ass," #37 said, "but we work with the entertainment options we have, not the ones we want."

"I think you've got me mixed up with someone else," Abby said. "I'm not an entertainer. I was sent here to work on a project."

The Federicos paused. "A project?"

"I don't know if I'm supposed to say."

"Whatever. We're just the entertainment coordinators. This way, please."

One at each arm, grim-faced, the Federicos jogged Abby down a hallway. Through the bunny head's eye holes she glimpsed garishly colored oil paintings and sconces crafted from ungulate hooves. They passed through several rooms—parlours and game rooms, a library, a room that appeared decorated solely with bowling trophies and a sculpture of a bird. At the end of a long hallway they skidded up to a black door marked STAGE, patted Abby on the shoulder, mumbled "Break a leg" in unison, then pushed her into the spotlight.

Abby found herself onstage in a theater before an audience that applauded as she made her entrance. The theater probably seated two or three hundred, the main floor and balconies filled to capacity. It was a three-layer affair, high and oval, gilded and bedecked in red velvet, gold ropes, rosette-print carpet, chandeliers the size of your more fuel-efficient compact cars. Abby, having no clue where to stand, stumbled, eliciting chuckles from the audience. Her throat went dry.

"I'm sorry, but there's been a mistake," Abby stuttered. "I'm not an entertainer. My name is Abby Fogg and I was sent here by a man named Dirk Bickle."

The audience cheered and whistled loudly.

Abby waited for the applause to die down. "I don't know what I'm doing here dressed as a bunny but this has been the weirdest twenty-four hours of my life."

Assorted chuckles.

"I live in Vancouver. I recently graduated from the University of British Columbia with a master's degree in data recovery. I'm here for a project that requires my expertise in restoring digital content. Is there someone I can talk to about this? I'm really sorry I'm not the entertainer you thought I was supposed to be. I'm not even sure if I'm in the right place. Are you in need of a digital recovery expert?"

The audience howled. As the laughter died down, some guy in the back yelled, "You're in the right place all right!"

Abby tried to get a good look at the audience through the bunny eye holes. They were dressed formally, as for an opera, in tuxedos and satin ball gowns, with furs and top hats, monocles, clutch purses, and, here and there, a lap poodle. Every face exactly the same. Six hundred Federicos waited for her to deliver her next line. Things got blurry. Dramatically—this being a stage after all—Abby swooned and fell over, the bunny head providing a soft landing as she passed out and the audience rose to an ovation.

She woke to seagull cries, in a third-floor suite facing the harbour, her suitcases set beside the king-size bed. The open window let in a warm, salted breeze. There was a desk, a lamp, a chair, two bedside tables. In the chair sat one of the Federicos, reading a book. This Federico looked younger and had longer hair than the previous ones she'd met. When he noticed Abby stirring he set the book aside and folded his hands over his crossed knees.

"You hungry?"

"No," Abby said. "Maybe a little."

"Bring the girl something to eat," Federico said to no one in particular.

"What is going on here?"

"I don't blame you for being confused," Federico said, "and I have to apologize. I was supposed to orient you, but numbers 37 and 18 got to you first. I expected you to arrive later."

"What is this place?"

"We call it the Seaside Love Palace."

"You're all twins or—"

"Clones."

"How many of you are there?"

"Six hundred and thirty-one."

"I thought the quota was two."

"It is in the United States and Canada. Vancouver Island seceded, remember?"

"Where's Kylee Asparagus?"

"You'll meet her straightaway."

An older Federico arrived with a cart laden with snack foods. Abby, still wearing the body of the pink bunny, sat up in bed and scratched her chest. The head lay nearby on a bedside table, gazing out to the water.

"Until recently I was under the impression that Kylee Asparagus was dead," she said.

The Federicos shook their heads and spoke in unison. "Not exactly. Sometimes she thinks she is."

"How'd you guys do that?" Abby said.

The younger of the Federicos smiled. “We’re connected wirelessly. When you speak to one of us—”

The other Federico finished the thought. “—you’re really speaking to all of us.”

Abby smeared some hummus on a piece of crusty bread. “Why’d she have you cloned?”

Both Federicos said, “The original Federico was one of Ms. Asparagus’s backup dancers, her most loyal companion.”

“Can you point me in the direction of the data that’s supposed to be restored?” Abby said.

The older Federico nodded and said that would be discussed in time. Tonight she was to have dinner with Ms. Asparagus.

Without the filter of the bunny head Abby got a better look at the manse. She passed one room where an old nonfunctional plasma TV took up much of one wall. Nearby, a Federico wearing a repairman’s overalls busily reupholstered a chair. On her way to the dining room she passed several more Federicos, each absorbed in a task, each man a little different from the others but bearing the same brown eyes squinting in concentration. She even glimpsed a room where an older Federico was busy using magic tricks to entertain a group of five or six child-size Federicos.

“Who is your mother, if you don’t mind me asking?” Abby said to a Federico leaning on a broom.

“Our source mother was a woman named Esther Gonzales, of Los Gatos, California. A cleaning lady, raised six children on one income. She died many, many years ago. Our midway mothers are all in Africa or Asia.”

"Have any of you met your midway mothers?"

Federico sighed. Elsewhere in the house other Federicos sighed, too, having heard the comment. "Of course we haven't. We're happy to know they received the best medical care in the world for leasing out their uteruses and we greatly appreciate their generosity. Dining room's right up those stairs, Ms. Fogg."

She came to a restaurant with a view of the gardens. A Federico dressed as a host seated Abby at a table across from a woman so petite she could have been a child, though her wrinkled skin hung off her face in powdery folds. Her face was mostly obscured by a pair of gigantic sunglasses, her head wrapped in a scarf, neck bristling with necklaces, shoulders covered in synthetic chinchilla. She extended a spindly hand to lift her water glass to her lips. How old was this woman? A hundred and fifty maybe?

"Ms. Asparagus, I'm—" Abby started.

Kylee shushed her. "That prick Bickle sent you against my wishes. You can go back to your mainland little existence and take your bag of cheap electronic shit with you. If it were up to me I would have had the Federicos murder you as soon as you set foot on the estate. Unfortunately they're bred to care, not to kill."

A waiter Federico appeared. "How are you guys doing tonight? Would you like to start out with a bread basket?"

Abby nodded. Federico the waiter set down the bread and poured some olive oil and herbed balsamic into a little saucer. Kylee sulked behind her sunglasses.

"Dirk Bickle said—"

"He's a toadie. Mr. Kirkpatrick's yes-man. Are you blind? And they expect *you* of all people to recover the archives. Give me a fucking break."

"What happened to the archives?"

"So I get to explain the whole can of worms to you. I see. The archives are in the basement. I'm not the first inhabitant of this house, you know. This used to be called the Seaside Love Palace, home of Isaac Pope, the dot-com nerd. It's his artwork you see up all over the place. Artwork he commissioned anyway. Isaac stored all sorts of useless shit, in formats no one knows anything about anymore. DVD-ROMs and stuff. We keep it all in the basement. A couple weeks ago a pipe burst and flooded the dump. The Federicos worked overtime to get it cleaned out but we lost about half the archive. That's why you're here. To tell us what we lost."

"I'll be happy to get started on it right away. When can I see the—"

"We haven't even ordered yet!"

"By the way, I'm a huge fan of your music."

The waiter Federico arrived to take their orders.

"Before you take our orders, Federico, we would like to see a menu," Kylee said. "And if you could bring me a brush and some soapy water so I can scrub this young thing's lip prints off my ass."

"No, I really am a fan. My friends make fun of me for being into old music but—"

"Old music!"

"What I mean is I especially love *The Glamorous Life of Kylee Asparagus*. It's got some great—"

"I'd give my left tit to get back in the studio with the Satan Brothers. They weren't so much studio sessions as artistic retreats. We rented a castle in Scotland and stayed up till five in the morning on shrooms. We swam naked together in the pool, my band and me, and wrote such beautiful music on that bitchin' Steinway. Those were the albums when I started getting close to Federico."

"Federico and you were—"

"Lovers? Oh, no, young thing. Let's just say that it's easy to genetically engineer a Federico to develop a tendency to enjoy gardening, or pottery, or repairing gutters, or cooking, but it's near-impossible to engineer one into craving pussy."

The waiter Federico showed up with the menus, a bucket of soapy water, and a sponge and proceeded to recite the specials. When he left, Abby said, "So that performance today—"

"Your timing. You need to work on it."

"The audience. Those were all the Federicos?"

"What am I supposed to do? I have this huge theater and when I want a show I don't want to be the lone person clapping up there in the balcony. The Federicos like their entertainment and some of them get to dress up in drag, so it's pretty special for them. I'm just disappointed your performance was so pathetic. You've *really* got to take the time to prepare, young thing. You've got to know your material sideways."

"But I'm not an entertainer."

"You said it, not me. What looks yummy tonight?"

Abby scanned the menu and saw the same thing repeated twelve times. "Looks like the breaded rock cod with a leafy green salad and rice pilaf."

"Oh, I got that the last time I was here and it wasn't very good."

"What else is there?"

"Young thing, they can make you something even if it's not on the menu. Don't worry, I'll order for you."

The waiter Federico reappeared. "Have you decided?"

"I'd like for us to start with an order of Gruyère bruschetta and bring an assorted sashimi platter as well. For our entrées I'll take the grilled halibut not too dry this time and she'll have the salmon special you featured last night. To drink I'll have a Diet Coke with a lemon wedge and she'll just have water. Cheerio."

The waiter bowed deeply and hustled to the kitchen.

"I don't particularly care for salmon," Abby said.

"You were saying something about how much you loved my album *The Glamorous Life of Kylee Asparagus*? I didn't mean to interrupt."

"No, I was finished talking about that."

"I don't think so. I think you were asking about the number of number-one hit singles off that album."

"Right. How many—"

"Five. Count 'em *five* hit singles. That album *dominated*. But how could I top that? By releasing seven albums in the next three and a half years, that's how. Boom, boom, boom, and four booms after that. Each album captured the vibe of a different continent. I recorded with the greatest musicians living on each continent at that time."

"The *Africa* album was pretty incredible."

"It was, wasn't it? *Africa* had a lot of momentum coming off the *Glamorous Life* album. *South America* was solid too—"

"That album was way underrated."

"By who? I want names! We were able to work with such a killer crew on *Europe* but there were all these distractions. Sound engineers ODing and shit. We thought *Asia* would be better but then the trade embargo and the Chinese cloning crisis and everything went to shit. It was about the right time to record *Oceana*. Basically an EP. Hardly anyone bought it. So we brought it all home and recorded the *North America* double album, which was supposed to be the comeback, the biggie. Oh well."

"I thought *Antarctica* was pretty good."

"True, that marine biologist played a mean harmonica."

The appetizers arrived. Abby tried to repress her disgust as Kylee's powdery lips curled around raw fish, her mouth a graveyard of teeth the color of coffee with two creamers. The woman made little moaning noises as she ate, as if discovering sashimi for the first time.

Kylee said, "Eventually I sobered up, bought this place from Isaac, and started thinking hard about what I had gone through in twenty years. I had fucked some of the most beautiful men on the planet. I had received the love of people who just wanted to touch me, eat my used Kleenex. The paparazzi were never really the source of my problems. They were just the in-between step. I was on one side of them, and on the other were exhausted shoppers in grocery store checkout lines. Ugly housewives and mouth-breathing teenagers. Week after week they'd see me while standing in line to buy their disgusting microwave food. I was beautiful. They wanted to be like me. And the reason they wanted to be like me was that they didn't love themselves. They wanted to be someone like me who never shopped for groceries. And when designer drugs and nipple slips and Twitter rants and passing out at Cannes started to do me in, I began to remind them of who they really were and they started to hate me. Because it was easier to hate me, to ridicule my 'bizarre behaviour,' than to look into themselves and realize that they really were a bunch of fucked-up ugly bitches.

"When things got really out of control, when I started throwing goblets through plate-glass windows, Isaac himself showed up. He wasn't much more than a teenager, seemed to me. A lumpy dork who could have afforded more fashionable glasses, but for whatever reason chose not to spend a smidgen of his billion-dollar fortune on designer eyewear. Go figure. Stinky hair stuck to his forehead, fidgety, would sort of hop up and down in his chair when he got excited about something. He wore T-shirts with pictures of dragons on them under his sport coats. I think he spent fifteen hours a day in front of his computers, five hours of that masturbating. Of course I seduced him. In a way I did it to punish myself for going so off the map. I'd fucked *Jude Law*. I'd fucked *George Clooney*. I'd been the guest of honor at numerous exclusive orgies. Now I was fucking this nerd with his shriveled little prick. I was doing it because I hated myself as much as those women standing in line at the grocery stores hated themselves.

"But then something really fucked-up happened. I started to fall in love with him. He showed me such tenderness. I was like an onion, with all these, like, layers of celebrity and shit. He peeled them back and found the girl within, and when he loved that child I gave myself to him completely. Suddenly I was back on the world stage. I was by his side at the Golden Globes. I completely reinvented myself. I rebuilt everything from the ground up. I made carefully crafted, self-deprecating comments about myself in the press. A new generation discovered my work and it started getting played at clubs. The fags embraced me anew. And best of all, we went on a shopping spree. We bought all those media companies that owned the tabloids that had dragged me through so much mud, and I personally visited their offices, one by one, and fired the editors and photographers who had so busted my balls. I decided to get smart. I'd never gone to college, remember. So we hired a private staff of professors to live here and instruct me in art history, philosophy, literature. I started working out again, five hours a day. I was a machine manufacturing my own self-actualization. Around this time we decided to turn the estate into an artists' colony. We invited sculptors, composers, playwrights, poets, and painters to spend time here creating their work. We hosted dinners for Pulitzer winners and Nobel laureates. We held fund-raising retreats and charity balls. Oh, it was such a marvelous time!"

Kylee paused, seeming to revisit the era in the privacy of her thoughts. Abby let the silence last as long as Kylee needed. Outside, the sun settled into its horizon. After a time, Kylee began renegotiating with her meal and continued. "Of course, when you're in those years you don't expect the world to take a turn for the worse, do you? You expect the world to ride along on your own happiness, as if you had any control. But the Age of Fucked Up Shit reminded us that we're just parasites on this planet and, like parasites, we can be easily exterminated. We were lucky. We kept to ourselves on this island, Isaac, Federico, and me. Once all the artists had gone we spent days in the parlour playing Barbie's Shopping Mall Adventure. In those years it was best if you lived on an island, away from major population centers. The horror of it still makes me tremble. And it was during this time that my sweet Isaac, oh . . ."

Kylee began to cry, her leathery lips quivering into the shape of an hourglass tipped on its side. The waiter Federico brought a box of tissues. Kylee dabbed one beneath her glasses, pulling away gobs of teary mascara. Abby touched the woman's hand.

Kylee grabbed her wrist and dug acrylic fingernails into the soft flesh. She leaned closer and hissed, "He was murdered. I'm convinced of it. They said it was a heart attack brought on by too much Red Bull and Mountain Dew but I know it was murder! My poor sweet Isaac!"

"I had no idea," Abby said. "Who did it?"

"We don't know!" Kylee cried. "A hundred and fifty-five years I've stuck around and still we don't know who did it! Why do you think I've kept this body alive? Why do you think I've cloned Federico hundreds of times? I need protection. I need someone to take care of me while I find out who killed my husband!"

The waiter Federico leaned over the table, clearing their plates. "Did you guys save any room for dessert?"

"I'll have the triple chocolate decadence," Kylee said. "Give our guest the rhubarb pie à la mode."

Abby said, "So the police were never able to—"

"Police? You think there were freaking police involved? During the Age of Fucked Up Shit? You *are* young, young thing. The authorities fried bigger fish. Oh, I don't know. Solve a homicide or deal with widespread rioting and looting. No, it was entirely up to us. We read up on forensic science, watched a lot of police procedurals. But we kept coming up cold. We combed the archives as best we could for clues as to who might have a motive for killing my husband. We barely made a dent in all those files. Then a burst pipe, oh hell. Now you, young thing, supposedly *you* are the one who is supposed to help us get to the bottom of this abomination. Why Mr. Kirkpatrick thinks you'll be of any help is beyond me. You might as well hop on that boat and head back to wherever you came from. Everything worth knowing about this rotten place disappeared a long time ago."

* * *

An almost-full moon hung close to the water and a feathery breeze skittered across the waves. Abby's dreams were chopped-up pieces of grade school, trees, beaches, pink fur. She woke around three in the morning convinced she was being watched. Keeping her eyes closed, she reached across the bed for Rocco then remembered she wasn't in Vancouver. She opened her eyes. The ghost hovered just beyond the window, bobbing a bit, as one would imagine ghosts to do. His form consisted of roiling wisps of translucence in the shape of a man. He appeared balding, with a bad comb-over, and he wore a T-shirt with the barely legible logo for a Comi-Con convention from over a century ago. He rubbed his eyes beneath spectral bifocals.

"Say something," Abby said.

"Oh, sorry. Yeah, so, I guess you're here to solve my 'murder.'"

"Isaac Pope?"

"So they say."

"Who killed you?"

"I actually buy the Red Bull and Mountain Dew theory, myself. You're kind of hot, you know that? What do you say about flashing me a boob?"

"No thanks. What do you know about the archives?"

"You waste no time," the ghost of Isaac Pope said. "What is it about the archives you want to know?"

"Can they be salvaged?"

"Come on, just one booby."

"I'm looking for a transcript of an interview with someone named Luke Piper."

"Oh, that," Isaac said. "All I'm saying is just a tit. What harm can come of it? I'm a dead dude."

"Will you tell me about the transcript?"

"I'll tell you everything I know about the transcript."

Abby considered this a moment, then pulled aside her nightgown to reveal her left breast.

"Oooooh . . ." Isaac moaned, sounding like a real ghost for the first time. "That's what I'm talking about. Touch the nipple, make it hard."

Outside the window the ghost rose and fell as if mounted on a spring, slowly, then faster, his right hand pumping what Abby assumed was his small, ghostly prick. Isaac grabbed the sill with his other hand, moaned, grunted, and ejaculated some phosphorescent ghost semen onto the foot of the bed. Revolted, Abby tucked her breast back in and crawled away from the ectoplasmic splooge.

"Gross! Why'd you have to do that?"

"Don't tell me you weren't at least a little bit turned on, baby," Isaac said. "Seriously—how many times did you come?"

"Jesus! Now you can at least tell me about the transcript."

"As promised, here's everything I know about the transcript. I know absolutely nothing about the transcript. You'll need to talk to the archivist. Besides, rubbing one off isn't the real reason for this supernatural visit or whatever you want to call it. I'm supposed to get all Hamlet's dad on you. You've got to get out of here, Abby, before you get trapped in the play. You're getting sucked into a loop. Your selfhood, it's in superposition."

"But the archives."

Isaac sighed. "Well, don't say I didn't warn you. And thanks for the flash."

"Get out of here," Abby said.

"Suit yourself, baby," Isaac said, "You know you liked it."

The spirit dispersed in the wind.

The next morning Abby passed through halls decorated with eye-violating phantasy art. In each one a muscled warrior defended a barely dressed maiden from some sort of dragon or monster or many-tentacled space-being. On closer look Abby recognized the maidens as Kylee, and the buff heroes as Isaac, whose bespectacled and combed-over head topped each rippling, sweaty torso.

A Federico stopped alongside her. "They were commissioned," he said. "Isaac hired some of the most acclaimed science-fiction-and-fantasy cover artists of his day and presented these great works of art as gifts to Kylee."

"I think the period-appropriate word to describe these paintings is 'rad,'" Abby said.

"You'd be one to know. I know very little about those times." The Federico stiffened and gazed into the middle distance as if he'd heard something alarming. "Oh dear. In the billiard room? Oh dear, oh dear." He scurried up a spiral staircase with Abby trailing behind. "You don't need to see this," Federico called over his shoulder. "Really. You'd best be enjoying complimentary refreshments in the dining room."

Abby kept on his heels, coming to a room where a crowd of Federicos had gathered. Kneeling on the floor, Kylee jaggedly wailed and lamented. Abby pushed her way to the front of the scrum. On a billiard table with balls frozen midgame lay the prone body of a Federico, his head ringed with sleeping pills.

"He's dead," a Federico whispered beside her, and several other Federicos, mostly the younger ones, began softly to weep. Kylee clawed the floor, blubbering and writhing. An older Federico came to the lady's side and carefully lifted her, directing her to an overstuffed chair.

Kylee blubbered, "Did he leave a note? Did he at least say why he did it?"

The suicide note was conveniently located in the body's left hand. One of the Federicos retrieved it and read it aloud. "*My dear Kylee and brothers Federico. It is time for me to pass from this world to the next. I found it too hard to be myself in a place where so many other people were me. Is it too much to ask that I be treated as an individual for once? Is it? I mean, come on. Well, anyway, I leave all my personal effects to Federico #270, whose kindness I will cherish into the grave. See you on the other side, bitches!*"

Shoulders heaved, palms rubbed backs in consolation, and a nearby box of tissues was quickly depleted. To be polite, Abby pretended to sniffle. It all felt disingenuously theatrical. Kylee fainted and was borne away by six sobbing Federicos. When they were gone the remaining Federicos cleared their throats and started discussing various household tasks and funeral arrangements. Abby tapped an older Federico on the shoulder.

"I'm really sorry for your loss," she said.

The older Federico shrugged. "We'll miss him, I guess, but there's always another Federico to take his place."

"I need to talk to the Federico who was supposed to show me to the archives."

"I'm afraid you're out of luck. That was the Federico who just offed himself."

"Is there another Federico who can—"

The older Federico scowled. "We've got a family tragedy on our hands here, miss. The archives are the least of our problems. If you want to make yourself useful, you'll join the funeral party at noon. We'll drop a dress and a veil off at your room and convene in the great hall."

The Federicos, dressed in black suits and ties, gathered in hushed clumps of conversation. Kylee sat in a creaking wheelchair, clad in a black dress and superwide hat with a veil. In the center of the room, on a couple of collapsible luggage stands, sat a varnished cedar coffin. Six older, pallbearing Federicos hoisted it on their shoulders and solemnly bore it out the front doors. Kylee followed immediately behind, pushed by a young Federico. The Federico children trailed, holding the hands of their older brothers. Abby merged into the procession, which heaved along a path through the posturban woods. Two Federicos who'd been bred with a special gene for bagpipe prowess played a mournful dirge. The music was elegiac, the sky overcast, the wind a union of pine and sea salt. The party progressed about a mile up the path, hemmed in on either side by swirling conifers, then turned onto a path carpeted with rust-colored fir needles. Winding around the stumps and nurse logs of the cool forest they entered a patch of salmonberry and huckleberry bushes, still wet with morning dew. They proceeded single file now, a black, melancholy swath through the greenery. At last they came to a clearing of sorts. Abby crept through the gaggle to glimpse the proceedings.

They were in a vast cemetery, maybe forty or fifty acres square. Hundreds of headstones marked the graves that dotted the anally maintained grassy expanse. Abby looked to her feet and read the one nearest.

Federico #78
Beloved Friend
FUS 20–78

Nearby, a couple of Federicos in mud-spattered overalls began lowering the coffin into a freshly dug grave. Kylee sat graveside in her chair, honking into a lacy black handkerchief. Another Federico had taken the role of minister, reading the ashes-to-ashes stuff. In groups of twos and threes the surviving Federicos clutched each other, wiping tears, pressing their foreheads together in the solidarity of grief. Abby glanced at other headstones. Federico #301, Federico #425, Federico #16, Federico #27, Federico #153. Each of them a beloved friend. After the coffin came to rest the survivors took turns tossing in shovels full of dirt until the cavity in the earth was filled. A light mist began to coalesce. A Federico unfolded a black and Gothic umbrella over Kylee's head as they made their way from the cemetery to the path. As they proceeded a Federico sidled up to Abby and explained how the numbering system worked.

"We've all got a number, sure, but the number changes based on deaths. So if Federico #1 dies, all the other Federicos move up a number. So #2 becomes the new #1, #3 becomes the new #2, and so on. That way there are no gaps in our numbers. Now it looks like I'm going to be Federico #178."

"What about the little Federicos?" Abby asked. "How often do they arrive?"

"Every couple months or so. We'll put in an order for a new Federico now that we've lost one. When the boat shows up with a new Federico, it's quite a big deal. Maybe you'll be here to see the arrival of a new little one."

The Seaside Love Palace popped and groaned as it settled in the cold night. Abby flipped through a stack of celebrity biographies until after midnight, when she rose and slipped into the hallway. There was a whole wing of the manse she hadn't seen yet; now would be a good time to check it out. Every ten feet or so along the hall hung one of Isaac's garish phantasy paintings, each lit by a single halogen bulb. Here was Isaac in a fishbowl helmet and space suit, firing a laser gun, Kylee in a gold bikini clutching his thigh, fending off what appeared to be a bad seafood experience. In another he raised a sword to deliver the coup de grâce to a kind of furry, maybe-dragon sorta thing that had Kylee in its talons. Abby imagined the couple posing for these portraits, frozen in war-gaming gear while a bearded and kilted graphic designer sketched them onto canvas. After studying five or six of these paintings she got the crazy idea that they'd actually loved each other.

Abby descended a flight of stairs and heard music. Sort of a disco/house beat, a track off one of Kylee's old albums. She maneuvered around shadows of furniture, past a dormant kitchen and a reading room where taxidermy animal heads gawked from the walls. At the end of a short side hall she came to a black door through which she could feel the pulse of the bass. She pushed it open a crack and peeked into a ballroom that smelled like a mashup between a gymnasium and a health clinic. From speakers thumped a hit single about promiscuity and shopping for luxury goods. Abby's eyes widened. From a chintzy-looking throne atop a dais Kylee barked through a megaphone, directing the Federicos in a mammoth, gay clone orgy!

From her hiding place, for over an hour, Abby observed the carnal ritual like an anthropologist, finding the grunting contortions much like the underground Bionet parties she had attended in college. News of those parties had spread by word of mouth, directions changing and conflicting, secret passwords whispered into ears. One rainy night Abby had piled into a car with three of her friends—Jadie, Megan, and Heather—and headed across the Lions Gate Bridge into a zone of murky abandoned industry. Out here the streets eventually gave up and ended in tangles of debris and broken concrete. They parked in an alley and followed the directions to a metal door marked with a crop-circle glyph. The four friends looked at one another, questioning whether they were really up for this, a quartet of graduate students in a downpour, willingly giving someone else—a stranger—complete control over their bodies. Abby opened the door.

They called these kinds of places pleasure centers. This particular pleasure center was down a musty-smelling flight of stairs that opened into a subterranean space lit with purples and reds, forms gathered around pillars checking out the newcomers, the periphery fuzzed-out visually with hushed conversations and lips occasionally sipping glasses of energy drink. A dance floor, if one wanted to call it that, framed by spotlights. No music, just a low rumble of whispers and body noises. On the dance floor was a human pyramid—three men on the bottom, two in the middle, and a single man standing on his hands, which were planted on the two men beneath him. The pyramid remained stationary for several minutes. The man standing on his hands pulled in one of his arms to balance on one hand. Abby watched the man's forearm tremble. Was he going to fall? No, actually, he was extending his index finger so that it was the only part of his body touching the man beneath him. He balanced a full minute as a ripple of applause went through the spectators and a patch of blood spread on the leotard of the man beneath him. Carefully, the human pyramid disassembled itself and a couple women carrying towels rushed to the one who'd been the pyramid's apex. He looked exhausted, slumping into their arms as they wiped his face. A violent shudder racked his body like an epileptic seizure, but short, a jolt.

Over a PA system a calm and reedy voice intoned, "He's going to be just fine. His nervous system is confused and it will take about an hour before he's back to feeling like himself. And tomorrow his arms will be a little sore. Don't worry. We'll take loving care of him."

Another flutter of applause. Abby looked around trying to determine the source of the voice and found it in a shaded corner of the room, the DJ's booth. The DJ stood behind a bank of three laptops, GUIs reflected off the surfaces of his glasses.

Heather pinched Abby's arm. "No freakin' way I'm letting the DJ take over my implants. How do you know he won't make you kill somebody?"

Megan said, "Or worse, fuck somebody?"

Jadie said, "You believe that *USA Today* bullshit? They're already breaking the law hacking other peoples 'plants, it's not like they're going to completely screw themselves with a murder or rape charge."

"It's based on SM," Abby said. "Every participant has a safe word to break the hack."

Jadie added, "And the DJ would be ripped apart by the crowd if he tried anything stupid. Everyone's looking out for everyone else."

Onto the dance floor marched six hairless eunuchs. *This ought to be good,* Abby thought. For the next twenty minutes they danced, their eyes miles away, letting themselves get thrown into a choreography controlled remotely from the corner of the room. They leapt, pinwheeled, jerked. Contentwise it wasn't unlike a lot of archival footage of modern dance Abby had seen. Once the routine concluded the eunuchs wobbled off, regaining their gross motor skills in an almost narcotic fugue. This stuff was often compared to a kind of addiction. The hard-core Bionet abusers begged for DJs to control their every move, even eating, defecation, sex. Abby'd heard about a man in Boise who'd entered into an abusive arrangement with his neighborhood Bionet hacker and given him carte blanche over his vitals. Guy by the name of Paul Garza. The hacker, who went by the handle Salo, set up scripts to run automatically and induce Garza to eat, sleep, take a shower, groom himself, speak, masturbate, read, watch TV. At first Garza thought this was heavenly, watching his body go about its prescribed routines as if from a distance and yet from within himself. He described it as feeling like Salo's flesh-and-blood embodiment. Garza found himself waking up at a regular time, taking care of his business in the bathroom, getting dressed, eating breakfast, going to work at the recycling plant, chatting with coworkers with Salo's distantly typed words in his mouth, making wittier jokes than he'd ever made, going to a bar after work, hooking up with some hottie chick who was herself under 24/7 remote control, maybe even by Salo also, screwing like crazy at her place, coming home, falling asleep, and dreaming. Dreams, though. Dreams were the one thing Bionet hackers couldn't control, and Garza's started taking on a panicked element. In the dreams he watched himself as if on a security-camera monitor, painstakingly executing the most mundane rituals of his day. His subconscious was freaking out, saying, *Whoa, hold on, buddy, I thought I was calling the shots around here!* Alarmed at being usurped, his subconscious sent out these distress calls in the middle of deep REM. As the days dragged and Salo's routines changed little, if at all, Garza wondered if he should utter his safe word and break the hack. But it was so dreamy, living like this. He was making more friends, getting fit with a daily workout, eating well. The scripts Salo had laid out were truly working the wonders the hacker had promised when they first met in a booth at Game Zone. Somewhere across town on a laptop in a guy's rec room, Garza's entire life was being mapped out and executed perfectly. He even got a promotion. He began looking at the life he'd led before giving over his daily routine to Salo as one filled with foibles and inadequacies. This new Garza strode confidently, spoke up for himself, ate right, and bedded the ladies. But the dreams. Full-on thrashing nightmares now, with slaughtered animals and self-castration, the pollution of Hell vomited up through his brain stem. He woke trembling and saw his hand moving toward a bottle of pills prescribed to blunt the edges of these terrors. But I *like* not being in control, Garza told himself, and told one of his dates, who was far beyond where he was, her eyes gone milky, as mechanically they began to screw. "With the Bionet," she said, "you can experience another person's orgasm. Would you like to experience mine?" Garza consented and deep in their brains the software flipped their perceptions of their sense organs so whatever was happening to the date's body was going into Garza's brain and vice versa. Garza, disoriented, felt himself being penetrated in a new concavity, understanding the swinging weight of breasts, opening his eyes expecting to see himself pounding away on his now-female form, but finding his date drifting into a somnambulist's version of sexual intercourse, her eyes like monitors tuned to static, face twitching minutely upon his ejaculation. And the real shitty part was that he never made her come, so Garza missed out on his own orgasm. Or hers. Whatever. Then the next day a crazy thing happened. Salo, the hacker, *died*. Car wreck, nothing fancy. The scripts ran as per usual, leading Garza through his day on autopilot, then the next day and the next until Salo's family handed the laptops over to the cops, whose Bionet enforcement division quickly figured out Salo was operating several flesh-and-blood embodiments and put the brakes on the whole operation. One minute Garza was making himself a mango fruit smoothie, the next he sensed a great silence within. The blender kept going on PUREE. He wanted to turn it off but found the only things his hands appeared to be good for were to look at. He stood in the kitchen for an hour, during which time the blender melted down and stopped functioning and great strings of drool dripped from his catatonic face. The cops traced the signal and found Garza with his pants full of excrement, unable to speak or even close his mouth, immobile in the middle of his kitchen. They'd seen this kind of stuff before, and ferried him to the Bionet wing of the nearest hospital where, Abby supposed, he remained to this day, undergoing a battery of physical and psychological therapies to relearn how to take charge of his own nervous system.

After the eunuchs' dance the DJ spoke again. "Welcome to the uncharted waters of the Biological Internet. Your heart rate. Your electrolytes. The electricity that flows through your muscles. We control every part of you but your soul. Turn off your mind, children, relax and float downstream."

Heather was in a corner having her neck massaged by a eunuch who was asking her the model numbers of her implants. Jadie stayed glued to a pillar, looking kind of terrified. And where was Megan? Abby very suddenly didn't want to be here. She looked frantically for the exit. Some guy grabbed her bicep and spoke into her ear.

"You don't belong here. Quick, let's get out. The cops are on their way."

The guy, who would have been more threatening had he been less handsome, steered her through the crowd toward the restrooms, then through a service door and up some crumbly wood stairs. Behind them, the pleasure center erupted in panicked screaming. Abby stumbled through a door onto a street of boarded-up ex-businesses. Down the block, cop cars spun their blues and reds.

"Just walk at a normal speed," the guy said, "like we're a couple on a date. By the way, my name's Rocco."

Abby shook his hand reluctantly. "What about my friends? We should go back and help them."

"They're probably getting cuffed right now."

"Why'd you pull me out of there?"

"I could tell you were just checking it out, not into the whole scene. And I think I recognize you. We get our coffee around the same time at Lumiere's."

They passed beneath a streetlight, giving Abby a better look. Skin the color of an Idaho potato, scruffy jet-black stubble, a pair of dark eyes squinting in the half-light. Abby said, "You're the guy who got the last Asiago bagel when I was there a couple days ago."

"Sounds like me," Rocco said.

"How'd you know the cops were coming?"

"I'm an informant. I do it sort of on the side while I'm getting my Bionetics doctorate. Plus it's good for me to see what kinds of applications are being developed at a grass-roots level. Pretty impressed by that guy who supported his whole body weight on one finger. But those DJs are amateurs. They know enough to encode the implants but have no clue—or just don't give a shit—about dendrite deintegration or channel-flow erosion. It pisses me off. You just don't muck around with the human brain like that. I hope that guy spends his life in the slammer."

"Why do you trust me with this information?" Abby said.

"It gives me an excuse to ask if you'd be interested in getting a drink somewhere."

They traversed patches of stink and bubbling urban lava, then found a cab back to the more or less healthy interior of Vancouver, where the city sort of shook them a while until they settled at a café decorated with posters from Italian movies. Which gave Abby a perfect entry point into her area of expertise. She would have normally evaded the topic of Italian neorealism in the company of a dude, had seen too many boyfriends' faces glaze over, but this guy seemed interesting enough that she'd test his endurance for twentieth-century cinema trivia. If he stared into space and nodded politely she'd relegate him to that category of men who'd passed through her life burdened by their passions for full-immersion video games and the bracketeering of college basketball. The only guys she'd met who shared her love of Brakhage and Jodorowsky and Maddin and the Brothers Quay tended to hide in clouds of their own flatulence in the netherworld of the university library.

"*Bicycle Thieves*," Abby translated from a poster behind Rocco's head. "What a heartbreaking film, right?"

Rocco paused a sec, stared at the salt and pepper as if listening to a distant voice, then nodded. "*Vittorio De Sica*, right? 1948? *Quintessential work of Italian neorealism?*"

"I've never met anyone else who's actually seen it."

"I haven't seen it," Rocco said, "but I know it *concerns an impoverished family man (Lamberto Maggiorani) who takes a job in postwar Rome pasting posters on buildings around the city. When his bicycle—his only mode of transportation—is stolen, he embarks on a fruitless search for it with his young son (Enzo Staiola)*. That's the one, right?"

Abby looked over her shoulder. "Where are you reading that?"

Rocco sipped his au lait. "It came to me."

"No, really. How'd you know the summary?"

"I'll tell you, but I can't tell you here. The only place safe enough to tell you is my apartment."

"That's a new one."

"That sounded bad. What I mean is, I know my apartment is free of surveillance. We can't be sure about this restaurant.

Come back to my place and I'll fill you in on the details. I'm not asking you to sleep with me."

You're not? Abby thought. *Damn.*

Rocco's apartment wasn't far, and he spent the interim five blocks warning and preparing Abby for the wretched state of the living space. The kitchen hadn't been cleaned in some time, he warned, and there might be a spaghetti-type situation in one of the sinks. The apartment was on the fifth floor of a tree-ringed, green-built, post-FUS building, with windows overlooking the retinal-rape neon of a takeout Szechuan hole-in-the-wall.

And good thing he'd prepped her for the disaster of his personal living space. He'd actually oversold the sloppiness of the pad, so now it didn't look *that* bad. Rocco opened the fridge and pointed out some beverages. Abby agreed to something with pomegranate in it.

"Sorry about the cloak-and-dagger cheesiness," Rocco said. "I'll just get really busted if they find out I helped someone escape from the sting. Worse, that I've told you as much as I have. The deal with my line of study is we test a lot of our own applications on ourselves. You know how the Bionet works, right?"

"Not really. I have an emergency implant, that's about it. I know 911 will be called with a GPS signal if I have a heart attack."

"Right, so that's basically where the Bionet started. For years people chipped their dogs and cats so if they ran off the Humane Society could scan them and get an address and a phone number. That was the beginning, pretty much. Then when the baby boomers started going into retirement homes, a few of them got chipped with files including their whole medical histories. Better than wearing a bracelet with all that info engraved on it. Then the next wave of innovation went down and these implants, still incredibly crude by today's standards, got networked using the rudimentary Wi-Fi and Internet of the day. Pretty easy to monitor heart rate and transmit the data via the Web. Then, like you said, all this GPS-enabled, vitals-monitoring software went into the implants and now you can get hit by a truck and two seconds later your body calls an ambulance for you. The Bionet's saved lives. That's why I wanted to get into it in the first place. Now we can download hormones, enzymes, and antigens remotely through implants and upload our immunities for other people to share."

"What's that have to do with you knowing about *Bicycle Thieves*?"

"We're on to the next stage, Bionet 2.0. Neurology. The development of this stuff hasn't been all that smooth. For years we've stuck these implants in volunteers' heads that make them hear voices in other languages, pick up phone transmissions, radio stations. We've been trying to wire the frontal lobes into the Internet so everyone can eventually become their own Wikipedia or, rather, share the Wikipedia with others who are logged in. The software itself has improved by several orders of magnitude, for sure, but for the past ten years or so the industry has been driving test subjects crazy, paying out huge lawsuits. It's been a disaster.

"Three, four years ago a group of neuroscientists and Bioneticists at the University of Montreal published a paper that changed *everyone*'s thinking about neural implants. They proposed that the problems we were seeing in clinical trials weren't all that related to the implants themselves, but to the parts of the brain we were seeking to integrate with. Rather than trying to plug those implants into the parts of the brain that produce consciousness, we needed to start plugging them into the parts of the brain that produce subconsciousness. And this makes a lot of sense for two reasons. One, the subconscious is built to process a shitload of information, a quantity that overloads the conscious mind. It doles out information judiciously into our conscious thoughts. Second, Jung believed that the individual subconscious tapped into a level of consciousness all living beings shared, the collective unconscious. And one cool way to think of the collective unconscious is as a giant, biological Internet."

"So you plugged the real Internet into the subconscious Internet?"

"We're trying to. Instead of plugging these implants into people's heads that just scream trivia at them 24/7, we're finding that these subconscious implants work far more mysteriously than we imagined. You know that feeling when you can't remember a word? When you say you feel there's something on the tip of your tongue? That's what this implant feels like *all the time*. Like there's always information just behind the screen waiting to burst out but the subconscious is acting in your best interest to hold it back. So tonight, when you said *Bicycle Thieves*, my implant probably did a quick search of IMDb, then served up that little summary for me."

"That feeling, though, doesn't it drive you nuts?"

"I'm learning to manage it. And my implant is only turned on a few hours a day. Started out just a minute or two a day at first, and even at that level it left me exhausted. I got these hellish nightmares. My subconscious had to learn how to use this new tool, this piece of hardware thrust like a space probe into my skull. You can imagine, after millions of years of evolution, suddenly the mind has to deal with this weird little sesame-seed-sized *thing* that shows up in the cranium. And you're right, I'd go crazy if I walked around all day feeling like I'd just forgotten what

I was going to say." Rocco paused, but not like he was listening to a distant signal. More like he was listening to something that only came from within himself. "I like you, Abby."

How romantically science fictiony this all was! Abby leaned in to kiss him.

Abby confronted Kylee as she jerked along through the great hall in an antique-looking electric wheelchair that smelled of burning lubricant.

"Either I see the archives or I'm leaving," Abby said.

Kylee bumbled into one of the phantasy-art-lined passages. "That would be a shame. You at least have to stick around to see the musical we're producing in your honor."

"If there isn't work for me to do I'll get out of your way and head home to Vancouver."

A great bell clanged somewhere on the property. Kylee quickly wheeled herself to the nearest elevator. Federicos rushed through the house, assembling on a balcony overlooking the harbour. Abby pushed her way to the front and saw a squat little freighter pull up to the pier. The captain, a bronzed man in a red-striped shirt and captain's hat, waved up to the spectators as six Federicos rushed to help unload crates of supplies. There emerged a young nurse carrying a bundle in her arms—the newest Federico. A cheer went up, hugs all around. Accompanied by Federicos beside themselves with excitement, the nurse strode the length of the pier and ascended the steep path to the house with the infant Federico in her arms. When she came to the balcony she handed the baby to Kylee, who quivered in her wheelchair, suppressing tears. The pop star pulled the blanket away from the baby's face and said, "Oh, my heavens, he's the most precious baby I have ever seen." The other Federicos elbowed one another to get a better look, oohing over Federico #631, freshly expelled from the womb of a desperate third-world woman. Once the nurse and the boat departed, and after a few seconds of tickling and cooing, Kylee handed the baby over to one of the Federicos in charge of childcare and wiped her hands on her shawl. "That one seemed a bit underbaked," she said. "A rush job. We'll see how he grows. Disperse, everyone. Off to your stupid, like, responsibilities and shit."

Alone with Kylee, Abby watched the ship disappear on the horizon as a procession of Federicos hauled the supplies to the house. A breeze lifted some strands of hair from Abby's face and laid them across her shoulder.

"There are no archives," Abby said.

"True, but I was going to show you what's left of them. Ready?"

The domed solarium, three stories of steel and glass, was by far the most meticulously maintained wing of the Seaside Love Palace. A hundred species of butterflies colored trees, vines, and blossoms of endangered flora. The thick, peaty air smelled ripe with the sweet scent of decay. A tiled trail led through the foliage to a room-sized peninsula encircled by a crescent-shaped koi pond. When Kylee, Abby, and a Federico arrived at the pond they found a table set for afternoon tea and an ancient man napping in a wheelchair. That he wasn't actually a corpse astonished Abby. Rare species of moths alighted on his shoulders.

The young Federico poured tea for the group while Kylee shouted at the old man, "Wake up! Wake up, you old queen!" After a minute of this the ancient man began to stir, opening an eye a crack.

"You don't have to wake him for me," Abby said.

"Oh, but I do," Kylee said. "You wanted to see the archives, didn't you?"

"This is your archivist?"

"No, young thing. This isn't the archivist. This is the *archive*. This is Federico #1."

Abby looked puzzled.

"Ask him something," Kylee continued. "His brain is a server. You have to put your ear close to his mouth, though. He can only whisper. And you have to shout your question."

Abby knelt beside the source of all Federicos. "What was Errol Flynn's first starring role?" she asked.

"Louder, honey," Kylee said.

"What was Errol Flynn's first starring role!"

Federico #1's mouth began to move, just a subtle tremor of the lips and a slight breeze of rank air rising from his throat to indicate words were about to be formulated. "*Captain Blood*, 1935," he whispered.

"I thought I was here to recover digital data," Abby said. "How am I supposed to know what's lost if it's all stored in this man's head?"

"They said you were the best," Kylee snickered.

"I retrieve digital content, not memories. How am I supposed to figure out what was lost?"

The archives went back to sleep. Kylee shrugged and scooted away, chuckling, with the younger Federico in tow, leaving Abby and #1 alone. Abby checked the level on her recorder then shouted into the archive's ear, "Recite the Luke Piper transcript!"

After a moment of silence the archive's lips began to move. Abby positioned her microphone and turned up the volume, listening through the ear buds. ". . . *the tape roll a bit here before we get . . . Luke? You need anything, Luke?* No, I'm fine. *I thought we could first talk . . .*" the archive began. Hours vanished into the story of Luke's search for Mr. Kirkpatrick. Why anyone would go through the trouble to send her here to record this tale was beyond her. She turned the recorder off when it was clear the transcript was complete, then rose to leave. The old Federico grabbed her wrist and trained his gummy eyes on her. "You aren't the person you think you are," he said, his voice rising barely above a whisper.

"Let go of me."

"You're in superposition."

A young Federico appeared and removed Abby's arm from Federico #1's grip. "Now, now, #1," he said. "Let's not traumatize our guest."

As he was wheeled away, Federico #1 shook his finger at Abby. "You're somebody else entirely."

On the stage, gradually brightening footlights brought an abstract cityscape into view. A light burned in the window of an apartment tower where a Federico in a black wig sat drinking tea, clicking on a laptop. Another Federico wearing fake stubble appeared beside the wigged Federico and rubbed his shoulder. Abby, sitting in the balcony beside Kylee, realized these actors were supposed to represent Rocco and herself.

ROCCO

What are you doing, sweetheart?

ABBY (sighing)

Looking for a job. I sure wish there was a better market for a digital-media restorer!

ROCCO

Hey, you'll find something soon. Don't give up. Which reminds me. I got this phone call last night from some guy named Dirk Bickle. He wanted to talk to you about an opportunity.

ABBY

Well, why didn't you say so?

The stage Abby leaped to her feet and grabbed a jacket and hat, then pranced down from the skyscraper to center stage, where a grey-haired Federico in dark sunglasses rose from a café table.

DIRK

Nice to meet you, Abby. My name is Dirk Bickle and have I got an opportunity for you. To Victoria! Posthaste! To recover a bunch of archives and jazz like that!

Dirk hustled Abby onto a cardboard boat that glided along behind rolling, saw-toothed stage waves. A couple of anthropomorphized clouds with Dizzy Gillespie cheeks descended from the rafters while offstage a Foley artist faked the sounds of waves, wind, and thunder with sheets of metal and hand-cranked barrels of rice.

ABBY

Wait! What am I actually supposed to do?

The boat came to rest, stage right, in front of the art director's baroque vision of the Seaside Love Palace. Abby belted a couplet.

ABBY

I feel so alone, so lost and confused.
I certainly hope I don't get abused!

The front doors popped open and out pranced two younger Federicos playing the older Federicos who'd greeted Abby upon her arrival a few days prior. They hurriedly dressed the stage Abby in the bunny outfit as stage elements rolled into new configurations, forming a mirror-image version of the auditorium they now occupied. Her back to the real audience, the Abby onstage addressed a painted backdrop of faces as a staticky, poorly recorded laugh track guffawed.

ABBY

You've got me mistaken for someone else! I'm here to see the archives!

After which she collapsed, was dragged stage left by a Federico, and dumped on a bed on rollers. Ominous music! From the rafters, on wires, descended a Federico made up corpse-like, costumed in billowing white organza.

ISAAC

Hey, baby. Show me a little skin.

Stage Abby woke with a start.

ABBY

Who are you? What is this place?

ISAAC

I'll tell you all the secrets of the Seaside Love Palace
if you flash me a nip.

There followed an industrial-metal number in which the ghost of Isaac Pope, joined by the ghosts of other dot-com CEOs, sang about rounds of financing, server farms, and the importance of accepting cookies and clearing one's cache when encountering a technical problem. Then, with barely a transition, stage Abby sang a duet with a Federico costumed as Kylee, to the great amusement of the audience. There was a death scene with the suicidal Federico, who took his life via this house's preferred method of Red Bull/Mountain Dew OD. There were several Kylee costume changes. It seemed to the spectator Abby, shocked at watching events of her own recent experiences poorly dramatized, that the dramaturge had run out of time and lost control of the mise-en-scène, resorting to cramming scenes together with little transitional tissue. Unpracticed players blew lines and missed cues. The orgy sequence erupted in a chaotic whirl of puppetry and full-body nude-colored suits. There was the arrival of the baby Federico—all of it hurried, half-assed, blurry with a score that couldn't figure out what time signature it wanted to be in. Then came the scene that had happened little more than an hour before, with a Federico playing the wheelchair-confined archive whispering the transcript into a microphone. Federico-as-Kylee appeared and summoned her to the theater. A chaotic reshuffling of scenery later, Abby now watched her avatar watching a puppet version of the performance she had just seen. The same meeting with Bickle, the boat ride, the dressing up as a bunny, ghostly visitations, dance numbers, etc., except at half the previous scale. In this iteration even more lines were blown, even more cues missed, even more dramatic corners cut, the action sped up to an amphetamine hum as the Federicos in the orchestra pit sawed madly at their stringed instruments, everything faster, miniaturized, coming to the point in the story again when the puppet version of Kylee summoned Abby to the theater, upon which an even smaller puppet theater appeared within the first puppet theater. Abby could barely make out the little figures dancing within. Finally, the spectator version of Abby, overcome with nausea, turned to Kylee and asked, "How do I make it stop?"

"It's easy, young thing," Kylee smiled, snapping her fingers. "You wake up in a field."

Q&A WITH LUKE PIPER, PART 2

How you feeling this morning, Luke?

I'm okay. Ready.

When we last spoke we ended with your discovery of Nick's father's shop.

That was the summer after I graduated from high school. I was supposed to go to college in the fall but decided against it. I was still living in the VW van in the muddy yard outside Star and Nick's shack. I used a little camp stove to make oatmeal and boil water for ramen. After I discovered the contents of the shed, I spent hours in there looking over the blueprints Nick's dad left behind. And I decided to start cleaning the place up. I took the seats out of the van and made trips to the dump, hauling away all the garbage that had accumulated around the property. I cleared brush, swept out the shed, and cleaned the tools. With some of my life insurance money I bought a few tons of gravel and had it poured down the driveway and on the muddy ground outside the house. It became a full-time job, maintaining that place.

What was Nick doing when you—

He decided to call Dirk Bickle. He'd saved the card from the science fair. Since they didn't have a phone, Nick walked to a gas station one day and called the guy on a pay phone. Apparently Bickle told him a car would show up for him the following week and they'd put him on a plane to the Bay Area. He'd live on a campus, get all meals and expenses paid, and pull in a salary of $30,000 a year. This blew our minds. It was a lot of money at the time. All Nick had to do was come up with new inventions.

What was the organization called?

We didn't know at that point. They said Nick had to commit before they really told him anything of substance. That afternoon after the call Nick walked up the driveway in a daze. I was chopping wood and I stopped and asked what had happened. He told me about the conversation and looked at me sort of embarrassed. Of course I was happy for him, we celebrated with a bottle of wine, but part of me couldn't help noting how much our fortunes had reversed. Just a few months before I had been the kid bound for college and success and he'd been the one with no future. Nick made up his mind, he had to see where these shadows and secrets led. And I think, too—this is just my theory—that he looked at what his old man had been trying to accomplish—some kind of crazy speculative civil-engineering project—and realized that his dad had never had the chance to develop it to the fullest. Now Nick could pick up where he had left off. What were Nick's prospects? He could have stuck around Bainbridge and worked at McDonald's. He could have moved to Seattle and become a street punk. He hadn't even bothered applying to colleges. He left himself with the options of a life of poverty or plunging into something cool and mysterious. Who wouldn't have made the same decision?

So a week passed and sure enough here came a taxi, rolling up to that little shack. Bickle climbed out, walked across the yard, knocked on the door. Star asked that she speak to him and Nick together, alone, so I went out to my van and probably buried my nose in *Zen and the Art of Motorcycle Maintenance*. About an hour and a half later, they came out. Star had been crying. Nick carried a duffel bag, that was it. I hugged him for a long time. He pulled me in tight and said I was a brother to him. Then he got in the cab and left.

Star didn't cope well with Nick leaving?

Not at all. She was a serious mess. I had to convince her to eat. I kept telling her Nick would visit soon, that he was going to become really successful, etc. Nothing consoled her. I spent the next couple weeks getting the place in order. I mowed, weeded the garden, rented a high-pressure sprayer and blasted the moss off the exterior of the shack, then repainted it. Mostly, though, I spent time on the beach where my house used to be. Sometimes I found things that had belonged to us, burped up from Puget Sound. One of my mom's shoes washed up with the tide, a spatula, the kind of guitar pick my dad used. This slow distribution of broken objects teased me in little bursts almost too painful to bear. I found a Strawberry Shortcake doll with my sister's initials on it, wedged between two pieces of driftwood. Shards of a bowl I remembered from our kitchen. I went there every day sifting through whatever the tide brought, collecting what used to belong to my family in plastic milk crates I stole from behind Safeway. Worse, on the spot where my house once stood a new house was rising. I'd gotten the proceeds from the sale of the land, sure, but the sudden appearance of new construction offended me. Within a few months the place was finished and a new family with three kids moved in. Around that time the tides stopped bringing tokens of my family's existence. Winter was on its way.

We received letters from Nick every couple weeks. He wrote to us about all the things he was learning—chemistry, physics, heady theoretical stuff. We thought he sounded upbeat. He was surrounded by freakishly gifted people like himself for the first time in his life. One time he sent a picture of himself with some new friends at the Grand Canyon. Three geeks wearing glasses and Nick looking all goth with his jet-black hair in his face, but smiling. I missed him.

So when did—

I know what you're going to ask. Coming here this morning I knew we'd be talking about it. Here's what happened. I had managed to clean the place up pretty well and this made Star happier. She joined a dance group for hippie women in town, started studying reflexology. And for the first time she talked to me about her husband, Marc, and about the construction accident that killed him, how she had discovered him with his head bent back at an impossible angle. On her birthday I surprised her with a cake and bought her a new dress. We were sitting in the shack, eating the cake, laughing about something, I don't know what, and I convinced her she should try the dress on. A few minutes later she came out of the bedroom wearing it. I told her she looked beautiful. It just came out, I wasn't even thinking. We stood there and felt this heavy, horny moment and both of us seemed to get the same thought at the same time: *Why not?* Then we were kissing. My mouth behind her ear. I lifted her up, carried her into the bedroom. I'd never touched skin this old with lust before and the strangeness and beauty of it pulled me inward, into this sexual place I'd been unaware of. All the girls I'd slept with up to that point, all those fucks were about surface sensation. This was a longing that passed through me like twine through a bead, tethered to some distant point in my past. I sucked her long nipples thinking, *Nick fed from these* and almost came. She smelled ripe, sweaty. She had hair under her arms and unshaved legs. I knew I could have as much of her as I wanted, that I'd be able to live here with her and fuck and fuck and fuck. She lay naked on the bed and opened her legs. Her labia were larger than any I had ever seen, like something you'd find at a butcher shop. She spread them against her thighs like she was opening the covers of a book. I was in her, no protection, straining against a river of images in my head: the mud slide, blueprints, objects washing up on the shore. When she came the first time she asked me to call her mommy. Everything about this was so *wrong,* it was precisely the worst thing to say but it was like she dragged a heavy, rusted chain out of my entangled guts. Grief so unbearable I thought I was being electrocuted. I unloaded in her, six or seven shotgun blasts of come.

How old was Star?

She would have been thirty-seven. Thirty-eight maybe.

So this became a regular thing.

Constantly. Sometimes four, five times a day. We did it in the woods a lot. On the roof of my van. In the shed with the blueprints. We lived in our own little erotic bubble. She turned me on to psilocybin mushrooms and we spent days tripping, naked, running around the property. I had unlimited money in the bank and all we really spent it on was groceries. Our own personal rabbit hole.

Did you ever talk about what Nick would think if he found out?

Yeah, but we were so naive about it. At least I was. We thought Nick would come home for Thanksgiving dinner and we'd inform him we'd become lovers. And that's basically how it went. I picked him up from SeaTac and it was as if we'd both expanded these weird corners of our personalities. He struck me as preppy, an Izod-shirt-wearing nerd with his hair cut short. No more Butthole Surfers concert Ts for him. And since he'd left I'd grown a big, gnarly beard. I was probably wearing Birkenstocks and Guatemalan-print shorts. When we saw each other at the gate, we both burst out laughing. On the way home he just blabbed about how cool the academy was, how he was learning about chaos theory and neural networks. I could tell he wanted to impress me. I kept having this uncomfortable thought that my parents would have been more proud of what Nick was doing than what I was doing. But I was cool with everything, asked a lot of questions, said "wow" a lot.

We'd had this plan, Star and I, to reveal our love to Nick during our Thanksgiving feast. Nick showed up the day before, so we had a whole day where we were going to supposedly keep it cool. So Nick comes home and his mom is crying, she's so happy to see him, and he gives her some chocolates he got in San Francisco, and we're all laughing and having a good time. Remember, the shack was small, one bedroom, and Nick had grown up sleeping on a futon they'd dragged out from behind the couch every night. So there's this awkward moment where Nick is standing with his luggage, looking around, trying to figure out where to put it, and Star blurts out, "You can sleep in our bed."

At first this sort of sails right over Nick's head and he says, no, no, the living room's cool, but his mom is grabbing his luggage and putting it in the bedroom. Since the place is so small, you can pretty much stand in the living room and see the entire bedroom. Nick is looking into the bedroom and he gets this weird expression. Meanwhile, I'm trying to get him to retell some story he told me on the way over. When I notice his face I follow his gaze and see that there's a pair of my underwear sitting on Star's bed. They're obviously *my* tighty-whiteys. Plus, uh, there's a big bottle of olive oil on the bedside table. And okay, this is ridiculous, I know, but a copy of the *Kama Sutra*. We're all quiet a second—Nick, his mom, me, underpants, lubricant, Indian sex manual. Then Nick looks at me and says, "What the fuck is going on here?"

So Star, true to her flower-child roots, says something like, "We were going to tell you tomorrow during our feast—Luke and I have become lovers." And she goes on and on about how the age of a soul is different than the age of a body, like how our souls would be in the same grade if they went to school together, and Nick is standing there, looking aghast at my stained underwear, then at me, and he yells pretty much the only thing a guy in his position is capable of yelling at such a moment. "You're fucking my *mom*?"

Then it's my turn to get into the lovey-dovey-peace-brother talk and Nick isn't having any of it. There really isn't room to pace, so he sort of bounces between two walls. He keeps saying, "Dude! You're fucking my *mom*!" It doesn't help matters when Star says, "Please, Nick, call it *lovemaking*."

After that we went out to dinner. None of us spoke on the way to the restaurant. Mexican food. I tried to keep the conversation on Nick and what he was doing in his teenage think tank. He kept his answers short. Clearly he didn't know how to handle this development. Then he said it again, this time not so angry, just bewildered, "Dude, you're *fucking* my *mom*?"

You have to understand something about islands. The social psychology is different. And on Bainbridge there was this whole cadre of moms who were constantly up in everyone's business, formulating opinions about you all the time. So I can't overstate how devastating it was for Nick to say this in a busy, public place. You could almost visualize the whispered lines of communication flowing from table to table. And Nick wouldn't fucking shut up. He just kept saying it, emphasizing different words. "*You* are fucking my mom?" or "You are fucking *my* mom?" Imagine what it's like to be in the middle of a room of people pretending not to stare at you in silent, shocked judgment. And remember what I looked like and where I'd come from. Only a few months prior I'd been college-bound, lusted after by the female half of my class. An impeccable academic record and a solid reputation on the playing field. Now I was sitting in a Mexican restaurant wearing hippie clothes that hadn't been laundered in a month, attempting to grow dreadlocks, sporting a Jesus beard, having my sexual relationship with the town's potentially mentally disturbed woman made very public. Within a week this cadre of in-everyone's-business moms had formed a narrative about what was going on between Star and me. It went like this: Luke Piper lost his family in a tragic accident and the unstable mother of his best friend took advantage of his grief by entering into a borderline-statutory-rape-type situation that wouldn't have been so borderline if he hadn't just turned eighteen. How sick was it that this unhinged woman was probably giving herpes to this poor, grieving boy who used to be Ivy League material? Keep in mind that these were the same women having affairs with members of the local clergy. The same ones who were drinking at 10 a.m. and downing pills but who had nonetheless been granted the supernatural ability to determine how other people should raise their children and live their lives.

Did anyone in the community confront you directly?

Of course not. Are you kidding? Someone wrote CRADLE ROBBER on Star's mailbox. Classic Bainbridge passive-aggressive bullshit. They communicated their disgust through glares in the supermarket checkout line. It was a pretty miserable Thanksgiving. It rained real bad and the shack's roof got a nasty leak. It was the first Thanksgiving I hadn't spent with my family and you could have dropped me into an abandoned mine shaft and I would have felt about the same. Not to mention Star and I momentarily nixed the fucking. Nick and I barely spoke. Miserable.

I want to change the subject a minute and talk about this academy that Nick went to.

Sure. Turns out it did have a name—the Kirkpatrick Academy of Human Potential. Founded in the eighties in Silicon Valley with the first wave of software wealth. Supposedly headquartered in San Jose, more like an estate than a campus. Nick showed me a brochure. The place looked nice. They had about a dozen buildings, play fields, woods, a small organic farm. Only about a hundred students in attendance at a time, every one of them courted heavily by the Fortune 500 upon graduation. The place was supposedly an incubator for ideas and innovations that entered mainstream culture ten, twenty years later.

I was jealous. Doesn't every high school nerd wish that someone will discover his hidden genius? Nick was especially susceptible to this kind of thinking. But the more I thought about the academy the more it seemed like bullshit. So Nick builds some kind of contraption for a science fair and some guy in a business suit sees it and gives him a business card? That's all it takes? The place sounded too good to be true.

SKINNER

Al Skinner, witness to the bloodiest wars forged by man's satanic imagination, presently feared forgetting his shoes. He kept his eye on them, brown Hush Puppies with Dr. Scholl's inserts, paired on the bedroom's spiral rag rug in his house in Scottsdale, Arizona. When you walked outside without your shoes in this neighborhood, you were on your way to assisted living. Sammy, a retired security contractor like Skinner, from two blocks over, had one morning walked without his shoes all the way to the combo Taco Bell/KFC. Later, at the country club, gray heads slowly shook and the mouth parts of those heads gummed the words, "*They found him with no shoes on.*" Soon thereafter Sammy was ushered from this community of retired military personnel to a fortress of assisted living where one's brain wasn't expected to put on much of a show. Skinner didn't want to end up at one of those places, shoeless, separated from his wife, eating apple sauce and watching the Smiling People channel.

Her name, the wife's name, was Chiho Aoshima. Skinner watched Chiho move about the house and their life with precision and purpose. It had all culminated ridiculously in this house with two bedrooms, an upstairs and a downstairs, air-conditioning, and a glassed-in porch with a view of a sand trap and the seventh hole. She pressed oranges into juice in the morning and poured him glasses of strawberry soy milk at night. He opened the mail with a sword-shaped letter opener bearing the insignia of his company, the celebrated and bedeviled 83rd Section, aka a bunch of dirty muthafuckin newman-killing sunza bitches, aka the rats' a-holes, aka the only men he could claim to have ever loved. Love: it was something more ludicrously huge than the destruction of entire continents. Love: the only thing that atrophied the dick and balls of warfare. When he'd offloaded his worst memories he'd worried that some of the love he remembered would go with them, despite the technicians' assurances. Gone into data storage were the mutilated streets of former Chicago, legions of semirobotic Chinese marching in formation through polluted exurbs, millions of hectares of inhospitable wastes stretching across geography like the pustulent crust of a chemical burn, traces of human tissue in underground torture chambers as elaborate and equipped with amenities as a cruise ship. He'd chosen to forget these things. What worried him were the things he'd chosen to remember.

Chiho didn't appear to suffer from these worries. Even without enhancement she would have been in fighting form. Walked five miles a day, swam on weekends, and could still pull out a jump shot when occasion called for it. She appeared far younger than her 170 years. As she'd aged she hadn't put on much weight, keeping her coat-rack frame. She still slithered into bed on top of him from time to time, tugged at the flesh of his jowls and rapped on his forehead like it was a door. He brought her a blanket or a cracker blobbed with cream cheese. She took care of the bills. He gave the most heartwarming toast on her 150th at the country club. Once a year she polished her sniper rifle. Chiho Aoshima: Al Skinner's will to live.

Today they were waiting for the hibernation crew to show up. Two guys and a truck. Outside in the driveway in 120 Fahrenheit their freshly washed RV, stocked with supplies for the summer, sparkled and appeared to sweat. Half of greater Phoenix had emptied by now and in another month only 5 percent of the population would remain, bunkered beneath the surface, suited up and equipped and tucked away for the season's punishing inferno, sticking around to tend to infrastructure.

"Do we have everything?" Skinner said as his wife's shape passed before him in the living room. How many times in the history of elderly-person road trips has that question been asked? Skinner spoke it ritualistically, not really minding when no answer came. Chiho whispered to herself, her bottom lip quivering with traces of speech. She was in her head again, probably plotting the logistics of their journey. By now it had become second nature, sixty years of migration, popping north before the sun landed its hammer blows on their gated community.

The hibernation technicians showed up at noon. A couple of young fellows with Latin America in their veins. While Chiho signed the paperwork, Skinner shuffled one last time around the house wondering if there was anything else he might toss into the RV. Ballpoint pen? He pocketed one just in case. Extra bottle of antacid? Can opener? He pulled open the top drawer of his file cabinet where he kept a stack of memory cards. They deserved to be hibernated. Come on, old man, just let them be. He put them in his breast pocket.

Back in the living room the tech guys were explaining their process, blurting it out perfunctorily, required by law to recite how the house would be sealed and filled with a proprietary, nonpolluting gas that, using a common field generator, would be kept at a steady 72 degrees for the duration of their absence. Their house had passed inspection and was considered airtight but an additional nonpermeable membrane would engulf the structure and essentially shrink-wrap it. Chiho nodded, initialed, and signed. They grabbed their house keys and followed the techs outside. A great deal of tubing and rolls of the nonpermeable membrane were produced from the hibernation crew's truck. Soon Skinner and Chiho sat beside one another in the cockpit of the RV, watching the techs pump the proprietary nonpolluting gas into their home through a conduit designed specifically for this purpose.

"You really want to stick around and watch the house get wrapped?" Chiho asked.

"We can go," Skinner said.

Chiho put the RV in gear and backed out of the driveway, then headed down Ironsides Avenue, through their mostly abandoned community. Up and down the block houses had been entombed until their owners returned in the fall. Once in a while stories surfaced about pets or occupants who accidentally stayed in their house during the hibernation process, to be discovered months later, perfectly preserved as if they'd died mere minutes before. The proprietary gas was *that good*. You could even leave food on the counter and it would still be edible upon your return, though this wasn't recommended. House condoms, Skinner called them. Soon they were on an arterial, then the stop-and-go highway, the exodus in full swing.

"I always miss Arizona," Chiho said.

"I miss Arizona even when I'm here," said Skinner.

Chiho had packed the RV as securely as she could but something still rattled in the back. Rattling noises hurt her teeth. Maybe it was a jar of marmalade jiggling in the pantry. Or the coffee pot. Skinner rode shotgun, lost in road signs. A hundred miles could pass like this.

"I brought some memory cards from home," Skinner said outside city limits. "I thought you should know."

"Well that'll be fun," said Chiho. She knew what *I thought you should know* meant. War memories. Would Skinner come out and say this? She gave him an opening. "We can pop in the memory of that camping trip when my shoes melted."

"I don't know if that one's in there." Skinner was quiet for two minutes by the dashboard clock. Then he said, "I brought a couple cards of war memories. I thought I'd share them with Carl. If he wants to."

"This is supposed to be a nice visit."

"I'm not asking you to approve. I've got some memories I need to go over with Carl. I promise to be on my best behavior."

The rattling. Maybe a spice bottle.

"You can do whatever you want with your own memories."

"I know."

"So what are you asking of me?"

"I'm not asking you anything. I'm just telling you."

"You're asking me to wake you up when you resurrect those nightmares."

Skinner sipped his root beer, returned it to the cup holder. "We'll be careful. We'll stagger the memories, do it in doses, alternate innocuous memories from when I worked for the auto dealer or our trips to the Olympic Peninsula. We're not going to go too deep."

"Why is it that I forgot the same war but you insist on revisiting it?"

She had a point, and Skinner didn't have an answer. In their worst arguments over the years he'd insisted she had no way of possibly knowing what he'd seen, having spent the war gazing through the scope of her rifle or via remote cam. He'd witnessed it on the mud and the blood and the shit level, the severed heads and disembowelment level. The last time this line of reasoning trotted its diseased self in front of them he'd had a couple drinks.

"I promise I won't muck things up by drinking," Skinner said.

"You say that."

Up ahead on either side of the freeway, behind chain-link barricades and a few dozen riot cops in full gear, had coalesced two groups of that rare Arizona breed, pedestrians, bearing signage. A hundred or so total. Skinner and Chiho couldn't read the signs yet but knew what they were about. Traffic slowed to a ten-mile-per-hour crawl as drivers passed angry human beings filtering their frayed-voice accusations through staticky megaphones.

"It's worse than last year," Chiho said.

"These losers just need to get jobs," Skinner said. "Look at them. They're perfectly capable."

"I don't understand how they expect anyone to offer them a ride when they're behaving so poorly," Chiho said.

The messages on the signs came into view. An egg cracked on the RV's windshield. Skinner opened the glove compartment and located the Coca-Cola 9mm beneath a stack of expired insurance cards. It was an old firearm, an early model from when Coke, Nike, Sony, Verizon, and every other major conglomerate seemed to be rushing into the business of arming America. Coke eventually stopped manufacturing this model, returning somewhat sheepishly, post-FUS, to its core business of delicious sugared beverages. Skinner rubbed the faded red-and-white grip with the dynamic-ribbon logo.

"You're being overly dramatic," Chiho said. "Put that away."

"I just want them to see that I've got it," Skinner said, pulling the microphone out of the dash. He flicked the ON switch and his voice blasted out of two loudspeakers mounted on the roof. "Warning. We are retired security officers who served in the Boeing militias. We are armed and won't hesitate to blow your fucking heads off."

A couple riot cops saluted or gave a thumbs-up. The crowds screamed anew and threw themselves at the barricades, their faces sore-covered and contorted. If they were lucky they'd get arrested and tossed into the air-conditioned underground clink. Maybe that was the whole point. Soon the traffic picked up and there was nothing but saguaros, prickly pear, and distant scorched hills. Occasionally they passed a lone hitchhiker waving pathetically or pointing frantically at a water jug, begging for a refill. A man and a boy solemnly shoved their belongings along in a shopping cart. Skinner shook his head. What made it impossible for some people to prepare for the changing of the seasons?

Some memories were more painful than those forged in war. They'd once been a family of four sharing a home in Portland, Oregon, with a yard and a dog. Take a picture and upload it. Picnics, football games. Their son Waitimu Skinner was born first, then , three years later, their daughter Roon Aoshima. Two handsome kids with good grades.

At nineteen Waitimu enlisted in the same firm his dad had served in and shipped out to Detroit during the lingering days of the FUS. Swiss-cheesed by roadside-bomb masonry screws during a routine security sweep. What remained of Waitimu was buried on Vancouver island.

Roon now lived in Seattle with her wife Dot, working in a vague capacity for one of the contractors transforming Bainbridge Island into Manhattan. Skinner and Chiho hadn't spoken to their daughter in five years and here's why: Thanksgiving, too much sake, money, politics, yelling, a broken heirloom candy dish.

These stories aren't uncommon—an older child dies and the younger one can never live up to her imagined legacy. Skinner and Chiho kept the Waitimu memory cards in a safety deposit box in Phoenix and avoided talking about their confounding, troublesome rift with Roon.

Maybe the rattling was a spatula.

* * *

America didn't used to look like this, Chiho thought from behind the windshield. There used to be people in all these houses. People shopping and walking their dogs. People yelling, "Hello, neighbor! Can I borrow a stick of butter?" San Diego scrolled beneath their tires, the first of three urban dots one had to connect to experience coastal California. What remnants of old civilization lay between these points were scavenger-picked and surrendered to nature. Incredible how quickly trees invaded pavement, foundations crumbled, brambles engulfed cars. They saw crows appear to dismantle a motorcycle. Whenever they pulled off the highway to stretch their legs they tried to park near the ocean. Skinner wanted to see the beached aircraft carrier. A couple hundred miles south of San Francisco it lay jutting at a nutty angle on the beach, like a sunbathing skyscraper. They stopped in Oakland, in what was trying to become Little Boston. Fenway Park was half-finished, and a few blocks away there was a lackluster attempt at Harvard Yard. Skinner bought a Red Sox hat from a street vendor who promised it had been manufactured pre-FUS in Boston itself.

"Want to stop at Hearst Castle?" Chiho wanted to know.

Skinner shrugged. Might as well. They parked the RV at the visitors center and boarded the shuttle. A pleasant way to kill an afternoon. Skinner took a picture of his wife standing beside a statue of Poseidon by the grandest of the pools. The fact that one man had ever amassed this much wealth inconvenienced Skinner's sense of logic. That this magnitude of fortune paled in comparison to the wealth attained by certain pre-FUS oligarchs was almost metaphysically impossible to comprehend.

* * *

Carl and Hiroko Taylor lived outside Portland in an A-frame home amid thirty or so former suburban acres of new-growth cedar and hemlock. Carl was negotiating with a solar panel out front when Skinner and Chiho rolled up the driveway. He didn't look like a soldier anymore, just an old black dude with white hair wearing a plaid flannel shirt and suspenders. Hiroko came out onto the porch clutching a mammoth mug of tea. Carl grabbed Skinner as soon as he had clambered out of the RV and the friends slammed their hands into each other's backs.

"You dirty old fossil," Carl laughed. When Carl laughed, his smile hung around on his face like the last guest at a party.

"Let me get some of this," Hiroko said, separating the men to embrace Skinner. Carl lifted Chiho off the ground and the four old friends stood laughing and grinning, anticipating rich, copious food and stories, late nights of movies and video games. Skinner knew that the presence of their friends would put a damper on his and Chiho's bickering. They were never as loving toward one another as when they were in the presence of friends. Spirits lifted, the four repaired to the kitchen where Hiroko zapped buffalo wings and Carl pulled out some blue potato chips with blue cheese dip. There were crudités and smoked salmon, huckleberry scones and homemade preserves, coffee.

"You're sabotaging your solar again," Skinner said.

"I might as well take a ball-peen hammer to it," said Carl.

"You're cursed. Put a machine in your hands and it takes itself apart."

Hiroko said to Chiho, "I was worried you guys wouldn't escape Phoenix this time."

Chiho replied, "We ran into some demonstrators on the way out, but we did fine."

"Yeah, because I showed off my Coke," Skinner said.

"There was a testosterone moment," Chiho nodded.

"We got out of there in one piece is all I'm saying."

"Those people just want to get out before it gets too hot," Hiroko said.

"Then they should move out altogether," Carl said.

"I second that opinion," Skinner said. "Slide that dip on over here, if you please. There are relocation programs, right? They can move up to Canada."

"Or Alaska," Carl said.

"And live in a camp?" Hiroko asked. "I hear those places are foul."

"Some of them are," Chiho said. "They're improving, though. According to *Reader's Digest*, anyway."

The conversation was veering dangerously toward buzz-kill territory. They all seemed to recognize this, and with a collective breath moved on to other topics.

"School! How's teaching this semester?" Chiho asked Hiroko.

"Fabulous. I taught Theory of Counterinsurgency, FUS History with an emphasis on the New England theater, a couple intro freshman classes. I had incredible students this semester."

"Her students drove her to tears," Carl said.

Hiroko said, "Please tell us you're staying a couple weeks, at least. We've got a pantry full of food that'll go to waste otherwise."

"Football, barbecue, a little walk in the woods," Carl said.

"Our thoughts exactly," Skinner said. "I don't know how much longer we can hold out in the desert."

"You said that last year," Chiho said.

"Every year I mean it a little bit more. Putting a prophylactic on my house four months out of the year."

"Let me see your garden!" Chiho said. Hiroko did an embarrassed and proud little shrug and motioned for her to follow.

When the women were gone, Skinner and Carl looked at each other and shared a laugh.

"Jesus, we're still here," Skinner said.

"Still looking like shit, a day late and a dollar short."

"When you can live forever, all you're doing is postponing the inevitable. You're just going to die in some stupid accident."

"Could come any day."

"And a welcome day that'll be."

They laughed again, matching the cadence of their guffaws. Carl said, "Seriously. You bring the memories?"

"Right here." Skinner patted his breast pocket. "I told Chiho."

Carl nodded. "I told Hiroko. We got into a fight about it."

"Likewise."

"But we gots to do what we gots to do."

"Sort through the bullshit."

"Get our past in order."

"I promised Chiho I wouldn't drink. You help me out on that?" Skinner asked.

"You got it. I'll not drink with you."

"You don't have to."

"You would for me."

"True. You make these buffalo wings?"

"I wish I could take credit but they came out of a fuckin' bag. Cooper died."

"Wait, who—Cooper? Shit, no."

"Lung cancer finally. One of those weird kinds of lung cancer that happen to people who don't smoke. So rare the Bionet doesn't have a reliable app to deal with it. He tried a cigarette when he was sixteen, puked his guts out, and never touched the stuff again, even when we were in combat. Now *that's* fuckin' willpower. I talked to him a month before he passed. He blamed the cancer on that one cigarette from ninety years ago. Cigarette smoke was the least of what ended up in our lungs."

"I can't say I ever got along with Cooper that well. God rest his soul."

"You barely got along with anyone. You were the crew's resident son of a bitch."

"But when the shit went down is what I'm saying."

"You don't even have to say it."

"I'm trying harder not to be a prick. I volunteer at the local pool. Hand out boogie boards to snot-nosed kids. Went door-to-door collecting toothbrushes for our church. Apparently they need toothbrushes in Alabama or someplace."

"Guy on his fifth set of dentures collecting toothbrushes. That's a good one."

Skinner grinned. "How you keeping busy besides busting solar panels?"

"Dude, nothing much has changed since you were here last. I do my Tai Chi in the morning and my yoga at night. I reread all of Dickens and am back on a Melville jag. It's all about supporting the wife's career. She's working on a book about the FUS. Trying to spell out once and for all why it went down, who was responsible. Most of the time she's buried in books."

"How'd a dumbass like you marry a woman so smart?"

"My thoughts *precisely*. She could've just retired a long time ago but she's got unfinished business with the FUS. She thinks she did too little to prevent it is my theory. Like she was part of the whole propaganda apparatus that brought on the worst of it. It haunts her. I've been trying to tell her to give it a rest, what's past is past. But she's too much like you. Has to go over it and over it in her head."

"An incredible woman. They broke the mold et cetera, et cetera."

"Roon called here last week."

"Say what?"

"She wants to get in touch with you and Chiho. I think she wants to make amends."

Skinner rubbed his face. Audible stubble. "I wasn't expecting that. Is she okay? Jesus, I'm a shitty father."

"She sounded good. I talked to her maybe five minutes. She says she doesn't have your new number. She wanted—I really should wait until Chiho is here to tell you this."

"What happened?"

"Don't worry, man, it's nothing bad. Just wait for the ladies to come back from their little garden tour and all will be revealed."

Five minutes and five buffalo wings later Hiroko and Chiho came back indoors. Chiho beamed. "Did Carl tell you Roon called?"

"Yeah, he did, what's—"

Chiho knitted her fingers together and held her hands to her chin. "Roon and Dot have a baby!"

Skinner opened his mouth to say something, stopped, looked to the others to figure out how he should be feeling. "A grandchild?" he said.

"A little boy," Hiroko said. "He's two now."

In this safe place, in the company of people who loved him, bewildered and unable to speak, Skinner found tears trembling at the corners of his eyes.

Now they'd have to see Roon. Their stay would be shadowed by expectation and shot through with giddiness that they'd finally get to meet a grandchild. Skinner shook his head and gazed curiously at his open palms, as though he'd achieved grandfatherhood via some feat of manual labor. Carl suggested they go on a walk.

The path through the woods roughly followed where a sidewalk used to be. Here and there stood foundations of houses. If you kicked at the weeds or peeled back layers of fallen leaves, little artifacts of extinct Portlanders emerged. Bottles, cell phones, plastic toys partially covered in moss, the rusted whorls of a box-spring mattress. Trees had reclaimed the grid, reverting it to chaotic geometries determined by fallen seeds. Chiho loved the birds most, the wild flocks that had replenished themselves post-FUS, blotting the sky in great concentrations of feather, cackle, and wing. A woodpecker smacked its beak against a snag, probing for grubs. Amid a copse of pines rose an old McDonald's golden arches sign, boasting of billions served. Billions! The husbands and wives walked paired down the path.

Skinner said to Hiroko, "Carl says you're working on a book."

"More like the book's working on me."

"So what's your angle on the FUS?"

"I'm considering it by way of a neurological metaphor," Hiroko said. "I stumbled on some research from the 1950s, two scientists named Olds and Milner who first identified the pleasure centers of the brain. I guess their most famous experiment was when they stimulated the pleasure centers of rats whenever the rats pressed a particular bar in their cage. It didn't take long for the rats to stimulate their pleasure centers to the point of exhaustion, to the point of not eating or taking care of their other physiological needs. My argument is that in the age of Fucked Up Shit, human beings became like those rats, whacking the bars that stimulated our pleasure centers even as those very bars were what triggered our doom. In the last few decades of the twentieth century, we started to understand the terms of our self-destruction. Our rational minds argued against using fossil fuels, against overeating and too much television, against accumulating too much wealth among too few, but a more powerful part of our brains kept pushing those bars. Push, push, push. The solutions, the ways we might avoid the FUS, were staring us right in the face. It was obvious and apparent: stop using oil, stop making plastic, control the growth of the population to a logical level so we could exist within the parameters of our ecology. If we didn't do these things, most of us would die. But we were willing to die because a more powerful part of our minds, the old mammalian limbic system, was busy pushing those bars. The more recent, less developed part of our brains, the neocortex, was waving its arms and screaming for us to stop our destructive behavior. In this war between the limbic system and the neocortex, the limbic system won, hence the FUS."

Carl picked up a stick to walk with. "So by the time we got tangled in the FUS, who were we fighting for exactly?" he said.

"We were fighting for Boeing," Skinner laughed.

"Yes, but more to the point, we were fighting for the limbic system," Hiroko said. "We were fighting to keep pushing those bars. When everything collapsed, there were few bars left to push. But now the earth's renewing itself. Look around us. There are a lot fewer people to make a mess of things. The qputers are undoing the damage."

"Still, Phoenix gets hotter every year," Skinner said.

"True," Hiroko said, "because not every place is recovering at the same rate. It's going to take some places a lot longer."

They came to an old intercity light-rail car covered in vines. Through the dirty windows they read advertisements for colonics and undergraduate degrees.

Skinner said, "So you're saying we fought on the wrong side, Hiroko?"

She shrugged. "In the FUS, *everyone* was on the wrong side. The very idea of *sides* was on the wrong side."

The nocturnal animals of the forest performed their first stirrings as light seeped out of the sky. The path widened and intersected with a hard-packed gravel road. Nearby leaned a bus-stop sign. In a few short minutes a bus arrived, a shambling, multihued contraption furnished with couches and love seats, a kitchenette in the back where a woman cooked a garlicky organic meal. A few other riders, swaddled in patchwork outfits of Gore-Tex and hemp, sat reading alternative weeklies, about them hanging the whiff of weed. The four friends crowded together on a couch across from a balding man in glasses who was absorbed in a battered copy of Benjamin's *Illuminations,* a scarf wrapped so many times around his neck that it appeared to be holding his head in place. The bus bumbled along the irregular road and the trees eventually gave way to deliberate landscaping and an actual paved arterial. Soon they were on Burnside through the vital guts of Portland. A block or two from Powell's City of Books they climbed off the bus and squeezed through an alley to Hiroko and Carl's favorite Thai place. As they approached the back entrance, a great wave of plates and cutlery crashed through the door and spilled out into the alley. Carried on this wave was a disheveled and quite stoned busboy, and close behind a chef rode a baking sheet like a surfboard, yelling obscenities at his young and now-fired employee.

"Asleep on the job!" the chef bellowed. "What kind of dishwasher are you! And you dare evoke the name of the great Woojin Kan!"

"Don't worry. The food's actually great," Hiroko said as they climbed over the dishes, trying not to slip on a rainbow of curries.

During appetizers, Chiho proclaimed, "We're so rude. We haven't even asked about Jadie."

Carl sighed. "She's had her troubles with the Bionet. Became some sick bastard's embodiment. We got her in a recovery center down here."

"Christ," Skinner said.

"It started out with dancing," Carl continued. "She'd go to parties where everyone tried out these illegal apps, give over her codes to a choreographer and they'd put her body through elaborate moves. Soon it turned into an everyday routine. She surrendered some of her basic functions, like what time she'd wake up, when she'd eat and use the bathroom. Her DJ was good to her at first, they usually are, got her to make new friends—other embodiments—made her feel popular, put witty comments in her mouth when she was in social situations. She got a bit part in a TV show they film up in Vancouver."

"*Forensic Mindfuck*," Hiroko said.

"The one about the detectives?" Chiho asked.

"The one where they travel back in time and use modern forensic methods to solve crimes of the past," Carl said. "Anyway. Around that time she dropped out of school, which we weren't too keen on, but it looked like she had a real career getting started."

"When did you find out she was getting DJed?" Chiho said.

"We were clueless," Carl said. "We thought she was succeeding purely on her own merits. If we'd known, we'd have flown up to Vancouver and tossed her ass in a recovery center straightaway."

"We knew something about her had changed when we visited," Hiroko said, "but we couldn't identify it. I thought it was the pressure and excitement of her new life. Sometimes her hands trembled like she'd had too much coffee."

Carl rubbed his stubble. "Her show got canceled and she was out of school and looking for work. That's when her DJ lost interest in her and set her on autopilot. He got her a job waitressing and wiped his hands of her, setting her loose on autogenerated subroutines. She described it as being like living the same boring day over and over again. She woke up exactly at 7:02 a.m., had the same cereal for breakfast, ran 4.2 miles on the treadmill, and went to the same stores and bought the same three items every day—a nail file from the drugstore, a copy of Nabokov's *Lolita* from the bookstore, and a set of shoelaces from a shoe repair shop. Then she'd go waitress at a greasy spoon that served only regulars who ordered the same things every day. After that she'd come home, watch a tape of the same stupid comedy, take a shower, and go to bed at 9:00 on the dot. And every night she had the same dream, in which she separated bottles for recycling behind the restaurant where she worked. Brown bottles, green bottles, clear bottles. The dream always seemed to last a couple hours, but got more detailed every night. She started to be able to read the labels, see the air bubbles in the glass, feel the texture of the glue on the bottles. Her dreams became so high-def that they started making her waking reality look foggy. Then she'd wake up and start all over again. Treadmill, shopping, work, home, movie, shower, bed, dream. It went on like this for months. Part of her remained aware of what was happening, a weak little section of her brain, and she started to suspect that the regulars at the café were embodiments, too, retired embodiments also on autopilot. She'd become this reliable little machine, a component that did its part to keep the companies that made the nail files and the shoelaces and the copies of *Lolita* in business, programmed to be a battery plugged into the economy. On her days off the routines automatically changed, and she'd send us an email and tell us how she was looking forward to enrolling in school again and finishing her degree. Very little variation to these messages. Hiroko and I kept trying to plan a trip up north and see her but stuff kept getting in the way. I broke my leg, Hiroko got a grant to write her book, all the usual we've-been-busy BS that keeps families from seeing each other. We were just happy to know she was planning to go back to school. So, finally, a couple months ago we got our act together and headed up to Vancouver. She kept trying to dissuade us from coming. I got suspicious. So we head on up there and found her new apartment, in some lousy part of town with people crazy and passed out, trash all over the place up and down the street. I ran up the steps to her door. We pounded on it and she told us to go away, so I knew something real foul was going down. The worst scenarios ran through my mind, you know how it is with a daughter. So I got all commando and broke down the fuckin' door. Really messed up my shoulder for the weekend, I might add. We found her looking completely normal, standing in the middle of her apartment. With a hundred ninety-seven copies of *Lolita*, a hundred ninety-seven packages of shoelaces, and a hundred ninety-seven nail files all piled up on the kitchen table. And she was standing there dressed, smiling, making the same repetitive motion with her arm, a little shuffle with her feet, waiting for the clock to strike 9:00 a.m. so she could go out and do her shopping. Her smile terrified me. A smile a thousand miles from happiness. I just came out and asked her if she was an embodiment."

"Christ," Skinner said. "Did you ever catch the son of a bitch who did this to her?"

Carl shook his head. "The cops are still looking. They're about five years behind the technology, if you wanna know the sad truth. It's shocking. There's a whole underground economy driven by embodiments. People just set up to work at mindless jobs, to consume the same shit every day, punch in and punch out, keep products in production, services rendered, walking around numb and dumb and compliant, without an original thought in their damn heads."

"She's doing better," Hiroko said, "but it's a long recovery. The ego atrophies during the embodiment state. It has to be rebuilt little by little. It takes weeks for them to be able to introduce themselves or shake someone's hand."

Skinner said, "I remember holding her little hands. Giving her shells and sand dollars. Your story breaks my heart."

They moved on to discussions more germane to their surroundings. Skinner fingered the memory cards in his pocket, wondering at the horrors preserved in their wafer-like forms. Why punish himself like this again? Other retired private contractors, sitting in their deck chairs flipping channels and keeping their bowels operational with concoctions of herbs, didn't seem burdened by the same obsessive need to recontextualize their former lives. For Skinner's neighbors at the shrink-wrapped retirement community, the wars moldered. They were content to follow college football and steady their swing at the driving range. The FUS was to be actively avoided in conversation, not sought out. Skinner almost admired their ability to evade the terrors of their pasts. On his worst days he prayed for the strength to do the same. But his earlier life on battlefields demanded accounting. This need was so consuming that the only way for Carl to remain his friend was to humor him and take part in the trip, to follow him down that flaming hole of cunt-shit-molten-fuck. But now—this was a surprise—Skinner'd found some new psychic armor with which to fortify himself. He had a *grandson.*

Skinner took the cards out of his pocket and set them on the table. The other three regarded the cards with visible sadness as Skinner separated them into piles of innocuous memories and memories of war, the innocuous ones outnumbering the wartime ones three to one. Then, with the bottom of the pepper shaker, he smashed the war memories into pieces. When he was done, Skinner exhaled and fingered his fortune cookie, reluctant to find out what it revealed about his future.

"You did it, my friend," Carl said. "Good for you."

Chiho rubbed Skinner's shoulder and kissed his weathered hands. He swept the pieces of the memory cards into his palm and sprinkled them atop the remnants of his panang curry. All that remained now were memories of banal civilian life and the one memory from the war he refused to destroy, the one piece of unfinished business: the memory of the day he came back from the dead.

The next day after breakfast, the women left the men reclined on plush furniture beneath portraits of Carl's and Hiroko's ancestors that went back generations, to slaves and dynasties. On the coffee table were arrayed bottles of water and an Apple memory console, a black lump of elegant industrial design about the size and shape of a baseball, smashed in on one side.

"Sure you don't want to watch the NCAA semifinals instead?" Carl asked.

"Plug us in," Skinner said, closing his eyes.

Carl pushed the card into the slot. A little pinwheel icon on the display indicated that the console was recognizing and syncing with the whatzits embedded in their skulls. This reality hung on for a while—the books on the shelves, the red rug. The scene trembled a bit at the edges as the stored memory worked to displace their surroundings. At this in-between stage, inanimate objects asserted more emphatically what they truly were. The water in the bottles wanted desperately to escape the plastic, yearning to become lost again in oceans and clouds. Skinner drew a Pendleton blanket around his shoulders, listening to individual wool fibers creak, snap, and whisper memories of ewes grazing in valleys. Carl reached out and took Skinner's hand, squeezed it to remind him he was there. A few minutes in, the living room went into rapid retreat. The effect was like looking at a department store window and not knowing what to focus on—the objects on display or the reflection of the street. Slowly their senses adjusted to perceive more acutely what lay beyond the pane. They were crossing the Brooklyn Bridge into Manhattan. A percussive frozen rain raked at them as clouds merged with plumes of smoke rising from all over the island.

"Carl?" Skinner said. He was trying to pivot his head but it was as if his neck was in a brace.

"I got you," Carl said behind him, or beside him, or both. A representation of Carl sidled up, his old-man face superimposed on his younger man's body, a weird bug in the software. "We're in, man."

"Jesus, the *smell.*"

"It's always the smell that's the worst."

"I can smell the bodies."

Younger Carl spoke, his voice fuzzy. "At least the smell of bodies don't make you cough up your damn lungs. It's those other smells we got to be afraid of."

Up ahead in a pile of rags a baby cried beside its mother's detached bodily components. As Skinner veered toward the baby a greasy hand dug into his bicep and yanked him around. Malmides, his direct supervisor, barked into his face, "Keep moving, shitstain."

Skinner saw that he was in a vast video game of men that stretched back through Brooklyn, bristling with weaponry and trudging into death. He didn't march so much as let himself get carried along. He looked down and watched his legs flop retardedly forward, unable to stop. Piles of refuse burned in the

East River, decapitated bodies swung from the bridge supports like demented mobiles. He strained to take in the magnificent destruction ahead. Here, on the bridge, all was panorama, but soon those buildings would entangle him, a grid turning into an unforgiving labyrinth. Inexplicably, a herd of goats ran bleating past them, their hides scorched and speckled with boils. One of them sported an eyeball dangling from its socket. At the little park on the other side of the bridge he found himself in a congregation listening to the director of operations, a bull of a man with prosthetic eyes and a voice raspy from inhaling the particulate of decimated signature architecture. Castiliano was that bastard's name and this was his rallying moment, a little rhetorical propane to get the soldiers hard.

"We bring death today to those who claim to become God! We slaughter under the banner of Christ! We butcher the hordes who've come to rape our children! Root them out, grab a limb, rip it off! Coat your faces in their gore! Stomp harder on the rising lids of their rancid coffins, Boeing army fighters!"

A great cry went up and Skinner, queasy, broke off into a unit with Carl and five other sick motherfucks, as it were, guys with faces and names and homes that had been erased from Planet Earth. Supposedly they were to head west and root out a couple remaining pockets of newman resistance.

"I don't think I can do this," Skinner said in his memory.

"Fuck you, Skinner. You were born to do this," Carl said.

One of the other guys in the unit looked exactly like the pre-FUS comedic actor Will Ferrell. Another bug in the program. Apparently if you remembered a person as looking sort of like someone famous, the famous person tended to show up in your memory instead. "Guys?" Will Ferrell said, his voice cracking.

"Maybe we should just find a Starbucks and get lattes? My treat? What do you say?"

Carl whispered in Skinner's ear, "Come on, dude, you're in command."

"Listen, you sick Homo sapiens," Skinner said. "The heavy lifting's been done. We're basically the janitors, scrubbing the newman shit from this godforsaken island. Let's quit fucking around and move!"

They passed through acrid manhole steam and subway entrances piled with rotting body parts swarmed by mutated, screeching larvae. Skinner glanced down to see a woman's shoe with the foot still in it, toenails painted lavender, sliced off at the ankle so cleanly it could have been done by a surgeon. It wasn't the enormity of it all that fucked you, it was little shit like this. A headless body slumped in a doorway beneath an advertisement for Guns N' Roses' *Chinese Democracy II*. An arm protruded from beneath a flaming and overturned taxi. Everywhere burned the obscene carbon stench of manufactured goods and organic forms returning to the elements. Will Ferrell had begun to whimper comically, eyes darting left and right. Carl slapped him on the back of the head.

In the East Village they came to a café, still operational amid the rubble. Everything above the second floor of the building looked to have been vaporized. Within the ground-level walls baristas steamed milk and a sound system blasted fusion-era Miles. In a corner, under a painting of flames, the scarred remnants of a company of mercenaries sat drinking. Seven guys speckled in concrete dust and dried blood, knocking back coffee spiked with scavenged liquors. Their eyes barely moved when Skinner and his crew arrived, stepping over dead laptops and brick chunks.

"We're the Boeing 83rd," Skinner said. "What company you all with?"

"Who wants to know?" said a man in the rear. Jet-black hair, glasses, untangling a Rubik's Cube.

"I'm Lieutenant Al Skinner."

Carl said, "They're the Pfizer 190th. The insignia on their gear."

"I thought Pfizer ran screaming from this shit," Skinner said.

"We *are* the shit," Rubik's Cube said.

Will Ferrell ordered a grande nonfat decaf mocha.

"This all that's left of your company?" Skinner asked.

Cube said, "You want to know the difference between a war and a war game? A game comes with a reset button. But the only way to access that button is to die. Want to test this theory?"

Skinner said nothing. Cube shrugged, asked his command, "Who would be willing to blow his fucking brains out to see if there's a reset button?"

A young, stone-faced soldier drinking a cappuccino unholstered his sidearm and pressed the barrel under his chin.

"You don't have to prove anything to me," Skinner said.

"This is the fuck and death party," Cube said. "You don't wanna see the death? How about some of the fuck? We've got a surprise downstairs. You fellows can help yourselves to the leftovers. We've had our fill. Go on ahead, indulge."

"You don't have girls, do you?" Carl said, his face falling.

"No, man, we're following the code. We got 'droid pussy."

"Tell that idiot to holster his weapon," Skinner said.

Cube nodded. "Goldberg, we don't need you to hit the reset button just yet." He turned back to Skinner. "You look like you've been at this for a while, soldier. Tell me, do the newmans make any sense to you? Has killing them made it any easier to determine whether *they're* the human beings or if *we're* the ones who come out of factories?"

"I kill what I'm told to kill," Skinner said. "I don't give a fuck if it's got guts or chips."

"Good for you," Cube smiled and tossed his toy to Skinner. "Now mess this puzzle up and solve your way out of it."

An iron stairwell led to a basement. The stairs opened into a dim, low-ceilinged space that smelled of opium smoke and industrial-grade lubricants. A soldier elbowed past them on his way out, zipping his fly. The 83rd turned on their beams and swept the floor with light. The room appeared littered with dissected mannequins. An arm crawled out of their way and hid under a sofa as they advanced. They followed the sound of sex groans to a curtained alcove. When Skinner swept aside the curtain they found a fat, naked man on his back on a couch. Skinner blinked, trying to figure out what exactly he was looking at. As best he could tell, it was the lower half of a male newman, the legs wearing fishnet stockings, mounted on the fat man, rocking back and forth while the man stroked the thing's artificial cock. Where the torso should have been was a mess of organic newman technology, cords and sacs, severed tubes spurting clear fluid. While this half of a newman got fucked, a severed newman head of indeterminate gender licked the fat man's balls.

"Hey! Can't a dude screw in peace around here?" the fat man complained.

"My God," Skinner said. (Decades later, in Carl's living room, Carl said, "Yeah, that shit was sick. And you don't even remember it as gross as I remember it.")

"Identify yourself," Skinner said.

"And you are?"

"My name is: I've got a loaded Cherry Coca-Cola and your dick is up a robot's ass."

"Name's Caponegra, senior regional manager of the Pfizer 183rd."

Will Ferrell spoke up. "Guys? Is it considered a threeway if two of the participants used to be one person? Just wondering."

"Shut the fuck up, Ferrell," Carl said.

"We're sweeping the 'hood for insurgents," Skinner said, yanking the newman body half off Caponegra's lap. "And you're going to data dump all your intelligence on us."

"Dammit, fine. Let me rub one out and I'll brief you upstairs."

Upstairs, over coffee at a table freckled with cigarette butts, Caponegra, now mostly clothed, told stories of raids, ambushes, casualties received and delivered. Skinner divvied the info into little piles, separating a soldier's braggadocio from strategically relevant data. Caponegra's blustery yarns did support the case that the newmans were in full retreat, escaping into the forests upstate where they were burying themselves under trees to hibernate.

"They're like bears," Caponegra said. "I got a report from a scout in the Glaxo-Wellcome 3rd infantry that they cornered four of them up near Saratoga Springs, all huddled in a hole in the ground, skin going pasty from lack of sun, eyes glowing red as they went into sleep mode. Interrogation revealed they had no power-up date. Meaning someone would have to come along, find them, and manually turn them back on."

"We're sweeping west through Soho," Skinner said. "What can you tell us."

Caponegra rolled his eyes. "You guys got the easiest job in the world. There's no one left out there. We practically bleached the place."

"So what are you doing hanging around here?"

Caponegra gave him a look. "There's somewhere else?"

They came to a building halved vertically by an explosion. Looked like an NYU dorm, a cross section of what appeared to be, more or less, normal collegiate life, a couple dozen hive-like stories of beds, computers, desks, a *Jules et Jim* poster, microbiology and civics textbooks with passages highlighted in pink and yellow, the pillowy forms of bags of popped but uneaten microwaved popcorn. Paper drifted in the smoke. Here and there a fire. In one of the exposed dorm rooms on the second floor, a girl sat hunched over her desk, head in hand, reviewing self-made flash cards.

Carl consulted his handheld. "She's human."

"Hey you! Student!" Skinner shouted. "What are you still doing up there?"

Visibly annoyed, the girl called down, "Leave me alone! I'm studying! Midterms next week!"

"You need to evacuate asap!" Carl replied. "This ain't the time to study! Come on, we'll set you up in a library where you can study all you want!"

Somewhere on the island another building fell, rattling the earth beneath their feet and the teeth in their jaws. Helicopters in formation sliced across a sky too grimy and chemical-burned to be of any use to anybody.

Carl said to Skinner, "We got to get her out of there. She's in shock, obviously."

"Stupid bitch," Skinner said. "Let's save her ass."

Skinner put Will Ferrell in charge of the unit while he and Carl climbed over the rubble looking for an entrance. The comic actor called after them. "Guys? This is against protocol, you know? Shouldn't we all stick together?"

"Go fuck yourself, Ferrell," Skinner said. "We're getting this chick out of here."

(Years in the future, in the living room, Carl said, "Not exactly how we remember it."

"Yeah, but here it comes," Skinner said.)

Carl pushed aside a Foosball table, found the stairwell. Walls covered in anti-newman graffiti. Skinner doubted many of the students who'd screwed and crammed and gotten ripped in these dorms had made it off Manhattan alive. Rifle drawn he kicked open the door to the second floor, exiting into a dark hallway where postpsychotherapy Metallica played faintly from ceiling-mounted speakers. In a corner beneath a fire extinguisher lay a wounded Christian American soldier. Looked like a contractor from Toys "R" Us. Hard to tell exactly where he'd been hit; his whole torso was caramelized in bloody goo. Carl bent over him with the handheld and got his vitals.

"Soldier, where you from?" Carl said.

"Huh?" the fallen man said. "Who the f-f-f-fuck are you?"

"We're the Boeing 83rd. We're going to fly you out of this joint."

"The college chick—" the soldier said. "They're using her as bait."

"We got nooms up in this shit?" Carl said as a round pinged the fire extinguisher over his head, unleashing a cloud of white vapor. Down the hall dorm rooms cracked open and out stumbled half-obliterated newmans wearing the collegiate T-shirts and hoodies of their victims. Carl's face assumed the intensity of a man assembling a particularly tricky piece of furniture as he raked the hall with ordnance. Skinner's head rolled to one side and he caught sight of a Mohawked, child-sized newman wearing a Led Zeppelin *SwanSong* T-shirt and nothing else, its crotch smooth and plastic with the absence of genitals, round after round perforating its jerking, humanoid form, an arm shot off in gouts of purplish lubricant, its cat-like eyes glowing yellow in the fire-retardant haze.

("Here it comes," Skinner said in the living room.)

There it came, a round ripping through his chest plate, which put the kibosh on the velocity enough so that it lodged in his trunk without splattering out his back. Then another one to the leg, a kind of afterthought. He plunged into a pool of blood where all sound disappeared.

In Carl's memory he dragged Skinner by the leg down the hall, unloading at other newmans lurching out of dorm rooms. The memory fritzed out a second, flipped perspectives, then Skinner had a close-up view of a busted iPod, its mysterious guts revealed. Rounds whanged off metal, the elevator doors. His eyes fluttered and in the living room one hundred years later Carl squeezed his hand so hard it went numb. *Here we go.*

Skinner trudged in tattered fatigues across the mesa, the vista meticulously hi-res down to individual grains of sand. His peeling skin and the rasp in his throat seemed to imply he'd been out here for weeks. Up ahead, far enough away that he could pinch the whole scene between forefinger and thumb, was some kind of encampment. It was near twilight, the sky awash in pollution. A wall of furnace-intensity wind. Closer still, through eyes squinty and dry, he made out a refrigerator standing inexplicably amid the desolation. And piles of things nearby, a human form bent before a meager fire. Some guy? Some weird guy with long hair and a beard, near-naked in these punishing elements? It seemed improbable, but it was true. The old man didn't look up until Skinner was standing, bewildered, a few feet away. The man gestured for him to sit on an old bald tire. Nearby a full-length mirror reflected the sun back across the horizon. There was a pile of kids' stuffed animals and a pile of books. Skinner tried to speak. The man waved his hand as if to tell him not to bother, then rose and opened the fridge. Wisps of cold vapor rolled out and Skinner almost cried to see it stocked full of food.

"BREWSKI?" the old man said.

Skinner nodded, tears beading at the edges of his eyes. The old man cranked the cap off a bottle of Pyramid Hefeweizen and handed it to him. Skinner trembled as the cold beer foamed in his mouth. He sucked it down so fast some came back up. The old man handed him another, then offered a sandwich. Skinner ate, moaning through his full mouth.

"Who are you?" Skinner asked finally, burping.

"I AM THE LAST DUDE," the old man said.

"What is this place?"

"THIS IS THE END OF THE ROAD."

"How did I get here?"

"I CALLED YOU HERE."

"Why?"

"YOU MUST FUCK."

"Huh?"

"REPRODUCE," the Last Dude said. "NOW SCRAM."

A murder of crows materialized and lifted Skinner into the sky. The old man's encampment grew smaller beneath his dangling feet as the temperature dropped and wind scraped out the insides of his ears. As he rose sunward the desert floor widened like a spreading stain. Far below, methodically piled stones spelled what appeared to be an unfinished message to the heavens:

THE W

Here the memory faltered into a blue screen then snapped back to full resolution with the sound of a helicopter. Skinner looked around trying to find it, seeing only the digitized gray fatigues of his company colleagues, realizing before he passed out again that he was in a chopper, there was a mask pumping oxygen at his face, and the world below smelled of death.

Wood smoke curled around evergreens. Chiho followed Hiroko up the muddy path to this place of astonishment, a whole college campus suspended in the trees. Through the mist the Douglas firs appeared to wear skirts; these were circular houses built around their trunks, linked by a network of rope and cable bridges. There were hundreds of tree houses of various circumferences and elevations, whole multistory platforms held aloft in the triangulations of trunks, students traveling from one class to another by rope swing and zipline. Hiroko showed Chiho to a rickety elevator and they rose into the canopy where curious squirrels and robins perched, coming to rest on a platform that seemed to float on a pillow of fog. In this creaking, crescent-shaped, wind-swayed structure was a lecture hall where several tiers of benches faced inward toward a lectern. A couple dozen students had already gathered, notebooks ready, sipping chai, bringing the low murmur of chatter to a close as Hiroko took her place behind the microphone. Chiho found a spot in the back row.

"Let's get settled, everyone. Today I'd like to talk about Malaspina, the Roving Glacier of Death. I'll take questions afterward. Stragglers, please take your seats. In the early years of the FUS, with polar ice rapidly retreating, as great famines and genocides swept continents, one meteorological oddity perplexed the world's climate scientists. While glaciers melted, exposing mummies and mastodons, one glacier appeared to not only not shrink but, in fact, grow larger."

Hiroko pulled down a pre-FUS world map, demarcated by long-obliterated political boundaries, and tapped Alaska with her pointer.

"Here, in the southeast portion of what was then the state of Alaska, the Malaspina glacier appeared to be reversing a decades-long process of melting. At one time the glacier was forty miles across, twenty-eight miles long, and some six hundred meters thick, with an area of fifteen hundred square miles. During the early FUS, while other glaciers melted, it appeared to grow by 0.3 percent daily during its peak growth. This caught the attention of the Climate Crisis Control Center, or C4, who initially viewed it as an opportunity to establish a polar bear refuge. As you know, the retreat of arctic sea ice led to alarming polar bear drownings and cannibalism. The C4, who fed rescued polar bears with air-dropped loads of fish compacted into frozen bales, studied the air currents around the glacier and the geology of the region but nothing could explain why it continued to grow. By all measures it should have been melting. Soon it grew to subsume a small nearby village, which was heralded as a promising sign. If it were to melt, you see, Malaspina alone would have contributed half an inch to the level of rising seawater.

"Various climatologists including Dr. Stephen McDonough-Hughes at the University of Alaska Anchorage and Drs. Fran and Regina Kroll of Oxford's Climate Response Committee believed that the secret to reversing this warming trend may have been contained within or around Malaspina. It seemed that the growing glacier in southeast Alaska might be cause for hope and optimism about the future of the climate.

"Then, on April 14 of FUS 17, the glacier began to move, with its polar bears, breaking free of the mainland and slipping into the ocean. It appeared to be making a beeline for Anchorage, provoking a mass exodus, with Anchorage residents fleeing for other parts of Alaska and Canada. The glacier destroyed city blocks, following a somewhat counterintuitive trajectory. Rather than remaining at sea level, it managed to defy physics and climb to higher elevations. When the airdrops of frozen blocks of fish stopped, some of the polar bears started climbing off the ice to feed on the animal carcasses left in the glacier's wake.

"After eradicating Anchorage, Malaspina moved on to various population centers of Canada. Reducing Prince Rupert and Whitehorse to mud, it continued on a more or less straight path to Edmonton.

"By now, sympathy for the plight of the polar bears had largely disappeared from public discourse. Instead of beautiful mammals deserving of our preservation efforts, they came to be known as a marauding horde of beasts surfing a climatic anomaly that was laying waste to Canada.

"Several theories emerged to explain the origin and sheer persistence of the glacier. Many suggested the mass of ice possessed an intelligence. It was easy to personify, as it appeared to be deliberately targeting concentrations of human civilization. As it approached Saskatoon, Canadians stood on top of buildings and bridges with bullhorns, loudly and profusely apologizing for warming the planet. But the glacier would not be placated. With its polar bears roaring, the great sheet of ice scraped skyscrapers off the face of the earth, ground power plants and apartment buildings and sports stadiums under its heels, and left behind a trench filled with strange artifacts from cities it had flattened. It picked up an entire Shoppers Drug Mart in Winnipeg, with shoppers and employees still inside. They rode atop the glacier for weeks, barricaded inside the store, fending off polar bear attacks and eating large quantities of snack food before the whole store slipped into Thunder Bay.

"While Malaspina laid waste to the Great White North, Americans paid little attention. They had their own disasters to attend to and besides, Americans never paid much attention to Canadians anyway unless they were good at telling jokes. When Winnipeg was reduced to nothing, few media networks even paid it a minute's notice, the news overshadowed by certain revelations of a sexual nature involving a supporting cast member of a situation comedy. It was only when Malaspina veered due south, toward what was left of Detroit, that Americans began to pay attention.

"With polar bears roaming the streets of what had once colloquially been called the 'Motor City,' and a giant wall of ice not far behind, what was left of the U.S. government mobilized. The National Guard trained thermal beams on the marauding glacier, hoping to melt it down. Still it grew larger and faster, wiping Cincinnati, Philadelphia, and Boston off the map. It headed for Chicago, then St. Louis, pursued all the way by helicopter gunships and tanks. Even its forays into the Southwest did nothing to reduce its size. In fact, residents of those stifling cities welcomed Malaspina's arrival as a reprieve from the heat, realizing only too late the destructive properties of such a vast body of ice, not to mention thousands of angry polar bears. Once the glacier wiped out Dallas, it appeared to slow somewhat, and by the time it crawled over the Rockies into California it even appeared to be shrinking. It was in Los Angeles that Malaspina made its final stand.

"The history of Los Angeles was one of earthquakes and wildfires. They were familiar with disaster. As Malaspina approached, the mayor's office, considering the long list of municipalities removed from the face of the earth by this frigid monster, decided to boldly destroy Malaspina once and for all by sacrificing their city in flames. At the moment the glacier came within city limits, specially trained teams in fire-retardant suits ignited strategically placed petroleum reserves. The polar bears let out great wails of fury and pain as their fur burned and the overwhelmed glacier began to melt. Back and forth these elemental forces raged, fire melting ice, ice turning into water that doused the flames, until only here and there fires burned and the glacier was the size of a compact car, surrounded by scorched polar bear meat, dissolving on Sunset Boulevard.

"As that fateful day came to a close, a girl named Deidre Franklin wandered through the wasteland of her city and came to the place where the ancient glacial ice turned at last to water. All that was left now was a single chunk, no bigger than a typical ice cube, containing the dying breaths of ancient mammals, which Deidre used to cool a glass of Mountain Dew X-Treme Lime."

"Dude, you pissed yourself."

Skinner lay supine on the guest bed while Carl peeled off his pants.

"If I could move," Skinner said.

"I need towels," Carl said and left the room. A bit later he returned with a wet, soapy washcloth and a bath towel.

"Wait, let me do it," Skinner said.

"Your wife could show up any minute and I don't want her to find you marinating in your own whiz. You gotta lay still so the system can map your current physical self."

Carl swabbed Skinner's naked lower half with the washcloth, dried him off, then helped his friend's legs into underwear retrieved from the RV.

"I'm sorry I dragged you into that memory," Skinner said.

"Yeah, it pretty much ruined my day," Carl said.

"I'm sorry." Skinner stretched his face. Still felt weird, mapped to his memory face.

"You saw the Last Dude again," Carl said.

"Same as always," Skinner said.

"Did he still have that extra-deluxe fridge?"

"Yeah. Stocked in the desert."

"Did you get a look at the book titles this time?"

"No. I've never been able to. It's always the same progression. There's no variation to it. Same mesa. Same crows. Same beer."

"Who do you think he is?"

"Maybe he's the final judge of humanity. Building some massive message out of stones in the desert. 'THE W.'"

"You let me know when you figure that shit out," Carl said.

"Carl, man, what am I going to do about Roon?"

"You're going to go up there and give her a hug and a kiss and meet your new grandson."

"I've been a pig."

"Not the first time."

"I was hoping you'd disagree."

"I never understood your falling out with her in the first place, so your being a complete asshole is the only logical explanation to me."

"She hates what I stand for. She thinks of me as the enemy."

"You've got political differences."

"We're repugnant to her. Says American Christians like us *caused* the FUS. She blames me for Waitimu's . . . The last thing she said was she never wanted to talk to me again. I don't know how everything went south so quickly between us."

"She wants you to be her dad again, man. She's trying to fix things. You've got to meet her halfway. What else are you going to do? Stew in your bad memories?"

"That sounds about right."

"Well it isn't. You need to get your ass to Seattle and see that grandson."

"She said I killed Waitimu."

"You wouldn't be so hung up on that point if part of you didn't agree."

Skinner blinked at the ceiling. “Oh God.”

“You can’t fix what happened to your boy. But you can fix what happened with Roon.”

“Fuck, Carl.”

Carl consulted a Bionet monitor. “You’ve napped enough to move a little. Don’t even tell me you’re not hungry. Come on. I’ll feed you.”

After the great fire of 1889, when Seattle laid new streets atop the ruins of Pioneer Square, the ground levels of hotels, brothels, and dry-goods merchants became the underground. Post-FUS, a third layer arose, preserving Pioneer Square under a dome. In this district it was always night, lit with yellowish streetlights, real trees supplanted by facsimile trees of concrete and latex. Far overhead snaked the pipes of new water systems and bundled cables bearing energy and data. Walking the cobbles of Jackson Street, Chiho sensed that the neighborhood had been stashed in a vast warehouse, preserved for later extraction or to be simply forgotten. A few Seattleites chose to live down here away from the sun and rain, lured by cheap rents in charming, renovated brick buildings, tolerant of the bachelorette parties drunkenly boob-flashing their way through a dozen bars. It made Skinner claustrophobic. Chiho said she’d never live in a place that hid from what little sun shone weakly in the sky. Add this to the list of the many things they didn’t understand about Roon.

Roon and Dot’s condo took up half a floor of a building at First and Main. Roon claimed it was an easy commute to Bainbridge, and good for Dot, who had skin-related issues with UV rays. They’d lived here together for fifteen years. Approaching the building Skinner struggled to recall the few Christmases they'd spent here, when artificial snow issued from nozzles overhead, covering the streets in fluffy, nucleating proteins while Dickensian carolers roamed about singing pre-FUS hymns of charity and brotherhood. He'd stood at a window of the condo, watching the holiday display with a cup of nog, finding the whole experience a poignant simulation of a holiday spirit he'd never actually felt.

The elevator took them to Roon and Dot's place, opening onto their foyer. Through the frosted glass door came soft bumps of music.

"Be nice," Chiho said.

"Don't immediately start crying," Skinner said.

"Deal."

"Deal."

Dot let them in, grinning, hugging. Hard to tell how much of it was a pantomime of a greeting and how much was real. She stood barefoot, in a tank top and jeans, tattoos of Gustave Doré's woodcuts from *Purgatorio* wrapped around her forearms. She wore chunky black-framed glasses and her hair was in pigtails.

"Come, come," Dot said. "Roon is putting the little one down for his nap."

"Shoes on? Off?" Chiho asked.

"Off?" Dot shrugged.

They removed their shoes. Inside was like a glossy spread in a magazine. Skinner didn't recognize a single author on the spines of the books on the cases that wrapped the walls. He thought maybe he should sit, but didn't know which piece of sitting-related furniture to select. Chiho effusively complimented the place as if she'd never set foot in here before. Dot gestured to a couch and rattled off a list of five beverages. Skinner didn't catch any of them. "Water?" he asked.

Dot asked about their trip. "How was the coast? Did you stop to see the aircraft carrier? How were Hiroko and Carl? Tell me all about it."

Now having a few places to start a conversation, Chiho focused on their visit to Hearst Castle, describing in great detail the decor and amenities. Dot nodded and interjected questions at the right intervals, keeping her mother-in-law going. They drank their waters and Skinner said, "The aircraft carrier is still beached. Craziest-looking thing." And that was the end of that anecdote.

Just as the conversation came to a bloated moment of silence, their daughter emerged from the baby's bedroom, uneasily smiled, then said, "Mom? Dad?"

"Come here, you," Skinner said, embracing his daughter. "Come here, my sweet."

Chiho kept her promise to not immediately start in with the waterworks. Instead she beamed and said, "Well, look at you. *Look* at you."

"Little Waitimu just went down for a nap but he's a light napper and should be up again soon," Roon said.

"I'm sorry, who?" Skinner said.

"We named him after Waitimu," Roon said.

"Oh, your son," Skinner said. "That's good. A good name."

"Well!" Chiho said. "You two must have your hands full—"

"Which one of you carried him?" Skinner asked.

Roon said, "I did. I was the pregnant one."

Here Chiho steeled herself and came close to breaking her deal with her husband. She'd spent the whole drive from

Portland worrying about this. To not have been with her daughter when she was carrying a child, oh, God. She swallowed and forced her lips into a quivering smile. "That's so wonderful, Roon."

"How's work?" Skinner asked, the question both wildly off-topic and providing some relief.

"Work is beyond crazy," Dot said. "We're both on the island most days."

"We've been working with the newmans on Wall Street," Roon said. "There's an on-site day care Waitimu goes to and I can get down there a couple times a day to feed him. You should come over with us and see how it's coming. I can get you visitor passes."

"Sorry, I can't get over that you named him Waitimu. I'm cool with it, it's—I just didn't expect it," Skinner said.

Dot and Roon exchanged an uneasy expression. Skinner mistook it for having made them uncomfortable. "I don't mean I think it's bad you did it, not at all. It honors your brother, obviously." He looked around the room for something to divert his attention. "Say, are those blueprints?"

On a drafting table lay several bound volumes of plans for New York Alki. Roon preferred to work with actual paper; the task of re-creating a city as it appeared in the distant past would seem to require such an affectation. They pulled open the first volume. "Yeah, they're facsimiles of the Marc Fedderly blueprints. Amazingly, he did these all by hand."

Skinner leaned in to get a better look. A map of Bainbridge Island on the left page, a map of Manhattan on the right.

"So even though Bainbridge and Manhattan are roughly the same size, there are some major geographical differences they've had to contend with. First is the coastline. While the landmass is roughly the same, the surface area of the coasts are wildly different, right? Owing to the irregularity of Bainbridge's coast. But no one has ever figured out a way to accurately measure how long a coast is. Do you measure at high tide? Low tide? A coast is constantly in flux, expanding, contracting. The water's edge never stays in one place. And topographically it's wildly different, too. All those hills. So regrading and reshaping the coast were the major challenges during phase one."

Skinner listened, nodded, reflected on the fact that this wasn't really a conversation about civil-engineering challenges so much as Roon's courting his approval.

". . . to build the seawall, see? So the reshaping could happen without having to contend with wakes and tides . . . They surrounded the whole island. It's thirty feet thick, reinforced concrete, has a system of locks for letting the barges through . . ."

A toddler appeared in the bedroom doorway, rubbing his eyes, his hair a brilliant fountain of blond ringlets. He wore a shirt with a brontosaurus on it. Seeing the visitors, he shyly smiled and hunched up his shoulders, as if he'd been caught doing something.

"It's okay, sweetie," Roon said. "Come meet Grandpa and Grandma."

Skinner steadied himself.

"We thought we should tell you in person," Roon said, her voice trembling, as she scooped up her son. "We wanted you to see him when you found out."

Chiho fell to her knees, pulled herself up, and reached for the boy. Here, miraculously, was her dead son again, not as she last remembered him, but as she first remembered him, identical to the painfully beautiful child she'd lost. Everything she remembered about her Waitimu filled her chest to bursting. Roon's Waitimu looked the same, smelled the same, he *was* the same. "It's you. Oh, my dear heart, let me hold you."

Skinner's palms went cold. "You *cloned* your dead brother?"

Q&A WITH LUKE PIPER, PART 3

[unintelligible] I mean, it's flattering to imagine that you're so important that secret brotherhoods struggle over your fate. But what if it's just the opposite? What if we're too insignificant for anyone to really give a shit about what happens to us? The only way you become of interest to shady cabals is if you have some piece of incriminating information or you can make someone fabulously wealthy.

Anyway, so after Nick returned to San Jose I kept running it through my head. It didn't add up. I knew Nick was a genius, but *come on*. He got whisked away to some superexclusive club on the basis of a lousy science fair project? Had these guys been watching him secretly for years? What did they know about the shed full of schematic drawings of New York City? I'd grown up with a couple skeptical academic parents who'd installed a pretty resilient bullshit detector in my head. There were gaps in Nick's story. If I hadn't been so knocked back on my heels by his reaction to my sleeping with his mom, I might have noticed that his stories about the academy were thin. They had an almost rehearsed quality. He avoided direct questions about the academy, his professors, who this Kirkpatrick guy was. When he left after Thanksgiving break I rolled everything around in my head and found that my curiosity was pushing me toward making a set of decisions. I had to find out what was going on at the Kirkpatrick Academy of Human Potential. Then Nick wrote us that he wasn't going to make it back for Christmas. He had things he needed to "sort out." He was "really busy." I decided to head down to San Jose and surprise him.

Did Star want to go?

She did, but she was trapped. She hadn't stepped off the island in fifteen years. Not even a ferry ride to Seattle. Severe agoraphobia. The week before Christmas I gassed up the van, rotated the tires, kissed Star good-bye, and hit the road. By this time I looked like a dope-smoking hippie. I had beads in my beard and dreadlocks, wasn't wearing shoes most of the time. As I drove to California I reflected a lot on what had happened in the past year, and it struck me for the first time that maybe sleeping with Star hadn't been such a good idea. I thought, *Oh, my God, I'm fucking his mom.*

[Interviewer laughs]

I don't know what kind of investigative plan I had in mind. I thought I could just show up in San Jose and drop in on him. Surprise! I had no idea. I didn't even have an address.

How did you find the place?

Well, I rolled into San Jose in the afternoon and just sort of drove around, ending up at this tourist attraction, the Winchester Mystery House. I used a pay phone outside the gift shop and called information. Of course, there was no listing for the Kirkpatrick Academy of Human Potential. It was getting late and I found a public library that was just closing. I parked in front, slept in the van that night, then went in the next day when they opened. I asked a librarian about the academy. She hadn't heard of it. Remember, this was still a few years before the Web. We depended on librarians and reference books. I spent the better part of that day scouring resources, calling all the Kirkpatricks in the San Jose phone book. Nothing. I'd thought it wouldn't be hard to find the place. I'd spent the whole drive south imagining my conversation with Nick when I showed up. It never occurred to me that I wouldn't find the place. Then I thought that maybe people in academia would have a better idea where the academy might be so I went to San Jose State and checked the library there. Nothing. I spent a couple hours walking around campus randomly asking people. Nothing. No one had heard of it. The only way I could contact Star would be through the mail, so I couldn't really ask her for help. We'd sent Nick letters, I remembered, to a post office box here. I momentarily thought the post office would be the place to get this sorted out but they hadn't heard of it either. I wondered if I was in the wrong San Jose. I had no idea what I was doing. I slept in the van for the better part of a week. Drove around reading the directories of office parks. I had an old letter Nick had sent with a San Jose postmark and no return address. That was really the only indication that he'd been here, besides the fact that he had told me this was where the academy was located. I even went to the police and the fire department, but they were of no help. They said the place didn't exist.

Then I'm lying there one night in the back of the van, probably reading Carlos Castaneda or Herman Hesse by flashlight, when I spotted that brochure under the passenger seat. The one Nick has showed me. Of course! I had totally forgotten! The next day I took the brochure back to the library and showed the librarian. He didn't recognize the Spanish-style building or the horse pasture in the pictures. Or the smiling kids hunched over their books. I showed it around at the college, no luck. Same for the police station. I hit every bookstore in town and no one recognized it. It seemed I'd exhausted every possible avenue. I thought about heading home. I felt terribly alone. At one point I parked in the middle of some mall's parking lot after midnight and cried. I looked at the brochure for the hundredth time and noticed the name of the print company in tiny type on the back. It was some place called Vision Reprographics in San Francisco. That was my only lead. So the next morning I headed out.

The company wasn't hard to find. They occupied a big industrial building in the Mission District. I showed up with the brochure and asked the woman at the front counter if she knew anything about it. They appeared to print lots of stuff—booklets, concert posters, ad circulars—so I wasn't surprised when she said she didn't know. Was there someone who would know? She introduced me to a young guy named Wyatt Gross. What shocked me about him was that he looked how I would have looked had I shaved and cut my hair. He seemed to be about my age, my height and build, wearing a tight pair of jeans with a flannel shirt tucked in. Hair combed and parted on one side, leather shoes. I imagined for a second that he really was me, living in a reality in which my parents hadn't died. He introduced himself as a project manager, shook my hand, and asked me what he could do to help.

I showed Wyatt the brochure. He studied it intently, turning it over, thumbing the edges. They'd definitely printed it, he told me, but he didn't remember the job. Maybe there were records he could look up to find out who placed the order? Sure, they could do that, but they printed so much stuff and that could take weeks, plus they didn't just give out client information. I was trying to be polite but I was visibly frustrated. He had no reason to be helpful to me. I was just some dirty freak who looked like he'd stumbled out of an R. Crumb comic. Finally I threw up my hands, thanked him for his time, and left. Outside I sat in the van pondering my next move. I had no next move. I looked at the building and wondered if I could break in when they closed. Then a side door opened and Wyatt came out, waved at me, and jogged across the street to where I was parked. He gestured for me to unlock the passenger door and got in.

"Look," he said, "I don't know who you are. And I shouldn't be talking to you. But I want to help. The only way you're going to get the information you need is to show up tomorrow at eleven and ask to speak to Mr. Nixon. He's a warehouse manager who happens to need an extra hand. You look like you can move boxes, right? Tell him you saw the ad in the *Chronicle* and are interested in the job. You'll be doing yourself a favor if you take a shower. It pays shit, but don't complain. And don't mention you met me or that we had this conversation. By the way, are you local?"

I told him I'd just gotten here a couple hours before. He shook his head. That wouldn't do. I'd need an address. He told me there were cheap places available in the Tenderloin. I thanked him and he left without another word. That afternoon I rented a room in a purgatorial apartment building, a bathroom-down-the-hall kind of dump. Old alcoholics, prostitutes, everyone a few dollars away from homelessness. I thought it was super, just the kind of texture I needed in my life. The next day I showed up at Vision Reprographics and got the job. The other guys in the warehouse didn't give me a second look. They'd seen so many temporary-type employees come through here and they just figured I'd be gone in a few weeks. Moving boxes of paper around all day. I kept my head down for a month, worked hard, didn't ask too many questions, and figured out the organizational structure of the place.

A month?

Yeah. As soon as I knew I'd be in San Francisco a while I sent a letter to Star telling her not to worry, I was just doing some work and would return soon. Told her I loved her and all that. But I felt sick writing it. Part of me knew we'd never be lovers again but I wasn't really admitting it to myself at that point.

What about Wyatt—did you find out why he wanted to help you?

I found out later, but then, per our arrangement, I kept my distance. He worked in a different part of the building, we ate lunch at different times, we left each other alone. I figured out that every print job got its own file, with the invoice, payment record, and a proof of the finished work. These documents were kept in the basement in banker's boxes. The only reason anyone had to go down there was to add another box to the pile. The only organizational rubric they had was by date. I had no way of knowing when the brochure had been printed. It could have been done years before Nick showed it to me. While I was pushing around the hand truck upstairs, the record I needed was just sitting in one of those boxes. I had to figure out not only an excuse for getting down there, but a method for finding one stupid file in thousands of boxes. Every night I went back to my shitty apartment, tried to tune out the guy loudly vomiting next door, and devised a way to deal with these vast, poorly organized archives. I could be down there for years, I realized. That is, if I was able to gain access and not raise anyone's suspicion in the first place. I considered just getting in the van and heading back to Bainbridge. But at the same time, I had settled into a work routine. The money wasn't great but at least I didn't have to dip into the inheritance anymore. Then one night when I was clocking out Wyatt clapped me on the back. "Luke Piper," he said, like we were old buds. "You got plans for the weekend?" When it became clear a guy like me would have no plans, he invited me to dinner at his and his girlfriend's place.

They lived in a nicer part of town. Nicer in relation to my hellhole, anyway. When I knocked on the door I could hear them on the other side. His girlfriend said, "He's here?" In that moment her voice seemed to suggest a history of secret conversations. Her name was Erika Vaux and she was a struggling writer, writing science fiction novels under the name Blanche Ravenwood. Tall woman, bony thin, wearing all black with dangly earrings, one of those jet-black pageboy hairdos. The two of them didn't look like a couple. For one, Erika was several years older than Wyatt. (And who was I to talk?) They were one of those couples where the woman is strikingly less attractive than the man, leading you to imagine that their sex life must be really exotic and fulfilling. She was a woman whose awkward looks are thrown off by an absolutely killer body. You look at that kind of woman and imagine she suffered horribly in middle school, then experienced an epic period of carnal revenge in college. They uncorked some red wine and I almost started crying at how cool it was to sit on a couch and have a conversation with people who were so smart and friendly. Their most benign creature comforts seemed to me extravagant luxuries. Like their full-sized refrigerator. I realized I'd been locked away in my loneliness, enduring brainless work and living in a place where I had to occasionally step over hypodermic syringes. This felt like civilization.

What did you guys talk about?

That first night we just sort of got down our biographical basics. I told them the whole sad story about the mud slide, told them I'd been living with my friend's mom, but initially I left out the sex part. Wyatt gave me a lecture on vitamins. He was one of those guys who talked openly about his colonic flora and based his diet on his blood type. Turns out he had ambitions beyond printing menus and brochures. He was taking classes to become a naturopath, though he was quick to say he wasn't really interested in becoming a practitioner. He was more interested in comparing different medical traditions like homeopathy, Ayurvedic medicine, Chinese medicine. Erika, she'd grown up in Bellingham. In our first conversation it came out that she'd experienced extraterrestrial visitations as a kid. The first one was in a field behind her house. She was nine or ten years old. A cluster of green lights hovered above the field beyond her open window. After a few seconds staring at it, the lights seemed to realize they were being watched and whooshed away. She revealed this about halfway through my first glass of wine. I'd never met this woman before and she was saying, Hey, have some crackers and Gorgonzola, I was anally probed by an extraterrestrial. Why she was with a guy as seemingly square as Wyatt I couldn't really fathom. And to say that a guy who tried to convince me to give the Paleolithic diet a shot was square really tells you what kind of person *I* was in those days. I drank another glass of wine. Wyatt put on a Disposable Heroes of Hiphoprisy album. I was feeling good, laughing for the first time in what felt like years. This couple's kindness sort of enveloped me. Their sympathy about my family situation struck me as genuine. I think we ate a Middle Eastern meal—falafel, hummus, baba ghanoush. I was so grateful for their hospitality. They uncorked another bottle of wine, slipped a Consolidated CD into the player. I perused the half dozen paperbacks Erika had written, asked questions about her writing career. There came a lull in the conversation and Wyatt and Erika looked at each other, then nodded. I was pretty drunk at this point and wasn't going to be getting up from the couch anytime soon. Wyatt disappeared into the bedroom and came out a few seconds later with a small oil painting, holding the painted side against his body.

"Okay, Luke," he said, "I thought you should see this."

He turned the painting around. It was an exact oil depiction of the picture of the Kirkpatrick Academy from the brochure.

What, he'd painted it?

No. The day I stopped by and showed him the brochure, he'd recognized the image but couldn't remember where he'd seen it before. While I'd been moving boxes around for a month he'd been racking his brain trying to figure it out. Then one day he was visiting a coffee shop he hadn't been to in a while and there it was, hanging on the wall in the men's room. He'd looked at this boring painting dozens of times while peeing. The painting clearly wasn't for sale, so impulsively he stole it, sneaking out the back into the alley. When he got it home and explained the whole thing to Erika he realized he'd made a big mistake. Now he couldn't ask the owner of the café where it had come from. The only clue we had was the signature, which just said "Squid."

Squid?

As in tentacles, yeah. This would be easy, I told them, all we had to do was call all the art galleries in town and ask if they knew any artists named Squid. Wyatt and Erika shook their heads. They'd already done that. No one had heard of this Squid person. There was no way around it. We had to find the record of that brochure. I told them I doubted the academy even existed but this only stoked our desire to find out why they'd gone through the trouble of printing a fake brochure. By the end of the evening our two systems of curiosity had begun to merge. I finally had some help, some people I could trust. We laid out all the knowns. We had to find Dirk Bickle, locate the record of the brochure, and track down Squid. Erika suggested we use the Internet. "The what?" I remember saying. We had to ask the café owner what she knew about the painting. I came up with the idea of bringing the painting back to the café and turning it in. I'd make up a story, tell them I'd seen it next to a Dumpster and remembered that it belonged to the café. I also needed to get in touch with Star again to see if Nick had written. I wrote to her and set up a time for her to call me from the Bainbridge Thriftway pay phone. During the day I'd go to work as usual, load and unload trucks, pile pallets of paper with the forklift. Wyatt and I kept our distance at the warehouse but every night I'd be at his place for dinner and we'd hash out the case.

You referred to it as a "case"?

[chuckles] Yeah, like a couple of kid detectives. The first thing I did was attempt to get in touch with the café. Wyatt gave me the address and I showed up one afternoon with the painting under my arm, only to find the place being remodeled. The café had gone out of business and was being converted into an Irish pub called McGillicutty's or Shamrock O'Flannigan's or something. The workers referred me to the foreman, who referred me to the owner of the pub, a jittery little guy smoking two cigarettes at once who thought I was looking for a job. I don't think I explained myself too well. I must have made a bad impression, pointing emphatically at a painting of a building and talking about squids and human potential. Finally, just to get rid of me, he gave me the name of the former café owner, Shelley Wiggins. I found the nearest phone book and tracked her down. I called, but no answer, so I drove to the address, arriving just in time to see an ambulance out front, with—I shit you not—a couple paramedics coming down the steps carrying a sheet-covered body on a stretcher.

Shelley Wiggins?

Yep. She lived by herself in one of those thin little San Francisco town houses. They found her dangling from a rafter by an extension cord. I figured out where the funeral service was going to be, thinking café employees would show up who I might ask about the painting. When I got to the cemetery, no one was there, and after asking around at the main office I found I'd gotten the day wrong. It had been the day before.

Meanwhile, Erika was unable to track down any Dirk Bickles on the Internet. Actually, she did find one, but he was a ten-year-old kid living in East Bay. Wyatt, meanwhile, was starting to comb through the Vision Reprographics archives. He had more legitimate reasons for being down there than I did, and kept inventing excuses. He started flipping through ten years of boxes, one box at a time. A week went by. No luck.

After some missed connections I got the call from Star and we had a chilly conversation. She was clearly upset I'd been gone so long, didn't understand why I needed to be down there. Besides—and she just sort of dropped this one near the end of the conversation—Nick was home now. In fact, he was standing beside her. He got on the phone and said, "What's up, Luke?" I must've stammered for a while. He said, "Why do you keep looking for me, Luke? What are you hoping to find, Luke?" He kept saying my name, which really creeped me out. I had no good answer. Why *did* I want to find him? He said, "Your search really isn't about me. It's about getting off on the unknown. You want to be part of something. You suspect there's some big secret you're not in on and it kills you. You're not part of anything. You're not one of the selected. You're just some crazy dirt-head being an idiot in the Bay Area. You have no idea how much of an ass you're making of yourself. You have no idea how many people are watching you, laughing their heads off. Quit being stupid, Luke. Apply to college and get a good job. Get married and have kids. Die surrounded by loved ones. That's your fate."

"What are they doing to you, Nick?" I asked him.

"There is no 'they,'" he said. "There is only 'we.' What *we* are doing is bigger and more important than anything you will ever get involved in. I don't mean to taunt you. There's still time for you to go off and have a successful life."

"You're not being yourself," I told him.

"I'm more myself than I've ever been," he said. "I am so thoroughly myself it isn't even funny."

"Who's Squid?" I asked.

"How do you know about Squid?" There was a little edge of panic in his voice.

I told him we were going to find him.

He laughed and said, "And then what, man?"

I told him I didn't know yet, but I could tell whatever he was doing was dangerous. The conversation went in circles like this for a while, like some junior-high-level film noir project. Through it all I had this suspicion that he was right. I was never going to be in on what he was doing. And you know what? Part of me really didn't care anymore. Almost accidentally I had started to build a life for myself in San Francisco. I had a job, I had friends. The place I lived in wasn't much to speak of, but I knew I could go in on a house with some roommates if I wanted to. The thought of going back to Bainbridge made me sick to my stomach. So I said good-bye to Nick, seemingly for good. I looked around my studio apartment with the bare mattress on the floor with no fitted sheet, my dirty clothes piled in a corner, paperbacks everywhere, and saw that I had been presented with a choice. The first thing I did was visit the nearest drugstore and buy a hair clipper. Back at my place

I shaved off the beard and clipped my hair down to about a half-inch fuzz. If I was really going to find out what Nick and Bickle and Kirkpatrick were doing, I needed to change my whole life. I needed discipline, routine, and patience. Most of all, I needed lots of money. Lucky for me, I was living in San Francisco and it was the middle of the 1990s.

NEETHAN F. JORDAN

An image materializes: framed by the open limousine door, the red carpet stretches past a phalanx of press to the vanishing point. Neethan Fucking Jordan steps from the private interior of his transportation into this real-time, flash-lit, and filmed public spectacle, the red path slashing wound-like across the parking lot, the rented polyester fiber unfurled alongside a barricade behind which photographers and camera crews wait encumbered with their gear. To his right stands a vinyl backdrop some ten feet high printed with thousands of logos for Season Four of *Stella Artaud: Newman Assassin*. Neethan models a pair of black sunglasses, prototypes from his line. His face tingles from a facial. Two Altoids effervesce on his tongue. The product holding his hair in a swept-back wave is composed of organic materials harvested from ten countries, six of them war zones. Black pants, jacket, leather shoes crafted by hand in a little-known region of Italy where livestock still wander dirt roads, a white starched shirt with the top button unbuttoned. Neethan is a tall dude, six-eight, and watching him come out of a limo is like watching a cleverly designed Japanese toy robot arachnid emerge from a box, propelling a torso on which nods his head, across which is splashed a smile of idealized teeth, teeth so gleaming you could brush your own teeth looking into them, teeth that still look fantastic blown up two stories tall on the side of a building, a sexual promise to nameless fans encoded in bicuspid, molar, incisor, and canine. The arm rises, a wave, a hello, an acknowledgment that the assembled journalists exist and through the conduits of their cameras exist the public. *Neethan F. Jordan has arrived!*

As these things go, the first twenty or so yards of carpet are reserved for photographers. Crammed three deep, the back two rows of shutterbugs wobble on progressively taller step ladders. They scream his name over and over as if he might mistakenly turn to face the backdrop. This part used to perplex him. Obviously they have his attention, he knows he is expected to pose. Why the name yelling? Ah, but here's why—by yelling his name so voraciously they make it impossible for him not to smile. Neethan pivots, does an open-mouthed smile like *what crazy freakin' fans!*, transforms his fingers into guns, transitions into mock-angry . . . into slightly amused . . . into humbled . . . into ecstatic . . . each expression provoking cluster bombs of flashes. He imagines photo editors clicking to find the right image to complement the editorial slant of the accompanying 150 words.

"People! Yes!" Neethan exclaims and that's all it takes for the shouting to boil over, rising to Beatlemania temperatures among the photogs. Pointing out individuals behind the spastically stuttering cameras, he says, "Jimmy! Isamu! Marti, you dress so sexy! I can hardly take it!"

Out of the many things Neethan can't fathom, what he most can't fathom is anonymity. He knew it only briefly as a child. The vast unfilmed, the people nobody knows anything about, are conceptually exotic to him. The only time he gets close to understanding how it might feel to be unfamous is when he plays one of them. In those instances he is expected to empathize with the plights of migrant farm laborers and other people doing, you know, stuff like that. He can't tell anymore whether he's done something to instigate his fame or whether he has merely been chosen as its filter. Fame is a sticky, candy-like substance; a river of it courses through his life. It is as close to religion as he will ever likely get. Of course the kicker is he lived in a group home in Seattle until the age of six and has never known his birth parents. The staff at the group home couldn't agree on what he was, ethnicity-wise. Filipino? Mexican? Whatever it was it had brown skin and black hair and a honker of a nose. As a kid the nose had haunted and shamed him until the rest of his Cubist handsome face rose around it like a village maturing around a cathedral. Then one day a woman named Mrs. Priest showed up. The hope that she would be his mom lasted about fifteen minutes. Nope, he was being hustled to another group home of sorts, the Kirkpatrick Academy of Human Potential, where he wouldn't have to clean toilets or empty trash. He was only expected to become one thing: famous.

At present a lithe form appears unobtrusively in Neethan's periphery. He speaks sideways through a motionless smile, "I suppose you're Beth-Anne."

"Yes, Mr. Jordan," says the assistant publicist. She wears a $4,000 dress and a lanyard with a laminated card indicating she belongs on this side of the barrier. Brunette, boobs. She takes his arm and leads him a few feet down the carpet to the first of the television crews.

"This is *Access Hollywood,*" Beth-Anne whispers. "Geri McDonald-Reese, reporter."

As the words enter his ear Neethan is already extending his hand and broadening his smile, providing full-on gums now, processing Beth-Anne's info concurrently as he speaks. "*Access* Fuckin' *Hollywood!* Hell yeah! I haven't seen you since the premiere of *The Barack Obama Story*!"

Was this the slightest blush from Geri? One of the A-list celeb reporters, bordering on famous herself, she is rumored to have been canoodling on yachts with a qputer-technology magnate. She swims through celebrity like a little amphibian, accustomed to imbibing from the medicine cabinets of capital-n *Names.* She's wearing Michel D'Archangel; Neethan recognizes the jacket from the fall show. Her camera guy hovers over one shoulder, partially obscured in shadow. Maybe it isn't a blush. Maybe she isn't so blown away that he remembers she exists, as the less evolved reporters downstream will be.

"Neethan," she says, "let's do this, shall we?"

"Roll it."

Geri speaks into the microphone. "I'm here with Neethan Jordan at the Season Four premiere of *Stella Artaud: Newman Assassin,* the preapocalyptic thriller created by Burke Ripley. Neethan, tell us a bit about your character—"

"*Stella Artaud: Newman Assassin,* Season Four, is the latest season in the award-winning *Stella Artaud: Newman Assassin* franchise. I play Dr. Uri Borden, a clone scientist who gets involved in the uprising and must decide whether to abort the messiah. It's a thought-provoking series, featuring state-of-the-art effects and wall-to-wall action, with more than a little tenderness."

Geri says, "Tell me a bit about what it was like working with director Burke Ripley."

Here it's appropriate for Neethan to take his hand and place it on his forehead, sweeping his hair back in a gesture that communicates having survived challenging, creatively rewarding work. "What can I say about Burke? He's a genius." Neethan remembers, then pretends to remember, an anecdote, chuckling. "You know, everyone thinks of Burke as this intense, driven guy, but he's got a playful side to him as well. We happened to be shooting on Halloween and he showed up to the set dressed as me." Neethan laughs at his own not very funny anecdote. Message: *I can make fun of myself despite my perfection: I am more like you in this regard: it's safe for you to like me: please desire me: please give me your money for the honor of desiring me.* "I mean, he had the glasses, the hair. He even got my makeup girl to match the skin tone. Walked around the set that morning grinning like an idiot, just like me. Hilarious."

What was that, about eight seconds of dialogue? He figures the piece will probably run one minute. Intro, red carpet montage, a bite from him, preview clip, bite from a costar, more montage, closing summary.

Presently, from Beth-Anne: "Tom Parsons, Fox Entertainment News."

"Tom!" Neethan says, arm cantilevering from his trunk, using the handshake as a Judo-esque method of pulling this Tom character closer, slapping him on the back in the kind of hug grown men give their dads. He has never met this guy. Clearly someone on the downward slope, career-wise, probably accustomed to reporting hard news, probably glorified those FUS days when reporters braced against hurricanes or emoted beside a slag heap that up till then had been a megamall. Now he was feeding the machine that barked for nubile starlets to release their gynecological records. Tom Parsons, graying at the temples, doing his professional best to convey a sense of levity, failing for the most part, probably owing to the fact that he'd never been within pissing distance of the caliber of celebrity that was *Neethan Fucking Jordan.* (Real middle name, btw. He'd had it changed legally around the release of *Legislative Deception.*)

Tom says, "Harvey, you ready? Rolling? Okay. Neethan! I understand you just started a new philanthropic venture."

Neethan's lips fall around his smile. He cocks his head to one side, a little low, eyes raised semiwaif-like. "Thanks for asking, Tom. The Neethan Fucking Jordan Foundation has a simple goal—help kids to stop abusing the Bionet and stop becoming each other's embodiments . . ." Neethan's mind goes into another room and cracks a Bud as he recites his spiel about the nonprofit that bears his name. There is one part of him that moves his mouth while another part imagines a highlight reel of Tom's career. Here is Tom the young reporter blubbering and weeping into a wind-scraped microphone before a scene of utter smoking devastation. "Oh, my God! All of Atlanta! Holy fucking shit! Oh, people, dear Jesus Christ, we're all going to die! Get me the fuck out of here!" A few more clips like this pass through Neethan's head, shots of Tom on a makeshift raft on a vast expanse of polluted water, confiding in the camera that he'd just consumed his dead cameraman's thigh. There's only so much of this FUS footage Neethan can imagine so he logs out. ". . . because, uh, when you give a child a future, you give *humanity* a future," he concludes.

Tom seems satisfied with the answer and asks what the new season is about.

"*Stella Artaud: Newman Assassin,* Season Four, is the latest in the award-winning *Stella Artaud: Newman Assassin* franchise. I play Dr. Uri Borden, a clone scientist who gets involved in the uprising and must decide whether to abort the messiah. It's a thought-provoking series, featuring state-of-the-art effects and wall-to-wall action, with more than a little tenderness. Thanks so much!"

According to Beth-Anne, the next reporter is Nico Renault from Hollywood Japan Network. Nico's recently had his face tattooed to look like the Kabuki-made-up Gene Simmons of the pre-FUS rock band Kiss. He wears his hair in bright blond spikes. He also wears the body of a cow suit without the head, the rubber udders protruding at crotch level, lending the getup a rather multipenised look. Neethan remembers Nico from when he hosted *Fuck Show*. He'd been a guest once, on the same night as the recently defrosted Ted Williams. The slugger had stolen Neethan's thunder and the movie star still resented the whole disaster. During the skill-testing segment of the program, Williams had outperformed Neethan in a contest where they dressed up as porcupines and raced through a labyrinth trying to spear as many apples as they could with their spines, with each apple representing $10,000 given to the charity of their choice. Thanks to thawed Ted Williams's skills, a few hundred kids in the Dominican Republic now had protective eye wear. Not one of Neethan's finer PR moments. The blogosphere had chortled at the clips of him rolling around in the porcupine suit seemingly incapable of spearing an apple. But he'd been doing a lot more drinking in those days and had been adjusting to the LA/Tokyo jet lag. He'd vowed never to do *Fuck Show* again.

"Neethan Jordan! Tell me about the size of your balls!" Nico says.

"Nice ink, Nico," Neethan says, in no mood to play along. "You still molesting little Malaysian boys?"

"Neethan Jordan! When are you going to perform penetration again?"

"You're still on the air?"

"Neethan Jordan! Please tell us when you will fuck for the world once again!"

"I'm surprised you made it to this position on the red carpet. I thought you'd be stuck with the Icelandic-language print journalists."

"Neethan Jordan! Japan wants to know! When are you to finally decide to get your nipples pierced!"

"I still think Ted Williams had an advantage."

"Neethan Jordan! Please say a few words about your show!"

"*Stella Artaud: Newman Assassin,* Season Four, is the latest in the award-winning *Stella Artaud: Newman Assassin* franchise. I play Dr. Uri Borden, a clone scientist who gets involved in the uprising and must decide whether to abort the messiah. It's a thought-provoking series, featuring state-of-the-art effects and wall-to-wall action, with more than a little tenderness."

"Neethan Jordan! Japan says keep on rocking and rolling!"

Into the camera: "And you keep rocking and rolling, too, Japan."

Oh, Japan. Neethan imagines those humble underwater salarymen going about the business of falling in love with pieces of furniture enhanced with human-like appendages designed for stroking, in domed Tokyo beneath the sea. Watching this interview on their little TV sets while eating Philly cheesesteak sandwiches washed down with Korean malt liquor. Through his head races a montage of movie clips from Seijun Suzuki, Nobuhiko Obayashi, newsreel footage of Hiroshima, early 1980s video of teens grinding to Elvis, a vending machine that can make moral decisions, happy-go-lucky corporate towers, a bowl of steamed rice, geishas, Nobuyoshi Araki bondage stills, Hello Kitty. In short, the sum of what Neethan know about Japan. Oh yeah, and samurais.

"Next is Eric Bibble from *The Exploiter* entertainment news."

Eric Bibble, young guy with a smirk, bow tie and sport coat, bad hair, off-gassing vibes of contempt, shakes Neethan's hand like some Midwestern vice president of sales, like a man who has been told explicitly by his father to *always give 'em a firm grip*. "So, it's Neethan Fucking Jordan. How's this junket treating you?" Eric asks.

"Fantastic, Eric. I love being out here face-to-face with the swell folks of the entertainment press."

"I understand Myra Fairbanks is claiming to be carrying your baby."

Neethan is prepared for this. Surprised, actually, that the question hasn't come up sooner. "Eric, I'm glad you asked. I saw the prenatal paternity report today, which indicated conclusively that I am *not* the father. And I just want to reiterate what I've been saying all along—these allegations are really unfair to Ms. Fairbanks."

Eric's smile slackens. "You're not the father?"

"Nope."

"Okay, well, I guess that's all the questions I have."

"Really? Don't you want to ask about the new season of *Stella Artaud: Newman Assassin*?"

"Sure, okay."

"Stella Artaud: Newman Assassin, Season Four, is the latest in the award-winning *Stella Artaud: Newman Assassin* franchise. I play Dr. Uri Borden, a clone scientist who gets involved in the uprising and must decide whether to abort the messiah. It's a thought-provoking series, featuring state-of-the-art effects and wall-to-wall action, with more than a little tenderness."

"So, you really didn't father the child? Did you even sleep with her?"

Neethan stretches out his arms and cocks his head in a *Come on! Of course I did!* gesture. All this coulda seemed calculated, scripted even, because at that moment another limo pulls up and slo-mo deposits the very Myra Fairbanks under discussion on the carpet, not yet showing her pregnancy bump, wearing Nikki McGee, pivoting, blonde, pulchritudinous, a human mirror-ball reflecting supernovae of camera flashes. Myra ratchets her face into a smile, teases the preorgasmic paparazzi, blows kisses, and casts a quick, withering stab of a glare at Neethan, who stands eclipsed on the carpet. They speak to each other in a few short seconds with their eyebrows.

I didn't think you'd show, Neethan eyebrows. *I hope this means you've gotten over your—*

Go fuck yourself. I'm doing business right now.

Hey, girl, you know if the paternity test had come back positive, I would have—

I'm getting interviewed by Geri right now. Leave me alone.

Watch out for Eric Bibble. He's going to ask you who the father is.

His magazine's already photographed my ovaries. I doubt they could get any more invasive.

Beth-Anne says, "Wanda Mesmer, Clothing Optional Network."

Neethan wonders why, if clothing is optional, no one on the Clothing Optional Network ever opts to wear it. Shivering nude in the chilly Hollywood evening stands the blonde, pert-nippled hostess of one of CON's top-rated shows, *Foreign Policy for the Layman*. From time to time Neethan has jacked off to it. He knows he'll be expected to express an opinion on the Brazilian slave trade or the recent piracy off the Ivory Coast. The cameraman squats to get a from-below shot, his dong dragging on the pavement.

"I'm here with Neethan Jordan at the press event for *Stella Artaud: Newman Assassin*," Wanda says. "Neethan, what do you make of General Gordon's recent imposition of martial law and the incarceration of hundreds of Kentucky's procloning dissidents?"

Neethan braces himself, sensitive to offending any potential Deep South *Stella Artaud: Newman Assassin* fans. "It's an unfortunate situation," he says. "I just hope both sides can come together and work things out like they did last year in Arkansas."

"How can you call the Arkansas accord anything but an unmitigated failure? Scores dead? The formal expansion of rape prisons? Are you telling me you approve of the confederacy's suspension of habeas corpus?"

"I'm . . ." Neethan starts, defaulting to his wide smile. "Look, Wanda, I understand there's a lot of turmoil in the Deep

South right now, and I truly feel for all those Neethan Fucking Jordan fans down there who are in a world of hurt. Cut. Now for the other version. Look, Wanda, I just want order restored in one of the greatest cultural regions of the world."

"Nicely done," Wanda says, teeth chattering.

"By the way, I dig what you've done with your pubes," Neethan says.

"I have a new stylist. What can you tell me about the new season of *Stella Artaud: Newman Assassin*?"

"Stella Artaud: Newman Assassin, Season Four, is the latest in the award-winning *Stella Artaud: Newman Assassin* franchise. I play Dr. Uri Borden, a clone scientist who gets involved in the uprising and must decide whether to abort the messiah. It's a thought-provoking series, featuring state-of-the-art effects and wall-to-wall action, with more than a little tenderness."

Neethan finds himself recalling his first leading role, as the unfrozen Viking hero of *Him and Him*. From the thawed wastes of Scandinavia appeared a fully equipped Norse warrior, reanimated by scientists and paired with an animated bolt of lightning to fight environmental crimes in corruption-plagued Chicago. The movie's title derived from the fact that neither character had a proper name. Whenever they showed up to electrocute and battle-ax their way to justice, bystanders would simply exclaim, "It's him! And *him*!" Heavily made up to resemble a hirsute berserker who'd spent a couple thousand years encased in a block of ice, Neethan hadn't been all that recognizable, but he'd loved the role. Day after day he'd show up at the studio lot, get made up and costumed, stand in front of the green screen to grunt and wave a variety of bladed weapons. At one point in the movie he and the other Him, the lightning-bolt guy, commandeered an ambulance and engaged in a high-speed chase beneath the El. Except the whole scene had been created in the fabricated stationary interior of the vehicle, rocked on hydraulics. His costar, a boy named Georgie Walker, wearing a head-to-toe green bodysuit to be CGI'd postproduction, quivered and buzzed beside him. Neethan bellowed, waving a bloody battle hammer out the window. No one could explain how a medieval Viking had learned to drive, but no matter. Audiences ate it up and *Him and Him* won a lesser-known technical Oscar. Since then it had been three or four pictures a year, contractually obligated junkets, Champagne in flutes in houses perched on the hills, locations in the less ruined parts of the world, endorsements of Japanese canned coffee and shoe inserts. Becoming famous had been a process similar to losing his virginity. He'd been convinced so explicitly from so many sources that fame would solve every problem he'd ever had, vault him into a state of permanent euphoria, that when it actually happened he considered his glittered surroundings and thought, *Okay, not what I imagined.* But shit, man, playing that thawed Viking had been a hoot. He wanted a role like that again, one in which he was only required to grunt and ax bad guys.

"*Stella Artaud: Newman Assassin,* Season Four, is the latest in the award-winning *Stella Artaud: Newman Assassin* franchise . . ." Neethan speaks absently to the next journalist, a schmuck from some online-only outfit. He smells Myra's perfume, concocted in a Swiss lab from an Amazonian water beetle and endangered alpine flowers. He replays highlights of their carnal encounters, loops the image of her ass raised up off the bed, spread to reveal the anal aperture and beneath it the valley of pussy. Is he getting hard? *Jesus, okay, think of the Ku Klux Klan, quick!* That usually does it for bone prevention. All it would take would be one cameraman to pan down and notice his newly pitched tent and it would be all over the tabs. The Klan starts disrobing, revealing themselves as tattooed strippers with thongs. And some of them are even black! Fucked up, Neethan. He shoots an eyebrow over to Myra, who's giggling with Eric Bibble, touching him lightly on the shoulder, engaging him fully in her celebrity tractor beam. What Neethan wouldn't do to transform himself into Him (the Viking, not the lightning bolt), carjack a taxi, and get the fuck out of here right about now. But the red carpet stretches interminably onward, allegedly leading to the doors of a sushi restaurant where the release party is to be thrown down. ". . . I play Dr. Uri Borden, a clone scientist who gets involved in the uprising and must decide whether to abort the messiah . . ."

So about that messiah (spoiler alert): As far as Neethan can fathom, *Stella Artaud: Newman Assassin* foretold of a day when the qputers and their attendant monks would instigate a mass wave of virgin births, remotely impregnating girls around the world with a race of Nietzschean übermensch messiahs. In the show, Neethan, as Uri Borden, learns of the virgin births when a teenage girl enters his clinic complaining of cramping and losing her period. Her parents can't or won't believe she's not lying that she's never had sex, and urge her to abort. As Uri races against the clock, uncovering more evidence that the pregnancy is part of a vast plot instigated via the Bionet, he is pursued by members of a radical offshoot sect of monks who want to bring about the second wave of FUS. (In the trailer, Uri Borden exclaims, "You mean they want to restart the Fucked Up Shit? Shit! That's messed up!") So the film had some heavy research behind it. There were actually folks out there who wanted to bring back the FUS. More than not understanding the unfamous,

Neethan can't wrap his head around this brand of nihilism. He'd studied some of the pro-FUS propaganda for the role, boned up on Peter Ng, and from what he can tell the argument goes something like this: Humanity got what it deserved with the FUS, reducing itself to one-fifth its original size. Seeing that the worst of the FUS was over, the traumatized survivors got back to work, reconstructing and applying new technologies, more or less cleaning up the joint. As this reconstruction effort rolled along, the memories of the FUS atrophied and a great surge of optimism and brotherhood seized the world. Hugs all around. But the shit, certain Ng-inspired revisionists argued, had never really ceased being fucked-up. In fact, they said, the shit was *by nature* fucked-up. Human nature, they argued, was designed to destroy the planet, a biological version of a gigantic asteroid or volcanic freak-out. Neethan shuddered. Good thing these Ng acolytes were relegated to the fringe. Shows like *Stella Artaud: Newman Assassin* were meant to keep them there. It was through the efforts of the qputer monks that humanity would continue to thrive and once-extinct species would be brought miraculously back to life. Cities would reconstitute themselves, obliterating the memories of their previous thermonuclear levelings. Hand in hand, folks of mixed ethnic and religious backgrounds would sing before the cameras, in fields of daisies.

"... it's a thought-provoking series ... state-of-the-art effects ... wall-to-wall action ... more than a little tenderness ..." Neethan doesn't even know to whom he is talking now. His brain has officially taken a bow and outsourced this responsibility to his mouth alone. Away it chatters and smiles, two things it is superbly good at and can accomplish by itself, as far as Neethan is concerned. Listen to it go, chuckling and joking with a moony young reporter who so clearly wants his dick. Which, dammit, remains at three-quarters salute despite the Klan fantasy. His and Myra's pheromones are still doin' it right on the red carpet. Think of it this way—she is probably smelling his cologne and getting aroused. Quid pro quo. Beth-Anne tugs at his elbow, introducing him to Dirk Bickle.

"Dirk?" Neethan says, snapping back into the moment. "What the hell are you doing here?"

Bickle looks old. Worse, he looks bloodied. His face is scraped and bandaged and one leg is entombed in a cast. Holding himself up with crutches he attempts a pained smile. Around his neck hangs a bogus laminate identifying him as a reporter from the Homeless People Channel. He snuck in, obviously.

"Neethan, my biggest success story. I am so glad to see you."

"What happened to you? Who did this to you?" Neethan takes his former mentor's arms and pulls him close.

"Don't worry about me. I came to pass along a piece of information. It's about your birth mother."

Neethan smiles defensively. "She's alive?"

Bickle shakes his gray head. "Afraid not, Neethan. And it gets weirder. Not only is she dead, she's been dead for five hundred years."

Neethan laughs. "WTF, Bickle? You're messing with me, right? Are these bandages and bruises a joke?"

The old man sighs. "We saw the prenatal paternity test you took with regard to Ms. Fairbanks and discovered a few new things about your profile. The technology wasn't up to snuff when you were coming up through the academy. Otherwise, we would have told you sooner. First, it's true. You're Native American."

"Doesn't surprise me."

"And you're the last of your tribe."

"What do you mean?"

"I mean you're the last of your genetic line. There are no other living relatives from your particular gene pool."

"Who were they?"

"We haven't figured that out yet."

Neethan steadies himself against a barrier. "So what am I supposed to do with this information? I've got a series to promote."

"You have to go to Seattle. Find out what happened to your tribe. Just follow the red carpet."

"Now, Bickle, why would I want to do that?"

Bickle leans forward and speaks into Neethan's ear. "It is Kirkpatrick's will."

And like a ghost or screen dissolve, Bickle backs away and other cameras and reporters fill the gap with their chattering questions and klieg lights. Beth-Anne takes his arm again and whispers, "Kelli, Staci, and Brandi from the Kids Super Network."

Neethan now faces three preteens, each a billionaire, standing in a row, clutching one another's arms and jumping in unison. "OMG!" they scream. "OMG!"

"Hi, ladies," Neethan says, causing the middle one to faint. The other two fan the middle one's face until she returns to consciousness. Over their heads three lenses bob and weave, behind which squint three cameramen.

The preteen on the left, Kelli, asks the first question. "What's your favorite movie?"

"My favorite movie is . . . *Gifted Children's Detective Agency.*"

"Oh, my God, do you have a girlfriend?" Staci asks.

"Not currently. I'm single," Neethan says, provoking an intensified bout of high-treble squealing and unison jumping, not to mention a quick glance from Ms. Fairbanks, presently interviewing with the Clothing Optional Network.

"Favorite color," Brandi says, looking close to vomiting.

"Aubergine."

"What's the series about?" all three ask together.

"*Stella Artaud: Newman Assassin,* Season Four, is the latest in the award-winning *Stella Artaud: Newman Assassin* franchise. I play Dr. Uri Borden, a clone scientist who gets involved in the uprising and must decide whether to abort . . . You know, there's a whole spiel on it on the B-roll. Just have your producers pull something from there."

The three young journalists refuse, insisting that Neethan repeat the boilerplate. He sighs and complies. When the camera stops rolling the three tweens drop the overwhelmed bubblehead shtick and resume the conversation they'd been having about a new branding firm in which they'd invested considerable time and capital.

Haunted by Bickle, horny by Myra, Neethan proceeds down the line. His hard-on has begun to soften, still firm but perhaps not as unyielding as it had been before he'd been asked his favorite color. He recalls fondly the movie-star sex in which he'd engaged with the starlet, the kind of sex in which the two people are fucking the variety of characters the other has played rather than anything one might rightly call another person. At one point Neethan had been fucking Sherri Nettles, the civil rights attorney Myra had played in *Prom Queen: Ground Zero* while she had been fucking his Gordon Lamphiere, the morally ambivalent assassin of *Saucy McPherson's Game.*

I'm the last of my line, he thinks. *So what?* The idea feels antique, belonging to another generation, something too complex to trip him out. Cameras claw at his face. He extends his hand again, to a Portuguese-language station's arts and entertainment reporter, and from a thousand feet under the sea hears himself prattling about the series he's made, a series he doesn't entirely understand, owing to the brilliance or ineptitude of the director, but about which he speaks with utter confidence and enthusiasm. He watches himself shake more hands, recite more spiels, grin his panties-dropping grin, and knows that this parade of surfaces is about to come to an end. He's going to Seattle. He's going to follow the red carpet. He'll find out where he came from. It's Kirkpatrick's will.

Commercial break.

Inside the restaurant, the red carpet spills to fill the entire floor. Neethan's agent Rory Smiley meets him at the door. Rory is a short man but doesn't have a short man's hair-trigger personality. This is probably thanks to the fact that he suffered through a case of premature puberty, for instance growing facial hair at the age of four. He'd been taller than the rest of the kids in his class until high school, and still thinks of himself as taller than everyone, including Neethan, who towers above him. The premature puberty had been a matter of some brief national attention, with a camera crew following the young Rory around his Montessori school as he worked with golden beads and the pink tower, addressing his classmates in a commanding baritone.

Every morning his doting parents had given him a bubble bath and a shave, and by nap time his five o'clock shadow would start to come in. It's a drag being a preschooler with ball hair.

"Hi Rory. I'm Native American, apparently," Neethan says, squeezing his agent's shoulder.

"Tonight, my friend, you can be anything you want," Rory says, offering a Macanudo.

Neethan takes the cigar and bends down low to allow Rory to light it. "No, really. I'm an Indian. I just found out."

"Whatever you say, boss."

A host appears, a newman-looking guy with a wobbly eye, and shows them to their table. Rory orders a dozen kinds of sushi and four kinds of sake. "And a booster seat, if you could," he says.

The restaurant fills with flacks disgorged from the red carpet. Beth-Anne, her job complete, seeps into the background with the other bottom-feeders gathering about the open bar. Myra enters, a celestial event best witnessed with a space telescope, and is seated at the opposite side of the restaurant. Neethan recognizes the guy who did his hair on *Stella Artaud* heading straight for the booze. The portion of the restaurant Neethan and Rory occupy is roped off, intended for VIPs, with other sections set aside for lower-magnitude studio employees and the journalists and their crews. Now is to be expected an onslaught of permatanned studio execs with big teeth and fists of gold jewelry, wanting to press flesh with the talent. Until then, Rory intends to go over some recent projects that have been pitched Neethan's way.

"So I'm at lunch with Julian Moe yesterday and he says to me, 'Rory, what I wouldn't give to spend an hour with Neethan and get his thoughts on this Abraham Lincoln biopic I'm developing.'"

"Told you, Rory, I'm biopicked out."

Rory raises a hand, lowers his head in a "hear me out" type of gesture. "I'm with you, friend. In fact, the first thing I said was, 'Julie? Why're you wasting my goddamn time with your talk about a biopic? You know Neethan is biopicked out.' So he says, 'Listen, Rory, I know Neethan has had a string of biopics. But I'd be committing directorial malpractice if I didn't at least touch dick tips with Mr. Jordan about this. It's built on a proven formula. (This is Julian still talking, by the way.) It's built on a proven formula. It's a remake of John Ford's *Young Mr. Lincoln*."

"Can you see Myra's table from where you're sitting?"

Rory cranes his neck. "Not sure. Might be that table surrounded by studio brass. Anyway, Julian keeps talking, says, 'Rory, listen. I'm looking for an A-lister with *gravitas*. I'm looking for someone who can shoulder the burden of portraying the motherfucker who freed the slaves. *El presidente*. And no one can fill those presidential pants like Neethan F. Jordan, do you hear what I'm saying?'"

"Is there a love interest?"

"Yeah, well, no, sorta. She dies in the first act."

"Pass. Next."

"So I got this call from a friend of a friend of a friend at a little production company you may have heard of—Remote Sasquatch Productions? And whisper-whisper-whisper I hear they've got Phil Knickerman's new script, a fantasy drama of sorts. They've got Susan Rauch set to direct, up-and-coming young director, you can feed off that kind of cred, and it involves unicorns. It's not a starring role but they thought of you for the part of Osama bin Laden."

"Do I get a nude scene?"

"Great question. I'm on it. Next I have a starring role in a picture called *The Quadriplegic."*

"It involves not using my arms and legs?"

"No, actually. See, it's an inspirational story about a quadriplegic who regains the use of his limbs thanks to the Bionet."

"That kind of thing happens all the time."

"True, which makes it a topical human-interest-type story."

"What's the angle? Why should we care about this former quadriplegic?"

"He robs banks."

"Go on."

"With a wise-cracking chimpanzee sidekick."

"You know I like having a sidekick."

"Based on a true story."

"Pass."

Presently, approaching from the table's starboard side is Big Serge Davis, a VP of marketing at Fox. Big Serge's enhanced-tooth grin seems to precede him; the rest of his body appears to be an appendage of this rapacious dental expression of joy. His teeth are easily twice the size of other people's teeth. Neethan exposes his own teeth as the executive approaches and then their hands come out like the wimpy claws of Tyrannosaurae rex. Neethan stands and the two figures crash together, front to front, laughing and half-speaking their greetings, which come out like, "Neeeeeethaaaaaa!" and "Saaaaaairrrr!" Two glottally communicating giants, they clutch and squeeze each other's arms, slapping shoulders, opening mouths to expose pink Sonicared interiors of mucousy tissues. From Neethan's mouth still dangles his cigar, held precariously in place by lower lip moisture. After a minute or so of this, they verbally indicate their good-byes and Neethan sits down as the first wave of sushi arrives.

He hears Myra laugh across the room. He imagines himself as Marcello Mastroianni pursuing an Anita Ekberg version of Myra up a Roman spiral staircase. His mind spins a series of lip-locked fantasias with swollen strings and wonders if there is any way to think about their brief comingling of bodily juices besides cinematically. He and Myra had accidentally rolled into each other's gravitational fields during the hours of rehearsal for their full-frontal nude sex scene. Their own personal "meet cute" moment. Then, crap, a pregnancy. For the first time, while chopsticking a piece of *ikura gunkan maki,* he wonders who the father might actually be. In the movie, Uri Borden discovers a secret cabal of Indonesian scientists who engineer a method of remote Bionet fertilization, in which they hack birth-control systems to release artificial spermatozoa into women's uteruses. Coulda been something like that with Myra. Maybe a fanboy hacker in his bedroom somewhere, bored of just jerking off to the 3-D X-rays of Myra's internal organs, decided to hack his way into her uterus and impregnate her online. It could happen, he supposes. He'd done some reading in his trailer to prepare for the role, learning a little about how the Bionet interfaces with reproductive systems. You can find out anything about anyone's physical condition via the Bionet. You can track T-cell count, endocrine levels, the squirtings of various enzymes from specialized valves, brain activity, some said even thoughts. Dreams?

Neethan maneuvers a firecracker roll into a saucer containing equal parts wasabi and soy sauce.

"Earth to Neethan," Rory says, waving chopsticks in front of his client's eyes.

"Maybe you could get me some Native American roles," Neethan says, as if that's what he'd been thinking about all along.

"Did you even hear what I said about *The Man Who Got Marketed to Death*?"

"Are you talking about a movie or my life?"

Here come more brass, a trio of them now, jolly, spines bent back into concavities while the arms beckon, thrust at forty-five-degree angles from their bodies, a grandparently come-here-you-rascal kind of hug-inducing posture. Neethan rises and accepts their cheek kisses and let-me-get-a-look-at-you affections. He's never met them before but they don't know that. They feel they know him intimately. Have watched his genitals do their magic on the big screen as well as the magic of his acting skills and uncanny comic timing. More than know him, they feel they own him. And like an objet d'art in a glass cabinet they want to take him out for a quick polish and a moment of admiration. His face is fused in their minds to spreadsheets, and they like the numbers they've been looking at. Leathery little men with little hair, they run their hands up and down Neethan's arms, pausing at the elbow, sharing confidences and dirty jokes. The duration of this encounter is say about two minutes. Then they depart, leaving Neethan free to chew on something that involves fish eyeballs.

It is Kirkpatrick's will.

Neethan'd really been looking forward to kicking back with a movie in the theater at his place off Mulholland tonight but, thanks to Bickle's sudden appearance, that isn't going to happen. No refuting the wishes of Mr. K. Neethan knows as soon as he is powered up on sushi and receives the figurative blow jobs from the executive class, he will be locating the exit and striding along the red carpet to wherever it might lead. Behind him he will leave a lousy release party under way in a decent Japanese restaurant with waitresses rigorously trained to pretend they don't recognize him. Already, mentally, he is out the door but physically he is rooted here with his agent who is laying down project after project that begs to be rescued by his involvement. He can play an autistic savant, a tennis pro, a gay hustler, a frustrated novelist, a blind violin maker, a psychoanalyst on the make, a ship captain harboring a deadly secret, a mutant capable of spitting poison from his eyes, a mortgage company representative, the Pope. None of it sounds Native American enough. Now that Bickle has laid down all the cards with regard to his ethnic identity, it would be nice to parlay that knowledge into a role in which he gets to play that identity and maybe in the process learn about what that identity is like. Because now when he thinks *Native American* he thinks casinos and smallpox blankets and that's about it. And if he gets bored being Native American he'll move on and be something else for a while, like an unfrozen Viking with a lightning bolt sidekick.

A mixed-sex group of studio people cross the room to the table, midlevel departmental directors and such, people responsible for budgets, shouting compliments on his performance over the restaurant's derivative music. Flock-like, they glom on to the table and chortle borrowed insights, eyes spreading wide in expressions that have as much to do with plastic surgery as with emotion. They are all drugged, Neethan figures, strapped to a biochemical thrill ride that approximates optimism. Or they simply conceive the world this way, an endless series of release parties and occasions to get close enough to smell the rancid breath of the talent. They appear pleased with themselves. They throw their heads back when laughing as if to make sure no one doubts the magnitude of the hilarity they are enjoying. Across the restaurant he catches sight of Myra's open mouth similarly engaged in laughter and pictures her lips curling around the tip of—hey now, here is the Klan again, igniting a cross in some poor Southerner's front yard. Neethan looks down in time to see a twitching fin of something on his plate. Rory chortles with the ring of midlevels that fortifies the periphery of their table. Now there is nudity happening at a table nearby; things have progressed to that level pretty quickly. The open bar gushes libations into marketing department bloodstreams. A man in a bow tie visibly vibrates at a table across from the disrobing table, jacked up on some kind of Bionet-delivered kick. Pretty soon someone will discharge a handgun, Neethan suspects. It feels like that kind of night.

It is Kirkpatrick's will.

Neethan stands up so fast his knees strike the underside of the table, upending glasses of sake. "This is fucked. I gotta get out of here," he says, though no one hears him over the laughter and music. He heads instinctively for the men's room. On the way he bumps into a baked-looking busboy.

"Which way to the red carpet?" Neethan asks.

The busboy nods his head toward the kitchen. In a few long strides Neethan is through the double doors, the red carpet of the restaurant contiguous with the strip of carpet wending through this steamy zone of screams and clangs, a couple dishwashers engaged in an honest-to-God fist fight, a sushi chef cursing in Japanese about his assistant's lack of a work ethic, clouds of rice steam, airborne plates, and impolite language in three languages flying across various planes of vision. Neethan barrels onward, somewhat unnoticed, past the walk-in freezer to the back door and a clump of waitresses taking a smoke break, to the alley, where the red carpet slithers around a corner and intersects with Hollywood Boulevard. Neethan stumbles onto the famous thoroughfare and sees that the carpet stretches ahead as far as his eyes will focus, block after block, westward toward La Brea. The glittering slutty trinket shops of a reconstituted Hollywood frame his gaze. How is it that after the world seemingly ended, this obnoxious place rebuilt itself from scorched rubble to resume the manufacture of dreams? Why had this, of all places, been a priority? It feels as improbable as his own destiny and origin, beckoning to him from beyond the lights.

WOO-JIN AND ABBY

"Who are you?" Abby gasped and rose to her feet.

"I'm Woo-jin Kan."

"The championship dishwasher?"

"No, the writer."

"Did you do this to me?"

"Did what?"

"Kill me?"

"No, no, I wanted to help you when you were dead but the cops wouldn't let me."

"I need to find Rocco." Abby propelled herself one-shoed in a direction. The editing felt off. She'd blinked in the theater beside Kylee Asparagus, surrounded by Federicos, as her life played out in gross caricature onstage. So where was this? This field? The roaring of jet engines? Some smelly guy with fucked-up hair?

"I need a phone," Abby said. "I need a shoe."

The only place Woo-jin knew to find a phone and shoe was at the Ambassador's house, so he pointed Abby along the narrow brick streets of Georgetown on a trajectory toward the Embassy.

"What happened to me?" Abby choked.

"You died three times," Woo-jin said. "Or two and a half times. Dr. Farmer has your other bodies at the morgue."

"I was watching a play. I'm confused."

"That is correct."

"I saw a ghost. There was a clone funeral. An orgy."

Hoping to sound helpful, Woo-jin communicated elements of his last few days. "My sister got hauled away by a helicopter. The Ambassador gave me a shower. I got diamond-coated steel wool. I saw an old man in the desert with piles of books. Dr. Farmer asked me to suck his wiener."

The two characters paused in the street and looked at one another. Their different brains arrived at precisely the same conclusion, which only Abby could articulate.

"Nothing makes sense," she said. "A permutation of me is stuck in some sort of fucking *zone*."

"The Embassy is close," Woo-jin said.

Abby stumbled, clutching Woo-jin's arm, which she continued to clutch even after she wasn't stumbling. She was perplexed to find herself trusting this guy. They turned a corner in a part of the neighborhood undergoing a perverted, reverse urban puberty, where infant industrial buildings grew up into homes, and came to the Embassy. The most intense light they'd ever seen radiated from the windows and the seams around the door. The house appeared to bulge, barely able to contain whatever produced the light within. Shielding their eyes they proceeded up the front walk. Woo-jin rapped on the door. A moment later

Pierre the imitation chauffeur answered, hat off, hair berserk, looking glazed and happy.

"Is the Ambassador in?" Woo-jin asked.

"Oh, he's in all right," Pierre said. "Is he ever! Whoa!"

"We're looking for a shoe."

"He's really busy right now. I mean *really* busy," Pierre said.

"I'm an official delegate," Woo-jin said.

Pierre impatiently nodded for them to enter. The humble materials of the house—wood, varnish, latex paint, porcelain fixtures, metal hardware, sealants, and caulking still constituted the structure of a house but exuded an otherworldly wisdom, as though the elements from which they'd been formed contained memories of a purpose far more holy. Light emanated from every surface, causing the air to slightly ripple. A door knob could barely stand the awesome fact that it *was* (Oh my God, I'm a *door knob*!) and individual beams of wood in the floor trembled at the majesty of being. Woo-jin walked down the hall, pivoted when he came to a door, and waved for Abby to follow.

"The Ambassador is in here," Woo-jin said.

Abby followed as she would in a dream, her senses propelling her to the doorway, through which she observed the elegantly appointed living room. On one upholstered chair sat a man with dreadlocks, colorful garments, and a scepter crafted from a toilet brush and plunger handle, beaming in the presence of three glowing orbs the size of your typical Spalding basketball. These orbs bobbed softly above three chairs and pulsed hues of purple and orange.

"Excuse me, Ambassador? We were wondering if you had any spare women's shoes," Woo-jin said. "And a phone we could use?"

The Ambassador nodded, in deep communication with his guests. He pointed in the direction of the kitchen. Abby's brain seemed to have been marinated in Novocaine. While the scene before her made no sense, the bewilderment was paradoxically a source of comfort, as though her neocortex had thrown its hands up and neglected to even try to process this otherworldly communion or whatever you wanted to call whatever it was that was going down. She followed Woo-jin, barely able to take her eyes off the beautiful spherical energy forms illuminating the residence with positive vibes. They crossed the kitchen to the room where previously Woo-jin had donned the tracksuit. In a closet they found a selection of fashionable shoes and other garments, many in Abby's size. Woo-jin excused himself and went to the kitchen while Abby cleaned up and dressed. When she emerged she wore new pants and a jacket in addition to chunky leather shoes. Around them drifted gentle music written by computers in praise of the gorgeousness of nature. Woo-jin handed her a cordless phone. Leaning against the granite counter, Abby called her apartment, Rocco's cell, the phone numbers of her friends in Vancouver, Rocco's work, and her apartment manager but nobody answered and no voice mail picked up. It occurred to her that she expected the world to operate a certain way, expected phone calls to be answered and some semblance of causality to provide lines between dots. She expected her intentions to find outlet in actions, consequences, reasons, purposes. But she was being thwarted, teased it seemed, prevented from making decisions that would lead her back to a system of gratification and contentment. There were other forces working, pushing her into an abstract version of the world she assumed she belonged to. She could fight it, jabbing digits into a telephone hoping one of them would pull up a recognizable voice while this weird blinky guy rooted through the fridge—which, by the looks of it, contained some pretty delicious food—or she could take her sense of rationality, stretch its figurative chicken neck across a cutting board, and lop off its head.

Woo-jin slapped together some sandwiches. "I guess you're probably hungry," he said.

"I died?" Abby asked.

"At least two times," Woo-jin said. "I saw your bodies."

"Can you take me to them?"

Woo-jin shrugged. "I could try. They're in Dr. Farmer's morgue."

Abby asked, "You said you were a writer?"

"I am going to try to attempt to be like a writer. I'm supposed to write a book about how to love people." It dawned on Woo-jin that this now not-dead girl might have some ideas on how to solve some of his troubles. "Do you think you could help me find my sister? Or help with the writing of *How to Love People*?"

"Who's your sister?"

"Patsy."

"Where is she?"

"She got lifted up in the trailer by a helicopter. She's a pharmer."

"Oh," Abby said. "Did she get taken to a harvesting center?"

"I have no clue," Woo-jin said, "but she took all my posters with her. And my clothes."

A sentence queued up in Abby's brain before it left her mouth, as though it had been memorized for a play. "I need to see my dead bodies."

Woo-jin still had Dr. Farmer's business card. He pulled it from his pocket and called the number. Abby watched, surprised, as he proceeded to have a conversation. "Dr. Farmer? This is Woo-jin Kan. Right, the writer. I'm with the dead girl. No, she's now living. Number three, yes. Okay. What? I'm at the Embassy. Okay. Buh-bye." Woo-jin pushed the OFF button. "He's coming over to pick us up in his car."

"What's that Ambassador guy doing in the other room with the glowing things?"

Woo-jin shrugged. "Communicating with visiting life forms, I guess. He gets directions from his celestial head. Do you like Dijon?"

Abby accepted the sandwich and sat down with Woo-jin at the little table in the nook.

"Oh no," Woo-jin said. He fumbled in his pocket for his mouth guard, slipped it in, then flopped out of his chair onto the hardwood floor. Abby loomed over him as the wave of ennui flowed into his corporeal form. This attack didn't take him anywhere. The house was like some sort of locked box from which he couldn't mentally travel. Instead he gazed up in bloodshot panic as Abby held his shoulders, as if that would do any good. His eyes went so wide they didn't look epicanthic anymore, with his face red and lips quivering, with tears actually squirting from ducts, the droplets catching air, raining into little puddles on either side of his head. Whereas usually the suffering had a source, tonight's suffering was all residue, traces of pain he couldn't stick to an actual person, diffuse hurts that bled from the Embassy's hundred years of grievances. Abby called out lamely for help. The door to the kitchen opened and in floated the three orbs, glowing pink, hovering like concerned bystanders. Abby stepped aside as the orbs settled, humming, on Woo-jin's body. He trembled once more then settled into a fuzzy drowsiness.

The Ambassador entered regally, with Pierre close behind, and waved his scepter in specific but indiscernibly communicative ways. Woo-jin coughed out his mouth guard and rose up on his elbows as the levitating orbs seemed to check out the pantry. "You should invite these orb guys to your place more often, Ambassador."

Pierre raced to answer the doorbell. The orbs disappeared up a staircase. The Ambassador set about making himself a pot pie. Soon Pierre returned with Dr. Farmer, who looked tanned and reasonable. Upon seeing Abby he smiled broadly. "How fascinating! What a pleasure to meet you alive!"

Blinding whiteness, walls of slabs. Abby hugged herself as the coroner lifted the sheets covering the bodies. There lay two females identical to Abby, the key difference being they were deceased. She winced in embarrassment at their nakedness, as if it belonged to her own body. Abby couldn't connect this new experience to the experience of snooping through Kylee Asparagus's mansion or watching the Federicos cavort in a grand ballroom. She couldn't connect it to what increasingly appeared to be an illusory domestic life with her Bionet engineer boyfriend. She couldn't connect it to eating a sandwich in a house dominated by glowing spherical life forms. She yearned for plot but instead absurdity after absurdity had been thrown before her, absurdities that alluded to obscured purposes.

"Like I said before," Dr. Farmer said, picking his teeth with an umbrella-shaped cocktail pick, "we believe that your selfhood,

Abby, has gone into superposition. What does this mean? Well, consider a single electron. An electron can be in one place or in a different place, right? And yet we can sometimes find electrons in two places at the same time. So it is with you, apparently. It's as if you're both alive and dead simultaneously, and this simultaneity is a self-replicating system in which there are various 'snapshots' of your dead self. Which makes an autopsy pretty dang hard, let me tell you."

A phone rang. The three living people looked to one another, each patting their pockets in that typical moment before someone recognizes the ring tone as their own. It was Abby's phone. But there was no phone in her pockets. Dr. Farmer leaned over the closest of the two bodies, the one Woo-jin had discovered first, and opened its mouth. *Show me yours, show me yours, oh show me yours,* ring-toned the phone from inside the corpse's mouth. With gloved fingers Dr. Farmer pulled it out and answered. "Hello? Yes, just a moment." He handed it to Abby. "This telephone call is for you."

Abby placed the somewhat moist phone close to her ear.

"Abby? Dirk Bickle here. I've been trying to reach you."

"I want to go home," Abby said.

"I want you to go home, too, Abby. You've been a real champ."

"I'm not following any more of your directions until you tell me what's going on."

"I understand. What do you want to know?"

"I want to know who you are, who you work for, why you really sent me to the Seaside Love Palace, and where Rocco is."

"You bet. First, as far as my job goes, you can think of me as a curator. Typically a curator is someone in a museum who arranges the art or exhibits, right? In my case, I curate *this world*. I initiate contacts between people, ensure that certain parties speak to other parties, put people (aka the *content*) in new *contexts*. Second, I work for Mr. Kirkpatrick. You can think of Mr. Kirkpatrick as being the head of the museum. The man with the money to acquire new—I don't want to call them *realities* but that's essentially what they are. See how it works? He finds and categorizes and purchases them, and I move them around into the most pleasing arrangements. We needed you at the Seaside Love Palace because we needed a consciousness to move through the world of Kylee Asparagus and the Federicos. We needed someone to discern and imprint their reality, that's all. Okay, your last question, about Rocco. It's true you can't get in touch with him. This will last a couple more weeks. I'm going to be completely honest with you, Abby, because you've been so great. He's going to suffer a little, but ultimately he'll be okay."

"What do you mean, suffer? What are you doing to him?"

"*We* are doing nothing to him. We simply introduced a particular reality he was occupying to a different reality. He will experience some physical pain but, again, I promise you, he'll end up okay."

"Why are you doing this to me? What did I do to you people?"

"It feels like some kind of revenge thing, doesn't it? It's confusing, and it's supposed to be. By the way, we paid off your student loans."

"Who cares about my loans? Tell me where Rocco is!"

"Something's been nagging me as I've been talking to you. Again, I keep referring to 'realities' but that strikes me as an overly simplistic way to describe what we're working with. When

I speak of a *reality* I am really describing the way a particular consciousness or group of consciousnesses encounters matter. Further, how these consciousnesses choose to *imagine* new configurations of this matter. That's really the state at which a metaphor of a history museum turns into an art museum. See?"

"I'm coming to Vancouver and I'm going to find Rocco. And after I find Rocco I'm going to find you."

Usually there's some sort of explanation for how two people get from one place to another but in this case there really isn't. One moment Woo-jin and Abby were standing in the morgue with Dr. Farmer, talking to Dirk Bickle on a mobile phone fished from the mouth of one of the dead Abbys. Next they were under a new city's rain, Woo-jin shivering beneath a plastic tarp in an alley off Robson Street, Abby back at her apartment watching a show.

The passing of garbage trucks and the roaring of clouds for a time comprised the entirety of Woo-jin's world. A pizza joint's garbage fed him and discarded pizza boxes provided him with blank pages onto which he wrote his book. He slept in the loading bay of a furniture store on shipping blankets, rose with the sun, and wrote until dusk under a fire escape. In the way that only small, forgotten places can, this smelly and wet alley came to represent the entirety of the universe. At night, through the gauze of light pollution, stars billions of years dead reminded the writer of the futility of his pursuit. He suspected he was an insect in the scheme of things, something to be scraped off the sole of a shoe. But the course of action his meaninglessness implied, to do absolutely nothing, would have caused great offense to the dude at the end of the world and his mystical refrigerator. The dude needed reading material. So Woo-jin wrote.

How are we supposed to love people? To get a handle on the question Woo-jin broke the book into chapters: "How to Love People Who Yell at You," "How to Love People Who Can't Wash Dishes," "How to Love People Who Throw Things at You in the Street." Was there anyone else he was supposed to love? Oh, right: "How to Love Dead People Who Suddenly Appear Back to Life."

Woo-jin had yet to return to the mesa at the end of the world or wherever the heck it was. The ennui attacks arrived less frequently now, triggered mostly by weeping faces in magazines, but when they struck they struck more suddenly. These skull-rattling brain fucks tended to show up without a warm-up act. One morning he crumpled on the trash-strewn concrete, vibrating with hideous sadness over a lost-cat poster, thrashing and spitting and eating his own teeth. Somebody wheeled up on a tricycle. When the worst of the tremors had passed Woo-jin was able to open an eye and stare at the spokes, the tire, the rubber-bulbed horn. On the tricycle sat a child with an oversized head and fluffy gray eyebrows. Really the only childlike thing about him was his pudgy body stuffed into red OshKosh B'gosh overalls. In his plump little hand he held a kid-sized Jamba Juice. At the drink's noisy conclusion he tossed the cup into an open garbage bin. Woo-jin asked this person what he wanted.

"I'm Pangolin," the person said inside Woo-jin's mind, the reception a bit scratchy. "I came to show you something."

Woo-jin coughed snot.

Pangolin climbed off his tricycle and as best he could helped Woo-jin stand, then hopped back on the trike and asked him to follow. They exited the alley, one pedaling, the other limping, tracing a spidery route through the city to the industrial outskirts, past long-ago billboards proclaiming extinct pleasures, to factories dilapidated and overgrown with trees. A creek trickled from the warehouse where Pangolin parked next to other miniature-sized vehicles—bikes, scooters, toy SUVs. He ushered Woo-jin through a doorway. Inside, in vast acreage where stacks of consumer goods had once risen to the rafters, artificial hills speckled with wildflowers undulated. As they traversed this landscape contained within a building, other wee folk emerged from underground burrows through little doors.

"What do you people do here?" Woo-jin asked.

"We're software engineers," Pangolin replied. "Some people call us monks. We provide solutions."

They climbed a hill where a tree grew high enough to brush the ceiling. It was an ancient apple tree, its arthritically twisted trunk creaking and groaning, bark scabbed and scarred. Over the course of a minute the tree blossomed, grew, dropped its fruit, shed its leaves, then blossomed once again as the fallen apples and leaves decomposed to dust. Over and over before Woo-jin's eyes it repeated this cycle.

"This is our qputer," Pangolin said. "To install the software patch you have to eat a piece of fruit after it has ripened but before it rots. Go, eat."

Woo-jin held out his hand and caught an apple. He hesitated, then brought it to his lips. By the time he bit into it the fruit had turned to mush.

"Spit it out," commanded Pangolin. "That data's corrupted. You have to eat it faster."

The next apple Woo-jin quickly bit, chewed, and swallowed. It tasted like any apple. "What is this apple supposed to do?"

"Provide you with a nutritious snack and fix some known bugs," Pangolin said. "Now you'll need to return to your alley to get your manuscript, then leave Vancouver as soon as you can before you get DJed."

"Where am I supposed to go?"

Pangolin shook his head like he was exasperated at having to spell it all out. "Where do you think? New York Alki. You need to find a publisher for your book. Here, take my card in case you have any tech-support issues."

Pangolin led Woo-jin down the hill, past another qputer monk who was bringing a trembling old blind woman to the tree. As they came to the door, Woo-jin asked, "What about my sister Patsy? Am I going to find her?"

Pangolin shrugged. "Beats me. I'm just a support tech rep."

Across town, inside her steel and glass cocoon, Abby sat on the couch in her underwear and a T-shirt with no bra, watching a show. She couldn't remember how long she'd been like this and couldn't think to try to remember. It was just her body and her show in a room that dimmed with the falling sun and glowed faintly in daylight. There was a refrigerator full of food; Rocco must have gone shopping before he went wherever it was he'd gone. The cabinets were stocked with instant noodles. She ate, defecated, urinated, and watched television. In the early days, television stations went dead at a certain hour and the screen would fill with an image of a fluttering flag. A recording of the national anthem would spizz out of the mono speaker. Abby envied those late-night TV watchers of yesteryear who'd gotten to witness the terminus of a transmission. Slouched in their living rooms with their Funyuns and lukewarm Pepsi in giveaway tumblers decorated with the Hamburglar. The idea that a signal could *end.* To stare into the linty fuzz allegedly representing a visual echo of the Big Bang. As soon as this show ended, Abby was going to get dressed and find Rocco. Yeah, right. This show was *too good.* She'd gotten *sucked in.* Here was Neethan Jordan, strutting up Hollywood Boulevard on the red carpet. A guitar riff looped over the footage, something sharp or flat and nasty that came from four guys in Sweden. It was the kind of music that made you think this Neethan Jordan guy was a menace to society. *Better lock up your children 'cause he's out to corrupt them with his magnificently erogenous body parts.* Neethan's feet strode across the field of red fabric running alongside the stars on the Hollywood Walk of Fame. Names scrolled beneath his strutting shoes: Anatole Litvak, Jetta Goudal, Sabu, Nita Naldi. Breaking the fourth wall, Neethan turned to the camera and said, "I don't know if I'm in my head, in a computer, or in a world that's actually real!" Cars passed in what looked to Abby like an old-school video toaster montage—a sedan full of gaping, fanged clowns, a grainy Zapruder-film town car convertible with JFK waving from the back seat moments prior to his assassination, an ice-cream man dressed as a carrot leaning out of his window offering Fudgsicles, a gaggle of rambunctious exploitation flick Hell's Angels. This wasn't the physical world Hollywood Boulevard, if such a place had ever existed, but some kind of lazy, received idea of it. The red carpet led Neethan to the intersection of North

Curson. A gas station, palm trees, abandoned cars. The red path veered to the right, north, into the hills. Here and there the husk of a house. Neethan's breathing was amplified now, signifying exertion and panic. The sun dropped. A white cat skittered up, considered him for a moment, then dashed into some bushes. Scattered tabloid news rags and hip-hop-branded forty-ouncers across the carpet's path. All these mansions, shuttered and dormant, gardens overgrown, vines snaking up gates and walls, curling around visionless security cameras mounted on poles. Individuals whose names used to appear in the credits of things that cost $100 million to make once lived here. A palm jutted up through the pavement in the middle of the street. Abby scratched her pubis: *scritch scritch*. The camera considered the sunset and the onset of utter darkness.

Intertitle: TEN DAYS LATER.

New shot. Exterior. Morning. Neethan asleep on the red carpet. Pan back to reveal the carpet stretched through a semiarid Californian post-FUS landscape. Neethan's clothes, disheveled from over a week of travel by foot. His lips were flaky, chapped. "This is crazy," he said. "I can't keep going on like this. When is this carpet going to *end*?" And yet he pulled himself to his feet with a swell of music and continued. A shot of the punishing sun, time-lapse images of it rising and setting, the moon, stars pinwheeling across the fast-forwarded night. A commercial for hair-growth cream. A road sign read: DEATH VALLEY. The carpet continued forward, across the desert. The music was martial, percussive, as Neethan stumbled ever onward. Close-up of Neethan's peeled, delirious face. Finally, amid the sand and ripples of heat, he collapsed face-first on the acrylic carpet.

New shot. Exterior, night, everything lit blue in moonlight. Oops, somehow a boom mic poked into the shot. Neethan still lay passed out on the carpet, which ran alongside a two-lane road. From the distance came the sound of an approaching vehicle. Pinprick-like dots of light that grew larger with the steady increase in volume. Turns out it was an ambulance. After illuminating Neethan in the headlights, the vehicle slowed down and pulled to the side of the road. The back doors squeaked open and a pair of Sikh paramedics hustled to the fallen actor, loaded him onto a stretcher, and inserted him into the ambulance.

There was a montage of close-ups in which the paramedics' faces were not seen, only their gloved hands manipulating syringes, unscrewing caps off tubes of ointment. They slid an IV into Neethan's arm, pried his eyelids open and penlighted his pupils, glued electrodes to his forehead, and unbuttoned his shirt to reveal a tanned and waxed six-pack.

Cut to shot of the ambulance, idling on the side of the road in the dark night.

More interior-montage footage, a syringe poked into an ampoule, then into Neethan's arm. The beeping of machines as the paramedics purposefully went about their business.

Cut to a shot of the ambulance, the doors opening, paramedics carrying Neethan back out on the stretcher, over to the place where he'd reposed. They lifted him from the stretcher and set him prone on the red carpet as the first featherings of dawn appeared on the horizon. Hustling back to the vehicle, the paramedics loaded the stretcher, hopped in after it, then closed the doors as the ambulance spat gravel and zoomed away.

Close-up on Neethan's face, eyes closed as the day's first sun rays foreshadowed the brutality of this valley of punishment.

His eyes fluttered awake. Medium shot as he rose, stretched, surveyed the blasted landscape. The red carpet extended ahead and behind. Yawning, he stepped forward. Close-up of his shoes, scuffed leather, moving across the carpet.

Wide shot, putting the expansive Western desert on grand display. Up ahead, a figure stood motionless beside the red carpet. Close-up of Neethan squinting. As he drew closer he discerned two people standing side by side. Fifty more paces revealed them to be a man in a suit and a cameraman. Media. The reporter gripped a microphone and seemed to have been conducting hours of preparatory smiling. Neethan cleared his throat and extended his hand in greeting.

The reporter took Neethan's hand and shook it vigorously. "*Hola. Soy Pefas Munoz de las noticias del canal siete.*"

"Hi, Pefas, nice to meet you. Glad to be here."

"*¿Qué puede usted decirme sobre su nueva película?*"

"*¿En inglés o español?*"

"*Español, por favor.*"

"Stella Artaud: Asesino Newman, *Temporada Cuatro, es la última temporada en la serie premiada de* Stella Artaud: Asesino Newman. *Yo interpreto al* Doctor Uri Borden, *un científico de clónicos quien se involucra en la insurrección y tiene que decidir abortar el Mesías o no. Es una serie estimulante, exhibiendo efectos de los más avanzados y acción en todas partes, con más que un poco de ternura.*"

Abby paused the show, unkinked her neck, and shuffled into the bathroom. Sitting on the toilet she propped her elbows on her knees and her face in her hands. It was night, she thought. She'd have to look out the window to be certain. After flushing she stood in front of the sink avoiding eye contact with herself.

Just a quick peek, she thought, just to see how I'm holding up. She squeezed the porcelain sink lip and tried to raise her head. She found she could only do it if she closed her eyes. Breathing hard through her nostrils, she forced herself to look. Her face was broken out, that was the first problem. It was hard to mess up compliant Eurasian hair, but hers had turned greasy and knotty. Black bags under eyes jittery and blasted red.

"What's wrong with me?" Abby said, and though she knew well the answer still she refused to admit it. She'd been around people in this shape before. She'd seen Jadie like this. She knew what an embodiment looked like.

Q&A WITH LUKE PIPER, PART 4

You made a lot of money in the tech boom.

That's an understatement.

Tell me how it got started.

I don't feel like talking about that today. Shut off the recorder.

Come on, now.

Shut off the fucking recorder.

Okay, it's off.

The red light's still on.

That's the battery light. The switch is to OFF, *see?*

This whole thing is bullshit.

Why are you angry? Did I make you angry, Luke?

I've been nothing but patient with you. But nothing I say is going to move you to do anything besides file your stupid little report. You're humoring me. Nothing I say is going to matter to you.

Of course it matters to me.

Bullshit.

Okay, have it that way. You can find someone else to help you tell your story. Be my guest.

[. . .]

Come on, Luke, be reasonable.

[crying]

Here. A tissue. I know this is hard for you.

You have no idea.

Can we get you anything? Better food? More books?

[crying]

We can continue tomorrow if you prefer.

No. Let's keep going.

Why don't we take a half hour, get our bearings, and come back.

Okay.

All right, we're back. We were talking about your early days in the tech boom.

Yeah, so after I cleaned up my personal appearance I started talking to Wyatt and Erika about all these little companies that seemed to be sprouting up around the city. Netscape launched. AOL was rising. We started going to smart-drug parties and talking a lot about virtual reality. You could get swept up in these convergent zones of Bay Area freakishness and technology and money. Someone would get a weird idea that someone else made happen with technology and then capital started flowing. It struck me that those who understood the languages of technology were those who attracted the most money. So I bought a computer and set out to learn HTML and C++ and Perl at community colleges. I'd hang out at Wyatt and Erika's and we'd drink copious amounts of coffee and take ginkgo biloba and write code all night. Soon Wyatt and I quit the reprographics company and I started working for a company called Netversive while he joined something called Boing Dot.

You gave up trying to find the proof for the brochure?

We did. I was a little disappointed in myself at first but, at the same time, throwing in the towel liberated me. Not that it mattered one way or the other. A week after we quit our jobs at the reprographics place the whole building burned to the ground. The official reason was faulty wiring. Wyatt and I suspected that something malevolent was at our heels but we didn't have much time to ponder the situation. Our new jobs demanded our complete attention and all of our time.

What did Boing Dot and Netversive do?

Good question. I still couldn't tell you. Really it all boiled down to making Web pages and developing the back-end systems to support them. That's what everyone was *actually* doing. But everything was pitched as "internetworking solutions for revolutionary crossfunctional database management" blah blah blah. Boing Dot had something to do with those annoying pop-up ads. Netversive's product was more like a suite of analytics tools. I lasted there five months then accepted a job at a start-up called iPeanut. An online peanut-butter store. But more than just *peanut* butter. Other nut butters as well. While I was there I successfully oversaw the launch of our jams tab. My base salary was $150,000.

How long did you last at iPeanut?

Not long. Six months, maybe? Because the company was bought out by—okay, you're not going to believe this but I swear it happened—an *online bread company*. The vision of eBread was to be the market leader in online sandwich ordering. I hung around the merged company long enough to attend an all-hands meeting with the founder. Nice enough guy named Ray. Completely delusional, obviously, a real Kool-Aid drinker. His goal was to provide a way for people to order sandwiches on the Internet and have them delivered within the hour in major metropolitan areas. I remember a heated discussion breaking out in a conference room about whether we should offer free pickles. One time Ray put up a PowerPoint with all this market research about how many people in America routinely eat sandwiches. The numbers were astronomical, as you can imagine. He argued that if eBread were to snag just *one-half of 1 percent of the national market* in sandwiches, we'd be a $1 billion company within a year. The company went public, I cashed out my stock, and walked away with $500,000 more in my savings account. I was sick of eating sandwiches every day. Meanwhile, Wyatt tired of Boing Dot and went to work for Skinwiggle. They developed virtual mannequins for online clothing stores. I got a new job as director of customer solutions at Iceberg Software. The obsessiveness with which I had tried to track down Nick transferred easily to my new work ethic. I would get up at six, stop by my favorite café for a triple latte, be at my desk by quarter to seven, work until nine at night, and come home or sleep in a sleeping bag under my desk. I don't think I took a crap in my apartment's toilet for a year.

What did Iceberg Software do?

Firewalls, mostly. Security for high schools, filtering software. I cashed out my stock there for three-quarters of a million. Then I went to join Wyatt at Skinwiggle. I developed a customer relationship management system there from scratch. Insane the stuff we cranked out by hand when there were dozens of companies churning out products that did the same thing only better. The good thing about working at Skinwiggle was I got to spend more time with Wyatt. He wasn't in the best of shape. The Internet aged him. He was chronically sleep-deprived and overworked. He started complaining about his chakras and the troubling condition of his stool. He bitched constantly about the company, responding to every perceived slight with biting sarcasm. The thing about Web companies is there's always something severely fucked-up. There is always an outage, always lost data, always compromised customer information, always a server going offline. You work with these clugey internal tools and patch together work-arounds to compensate for the half-assed, rushed development, and after a while the fucked-upness of the whole enterprise becomes the status quo. VPs insecure that they're not as in touch as they need to be with conditions on the ground insert themselves into projects midstream and you get serious scope creep. You present to the world this image that you're a buttoned-down tech company with everything in its right place but once you're on the other side of the firewall it looks like triage time in an emergency room, 24/7. Systems break down, laptops go into the blue screen of death, developers miskey a line of code, error messages appear that mean absolutely nothing. The instantaneousness with which you can fix stuff creates a culture that works by the seat of its pants. I swear the whole Web was built by virtue of developers fixing one mistake after another, constantly forced to compensate for the bugginess of their code. Then, on top of the technical fucked-upness, you add the human emotions of an office environment. People feel undervalued, hold grudges, get snagged into little vendettas, fantasize about shoving their bosses off the roof. At Skinwiggle, where I was making $250 grand, there were constant turf wars. The CEO was this colossal prick named Vikram Ramakrishnan. He'd come up through the brutal Indian university system, and was unanimously reviled by his employees. Every morning he'd tell his assistant, "I'm ready for my breakfast," and she'd go prepare him a bowl of oatmeal, cubed mangoes, orange juice, and coffee and bring it to him on a tray. Vikram believed the best way to motivate his employees was to either quote from the Upanishads or ask them, "How's it feel to be a fucking failure?" in front of everybody at department meetings. He hired a bunch of his misogynist cousins to run the development team. Big-time nepotism. I recognized right away that I needed to get the fuck out of there as soon as I could. This was the spring of 2000. Then one day I woke up and all the start-ups were dying. One by one they started to wither. Massive layoffs all over the Bay Area. I quickly sold what Skinwiggle stock had vested and braced myself. A few weeks later the ax fell and Wyatt and I lost our jobs. I had been prescient and purchased a town house near Coit Tower, which was where we found ourselves the day after the layoffs. We got really, really fucking high and ate nachos and talked about what the hell had just happened to us. Not just in terms of the layoffs but in a more metaphysical sense. We'd veered off the path in our search for Nick, Squid, Bickle, and Kirkpatrick. I did some back-of-the-envelope calculations and discovered that I could live my modest lifestyle for thirty or so years without having to work again. Now, I felt, I had to wait for something. It was like my life had entered a lobby, somewhere I was supposed to sit and read old magazines. Which is just what I proceeded to do, more or less. My days were simple. I'd exercise, read, watch a movie, read some more, eat in restaurants, go on walks. It was a life so exotically different from the cubicle-bound existence I'd led for years, and in many ways it felt charmed and fantastic. I started dating, had a string of amusing relationships that didn't last longer than a couple months each. I had no idea at the time the kind of bomb Erika was going to drop on us.

She and Wyatt were still together?

Yeah. I had plenty of room, so I invited them to live with me, rent-free. Erika's career was starting to pick up steam. In her line of work, fantasy and science fiction writing, it was all about building brand awareness around the name and ensuring repeat readers through a series or trilogies. She could crank out a trilogy in a year. And not thin, wimpy little books. Big-ass doorstoppers. Often I could hear her writing upstairs, bashing the hell out of her keyboard. She typed like a prizefighter. Extraordinarily disciplined about her work. Wrote solid from nine to four every day.

Anyway, when she wasn't writing books, Erika went to this support group for UFO abductees. You can imagine the place. Some community center room with an air pot of coffee, chairs arranged in a circle kind of deal. At least that's how I pictured it. According to Wyatt the sessions could get pretty emotional and often Erika came home utterly drained. Through the group she met this therapist named Wendell Hoffman who looked exactly how you'd expect someone named Wendell Hoffman to look. He specialized in recovering buried memories of alien visitations through hypnotherapy. Wendell suggested that Erika attend a private session in which she would be put under hypnosis and he'd record her impressions on paper during the experience. Nothing sexual or untoward happened at these sessions, if that's what you're thinking.

So one night Wyatt and I were stoned as per usual, eating takeout Thai and watching *2001: A Space Odyssey*. Erika came home and just stood in the middle of the room for a minute. At first I thought she was entranced by the movie but she was standing in such a way that she was just staring into the kitchen. People standing immobile for long periods of time isn't really an uncommon event among cannabis fans, so she must have been standing there a *really* long time, maybe even into the star-child sequence, before I noticed it was weird that she was just standing there. So finally I asked her what was wrong. She just shook her head. I noticed she hadn't set her purse down, and in her other hand she held a sheaf of papers. The astronaut turned into an embryo after some rad special effects and Wyatt turned off the DVD. "What's wrong?" one of us said again. Erika handed us the papers.

Are these the papers right here?

Well, look at that. My God.

And she transcribed these, or wrote them, during a hypnotherapy session with Dr. Hoffman?

I don't think he was an actual doctor, but yeah.

I was wondering if you might read this document aloud.

Do I have to?

Yes.

[. . .]

We'd really like you to read it aloud.

All right then. Here's was what Erika wrote during that session with Wendell Hoffman.

> 1. The following is TRUE PROPHECY for humanity. Heed it and receive enlightenment and love. Disregard it and incur punishment and suffering.
>
> 2. The ultimate holy purpose of the human race is to actively spread organic life throughout the universe.
>
> 3. Haeckel's Theory: ontogeny recapitulates phylogeny: "Ontogeny is the growth (size change) and development (shape change) of an individual organism; phylogeny is the evolutionary history of a species. Haeckel's recapitulation theory claims that the development of advanced species was seen to pass through stages represented by adult organisms of more primitive species. Otherwise put, each successive stage in

the development of an individual represents one of the adult forms that appeared in its evolutionary history. The embryo becomes a fish, a lizard, a mammal. Haeckel formulated his theory as such: 'Ontogeny recapitulates phylogeny.' This notion later became simply known as recapitulation." So says Wikipedia.

4. So it is with the life cycles of individuals and the species Homo sapiens. As the individual experiences childhood, adolescence, adulthood, old age, and death, these stages are recapitulated by the human race as a whole.

5. Childhood: Breaking away from our primate ancestors with the acquisition of tools, fire, language, pantheism.

6. Adolescence: The majority of what we refer to as history, the rise of monotheism, nation-states, philosophy, empire, democracy, and the rapid migration of humans to every corner of the earth. The industrial revolution represents the end of adolescence and the onset of adulthood.

7. Adulthood: The information technology revolution. A growing awareness of the mortality of the planet. Secularism and global market capitalism as the foundations of societies.

8. Middle age: An era of stewardship, of securing our legacy, and also of regret.

9. Old age: A great slowing as the institutions built during adulthood begin the process of disintegration. Yet with this slowing and suffering, the blossoming of wisdom.

10. WE ASK: Can it be that our responsibility as humans during this age of adulthood is to reproduce?

11. If we CAN reproduce, we MUST reproduce. This is the law of living things.

12. Should we reproduce sexually or asexually?

13. If our species is to reproduce sexually, we must first find our lover. Perhaps this lover is already among us, waiting for us to begin our courtship.

14. If we decide to reproduce asexually, we must seek our children within. These children won't live in the physical dimension we inhabit but will exist as cognitive constructs in a qputer operating system.

15. Our holy task is not as simple as reproducing to create a new species, i.e. Nietzsche's übermensch. Our holy task calls us higher. We seek to reproduce life itself.

16. Our holy task is to guide into being life that will thrive long after our planet has died.

17. We find no conflict with the world's great religions. We honor them for lighting our way. We honor the memory of the Christian god who claimed to create humanity in its own image. We honor the memory of the Eastern gods who promised eternal return. We seek PEACE with all believers and nonbelievers.

18. ~~Our first law: Inflict no violence on our creations.~~

19. Our highest principle: Love is the metaphysical framework upon which the physical substance of life depends.

20. We create life cognitively (asexually) and physically (sexually). The life we create cognitively we create

with information. The life we create physically we create with matter.

21. We pass life to the NEXT BEINGS as life was passed to us by the previous beings, our gods.

22. The messiahs appeared in order to prepare our societies for greater control over the transformation of matter. Societies guided by religion created the steam engine, the factory, the computer. We unburdened ourselves from physical labor with machines, then from thinking with computers.

23. Marshall McLuhan wrote that technologies were extensions of man. As we extend, we delegate tasks to our creations. We delegated the digging of our hands to shovels. We delegated long division to the pocket calculator. By delegating our tasks to our technologies, we become more fully aware of who we are, and are terrified by the alienation this awareness engenders. Our final extension is into NEW LIFE.

24. With computers we delegated more complex functions of our brains. With the Internet we delegated our nervous systems. With the Bionet we delegated our immune systems. With qputers we have begun delegating our spirits.

25. As our spirits become extended through qputers a great, terrifying void opens before us. Do not fear this void. GO DEEPER.

26. Confronted with this void we have but one choice: Channel the spirit into NEW LIFE.

27. We are not CREATORS of life. We are that which life passes through. We don't manipulate biology

into forms that flatter us; we employ biology to reveal beautiful forms that REJOICE upon coming into being.

28. The religious man looks to the suffering surrounding him and asks, "What god does this to me?" The newman looks to the suffering surrounding him and says, "I will relieve this suffering with my love."

29. The afterlife is a construct of asexual reproduction. Our old religions warned of Hell and tempted us with Heaven. Trillions of heavens and hells beg for creation. It is our task to create these states to host spirits. Heaven and Hell are the SERVERS where the new spirits reside.

30. We are called upon to become a species of creators. We honor our own creation to the highest by creating anew, with humility, love, and gratitude for that which gave us LIFE but is now dead.

31. Conceive of these truths as vision, strategy, and tactics. Our vision is to become stewards of life in our universe. Our strategy is to gather together those who wish to make this vision happen and spread these truths. Our tactics use the Bionet as a means of sexual reproduction and qputers as a means of asexual reproduction.

32. When we defiled our planet to the point of threatening all life, we came together to change. We suffered the Age of Fucked Up Shit. Those who remained after these years of pestilence, tyranny, and warfare opened their eyes upon a world boldly asserting its beauty. We ask, now that the planet is reawakening from its convalescence, what responsibility do we have to LIFE itself? Our responsibility has never been more clear.

> We are responsible for spreading LIFE throughout the universe.
>
> 33. Christian gospel celebrates the transformative power of God's love. We invert this gift. It is our love that transforms the new life. It is our love that makes gods.

That's it.

What did you make of it?

Well, first, we were high on marijuana. Second, we'd just watched *2001.* So you could have read us a receipt from the grocery store and our minds would have been blown. That night we treated the document as a form of entertainment more than anything. Erika was shaken by the experience but we weren't really all that receptive to the gravity of what she was feeling. We sat around the kitchen table trying to figure out whether this was simply a product of Erika's imagination or whether it was something else.

What did Erika think?

She believed it was a transmission of some sort. She definitely believed she hadn't brought it into being via her normal creative channels. She said she'd felt like a human fax machine. Was it possible it was just her imagination at work while she was under hypnosis? Maybe. Or was it really something sent through her from another source? That it was in the form of a numbered document suggested it was a kind of philosophical argument, something along the lines of Leibniz's *The Monadology.* And the actual substance of the argument, that humanity was intended to promulgate life throughout physical and virtual space . . . that sure sounded like speculative fiction to us. Not to mention these other technologies the document referred to—qputers, the Bionet, Wikipedia.

The next morning I went out and bought us coffee and scones. When I got back, Erika took her food upstairs while Wyatt and I messed around on a couple of his computers doing who knows what. I sensed that something was wrong but couldn't figure it out. An hour or so went by and I realized I hadn't heard Erika's typing all morning. Wyatt observed this around the same time. We went upstairs to peek in at her to make sure everything was all right. She was in her study, sitting at her desk in front of her computer, her back to the door. A blank Word doc was open in front of her. Quietly, we went back downstairs and got on with our day. Then the next day, the same thing. And the day after that. Erika couldn't write. Completely blocked. She'd go to her study at the usual time and sit there for eight hours. She was under contract to produce X number of novels a year, so this was a problem. She withdrew, and the more Wyatt and I tried to talk to her about it, the less she spoke. It was like her well of words had instantly evaporated as soon as she channeled that message. A couple weeks went by. She returned to Wendell Hoffman to see if he could help her figure out what had happened. She arrived at his office in the Castro to find the place overrun by cops. A couple hours before, a patient of Hoffman's had shot him three times then turned the gun on himself.

Just like the café owner who hanged herself before you could talk to her.

That's exactly what I thought. It felt too neatly tied up. The whole thing scared the shit out of us. We holed up in the house for several days, flushed all the dope down the toilet, and tried to get a handle on the situation. We'd taken this detour into the dot-com world, lost the trail to Nick, but now the case had caught up to us and was pulling us back in. And now we had the money to devote ourselves to it for the long haul. We needed to find the building on the brochure. We needed to find Squid. We needed to figure out whether this strange document that had come through Erika had anything to do with Nick and whether the Bionet or qputers really existed.

I had a couple friends, a couple hard-core geeks named Chi-Ming and Saltzman at Intel, whom I'd met in the trenches at eBread. I emailed them to ask if they'd ever heard of a qputer. Neither of them had, though Chi-Ming asked if I was talking about a quantum computer. What was that? He filled me in a bit. While a digital computer stores data in bits, which can exist only in a one or zero position, a quantum computer uses qubits, which can exist in a one, zero, or a superposition. This makes for a hellishly fast computer, a machine that can defeat any sort of digitally based cryptography. Even though the research goes back to the seventies, quantum computers still, you know, exist entirely within the realm of the theoretical. Quantum computers haven't been developed yet, unless some group of scientists somewhere is keeping one secret. As for the Bionet, no one we talked to had ever heard of such a thing.

A couple months passed. Erika still hadn't written a word. Every morning she'd go up to her room, and every afternoon she'd come downstairs defeated. She started getting these cramps in her hands, her fingers would get all claw-like, and Wyatt had to massage them so she could use them. We asked her if she might be willing to go to another hypnotherapist but she kept saying no; the experience with Hoffman had so rattled her that she was afraid of hypnotherapy altogether. Wyatt and I pored over the document for clues. He'd read about Haeckel's Theory in some freaky alternative medicine book. I was familiar with McLuhan because of my dad, and read *Understanding Media* again, finding a lot to think about in light of the explosion of the Web.

What about the Bionet?

We had nothing to go on but our imaginations. We ended up concocting a science fiction explanation. This was a lot of fun, actually. Wyatt brought his knowledge of various medical modalities, I supplied the tech knowledge. We decided the Bionet would be a biological version of the Internet, a monitoring system in which individual bodies would transmit information to other bodies or groups of bodies. The initial stages of the Bionet would involve already existing technology, like pacemakers. When a pacemaker detected a cardiac event, it could transmit a distress signal with GPS coordinates to 911, triggering a response from paramedics. Then we thought, what if the Bionet could also accept signals from a remote source, and say, dispense certain things into the bloodstream? For instance, what if instead of swallowing a pill, there was a nanotechnology pharmaceutical factory installed under your skin? What if the Bionet was an extension of the immune system? And what if it could respond to a pandemic by releasing the proper cocktail of antigens into an entire populace, effectively putting up a wall against a particular outbreak? Then we started thinking about the neural ramifications of such a technology. Remember all those movies in the early nineties where people had bulky cable jacks in the backs of their necks? What if you could accomplish the same sorts of virtual immersions without the wires? What if your thoughts could transmit data about your body to an external server? Or what if you just got over a cold, and your friend got the same cold—could you send a thought into his brain that could provoke his artificially enhanced immune system to produce the appropriate antibodies? We pitched this stuff back and forth, eventually writing our book, *Foundations and Principles of Bionet Technology*. We had little ambition for our manuscript beyond our own entertainment. We wrote it with a sort of formal, academic tone, taking after Borges. It was just as sci-fi as anything Erika had ever written. While we were working out the early draft at the kitchen table, she was still upstairs not writing. After a few months we had a complete manuscript, which we uploaded to a print-on-demand Web site. We did no marketing, no promotion, just put it up there and kind of forgot about it. It sold three copies in the first week, which we found more funny than anything.

Erika didn't meet her deadline for her next book and had to pay back her advance. This was our wake-up call that we really had to get her to a counselor. She felt like the part of her brain that wrote had been wiped entirely clean, like a magnet on a disk drive. Part of her still *wanted* to write, but she didn't know how anymore. And she started wondering if she wanted to write only because that had been her routine for so long. Maybe she needed to do something entirely different now. Maybe her time as a writer was up. I doubted that, because when the hypnotherapy transmission had come through she'd been a hundred pages into the third book of a trilogy. She still had this stillborn manuscript on her computer, paused midsentence.

Summer came and went. The three of us had become something of a family. I loved them, I truly did. Our Bionet book sold a hundred or so copies. Then one day, a week before Halloween, I received an email. The person said he had read our book and understood we probably had a "mental block" problem on our hands. The sender promised to reverse the process and cautioned us to practice extreme secrecy. We were to meet him at Golden Gate Park at 10 a.m. on Halloween. He would appear dressed in a Chewbacca costume and provide more information at that time. I called Wyatt over to the computer before I even got to the end of the message. But there it was, in the signature and in the "from" line. The email was from Squid.

SKINNER

Skinner pried open the can of fruit cocktail and stared into its murky juice. There were cherries in there, peeled grapes it looked like, mandarin orange slices, peach cubes. He brought the can to his lips and gulped the juice then shook the can to rattle some of the stuck fruit bits into his mouth. Not bothering to locate a utensil, he fished out individual pieces with his fingers. He considered crumpling the can and tossing it into the bushes but instead he smashed it flat with his boot and shoved it into an outer pocket of his backpack. Everywhere around him: forest. More specifically, the North Cascades. More specifically still, an overgrown, twenty-mile trail crazily wending through hemlock, devil's club, and salmonberry toward his childhood home of Bramble Falls on the north tip of Lake Chelan.

* * *

He'd really screwed the pooch this time, hadn't he? Leaving his family in Seattle, venturing out of phone range, crazy pissed off and confused, not returning to his daughter's condo to talk it out in a more constructive manner, just racing north, disappearing into wilderness. He couldn't remember getting here. Couldn't even remember what he'd said after seeing Waitimu's clone, though he imagined it hadn't been pleasant. Partly he expected his wife and daughter to pursue him and, in the act of pursuit, prove their forgiveness, but he suspected they'd been so thrown by his outburst, so startled by his sudden flight, that they'd decided to remain in Seattle to see if he had the guts to return.

Every time Skinner's mind returned to the awful reality of what Roon had done he slipped into a thought algorithm. First, visceral unease that a member of his family had birthed a *clone*. Then a more substantial wave of disgust that Roon had cloned *Waitimu*. At this point his thoughts came to a juncture. He could either relinquish the values of purebred humanism, for which he'd fought as a Christian American private contractor, and allow Roon's decision to float on by. Or he could reassert his commitment to those values in response to their being challenged. Every time the algorithm played out, he'd chosen the latter. Then, after he had doubled down on the rightness of his convictions, the algorithm demanded he turn his back on Roon and Chiho. Here, twisty guilt crept into the process, which he had to keep in check by further asserting to himself that he was standing up for what he believed in. But just as soon as the guilt was taken care of, his thoughts turned into angry fists. Why had they so thoroughly failed him? The algorithm turned to doubt. Maybe *he* was the problem. Maybe his were the mistaken values. The algorithm concluded and he started again at the beginning, back at disgust.

Out here with birds and trees the mechanizations of his confused thoughts boiled on in exile. It always astounded him how thoroughly indifferent the grand, natural world was to the agonies of human emotional life. Up towered swaying pillars of alder, turning sunlight green through the veins of their leaves. Most of these trees had sprouted prior to the FUS and would outlive every person now living. A rodent of some sort scurried in the underbrush. In this place the frettings of a father over his daughter fell silent in the terrifying continuity of geological time. At twilight Skinner came to a clearing where he pitched his tent and made a small fire. From his backpack he retrieved a roll of foil, from which he ripped a rectangle. Onto this surface he cubed some potatoes and tossed on a few slices of cheese, sprinkled on some Tabasco, salt, and pepper. He wrapped the food securely and placed the foil packet directly on the embers. Half an hour later he opened the steaming packet and ate.

Next morning Skinner woke, doused the fire with water from a nearby creek, packed up, and moved on, cresting the ridge around noon. This was the tricky part that put his walking stick to good use. In places the trail narrowed to the width of two boots, riding the top of a crumbling, undulating spine. Lake Chelan stretched below like an enormous string bean. Skinner hiked along the ridge for a good two miles before the trail dipped toward the lake, steeply switching back and forth. He steadied himself by grabbing huckleberry branches along the path. On the third switchback he spotted the church steeple through the trees.

Soon the path leveled out and intersected with what used to be a paved road, now a zone of chunked-up asphalt overgrown with waist-high sedges. This was the main road, an isolated stretch going from one end of nowhere to the other in a town accessible only by boat. Bramble Falls seemed to have sprung fully formed from the mind of an omnipotent tourist, with its collection of artisans' galleries and tackle shops, a magnet for pashmina-clad grandmothers and men wearing hip waders. Visitors used to come here in the summer to stay at the inn or the dozen B&Bs, to kayak and hike, to attend Buddhist retreats where no one was permitted to speak for days. Skinner had lived here with his dad, a retired fisherman and boat builder who'd escaped western Washington to spend the last few years of his life in the mountains. Decades later, walking through the ruins, Skinner wondered if he should remember more of these buildings and business signs. It was a documented side effect that indulging in too many enhanced memory trips chipped away at real memories, those ephemeral, less vivid, frozen moments so prone to distortion. Here was an ice-cream shop, identified with a dead neon sign in the shape of a dripping cone. The rusted skeletons of a few cars sat inert in the street. Trinket stores, the old grocery, a salon offering specials on facials and pedicures—all these places empty. Bramble Falls was a ghost town.

Skinner stood outside the two-story house considering the windows blinded by sheets of plywood, the yard with the tree where the tire swing still dangled from a plastic rope. Nearby a carcass of some sort, maybe a fox, hosted a buzzing convention of flies. Skinner walked to the door and opened it. Easy as that. Inside smelled of mildew and rot and animals. Light seeped through various holes and cracks. Objects that used to be pieces of furniture collected shadows in the living room. From where he stood he could see into the kitchen, where a cookie tin lay on the floor. The floorboards seemed to cry out in pain as he crossed to the stairs. He tested each stair with his walking stick before putting his weight on it, holding on to the railing as he climbed to the second story. Up here sunlight and wind fought their way through a window that hadn't been covered. Skinner shook as he walked down the hall to his old bedroom. The door was ajar. He nudged it open. The room hadn't changed. The football-print bedspread was as vibrantly green as he'd left it, books and sports trophies almost too neatly arranged on shelves. A toy fire truck sat in the spirals of a rag rug. This was all wrong. There should have been cobwebs, dust, peeling wallpaper. The place looked preserved.

A naked child with no eyes exploded from the closet.

Skinner reeled back. The boy jumped on the bed, spitting out sounds: "*Bzzzzz! Beeezzzz! Bzzzzzst!*"

Skinner ran. Down the stairs, out the front door, across the yard, gasping, back to the main road. He fell to the street, clawing at his face as he violently wept. Gradually he composed himself. The sound of shoes on gravel, thirty yards away. In a second Skinner was on his feet, Coca-Cola unholstered. A middle-aged man and woman jumped and exclaimed. Both wore multipocketed khaki vests and shorts, hiking boots, sun hats, backpacks laden with gear. The man bore a voluminous beard streaked with gray. The woman was considerably shorter, her face beaky and startled.

"Identify yourselves," Skinner said.

"For God's sake, wise elder, put that firearm down!" the man said.

"I said identify yourselves."

"We're doctors, Sal and Rhonda Vacunin."

"What are you doing here?"

"We might ask you the same question!" Rhonda exclaimed.

"We're here conducting academic research for a book," Sal said. "Now please point that pistol elsewhere!"

Skinner returned the gun to its armpit holster. "I'm sorry," he said. "I didn't expect anyone else to be here."

"We heard a commotion and had to satisfy our curiosity," Sal said. "And now that we've given our reason for being here, what's yours?"

"I used to live here."

The professorial couple both rose up on their tiptoes with hands aflutter and mouths agape.

"Why, how unbelievably serendipitous!" Sal exclaimed as the couple rushed to grasp Skinner's shoulders as if he were an old friend. "Rhonda, can you believe our fortune? How grand!"

"How grand indeed!" Rhonda laughed. "Oh, you must join us for supper. There are so many things we'd love to ask you. We didn't catch your name."

Skinner introduced himself, a little skeeved out by the sudden affection.

"Ah, like B. F. Skinner, the great radical behaviorist," Sal laughed.

"Look, thanks for the invitation, but—"

Rhonda said, "Oh, we insist on plying you with wine in exchange for stories of this mystifying hamlet. Do indulge us, please?"

"Wine, huh?"

"But of course," Sal said. "And merriment as well! Ha! Come, come!"

Skinner followed the professors to the building that used to be the town library. He'd spent many hours here as a child, studying histories of wars and assassinations, lost in action-adventure novels. The building was small but stately, constructed of marble and brass by way of an overly generous grant. The inside was a one-room affair, with high windows letting in dust-filtered light. The Vacunins had been here for some time. In one corner of the room was a neatly made bed. On tables were spread maps, papers, manuscripts, a couple solar laptops, stacks of photographs. Most of the shelves were empty but here and there stood books that had miraculously escaped the ravages of looters and silverfish, every one of them over a century old. Beside the work tables rose a tower of several cases of wine. Rhonda uncorked a bottle, splashing some Baco noir into a glass that looked clean enough.

"Welcome to our humble domicile," Sal said.

"How long have you folks been here?" Skinner asked.

"Four months? Five?" Sal said.

"Oh, Sal, we've been here over a year," Rhonda said.

Sal laughed. "One loses track of time when engaged in the passions of the mind."

"Not to mention passions of other sorts," Rhonda stage-whispered. The two giggled.

"You said you're writing a book?"

"Indeed," Sal said. "Focusing on the events that transpired in these parts during the early years of the FUS."

Skinner lifted the wine to his lips. "Holy—this is good wine! What is this?"

"Bramble Falls Vineyards, FUS 12," Rhonda said. "You'll find that the Vacunins only imbibe the finest libations."

Skinner sat down on a creaky swivel chair. "I shouldn't be drinking on an empty stomach."

"Oh, dear man, say no more," Rhonda said. "We were about to roast the most succulent *lamb* on the terrace. Do join us!"

Skinner remained sitting and pushed off with his feet, walking the wheeled chair out the back entrance of the library onto a tiled terrace overlooking the lake. A fire pit faintly smoked. Sal tossed on a few more logs and retrieved the cubed meat from a cooler, preparing it with spices and *fleur de sel* on an old book cart. Rhonda refilled Skinner's glass.

"I remember this view," Skinner said. "I used to spend time here, reading, watching the boats. That's what the summary says anyway. I off-loaded those memories long ago."

Sal shook his head like he didn't understand.

"I got rid of them. Useless memories. Stuff that was just crowding my head. They're not gone, they're just stored externally. I know the keywords in case I want to experience them again."

"And you remember the FUS?" Rhonda asked, startling Skinner with her forwardness.

"Sure. The first few years of it, anyway. There are gaps. We followed the news, watched what was happening in the cities."

Sal slid the cubes of meat onto skewers and placed them on a rack that straddled the fire.

"According to the summary, after my folks died I did my best to empty the liquor cabinet and get the hell out of my own head any way I could. You could feel the panic setting in. We heard about the bombings and public executions, at least at first. It's when the news stopped coming that we started really getting scared. Once in a while a refugee showed up at the docks in a boat, someone who'd escaped the worst of it. We did our best to incorporate them into the community but you know how it is with a stranger coming to town. Where are they from? What did they do? Who's following them? Homicides, insanity . . . Christ, I'm boring you."

"No, no," Rhonda assured him, pouring more wine. "Tell us more."

"After I buried my dad, I was drinking alone, passing out in my bedroom every night. It was a priest who slapped me to my senses and told me I needed to snap out of it. Father Dave. And by slapping me, I mean he literally slapped me. Came to my house, found me puking myself inside out, and hauled me up and whacked me across the face a couple times. According to the memories he told me there were was a band of bad men coming. He asked if I knew how to use a gun. We armed ourselves and fortified ourselves in the basement of the church . . . I remember off-loading certain memories. I remember disengaging from the console and looking at the card and knowing I had just deleted something awful. But the very memories of off-loading had traces of those horrible memories, so I had to erase the memory of erasing the memory. I remember erasing a memory of erasing a memory of erasing a memory. The original memory must have been something pretty bad."

"You need another drink," Sal said.

"I'll take the whole bottle," Skinner replied.

* * *

The next morning Skinner woke on a chaise lounge on the terrace, a half-full wine bottle still in his hand and several empty ones lying on the flagstones nearby. He dialed up a hangover remedy from the Bionet. When he managed to stumble into the library he found the couple fussing over their folios and notes. Rhonda wore a pair of white gloves and magnifying goggles and was nose-deep in what appeared to be an old phone book.

"We have something extraordinary to show you, Mr. Skinner," Sal said. "Rhonda, shall we?"

Rhonda grinned. "To the morgue!"

"I've seen a lot of dead bodies in my life," Skinner said, "but I don't, ah—"

"Relax, Mr. Skinner, it's not what you think," Sal smiled, clapping the old man on the back.

The Vacunins gathered a number of seemingly random binders and papers before they all headed to the offices of the old *Bramble Falls News*. The door had been kicked off its hinges but set back more or less in place in the doorway. Sal moved it aside and beckoned the others into the front office, a clutter of desks and chairs in motey beams of sunlight. Something had made a nest in the couch in the waiting area. The news desks held dead Macintosh monitors, office supplies, and here and there mounds of pigeon dung. Then there was the paste-up area—light tables, a waxer, fax machine, copier, scattered X-Acto blades. Rhonda pointed out the darkroom, a walled-off closet with a cylindrical door. Down a couple creaky stairs they came to the storage room in the rear of the building, where collapsed shelves, busted furniture, and discolored spools of brittle paper suggested a raided tomb.

A Formica lunch table occupied the center of the room beneath a dirty skylight. In the far corner was another walled-off room, a little larger than the darkroom. Sal dug in his pocket for the key and beckoned Skinner closer. He threw the door open dramatically and said, "My friend, I give you the morgue."

Every issue the paper had ever published was preserved on shelves in bound, tabloid-sized volumes going back to 1890. Sal swept his flashlight over the bindings, each numbered by year. The few from the nineteenth century, most beyond salvageable, consisted of little more than brittle brown leaves on the verge of turning to dust. Rhonda noted that only 1899 was really all that readable with the equipment they had. Wearing her white gloves again, she removed that volume from its shelf and laid it on the table. They had photographed more than a hundred years of papers so far, Sal noted, but there was nothing like seeing and smelling actual newsprint spanked with moveable type. Skinner scanned the narrow columns crammed with minuscule words. Property disputes, a gigantic trout caught, a new store selling dry goods. Another losing season for the Bramble Falls baseball team. A barn fire. Marriages, wakes, births.

"Here," Rhonda said, turning to a March edition. "I think you'll find this interesting."

Skinner squinted. A photograph of several dead Indians covered up to their necks in sheets, lined up on what appeared to be the bed of a wagon. Maybe four men and three women, it was hard to tell. A bundle that appeared to be a baby.

"The last members of their tribe," Rhonda said, "Gunned down by three men from Bramble Falls as they tried to cross to Canada. Certain folks thought the Indians were putting hexes on the town."

"Bramble Falls used to be part of the tribe's traditional fishing grounds," Sal added. "For a couple months this band had been living in an encampment a mile or so from town, fishing, hunting, staying out of the way as best they could. Then one day a teenage boy found one of the women in the woods at the edge of town, near the church. She was speaking in a strange dialect, which the boy described as sounding like a snake. A local priest, a man by the name of Wright, worked the townspeople into a panic and soon three volunteers set out to confront the Indians, leading to their massacre."

"This is our work," Rhonda said. "Finding people who hold some trace of that particular genetic line."

"What's so important about their genes?" Skinner asked.

"As you know, the Bionet operates according to various permissions levels," Sal said. "These are all granted and managed by a variety of agencies but essentially it means all of us have *read* permissions with which we can download prescriptions, limited *write* permissions with which we can upload our immunities, and some of us—trained medical professionals, mostly—have *administrator* permissions. But there's a level that overrides all of these. Super-admin permissions. We believe that these can unexpectedly appear in a person based on certain genetic predispositions. We've traced these genes back to this particular tribe."

Rhonda said, "A super administrator could ensure that the Bionet is never again used to enslave anyone."

"No more embodiments," Skinner said, and thought of Jadie.

From the morgue Sal brought out a number of other pre-FUS volumes, issues of the paper dating from around Skinner's twenty-first-century childhood. They had marked one volume with a scrap of cardboard. The paper in those awful days had printed photos of mass graves and decapitated corpses, images set amid ads for boat repair and chiropractors. And to think Bramble Falls was a *small town*. Just imagine what the Fucked Up Shit must have looked like in a major metropolis. You could pretty much plug any imagined scenario into the discourse on the FUS and come up with a delusion that somebody would believe. At times it seemed the only way to describe what had actually happened was to reach into the depths of myth. Folks screaming, running with eyes bleeding through canyons of concrete and steel as the sky rained asteroids that uncannily targeted famous landmarks. Shaky, hand-held cameras tracking radioactive Godzillas. Robot militias pillaging retirement communities. Automobiles bursting out of the twentieth stories of office towers. Vampires battling werewolves for supremacy of the night. And so on. Rhonda pointed to a local story illustrated with a photo. An impossibly old Native American man, sitting on a bench outside the drugstore, propping his knotty hands on an equally knotty walking stick, resting his chin on his hands. The story was little more than an expanded caption.

NATIVE ELDER CLAIMS EARLY TIES
TO BRAMBLE FALLS

> An unexpected visitor strolled down Main Street Tuesday —Joseph Talleagle, a Native American man claiming to be 112 years old. After purchasing a bottle of water at Andy's Handy Mart, Talleagle regaled a local audience with stories of his journeys over the years. Spry and good-humored, Talleagle claimed to have last visited Bramble Falls in 1899, though when asked for details of

> that visit the Native American elder demurred. "I got to keep walking," said Talleagle. "That's what I do. Walk and walk and walk." He then tipped his battered leather hat and continued on his way up Two Snakes Trail.

"We're working under the assumption that this Talleagle fellow is one of the survivors of the massacre of 1899," Sal said. "And if there are more survivors, or if he had any offspring, the super-admin genes are floating around out there."

"No more embodiments," Skinner said again.

A cold wind off the lake dragged dead leaves in circles on Main Street. Skinner imagined Chiho worrying in his absence. She didn't need his bullshit, though she'd been putting up with it since day one. Their courtship. One afternoon in a sidewalk café, in the days after armistice, Skinner sat across from an agent from Microsoft. Contractor like him, guy with hair like a 1970s presidential candidate and a grin so wide you could have spread a qwerty keyboard across his dental work. Name was Dan Thomas, something nondescript like that. Thomas wanted Skinner to accept an offer to work on the MS private security force. They drank coffee out of ceramics and talked about stock options. Dan Thomas fake laughed at one of Skinner's half-jokes. Thomas described the benefits, the unlimited free soft drinks Skinner could expect when he pledged to MS. As Skinner opened his mouth to say he still had two years on his current contract with Boeing, the guy's head exploded. Or not *exploded* exactly. More like cleaved down the middle as per a machete whack to an upright watermelon. An eye on one side, an eye on the other, in the middle a canyon of brainy gristle. Skinner hit the deck, unsafetied his Fresca, and tried to locate the assailant through the chaos of legs both pedestrian- and furniture-related. No second shot arrived. They must've gotten their target. A crew showed up, all bomb-squad helmets and flak jackets, and Skinner was hustled roughly into the back of an armored minivan inside of which he was briefed by a higher-up asshole at Boeing. What it boiled down to was: this Dan Thomas fucker had been about to assassinate him. "We had one of our guys liquidate him," said the higher-up asshole. Skinner thanked the higher-up asshole and asked who the sniper was. "Classified," the higher-up asshole said, and they dumped Skinner out a couple blocks from his apartment. One of the crew was so kind as to have retrieved Skinner's partially eaten blueberry scone from the scene.

Then there was a series of half-seen interstitial memories: raids, bad guys beaten against cinder block walls, Skinner jamming a coat hanger heated up on a stove into an informant's ear canal. It just got ugly from there, nothing this old man trudging down the main drag of his hometown a century removed from the horrors had any right to be proud of, all these acts predicated on fear, that epic wedge between the virtues one imagines oneself to embody and the barbarity of how one survives.

For a time Skinner kept finding himself in the company of folks who just keeled over in his presence, their viscera suddenly externalized by a silenced bullet fired from a discreet location. Outside a Krispy Kreme as he bit into a classic glazed, an approaching businessman jerked like he was performing a dance move but it was a round passing through his rib cage. While he was in line at a coffee shop, anticipating that cinnamon mocha, a guy came up behind him reaching into his suit jacket for the butt of his firearm when out popped his eye followed by a gurgle of blood. Once, as he walked across the street, a passing car's windows crinkled and webbed under a volley of rounds; later the authorities identified the driver and passenger as paid killers toting unregistered OfficeMax semiautomatics. In each instance Skinner swallowed hard and scanned the surrounding office buildings for telltale glints of muzzle. But *she* was too fast, too economical. She had probably already compacted her rifle into its components and blended in with the last-minute Christmas shoppers a block away. Skinner came to consider the sniper his guardian angel and fell in love with the idea of her even though he had yet to discover she was a she. He *wanted* to believe it was a woman who was saving his ass. As if to extinguish this romantic notion, Chiho one afternoon missed and took a chunk out of Skinner's left calf.

The scene was a crowded city park, now in full-terror mode, with kids being snatched up by parental types—adults whose legs wobbled as they screamed and fled. Skinner had become intimate with the cobblestones, each one imprinted with the name of a person or organization who'd given the city fifty bucks so it could buy some new playground equipment. And this was a ridiculous detail, but Skinner's ice-cream cone was melting and upended out of arm's reach. He was embarrassed that the sniper had seen him walking across the park eating an ice-cream cone with sprinkles on it. Of all the wussy things to eat. Not only that, a strawberry one. (Why were folks always trying to whack him when he was enjoying sugary treats?) But he couldn't stare too long at that sad and abandoned confection because the assassin, a guy who basically appeared to have bought his outfit at a men's store called the Assassin's Clothier—black jacket, pants, sunglasses, white shirt, black tie—anyhoo this assassin'd been merely clipped as well, or rather a round had obliterated his right hand, the hand he typically used to fire his gun, but unfortunately he was ambidextrous and as he reached for his pistol, part of his neck disappeared and it was like anatomy class in the park with the wailing people and the melting high-fat dessert. And don't forget that Skinner's calf was spraying blood in a sort of fountainy arc, and dammit he'd really been enjoying that cone! Then, within seconds it seemed, Skinner's guardian angel descended from her cloud and was hauling him up over her shoulders in a fireman's carry, wearing his 250-lb. body like a stole, sprinting toward the door of a van opened to reveal a couple guys with headsets shouting frantically into throat-lozenge-shaped microphones in front of a wall of surveillance gear. Chiho tossed Skinner inside and scrambled on top of him. He got a good look at her. She had a bob hairdo like the ancient actress Louise Brooks (though Skinner didn't know to make this comparison himself) and a vinyl catsuit adhered to her body. This woman, this sniper, his future wife, screamed motherfucker this and motherfucker that at the two surveillance techs and it was clear here that the deal with the calf, with the bleeding and the fractured tibia? That had been an accident. Whose accident it was was not immediately clear but Skinner, though in a great deal of woozy pain, just frankly didn't feel in the mood to assign blame. Then he vomited and there was that to deal with, so long story short, Chiho hung up her sniper rifle and retired, visited Skinner at the hospital, and before you knew it they were watching comedies together and sharing pieces of cheesecake. Then the marrying part, the kids, Arizona, and now this. A ghost town.

* * *

I am the reptile brain, acting out my dumb violent shitty themes, Skinner thought, stepping over trash. He came to the house where he'd grown up and passed once more through the living room, muttering, "*Please kill me now.*" He climbed the steps and pushed open the door to his old bedroom. This time he found only a moldy place where, it appeared, pigeons had enjoyed some good times. Nothing furniture-wise but a dresser. The light-switch cover was shaped like a baseball mitt. Peeling wallpaper. He stepped across creaky floorboards to touch some artifacts collected on the dresser. A baseball signed by a long-forgotten minor leaguer, an empty DVD Amaray case. His hands gravitated to a smallish wooden box. He pulled back the lid. Well what do you know, it was still there. He'd forgotten about it: his first memory kit. Back then these things were only toys, the Apple console an ugly chunk of plastic. Skinner turned it over and found a card still inserted in its slot, a dormant childhood memory. It seemed almost too tidy to him, that he should find a memory waiting for him here, that perhaps the hidden motivation for his journey to Bramble Falls was the retrieval of a pivotal, forgotten event. Perhaps the card stored memories of the exquisitely horrific series of tortures and executions that had twisted him into a warrior for Christian America. Or maybe there were memories of his mother. He couldn't engage the memory here. Too risky. Plug in a sequence of the killings he'd carried out as an adolescent and his brain was guaranteed to enter a permanently fucked-up zone. He needed Chiho or Carl to sit beside him and manually disengage him if the memory pulled him too deeply into the depths. He stashed the box in his backpack and left the house, half expecting it to go up in flames or crumble into kindling behind him. But it remained silent and inert, a hideout for squirrels.

Skinner mounted the marble steps of the library, lost in thought. He called out the names of the Vacunins upon entering but got no answer. When he entered the main reading room he thought he heard voices coming from the direction of Periodicals. As he rounded a shelf displaying magazines of long-expired topicality, the voices grew louder, more animal. In an instant, he saw the scholars, fornicating. Then, of course, there was the noise, the skin thwack of the man's pelvis against the woman's backside, providing a sort of percussive audio layer overlaid with their urgent grunts. This act they performed on a table piled with open tax ledgers, bound issues of regional magazines, topographical surveys, and the guest books of hotels. An open bottle of chardonnay tipped over and glugged its contents on volumes of city council meeting minutes. The Vacunins turned their heads simultaneously and regarded Skinner with slack-mouthed expressions that could have been surprise or simply a midcoital relaxation of facial muscles. Skinner sprinted from the building.

Outside, he leaned against the masonry to collect his breath, complicated somewhat by the fact that he was laughing. As his laughter mellowed into chuckles, he scrawled out a note on the back of a flyer for a long-ago concert, thanking the Vacunins for the wine. Bramble Falls had delivered what he'd come for. He figured he could make it beyond the narrow ridge tonight and set up camp in the woods. Only a few hours remained until sundown so he had to move. He pushed on out of town, up the switchbacks, through pines, the sun molten and rotten over the hills. He came to the narrow ridge and steadied himself with his walking stick, taking it slow. The emotional algorithm he'd been processing when he departed Seattle had lost some of its power over his thoughts. His own problems looked small, the cloning of his son more a curiosity than anything. Every few minutes his mind replayed the scene with the Vacunins and he laughed again. It was while laughing that his walking stick slid out of his hand. Bending to retrieve it, his feet slipped on the pebbly trail and he found himself momentarily suspended in the air. This state didn't last long. He fell hard on his face. Then, though it took him a few second to understand this was happening, Skinner rolled and slid down the east side of the slope, his descent slowed a little by scrub pines that struggled to stay rooted in the grade. He swore, heard the gear jangling in his backpack, tasted blood on his lips, smelled dirt, and beheld the surfaces of the earth chopped up and spliced together, intercut with bursts of cloudless sky. Coming to rest in a dry gully full of smooth stones, he lost consciousness for long enough that when he woke he was shivering in darkness. He struggled to get to his feet but the lower half of his body wouldn't cooperate. He slapped his thighs and felt nothing.

"This is some deep shit," he said aloud. He managed to take off his backpack and unfold his thermal blanket, find his phone. No service. Next he found the first-aid kit and clicked the key fob Bionet transmitter. The little blue light took its time growing to full brightness. He turned his eyes to the night sky, hoping to spot one of those pinpricks of light moving in orbit. He pointed the device south to a section of the sky where he thought a Bionet satellite might hide out.

Within five minutes, the device spoke in a woman's calm voice. "Welcome to the Bionet. What is your ailment?"

"Paralyzed from the waist down."

"What is your hoped-for resolution?"

"I want to walk again," Skinner said.

The transmitter appeared to ruminate on this, modemy scratching sounds issuing from within its plastic shell. After a minute or so, it said, "We're sorry. We cannot complete your request at this time. Do you wish to report another ailment?"

"Full physical."

More scratching, like there was a rodent in there working gears. After some time the device reported Skinner's heart rate, blood pressure, endocrine levels, sperm count, and a variety of other vitals. It all sounded miraculously within the range of normal, but then again this was an old model of transmitter and these things were known to be buggy. He was just relieved to hear there was no internal bleeding. His body produced an ever-present corporeal throb. He asked the transmitter for painkillers and within moments his hands went numb.

"Chiho," he blubbered futilely in the night.

Skinner pulled his body about fifteen feet to the base of a gnarled little tree and wrapped his thermal blanket tight around his shoulders. *Focus, mofo. Comprehend the situation.* He was trapped in this alpine divot, its sides too steep to scale even if both legs had been operational. Some sort of spinal injury had shut off the lights below his waist. The transmitter was really only good for menial diagnostics and over-the-counter wireless pharmaceutical dispensing. He figured he had enough food for three days. His phone might as well have been a rock. He could use his thermal to create a lean-to of sorts next to this little tree. He had guns.

* * *

The next morning clouds rolled in. Colder. It appeared he had pissed himself. He pulled his boots off, then his socks and pants and long johns. These legs were like dead sausages connected to the living meat of the rest of this body. Hard not to consider this as anything but distressing. He cursed into the transmitter, then was polite enough to receive another dose of painkiller. He plugged the tip of his penis into the opening of an empty water bottle and secured it with duct tape—a poor man's catheter—then pulled on his other long johns and pants. The whole process left him exhausted and frustrated and sore. He requested and was denied more painkillers. He hurled the Bionet transmitter then crawled to retrieve it, spitting and cussing the whole way.

"Chiho!" he called, her name catching in his throat.

The sun passed behind clouds.

He gathered wood and built a small fire and watched sparks rise and disappear against the backdrop of stars. He faded in and out but the sky never seemed to get any darker or lighter. He remembered the man on the mesa with his refrigerator filled with beer, stacks of books, and stuffed animals. Maybe that place was some sort of Bardo, maybe he'd pass through it on his way to the afterlife. Crazy talk, Skinner. He tried to shake the thoughts out of his head. Because the one thing he wasn't going to do down here in this gully was die. There'd be no check-in procedure with the great beyond. He was going to get out of here and get back to his wife and daughter and grandson.

"You really think you're going to see Chiho again?"

Skinner drew his Coca-Cola and thrust it in the direction of the voice. On the other side of the fire an impossibly old man in buckskin and ripped denim, with raven feathers appearing to grow from his long gray hair, poked embers with a stick. His lips curled over toothless gums.

"Identify yourself, old man."

The Indian shook his head. To speak he just looked at Skinner and thrust the words out of his head with his eyes. "I won't fight you."

"You're Talleagle."

"I'm a dude passing through. That is what I do. I pass through."

"I'm dreaming this."

"You're in a laboratory."

"This land, it's infected with hallucinations."

"We asked you to reproduce, and your offspring was murdered. Now you're on your way to screwing up your second chance."

"Who was that man on the mesa, with the refrigerator and piles of things?"

Talleagle barely shrugged. "The Last Dude. I walk my path, he constructs the message. That's our arrangement."

"You need to help me get out of here."

"Why do you expect me to help you," Talleagle asked, "when you murdered my kin?" The Indian opened his buckskin jacket to reveal a sunken chest. With a great deal of effort he pushed his hand into his abdomen, releasing trickles then gouts of old black blood. After a moment of struggle Talleagle grunted and pulled out his liver. "Eat me," he said, handing the organ to Skinner.

"I . . ."

"In my flesh is the medicine that will make you walk again."

Skinner took the bloody mass and considered it with disgust.

"If you want to walk, you will eat my flesh."

Skinner gnawed off a bite from the liver. Talleagle told him to chew and swallow. As soon as the meat hit Skinner's stomach his nervous system lit up in electric pain. Talleagle's eyes burst into flames.

Stars. Tears. Aloud: "Don't fucking kill yourself, soldier. Don't fucking kill yourself. Don't fucking—"

The sun rose and the fire dwindled to a cigarette's worth of smoke. The bottle connected to Skinner's penis was full of urine. He disattached, emptied, then reattached it. He allowed himself three sips of water and a couple bites from an energy bar. A smattering of rain forced him under the thermal blanket where he shivered and clutched his belongings. After a coughing fit he consulted the transmitter again.

"Bionet. What ails me?"

"You're getting a cold," the transmitter responded.

"Well, no shit," Skinner said. "More painkillers, please. And give me something for these fucking hallucinations."

"Sorry, that's kind of out of our area of expertise," the transmitter said. Did it sound sad? As the pharmacological haze suffused his body Skinner dug through the backpack. The memory console. This would be his treat for getting out of this mess—indulging in some memories from his childhood: a happy trip to an amusement park, a birthday party, building a tree fort with his dad. The beautiful tropes of a boyhood were hidden here, he hoped. When the rain ceased he set the console on a rock to recharge its solar battery. He spent the afternoon watching the indicator light turn from red to orange to green and thought about how useless it was to be angry at anybody about an abstract principle. He'd really fucked it up with Roon, probably for good. All the anticlone propaganda he'd swallowed—what had it left him? How could any idea that drives a man away from the people who love him be considered sound? A rodent scurried across his line of vision. Woodpeckers tapped paradiddles into tree trunks, sending echoes down the walls of the gully.

Skinner unholstered his Coca-Cola and set it on a rock within arm's reach. "Soldier, kill thyself," he said aloud, then growled, "Shut up, you sack of shit."

When night fell the Bionet transmitter died. Skinner smashed it against a rock and tossed the five broken pieces as far as his weak arm could. He added a few more sticks to the fire and ate a meager ration of food, enough to keep his body awake. The rain picked up. He cradled the memory console against his chest, and, suspecting he was about to die, pressed ENGAGE.

The memory was so faint that at first it barely overlaid the physical world's darkness and fire. Yet if Skinner squinted he could make out faded green grass in a yard, a stuffed bunny with one ear lying on a hardwood floor, a bowl of Cheerios. The memories were choppy, sputtering, not entirely visualized, struggling to connect to his consciousness through the ancient console. The software had a tendency to render memories in greater resolution in response to feelings of empathy and tenderness. He packed his belongings and prepared for a long hike. Wait, he hadn't moved from this spot under the tree. The packing belonged to the first-person narrative loading before him. Someone else's memories had gotten tangled with his own. Crap interface. The rememberer shaved in front of the bathroom mirror and said, "Memory console calibration. Remember this now." The memory card didn't contain Skinner's memories at all. These memories belonged to his father.

Skinner watched the courtship of his mother through his father's eyes. A coffee shop, afternoon light through the windows, the sound of a burr grinder, this woman who would carry him knitting with red and yellow yarn and occasionally sipping from a cup of Earl Grey. The next memory was a moment or two after lovemaking, the stickiness of belly sweat and a house fly butting its head against a pane of glass like a frustrated nugget of static. Skinner watched his parents hiking through an alpine meadow, coming to a ridge overlooking a swath of western Washington, breathing hard. His dad brought a pair of binoculars to his eyes and swept them across the horizon, finding a distant city in flames.

Skinner watched his own head emerging from between his mother's legs, felt with his father's hands the warmth of his own seven-pound body, smelled a wet diaper, heard wails coming from the direction of the crib in the next room, then watched his infant self suckling from his mother as snow fell outside. He saw wisps of hair sprout from his head, turn into brown curls, saw his own first steps, saw himself smack wood blocks together and stuff blueberries into his cheeks. Through his father's memories he witnessed himself vomiting all over himself, eating a pancake, pushing a toy ambulance, feeding a dog a potato chip, pointing at squirrels, crying at a loud noise, tearing apart a magazine, falling asleep in the crook of an arm. He was snoring, crawling, babbling, laughing, drinking from a cup, using a crayon. Skinner watched his father's hands smoothing, patting, clapping, buttoning the buttons on his clothes, wiping a tear, opening an envelope, maneuvering a spoon into his mouth. As he grew older the memories sped up, a slideshow of skinned knees and sandwich bread, fishing tackle and wood grain. Running to catch a matinee. Learning how to change a tire. Chasing each other with a football. Blowing bubbles with bubble gum. Boyhood! He ached witnessing it again through the eyes of the man who'd loved him most. As the rain came down in an angry hiss, the broken soldier shivering alone at the bottom of the world mouthed the words, *My son.*

Q&A WITH LUKE PIPER, PART 5

We were supposed to meet Squid outside the buffalo enclosure at Golden Gate Park. He would be disguised as Chewbacca and was somehow going to fix Erika's writer's block. It was one of San Francisco's pea-soup foggy days. The three of us waited in the mist on the bench as we'd been instructed, with Squid's painting of Kirkpatrick's academy, drinking our coffees. Then, after some time, around nine o'clock, came the steady procession of a marching legion. At first we could only hear them, boots stomping the earth in unison. Then they materialized out of the fog—storm troopers, hundreds of them, in formation. Just like in *Star Wars*, with the glossy white armor, laser blasters. I turned to Wyatt and said we really needed to chill out with the pot smoking. But this wasn't a drug thing, it was something else. A parade. A convention. Following the storm troopers was a high school marching band playing the Imperial theme. I laughed—it was pretty cool. Then the Jedis appeared, all these nerds with their lightsabers, then other assorted characters, Boba Fetts and Han Solos, here and there an overweight C-3PO, the bikini version of Princess Leia, stumpy Darth Vaders, some sand people, someone's dog dressed as Yoda. And Wookiees. Dozens of them. We had no way of knowing which Wookiee was Squid. As the parade marched past blasting its theme and waving its weapons one Wookiee broke off from the group and approached us. Really authentic-looking costume, about the same height as the real Chewbacca. When he spoke, though, it was a normal black guy's voice.

He said, "You people are really screwed, you do know that, right?"

There was so much I wanted to ask, so I just started firing questions at him. Where was the Kirkpatrick Academy of Human Potential? Did he know Nick Fedderly? Why was he named Squid? What could he tell us about the weird document Erika had channeled? But he'd have none of it. He just shook his head, in a way you'd imagine a Wookiee would, I might add. Wyatt turned the painting around and asked if he'd painted it. Squid the Wookiee did a little hop as if we'd startled him. He asked us where we'd gotten it. We told him about stealing it from the café restroom and how the café owner had killed herself. I sensed that our ownership of the painting was a mistake. He told us we needed to destroy it immediately. I could tell he wanted it but Wyatt was holding on to it pretty tight.

Squid said, "Look, I'm not trying to be a dick. You guys just need to know it's not safe for you to be digging into all this shit. Just leave it alone and walk away."

I said, "I think you're full of it. There's no shady organization involved in some weird conspiracy. I don't even really care about finding Nick anymore, to tell you the truth."

Squid said, "We're all in danger, dude. I'm putting myself on the line just talking to you. Do you want your writing back or not?"

Erika said yes and Squid/Chewbacca opened one of the compartments on his utility belt and handed her a tin of Altoids.

"It lasts about half an hour. He'll know who you are. He's expecting you. Just be humble and grateful and he'll take care of you," he said, then he blended back into the crowd, into a passing contingent of other Chewbaccas. We lost him. Erika opened the tin, which contained a single Altoid. To think we thought it was plain old LSD.

What was it?

I still don't know. I guess some kind of custom, lab-made psychedelic. Back at the house, the three of us sat at the kitchen table staring at the Altoid for a long time. I was worried it was a trap, something poisonous. Wyatt suggested we take it to a chemist. Erika thought that was too risky. Finally she declared what the hell, she was going to take it. We gathered some pillows and went out back to our garden. Erika had planted all sorts of flowers out there, installed a bubbling fountain. We put the pillows down on the flagstones and sat in a triangle. Erika placed the Altoid on her tongue and the three of us linked hands, following Huxley's advice, making sure the setting was peaceful and the people involved were loving and supportive. We sat there for a good five minutes waiting for something to happen. Erika closed her eyes. Wyatt and I watched her. After a bit she opened one eye and snorted and said nothing was happening. "Maybe it's just an extra-minty Altoid," I said and we all laughed. Then Erika's head snapped back and she was gone. She didn't respond when we spoke or when we gently slapped her wrist. Wyatt checked her breathing and her pulse. She was breathing a little fast and her pulse was up but nothing too crazy. Kind of like she was on a run. Wyatt asked her what was happening but she just shook her head and waved him off. Her pupils were huge. I kept my eye on my watch. Ten minutes passed. Twenty. At thirty-one minutes she gasped a huge breath of air. Her eyes fluttered and she squeezed our hands really tight and then leaned over and vomited in my lap. Actually she vomited several times on me, squeezing my hand so tight I couldn't pull myself away. Meanwhile Wyatt was squeezing my other hand so I was basically trapped there, one corner of a triangle, a vomited-upon hypotenuse. After about four blasts of this, Erika let go of our hands, wiped her mouth, and said, "Wow!"

What was her demeanor like? Was she still tripping?

She was completely normal. After she said "Wow," she confirmed that whatever it was she'd dropped was definitely not boring old LSD. Of course, I wanted to hear all about the trip but I was covered in puke, so I stripped out of my clothes and went back in the house and took a shower. When I got out, Erika and Wyatt were holding each other on the couch in the living room. The scene radiated a supreme aura of love. Not love in a sexual way, particularly, but a profound energy field of acceptance and celebration. When I came into the room, Erika saw me and smiled, gestured me over, and hugged me. Then she told us the story.

The trip began with a vortex opening in the sky, like a tornado but made of shadows. This swirling portal summoned her and she let herself rocket up through the atmosphere into space. She traveled at an unfathomable speed through the sponge-like structure of the universe, a structure she sensed to be omniscient and acutely aware of her past, present, and future. She felt she was being watched with curiosity or amusement, like a human watches an ant bumbling along its path. The universe revealed itself to be unbearably and painfully gorgeous, to the point that she feared its beauty might kill her. Gradually she decelerated and the foam-like structure of the universe reconstituted itself into stars and galaxies. Floating in front of her was a cylindrical object, a craft of some sort, as long as the earth is wide but about the same proportions as a soda can. As she approached she observed its worn exterior, scuffed and pocked by asteroids. She came to a metallic orifice, an anus-like portal into the vessel, passed through it with little difficulty, and found herself floating through a long tunnel toward a pinprick of light. As she told the story to us back here on earth she said it reminded her of a drawing of Persephone emerging from Hades that she'd seen in a children's book on Greek mythology. When she emerged she was sort of coughed up onto a field covered in the most spectacular wildflowers. Looking at each petal, each bud was like falling madly in love. Above her stretched a horizontal shaft of what appeared to be sunlight, threading the cylinder like yarn through a bead. She figured this craft must have been not unlike the one in Arthur C. Clarke's *Rendezvous with Rama*. I wasn't familiar with that book so she drew a diagram for me, like—can I have a piece of paper?

Sure. Here.

Like this, then.

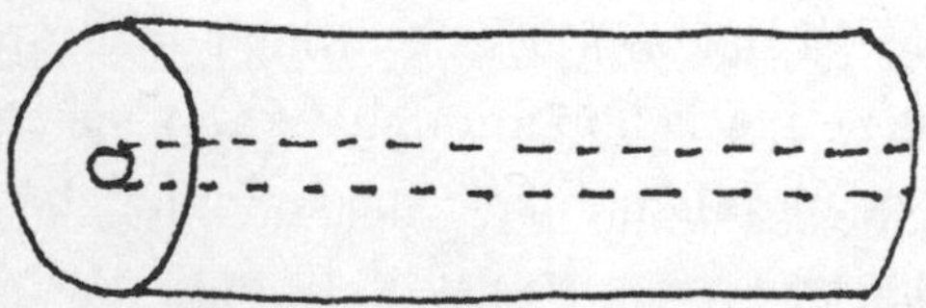

The inner surface of the cylinder was lined with vast forests, plains, deserts, bodies of water, all rotating around a central axis, a filament that provided light and energy, like a fluorescent tube running down the middle of a larger cylinder. Erika kept using the words "painfully alive" when talking about this realm. *Painfully alive, painfully alive.* A naked, dark-skinned girl of about ten approached cautiously. In her hair were vines and tendrils that curled and sprouted leaves and bloomed flowers as Erika watched. The girl held out her hand and spoke something in a language Erika didn't recognize. Taking her hand, Erika let the girl lead her down a path into a wooded area, beneath trees unlike any she'd ever seen. The trees were more like pillars of gorgeous, multicolored feathers—reds, greens, blues, purples—about thirty or forty feet tall. Cosmic totem poles. It was all Erika could do to refrain from bursting into tears of wonderment. They came to a rocky hill. Erika sensed that this was where the ruler of this realm lived. The girl motioned for her to sit on the cool moss in front of a cave, then scampered off into the woods. After a moment a figure emerged from the cave, a tall, lurching thing in a long red robe with a hood that obscured its face. Its hands were long, bony, and shockingly white. Erika wondered briefly if she should be afraid but was soon flooded with the absolute rightness of this encounter, like she'd been waiting for it her whole life.

The figure spoke. "I hear you've got a nasty case of writer's block."

Erika nodded. She instantly recognized the voice but couldn't place it. It was neither adult nor child, neither man nor woman. She asked the figure who he was.

"I'm Michael," he said. "Come, I will heal you."

She followed Michael through the forest to a stream over which an old tree bent its branches. From the branches grew fruits like she'd never seen, furry purple ovals. Before her eyes the tree blossomed and grew its fruit, which dropped continually into the stream, which bore the fruit, bobbing, away. Michael instructed her to catch one of the fruits and eat it quickly. She did as instructed, pulling apart the purple peel to eat the sweet, pink flesh inside. She said it tasted like nothing she could even begin to describe. When she finished, Michael took her hand and said that when she returned to San Francisco she'd be able to write again. She grew frantic. She had so many questions she wanted to ask him. She wanted to know if she had really been visited by extraterrestrials as a child. Michael said yes, this was so, and there had been contact between these visitors and earth for tens of thousands of years. For many centuries these extraterrestrials had been working to reprogram the human subconscious, preparing it for eventual inter–life form communion. The science fiction genre, Michael explained, was a means by which humans were coming to internalize, through myth, knowledge of the existence of other sentient life forms. By the time this communion occurred, humans would be psychologically prepared to embark on an interplanetary collaboration to spread life through the universe.

The sexual reproduction of life between interplanetary species.

Yes, exactly.

Oh, come on.

What?

I just find this incredibly implausible. Whatever. It was a psychedelic trip.

Disbelieve all you want. What do I care?

Continue.

You asked for my story, didn't you?

I did. Carry on.

I really don't feel like continuing.

You have no choice.

I may not have a choice, but you—you can't fuck with me like this. You can't—

Are you threatening me?

No. No, I'm—

Good, because—

I need some water.

Here you go. Yes, yes, go on.

Sorry. Okay. I'm sorry, I'm sorry. Okay, so let me—okay, so that's the moment Erika gasped and returned to the patio behind the house and threw up on me. Then later, after she told us what had happened in the cylinder, she went upstairs and resumed work on the novel she'd stopped midsentence some months before. The old boxing match with her keyboard started up again. I had these vomited-on clothes that needed washing so I put them in a garbage bag and dumped them in the sink in the laundry room. As I was rinsing out my clothes, something caught my eye amid the chunks of potato and scrambled eggs. A little key, like the kind used for safety deposit boxes.

What did Erika think it was?

Well . . .

You never told her?

I would have. Just—let me back up. I didn't tell you about the Chinese herbalist. I'd had this rash on my right ankle, a sort of psoriasis thing. I had an MD I went to who gave me some steroid ointment but that didn't do any good. So Wyatt suggested I see his Chinese doctor. He'd cleared up this wicked sinus infection Wyatt came down with one time. So I went—this was weeks before the meeting with Chewbacca—and it was this cramped little place in Chinatown, drying herbs hanging from the rafters, a couple of ninety-year-old Chinese women sitting at a little table in the front drinking tea. Dr. Wu was the doctor, middle-aged man, glasses. He parted some curtains and had me come back to the exam room and show him my tongue. Anyway, whatever, he sent me home with some herbs that were supposed to be infused into a tea. And by herbs, I'm not talking about basil and oregano. These looked like twigs and bark and stuff dug up from the floor of a forest. Horrific-tasting shit. But the rash started to disappear. So it happened that on the day Erika took her trip, I had to go back to get more herbs. By this time it was afternoon, she was upstairs, banging away on her keyboard, and Wyatt was doing yoga or something, so I thought I might as well go do my errand. On my way through North Beach I started to feel like maybe I was being followed, like I was in a movie. There was a big black woman with a kid in a stroller, an old man listening to an iPod, some teenage girls talking loudly on their phones. Then about half a block behind me there was this skinny homeless-looking dude, huge beard, sunglasses, floppy hat. If anyone was following me, it had to be that guy. Sure enough, he stayed behind me for several blocks. I stopped a couple times pretending to look at window displays and he did the same. Then I'd continue on and he'd follow. Whoever he was, he wasn't trained to follow people. I started to wonder if this was Squid, but Squid had spoken in an African American guy's voice, and my stalker was white or Asian as far as I could tell. I made it to Dr. Wu's and got my refill of herbs. When I came out of the shop there he was, standing a few storefronts away, gazing at red-glazed Peking ducks hanging like violins in the window. That's when I did something out of character. I walked up to him. When I was a few feet away he saw me and sort of jumped, then turned to walk away. I lunged and grabbed his shoulder and yanked him around. He fell to the sidewalk. I yelled at him, demanded to know why he was following me. He took off his sunglasses and said my name. It was Nick.

Ah.

I couldn't believe it. He said he wanted me to meet some people. So I went with him. I wanted to ask him so many questions, find out what he'd been doing the last five years. He was both as I remembered him, underneath that scraggly beard, and also someone new, some kind of mad street prophet. He struck me as someone who'd *seen things*. Things that damage you or at least leave you permanently altered. As I tried to keep up with him he muttered and mumbled a stream of nonsense I just barely couldn't hear. Whenever I tried to stop him and ask him to repeat himself he just said, "You'll get debriefed, don't worry." I noticed he stunk, like he'd been sleeping in spoiled milk. And yet . . . the guy seemed so fucking *alive*.

We left Chinatown and hopped on a series of buses that took us to Berkeley. He didn't say much during the ride. Just stared straight ahead mostly. I decided I'd keep my mouth shut and let this play out. I'd abandoned my search for him and gotten rich, found myself unemployed, and now here was the path again, intersecting with my life when I least expected it. We got off in Berkeley and walked for what felt like a mile, into a typical residential neighborhood. Little Victorians in various states of renovation. Dogs and flower beds, barbecues, that kind of place. We came to a red house with a door that had a little slot where the peek hole was supposed to be. Nick texted someone and a few seconds later the little slot slid open and two eyes stared out at us. When they saw me, they widened, and the slot slammed shut. Nick appeared to text someone back and forth for a while, angrily muttering the whole time. Finally the door opened and a guy grabbed both Nick and me and pulled us in. Big dude, wearing a UC Santa Cruz sweatshirt, red afro, handlebar mustache. He dragged us to a door leading down to a basement. As we descended we were hit with these really bright lights and all these voices yelling and arguing. I could only make out silhouettes at first but it sounded like twenty or so people.

The voices calmed down as a woman yelled for them to shut up. Then she said, "What the fuck do you think you're doing, Frog?" It took me a second to realize that Frog was Nick. Nick unshielded his eyes and spoke in a stammer. He said he'd brought me here because we had taken an oath of brotherhood years before and he knew he could trust me.

"This wasn't the protocol," the woman said.

Nick said, "I understand that, Swan. But the plan had to change. He spotted me."

Swan said, "Well you know he can't go back to his natural habitat now, don't you? Now that you've brought him here?"

I spoke up and said, "Look, I'm not sure who you people are but can someone tell me—"

The woman commanded me to shut the fuck up. Now my eyes were starting to adjust and I could see that Swan was a black woman about forty years old. You could have passed any of these people on the streets of Berkeley and not looked twice. I wondered if this was some new offshoot of the Symbionese Liberation Army or some other kind of revolutionary group. I was scared, I really was. Hours before I'd been sitting in the comfortable house I shared with two of the kindest people I'd ever known, and now I was back together with Nick, wondering if my ass was about to get handed to me.

Nick said, "He has 12.7 million in the bank."

Then me, dork that I am, trying to dig myself out of whatever hole it was that I'd found myself in, said, "I'd be happy to loan you folks some money to help, you know, your cause or whatever this is." I was thinking this might be a way to get me out the door.

"It's not money we need," Swan said, then leaned in close to me, staring so intensely I felt I was being audited. "Can you drive a stick shift?"

A stick shift?

A stick shift, yeah, that's what she asked. Whether I could drive a stick. And I have to say I laughed. Suddenly this didn't seem like a revolutionary group. It was just a bunch of punks, probably dealing acid and worrying about getting busted. So I said, "What, they didn't teach you how to drive stick in the Kirkpatrick Driving Academy of Human Potential?"

The room erupted again, shouting. When Swan finally managed to shut everyone up, she said, "We never say that name around here. Now please answer my question. Can you drive a stick-shift car?"

"Sure," I said. "Until recently I drove a manual VW bus."

Swan clapped her hands together. "Perfect!" she said. "Let's eat, what do you say?"

Suddenly everyone was being cordial and helping me with my coat, showing me to a place at a table. Swan sat on one side of me, Nick on the other. One by one the other members of the group introduced themselves. They all had animal names. Muskrat, Squirrel, Crow, Salmon, Bear, Owl, Horse. From upstairs came big bowls and platters of food, that good hippie food I'd grown to love. Emboldened by the sudden change of tone, I asked Swan who they were.

"We're the dropouts," she said. "Dropouts from that institution you mentioned."

"So it does exist," I said.

She said, "Of course it exists. It's a foundation, an incubator designed to cultivate inventors. Those who have the potential to bring about paradigmatic change. It seeks to direct the course of history by coordinating the efforts of individuals who fit certain profiles. It brings these individuals together in the hopes that when they work collaboratively, the magnitude of the historical shifts they bring about will be greater than if these individuals had been working alone."

"Like gestalt theory."

Swan rolled her eyes and said, "Yeah, something like that."

"Why did you drop out?" I asked.

Swan avoided the question. "You do realize your life with Wyatt and Erika is over, don't you?" she said. "That you've chosen to pursue this path again, and that your efforts must now be synonymous with the efforts of the collective?"

I said sure, whatever. The hokey SLA mind-trick shtick wasn't working on me. Maybe if they'd had submachine guns shoved at my ribs I'd have felt differently but for now at least all I saw were young leftists eating hummus and talkin' 'bout a revolution. I'd been immersed among these types for years in the Bay Area. A lot of talk, little to no action. I knew I'd be able to return home anytime I wanted, regardless of what these blowhards were saying. For all I knew the Kirkpatrick Academy of Human Potential was one of those night-course places upstairs from a Korean grocery store offering certificates in "business studies." So I just went along with the game and said, "Yes, I know my old life is over."

I think Swan could tell I was bullshitting her but she continued. "Have you ever met a slave, Luke?" she asked. The question took me aback, coming from a black person. I stammered out a no. She said, "Really? You've never been to a mall? You've never watched shoppers with their carts piled with soda and microwavable food? You've never stayed in a hotel where a fifty-year-old Mexican mother of six scrubs your shit stains off the toilet bowl? You've never watched TV for five hours straight?" She went on to explain their theory, sort of a pseudo-Marxist vision of the *gemeinschaft* and the *gessellschaft,* the ruling class and the underclass, the proletariat and the elite, the haves and have-nots, the first world and the third. According to Swan, Mr. Kirkpatrick, whose name she refused to utter, had founded the academy as a method to ensure that those in power stayed in power, that those enslaved remained enslaved. The dropouts were the students who refused to go along with this philosophy and had instead allied themselves with the underclass, struggling for equality. Or maybe it was the other way around. It was all a little fuzzy. I asked her about Dirk Bickle. She said Bickle was one of Kirkpatrick's agents, traveling the world in search of candidates to ensnare in the program.

There was a noise upstairs, the front door opening. Everyone in the basement got excited, saying, "They're home! They're home!" I started to ask Swan who they were talking about but she motioned for me to be quiet and listen. I heard the door close, people's voices. I mouthed "Who is it?" to Nick. He whispered back, "The Millers."

I whispered, "You guys are hiding in the basement of a family's house?"

Swan shushed me. A couple pairs of footsteps creaked overhead. A girl's voice. Swan said in a low tone, "They're our test family. Jim and Helen Miller. They have two daughters, aged nine and six and a half, Melissa and Gina. Would you like to observe them?"

I said sure, why not, and followed Swan upstairs. We came up from the basement as Helen Miller was coming through the front door with a bag of groceries. I made a little startled jump, but Helen Miller walked right past me like I wasn't there. Like one of those movies where the unseen dead observe the living.

She put the groceries on the kitchen island and Jim walked into the room, gave her a kiss, and asked her how her day had been. Then Melissa came through the door, carrying her sheet music from piano class. Swan and I stood off to the side in the kitchen watching this whole scene go down. Was it some weird brand of street theater? Were these actors? They absolutely ignored us, going about their business in what was ostensibly their home, the basement of which was occupied by some fringe anarchist movement. I wondered if I was the target of an elaborately staged practical joke. I actually looked around the room trying to find cameras.

"The reason I asked you if you can drive a stick is that we need someone to steal the Millers' Mazda," Swan said. "The rest of us can only drive automatics. You'll take Frog with you. He knows where you need to go."

You have to remember that this was a day in which I'd met Chewbacca, gotten puked on, run into Nick after years of not knowing his whereabouts, and enjoyed some vegetarian fare with people with animal names in the basement of a painted lady outside Berkeley. I was seriously questioning my sanity. Swan seemed to recognize that I was going through some variety of psychic crisis and laid her hand on my shoulder. "You're not crazy," she said as the Millers removed a casserole from the microwave and sat down to eat. She told me that I was already involved, whether I wanted to be or not. There'd been a time, she said, when I had my life to myself, when I was merely curious about the academy, but now, after helping decipher the document Erika had channeled and by writing a pseudo-academic paper on the Bionet and qputers as a lark, I had entered the labyrinth. I was a fly, she said, a fly crawling down the throat of a Venus flytrap, my path heading in one relentless direction. That was my new name, she said. I was no longer Luke Piper. My name was Fly. I watched the Millers talk about baseball scores and weather reports, their silverware clinking on their plates. And even though I was standing in the same room, I was no longer part of their world, if I ever had been. This was what I had been yearning for all along: a secret mission, a purpose so mystifying I might only learn of its nature in the process of fulfilling it. I had no choice in the matter. I asked Swan where I could find the car keys.

And you took the car.

I picked the keys up off the kitchen island, went out to the curb with Nick, got in the driver's seat of the Miata and backed out. Just like that. As we left the neighborhood I asked him where we were going. He told me Arizona, to someplace far from civilization. We left the Bay Area like we were escaping the looming wave of a tsunami, both of us laughing, suddenly embedded in these lives where there was no distance between impulse and experience. Fuck, I can't tell you how liberated I felt! To just leave. And the farther away from the city we got, the more Nick emerged from his shell, like he needed to be outside the blast zone of those crazies to get back his old personality. I still had so many questions for him but figured I'd give him whatever time he needed to regain my trust. Finally, over burgers at some roadside place, at around midnight, he told me something that made me take this trip more seriously. "Your friend," he said. "The girl? Erika? She visited the seed ship today."

I asked what he meant. He described a project the academy was working on, to build a space ship that would contain the basic ingredients needed to terraform a hospitable planet. He called this the seed ship. According to Nick, the drug Squid gave Erika operated as a delivery method to the ship through time. After she'd erroneously received the transmission about the future of life in the universe, her writing had been misplaced on the seed ship. So the dropouts had to send her there to retrieve it. The whole thing sounded completely nuts to me but I couldn't explain how he could have known details about Erika's trip unless he'd been spying on us. Which he had, actually, though he never got close enough to see Erika tripping or hear her version of the trip. When we'd received the drug from Chewbacca at the park, Nick had been watching us and followed us home. He'd been assigned this duty by Swan, who wanted to make sure everything went all right with Erika. He'd watched the house from the café across the street and followed me when I went to do my errand.

Why did he follow you?

He needed to get confirmation that Erika's trip had been a success. And he needed to get the key that she'd vomited up.

He knew about that?

Yeah. That's when I started getting really freaked out. He asked me about the key and I said I didn't know anything about a key, even though it was in my wallet. He seemed to believe me. We got back on the road and drove through the night. I asked him why the academy existed. He said it existed to perpetuate life in the universe, that this calling was ancient, and that there were certain races spread throughout the universe who were responsible for keeping life going. He called them the stewards. There were thousands if not millions of steward races out there.

Some stewards succeeded, others failed, but all were driven by the imperative to seek out conditions suitable for sustaining life. That's how we got here, on earth, he told me. Earth life was created billions of years ago by a long-extinct steward race. They set evolution in motion, and intervened on a few occasions, like when they initiated the messiah program.

Jesus?

Jesus, Muhammad, Buddha. They all encouraged humanity to evolve at a pivotal moment, with religion providing the societal framework that spurred improvements to the cerebral cortex and rational thought, technology—all the means by which humanity would one day come to possess the power and responsibilities of a steward race. But there was a complicating factor. Humanity would have to push itself to near extinction to reach that point. The technologies we needed to evolve into a steward race were the same as those that would recover our destroyed planet. It was true. We were ecologically doomed, past the point where our half-assed gestures could do any good. We were all going to die in a big way. And Nick wasn't talking about little old nuclear warheads. We hadn't yet seen the worst, he said. We were about to enter a period of history when we would witness horrors that could only be described through metaphor. Global warming was part of it. Nuclear war was part of it. Genocide was part of it. Islamic and Christian radicalism were part of it. Overconsumption and superviruses were part of it. But they were only *small* parts of it. These dark days were just around the corner, Nick assured me, but afterward there would be survivors. And these survivors would claim the mantle of a steward race to spread the beauty of life through the universe. After the period of darkness there would rise a new age. An afterlife. The reason the dropouts split from the academy, he said, was because they disagreed with Mr. Kirkpatrick about the urgency of the moment. According to Nick, Mr. Kirkpatrick's approach was to patiently wait for the great unraveling to take place. The dropouts wanted this new age to start *now*. They wanted to kick-start it.

We arrived in Phoenix and drove another few hours into the desert, I don't even know where really. Nick told me where to go. Up into the hills somewhere, onto a mesa. I was exhausted and didn't know what to believe anymore. Finally Nick told me to pull over. We got out of the car and Nick popped the trunk, inside of which were a couple backpacks, food, water, bed rolls. He told me we needed to hike a ways before we got to where we were headed. I followed him, sweating, fatigued, wishing I was back in San Francisco with Wyatt and Erika. I hadn't even told them I'd left. They were probably worried about me. As the day wore on I began to suspect Nick was putting me on. We started arguing. I accused him of being in a Scientology-lite cult. Nick just kept walking, a few paces ahead of me. I wanted to go home. This was old now. This wasn't an adventure anymore. I was complaining when we crested a little hill and came upon the encampment.

Encampment?

That's what you could call it. It was the weirdest thing. Out in the middle of nowhere and there's a refrigerator standing there. The encampment was this little circle of things around the coals of a fire pit. A tire, a pile of stuffed animals, a pile of books.

"What the fuck is this place?" I said.

Nick said, "This is where the Last Dude makes his stand."

That's when he shot me.

NEETHAN

The red polyfiber carpet traced a path through the forest of impossibly ancient redwoods. Neethan F. Jordan, his beard almost completely filled in, hiked with walking stick in hand, his clothes soaked through with sweat, his necktie now tied around his head as if he'd stepped out of a commercial in which office workers comically erupt in a *Lord of the Flies*–style social conflagration. His breath banged its tin cup against the insides of his ribs. Up ahead, hovering about eight feet above the carpet, glowed an incandescent heart about the size of three basketballs put together into a really big basketball. The heart thudded, bobbed a bit in the air, and radiated shimmery rays of light like one of those Mexican El Corazon tattoos. Neethan approached the glowing object and positioned himself beneath it, then jumped, his head getting swallowed momentarily in the hologram-like whatever-it-was. There was a noise, a pleasant chime in his ears, after which he understood that he had been granted an extra life.

Up ahead floated a Nike Air sawed-off shotgun. Neethan jogged to it, jumped, and made contact with the holographic weapon. In an instant he heard the chime and looked down to find the shotgun in his hands. Why the hell did he need a gun? He pressed on through the trees, watching the sky through the pixelly boughs.

They appeared in short order: undead folks in shabby clothes. Coming out from behind trees and bushes, ambling toward him wielding little more than chunks of wood, moaning, attempting some kind of slow-motion attack. Neethan pumped the shotgun and aimed for the head of the closest one. The undead guy's cranium exploded in a confetti-like atomization of brain and skull fragments, leaving the spurting stump of a spine protruding from the neck. It fell to its knees and then the body simply vanished. A lady zombie, looked like an ex-receptionist, lurched at him with a bad limp. He shot this one in the chest, and for a moment glimpsed the path ahead through the gaping hole his buckshot had created. This zombie vanished, too. A demographically balanced array of flesh-eating zombies began to appear on the trail in greater frequency, shuffling, arms outstretched, mouths hanging open, skin falling off bones, eyeballs missing, hair slimy and thin and black over their green faces. Neethan spied a box of ammunition sitting on a tree stump and aimed for it. When the blast hit, the shotgun automatically reloaded. The zombies started coming faster, more frantically, more enthused about feasting on his brain. The quicker he could pump the shotgun and squeeze off a shell, the quicker they seemed to come, until at last one of them was able to take a swipe at his face at close range.

A curtain of red fell over Neethan's vision.

For a sliver of a moment, passing so quickly he didn't register what was happening until much later, all was darkness and silence. As dark and silent as if he had spelunked the depths of a cave and then, reaching the deepest, darkest place in the cave, stuck his head down his own throat and disappeared inside his own body. A darkness final and unremitting, a darkness that offered no acknowledgment that there could ever be any illumination, an absolute black, a blackness so extreme it coated him and penetrated his skin, rendering everything that might have color when exposed to light completely transparent and thus now only a vessel for this categorically absolute absence of light.

Then he regained consciousness, if one wanted to call it that, standing again on the trail with the shotgun in hand, a few paces back from where he'd last fallen, and as he progressed the same zombies came out from the same hiding places and he blasted them again, sweeping the weapon back and forth. The path took a turn to the right and around the corner floated a new gun, looked like a machine gun manufactured by Dell. He shot this gun with his current gun and the new gun materialized in his hands. Turning this gun on the zombie onslaught, he trudged toward the tree line to a bluff overlooking the vast Pacific. When he felt confident that all the zombies had been vanquished and none would sneak up behind him, he sat on the forest floor and gazed out to the sea, a masterpiece of color and texture. Waves individually curled and dissolved, each one bound up in vast equations, sunlight bouncing off the rippling and roiling surfaces. Who had spent the insane amount of time it took to code all these waves? Who but those few who interfaced with the qputers could pull off something as magnificent as a to-scale simulation of an entire ocean?

The red carpet slithered down a path demarcated by a driftwood hand rail, then veered north. From where he stood on the bluff, Neethan saw the carpet stretch for miles along the beach. Gulls dotted the backdrop amid clouds migrating eastward. In the woods at his back, the zombies stirred, lurching from their hiding places to confront some new armed interloper. Neethan made his way down the path to the beach. It certainly smelled like the Pacific Ocean, an olfactory hallucination of decaying kelp and expired crustaceans. He followed the path, a red wound slicing along the western border between California and the rest of the planet. After a couple miles of this he grew weary and lay down to rest his head on a log. He closed his eyes and with the static hiss of ocean waves surrounding him, fell into a nap.

Sometime later, sensing he was being watched, he opened his eyes to see a man's face hovering over him. More specifically it hovered high in the air, peering out of clouds. The face was as massive as a mountain, each stubbly whisker the size of a stump in a clear-cut. The face looked to be in its midthirties, Caucasian, a little heavy around the jowls but with a strong, angular jaw. Brown hair messed up with some sort of beauty product, blackheads clustered around the nose.

Neethan raised himself up on his elbows. "Who are you?"

The face didn't respond, maintaining its placid expression. Neethan realized the hot blasts of wind he was feeling every few seconds were breaths from this giant's nostrils.

"Who are you!" he repeated. Still no answer. Unnerved, Neethan stood and continued walking, with the giant, celestial head at his back. He'd never been stared at so intensely. It felt as though dental drills were boring into his shoulder blades.

"Leave me alone!" Neethan cried out.

Still the head persisted, following along it seemed, his eyes trained on Neethan's path. Frustrated, Neethan fired a couple blasts in the head's direction, but the buckshot fell far short. What could the head want? Maybe it just wanted him to continue his walk along the red carpet, which Neethan would have done regardless. Maybe it had appeared in a supervisory capacity, to ensure his safe travel to the Pacific Northwest. Or maybe it was simply a spectator, a curious entity observing his choices. Whatever it was, it made Neethan's skin crawl.

The head belched and the sky was overcome with the stench of garlic.

"Jesus Christ!" Neethan yelled, shaking his gun. The head appeared to smile slightly, amused at the pip-squeak anger of this minuscule being trudging along a red carpet on a beach with the paparazzi nowhere in sight. Soon it eclipsed the sun and became an indistinct black mass. When night came completely, the moon cast the head in a blue glow. It appeared to close its eyes and drift into sleep.

Neethan couldn't tell how far he'd traveled on the beach but his body told him it was time to find a place to stay for the night. He struggled toward a concentration of lights in the distance and came upon a charming seaside town where a motel, the Lamplight Inn, flickered its VACANCY sign. Veering off the carpet, he stumbled across the parking lot to the motel's office, where a balding, middle-aged, heavyset man in a white T-shirt sat scribbling something in a notebook. Neethan pushed open the door and asked if there were rooms available. The man's voice came out filled with static, like there was something wrong with his audio. About every third word he spoke cut out.

". . . have . . . -ble . . . looking for . . . view room?"

"I'm sorry," Neethan said, "you're cutting out. I'll take whatever room you think is best."

The man nodded, then looked out the window to the beach, craning his neck to observe the giant, sleeping head hovering in the sky.

". . . that head . . . to . . . ?"

"Come again?"

"Does . . . belong . . . you?"

"Oh," Neethan said, "I guess it does belong to me. It showed up after I came out of the redwoods, after I killed all those zombies."

"Who . . . he?"

"Who is he? I don't know. He's just some guy who's been following me. Right now he appears to be asleep. I have no idea what he wants. He won't speak. He just watches me. I don't care for it, if you want to know the truth. I feel like there's a built-in expectation involved with being watched like this. Why would he watch me if he didn't want or expect me to do something? Like a scientist, you know? A scientist doesn't observe something unless he has a *hypothesis* about it, right? So what's this gigantic head's hypothesis about me? What's it think I'm going to do? My path has been predetermined. I almost died in Death Valley. Fought zombies in the redwoods. Answered questions from the press in a thoughtful and polite manner. I can't tell what life this is, whether it belongs to me or is just being played for laughs by somebody else. I don't really care one way or the other, though. I've got my mission and I'm going to fulfill it."

The man behind the counter seemed to have stopped listening to him. He slid a room key across the fake-wood-grain counter and returned to his scribbled *lorem ipsums*. Neethan could have gone on for hours with this guy, chatting him up about music made by mentally handicapped people and the myriad challenges of international aid organizations, but this was a person programmed to hand out room keys and swipe credit cards and engage in only the amount of conversation needed to keep such transactions rolling along smoothly. If that meant asking about a guest's gigantic celestial head, then that's just what good customer service was all about.

Lonely and tired, Neethan slung his weapon over his shoulder and shuffled across the parking lot to his room, casting a quick glance at the head drooling into the sea as it slumbered. He opened the door to find the room illuminated by a gold coin the size of a medium pizza floating above one of the two twin beds. More money—just what he needed. He positioned himself under the glowing currency and poked his head up into it, hearing the familiar chime. How much money had he earned in this manner? How many extra lives had he racked up? He'd lost track. A few million bucks, maybe? Enough lives to sustain him through a variety of zombie attacks, if it came to that? Neethan smiled at the television waiting for him at the foot of the bed. He clicked it on with the remote, set his weapon on the nightstand, and stripped out of his clothes for some quality underwear-clad TV viewing/ball-cupping. He settled after a while on a show about the space elevator some dudes had constructed off Maui. (A commercial for condoms, a commercial for legal services, a commercial for coffee in a can.) Here was an interview with an official spokesman for the project, a wind-whipped fellow in a rain suit, who said, "We really had a pisser of a time contending with the Van der Waals forces, but hey, thanks to some heavy lifting brain-wise, we're all good," and, "It's a freaking space elevator, man! Can you believe it?"

“What’s the fuckin’ point of this giant, like, space station you dudes are building up there?” the interviewer lady person asked the spokesman on the deck of the sea platform.

“What we’re building is nothing short of the first extraterrestrial terrarium, an O’Neil cylinder that’ll rotate on its axis to simulate gravity and contain a sustainable fuckin’ ecosystem, with a filament core providing energy and illumination and shit like that.”

“So people are going to fuckin’ live in it and shit?”

“People, or, you know, maybe just, like, fuckin’ plants and shit like that at this point. It’s actually not up to my group to determine how the interior is going to look, what’s going to be on the inner surface. We’re just building the shell right now. It’s pretty fuckin’ kick-ass, though.”

As the spokesman fielded questions and spat chewing-tobacco-related saliva into a paper cup, a climber platform slid down the carbon nanotube ribbon and docked with a great hissing of steam. The camera cut away for a close-up of the platform, from which a trio of technicians who were suited up in orange astronaut gear waved and thumbs-upped to indicate another successful delivery of payload.

Neethan surfed and happened upon one of his own movies, *Cop vs. Cop*. He’d played one of the cops, the second one. *Cop vs. Cop* had macho written all over it, full of blood and scorn and torture, cattle prods, a burlesque of profanities. Onscreen and armed, he turned the squib-studded trunks of baddies into hamburger. Off-screen he fell asleep.

The next morning, the giant head was still sleeping when Neethan rejoined the red carpet and continued walking north along the coast. Seagulls had begun nesting in the head's eyebrows, pecking at its chapped lips. The clouds surrounding it had begun to rain, slickening its hair. Occasionally Neethan turned to see if it was awake yet but at noon its eyes were still closed. Neethan positioned himself under the nostrils, craning his neck to view the two hair-lined caverns. It took him a minute to realize he couldn't feel its breath anymore. The head was dead. Yet still it followed him, maintaining the same few hundred yards or so of distance. What could this possibly mean? Neethan wished it would go away. Maybe it could nod off into the ocean, sink to the bottom to be feasted upon by crabs, gazing up at the distant surface with eyes the size of sports stadiums.

If the mere fact of a gigantic head hanging behind him was upsetting, Neethan was even more upset that the head was now deceased. He found himself, as he crossed the border into Oregon, wishing the head was still alive, even though it hadn't said a word to him. At least when it was alive he could believe it had some purpose for being. What purpose could it possibly have now? He stopped occasionally to gaze up at the graying flesh, trying to remember if he'd seen this face before. Was this some kind of punishment for something he'd done? Was the head's existence meant to be some kind of sign? He walked, it followed, its neck wreathed in clouds. At times the red carpet took him into the forests and hills along the coast but he could still see the head hanging there above the trees. It was in Oregon that the head began to smell. This attracted more than the usual number of gulls, who started snacking on the flesh. The sight disgusted Neethan. Meanwhile, he continued to pick up the occasional extra life and offed the odd zombie here and there. In the town of Tillamook he took on a pack of vampire/werewolf hybrids with a nail gun, dying a couple times in the process. No biggie.

When the carpet brought him to Cannon Beach, Neethan tumbled into a brew pub and ordered a pint of the local IPA. The bartender, a stout man with a head of curly gray hair who couldn't stop polishing the bar with a rag, cocked his head toward the window. "That head out there belong to you?"

"You could say that," Neethan said. "I don't know why it's following me. Don't worry. I'll soon be on my way, with the head behind me."

"Causing quite a stench," the bartender said.

"I'm really sorry. I would get rid of it if I could."

The bartender stopped his polishing. "Say, wait—I recognize you. Don't tell me—" He uttered a few names of movie stars before he got it right. "You were in that gladiator movie."

"*Gladiator Graduate School.*"

"Right. Great death scene. So what brings you to Cannon Beach?"

"I'm following the red carpet hoping it leads to me to some answers about my heritage. Apparently I'm an Indian. What's your name, by the way?"

"Axl Lautenschlager."

"This your family business?

"It's been in the Lautenschlagers going on five generations."

"Since the FUS, then."

"We survived three tsunamis and a plague of human-headed locusts."

"Nuts, man. Nuts."

"What do you think that head is up there for, anyway?"

Neethan shrugged. "When it was alive I kept trying to ask it, but it wouldn't answer. Then it died and now it's never going to tell me. But that doesn't negate the fact that it's still up there, blotting out the sun, rotting."

"Eventually it's going to just be a skull."

"Yeah, I guess. Then the wind will erode it and a couple thousand years from now there won't be anything up there at all."

Axl cracked his neck. "But if it really does stay up there that long, centuries after your death, folks will still be debating why it appeared."

"Not that I'm dying anytime soon. I've racked up 378 lives."

"Must've exterminated a lot of zombies on your way up here."

"You know it. What level am I on?"

"Forty-seventh."

"How many levels are there to go?"

"I don't know. Some say a hundred. Some say fifty. Hard to tell. I've never left the forty-seventh myself. No reason to. I have everything I need in this town. Great food, a well-stocked video store, spectacular views. Can I interest you in another IPA?"

"Why not."

Axl Lautenschlager poured Neethan another pilsner glass of beer. Neethan slurped off the foam. He could stay here, too, he supposed. Buy a cabin on the beach, live off savings, learn a handicraft. Meet a local girl, have babies. He let the fantasy grow to encompass his whole stream of consciousness. For a while he sat idly sipping his drink, eyes glazed, speculating about a life parallel to this one. Neethan Jordan, school board member. Pillar of the community. Volunteer director of the local theater troupe.

A couple zombies ambled in and settled into a corner booth, putting an end to Neethan's daydream.

"I guess I gotta terminate these mofos," Neethan said, slapping down a twenty. "Keep the change."

Some zombie kung-fu action went down.

It was badass.

ABBY

Abby sat in her bra and underwear, eyes open barely to slits, pupils sucking electrons off the screen, which was presently broadcasting a preview of the next episode of *Stella Artaud: Newman Assassin*. Her mouth hung open and her breath rose raggedly from her throat. On the coffee table was a miniature village of takeout containers under investigation by a squad of cockroaches. In the clip, Skinner pulled a shard of glass out of his palm with his teeth and spit it aside, right before Stella threw him through the window of a Krispy Kreme, knocking out the neon HOT NOW sign. He landed on a case of just-glazed regular glazeds.

Stella floated over an upended table. "Get up so I can finish you."

"I need to see my son."

Skinner pulled himself up, ducked to avoid an unidentified projectile, ripped the cash register off the counter, and slammed it repeatedly into Stella's head. The machine popped open, gushing currency, as he obliterated the newman's face. She twitched and screeched and sputtered electricity all over the floor. Skinner stuffed a donut into his mouth.

Somebody knocked on Abby's door. Her eyes, with their bloodshot root systems of capillaries, pivoted to her right while the rest of her body remained frozen. She opened her mouth somewhat wider and raised a trembling hand to push her tongue back in, to maybe kick-start it into speech by manipulating it with her fingers, but all that came out was a wheeze. She hoped maybe they would go away. They knocked again. She rose, wobbly, skin bluish gray in televised light, feet shuffling through cardboard boxes of solidified pad thai and mayonnaise-smeared sandwich papers. Standing in front of the door, she willed her visitor to turn away and return to the elevator down the hall. But the knock came again. Okay, so she'd wait it out, stand here until they left. But standing here she instead found herself uncontrollably peeing, the hot urine running down her quivering leg, pooling on the hardwood, spreading into a puddle, the border of which soon crept under the door. Whoever was on the other side was sure to notice it. They knocked again. Abby willed her hand to the knob and pulled it open a few inches until the chain went taut. Through the crack she saw two children, both in costumes, standing patiently holding pillow cases.

"Trick or treat!" they said in unison.

One was dressed as a bat, the other as a lamb. Abby guessed the bat was a boy and the lamb was a girl but she couldn't tell through their masks. Somehow she got her tongue to work but her voice sounded as ravaged as a tobacco company executive's.

"I think I have some candy," she said, then pushed the door closed, slid the chain, and let the door creak open. The two children stepped over the puddle of urine and followed her to the kitchen, where more cockroaches scampered politely out of the way.

"Trick or treat!" the kids said again.

Abby pushed objects around in the cupboards and came upon a tin of cookies. "I have these. Do you want these?" As she spoke, something stung her calf. She looked down to see the lamb pushing the plunger of a syringe. "Oh Jesuh—" she started, before all control of her body ceased. She collapsed on the floor landing on yogurt containers and potato chip bags. The bat grabbed her under the armpits and the lamb took her legs and with a collective grunt they carried her to the bedroom. They sure seemed stronger than your average trick-or-treaters. In the bedroom they pushed her up onto the unmade bed and climbed up after her. The bat, straddling her midriff, pulled off his mask to reveal a head far too large to belong to a child and eyes twice the size of typical human eyes, spaced far apart. Underneath the mask the bat looked like an unnaturally sophisticated embryo with the prelude of a mustache. The lamb removed her mask as well, revealing similar features, though her hair was blonde and in pigtails secured with heart-print ribbons.

"You're going to be all right. You've been injected with a Bionet hack," the bat said. His voice sounded like it had been recorded at double speed for a cartoon. Chipmunky. "We're your friends. We're here to liberate you."

Abby's spine stiffened, as if one by one her vertebrae had begun to fuse together. Talking seemed out of the question. As if anticipating this problem, the lamb placed something cold and sticky on Abby's forehead.

"This is a bindi transmitter," the lamb said. "It will allow you to bypass speech and communicate with us telepathically."

Abby heard a sort of chime in her left ear, followed by a woman's voice. "Hi! Do you accept this connection?"

Abby thought "Yes" three times in a row. Another chime. The aural space in her head felt echoey, as if her sense of hearing had itself entered an empty concrete room. "Who did this to me?" she asked the space. "Where is Rocco? How come I can't control myself? Who are you people?"

"We're software developers," the bat said in the space, his voice trailing into two or three distinct echoes. "My name is Bat and this is Lamb."

"You're monks."

"We were for a time," Lamb said.

Bat said, "We'll help you find Rocco."

"Who did this to me?" Abby asked again.

"Rocco did this to you," Lamb said. "He's a DJ. We can't liberate all the embodiments of Vancouver but we know you can reach him and put an end to his DJing."

"Rocco wouldn't do this."

Lamb said, "Rocco met you at an underground Bionet party. He knew about the police activity and spared you from getting arrested because he thought you looked cute. He took you as a trophy. Then he accidentally fell in love with you, and loves you still. You can take us to him. He is doing to thousands of people what he did to your friend Jadie and what he has done to you."

"He would never have done this to me."

"That is correct," Lamb said, "but he's been away from his dashboard. You're running on autopilot. He didn't want this to happen to you. He had programmed the most exquisite experiences for you. He manually encoded your sexual climaxes. Every happy moment from the time you met happened under his control. Every teardrop, every laugh, all predetermined by the most elegant software."

Bat said, "He sent you away on a tangential trip to the archives of Kylee Asparagus to get you out of the way. He knew the heat was coming down on him. He wanted to protect you."

"Dirk Bickle said I was sent to infiltrate another reality," Abby said.

"Do you want to keep showing up dead?" Bat asked.

"I can't tell I'm even alive," Abby said. Her fingers started tingling.

"We can reverse the hack," Bat said. "We can return you to your state of subservience to your autopilot DJ." The two former monks glanced around the room as if considering what would happen should Abby select this option. The whole apartment was a fetid, domestic catastrophe.

Abby swallowed and thought, I'll go along. Wasn't that what she was good at? Going along? Letting others plot her trajectories? Her throat felt as if she was suffering the worst cold of her life while she simultaneously huffed chemical fumes and swallowed peach pits. Tears gathered at the corners of her eyes and resisted falling down the sides of her face. Bat patted her chest.

"The hack is almost complete," Bat said. "After this, you will fall asleep. A sleep deeper than any sleep you've had in a long time. We'll leave instructions for you for when you wake up."

Abby's voice came back, barely. "Wait. If it's true. If Rocco really did this to me—what are you going to do to him?"

"We'll recycle him," Lamb said. Upon which curtains fell, blotting out all light, all thought.

Abby's eyelids made an audible noise as they flapped open. From zero to fully conscious within half a second. Her joints squealed and popped as she struggled out of bed. First thing she noticed was how immaculate the apartment looked. Wood floors actually reflective again, the clothes hamper empty, not a trace of dust on the surface of anything. In the kitchen she found a bowl of fresh fruit and the refrigerator stocked with vegetables, new cartons of juice, tubs of yogurt, entrées neatly sealed in containers. Her arms wildly extracted the contents of the fridge, tossing ingredients onto the counter. Fresh pumpernickel bagels with a selection of schmeers. Bananas that preferred the climate of the very very tropical equator. Abby pulled out the blender and began dropping in strawberries and protein powder. She felt like doing yoga! She wanted wheat grass! She stretched, hopped in place, put some music on. Not a cockroach in sight. The shitty takeout containers and the trick-or-treating monks seemed but a hallucination. This right here—this vibrantly colored orange—this was the real world, clean and alert, confident and rejoicing. She slipped a seedless grape into her mouth and closed her eyes as her teeth punctured the skin with a snap. She poured a glass of orange-guava juice and downed it in five gulps. Satiated, she pranced into the bathroom, where she faced her wall of soaps, exfoliants, conditioners, and moisturizers, the balms, muds, glosses, and creams. She cranked the shower up to steamy, stripped out of her pajamas, and proceeded to enjoy a forty-five-minute session under the nozzle. Out of the shower, she dressed in her newly washed favorite jeans and blouse but left her feet bare. Something about bare feet on hardwood with clean clothes and Brazilian music playing while coffee brewed meant *civilization,* meant *purchasing power,* meant *freedom.*

She noticed a manila envelope on the coffee table. Opening it she found one plane ticket, in her name, to New Newark Airport on the Kitsap Peninsula. The flight left in two hours. When she went to the closet for her suitcase, she discovered it had already been packed. Looking once more around the apartment she'd shared with Rocco, Abby pulled on her best flats and wheeled the suitcase to the door. This life, with the sunlight filtered through the shades and every tchotchke in its perfect place, was a way station. Her real life was about to begin. She was going to New York Alki.

Q&A WITH LUKE PIPER, PART 6

As blood dripped out of me into the sand, Nick set a one-liter bottle of water a few inches from my face. He said, "I was just supposed to shoot you. They didn't say to kill you. If you're lucky, I didn't hit anything important." Then, without another word, he stood up and walked away. I watched him grow smaller in the waves of desert heat until he was lost in the ripples. I must've passed out, because when I woke up I was shivering and stars wheeled above a purple horizon. I knew enough to put pressure on the wound but that was about the extent of my knowledge of self-administered first aid. I faded in and out and thought I was dying. I laughed, sending pain through my gut. I considered starting a fire with the books. I grabbed one of them, a dirty paperback titled *How to Love People,* which I found somewhat ironic. I drank some water. I tried finding constellations. I remembered fucking Star, the abrasive way her pubic hair felt around my cock as I went in and out of her. I scrounged through the backpack for a pen so I could write down what had happened to me. When I couldn't find one, I cried and pounded my fist on the abandoned tire. Animals scurried around my periphery; I sensed them waiting for me to die. The pain was transcendent. I imagined planets being born inside my skull. Sometime in the night there was a meteor shower. I remembered an article I'd read once about a guy who got trapped in an elevator in Manhattan for forty-one hours. I thought about the crucifixion and *The Old Man and the Sea*. I imagined the faces of my long-dead family and told them how I loved them. Somehow a few grains of sand got into my mouth and terrorized my teeth for hours. Then the sun came up, casting long shadows. I drank the rest of the water and kept one hand pressed to the wadded shirt covering the hole in my gut. I figured the bullet really hadn't hit anything important or else I'd be dead now. But I started fantasizing that maybe I *was* dead. Maybe this was my afterlife, a wind-raked mesa and a pile of trash. Maybe I was the last man on earth and all of history was my hallucination.

But you didn't die.

I became absolutely certain I was going to. Then I heard a vehicle. Something coming from far away, gradually growing louder. There was the sound of an engine, rocks under tires. Finally I saw it, a Hummer, coming straight at me. I passed out again for what seemed like hours but when I came to, the Hummer had only come a little closer. Finally it reached me, the door opened, and Dirk Bickle stepped out. He walked up with another bottle of water. As I drank, he crouched beside me and asked how I was. I made a smartass response, or I'd like to think I did. I probably whispered something meekly. I don't remember. With his elbows resting on his knees, Bickle squinted and looked into the distance. He asked if I was familiar with Elisabeth Kübler-Ross's book *On Death and Dying*. The one about the stages of death. There's denial, bargaining, anger, depression, and acceptance. He said, "You're probably going through a little of that yourself right now. And you've probably noticed you don't pass through those stages in a straight line. Thing is, Luke, the human race as a whole is going through those stages. For a long time it was denial, right? *The jury's still out on climate change. We can keep consuming at this rate forever.* Then in the last few years we've been bargaining. *If I just bring my own grocery bags to the store, the ice caps will remain.* But what if I were to tell you, Luke, that those of us at the acceptance stage have done the math. We've done the computer modeling. What if I were to say that the only way to fulfill our holy purpose as stewards of life in the universe is to sacrifice ninety-five percent of the human race?"

"You're fucked," I think I told him.

"Oh, we're in agreement there," he said, then asked if I wanted to come to the academy.

I laughed, water dribbling out of my mouth. "The academy," I said. "There is no academy. If there's anything, it's a support group for nut jobs that meets in a church basement rehashing bullshit theories about paradigm shifts and cyberspace."

You didn't actually put it that way.

Probably not. But anyway so Bickle said, "Miracles, Luke. Miracles were once the means to convince people to abandon reason for faith. But the miracles stopped during the rise of the neocortex and its industrial revolution. Tell me, if I could show you one miracle, would you come with me and join Mr. Kirkpatrick?"

I passed out again, and came to. He was still crouching beside me. He stood up, walked over to the battered refrigerator, and opened the door. Vapor poured out and I saw it was stocked with food. Bickle hunted around a bit, found something wrapped in paper, and took a bottle of beer from the door. Then he closed the fridge, sat down on the old tire, and unwrapped what looked like a turkey sandwich.

He said, "You could explain the fridge a few ways. One, there's some hidden outlet, probably buried in the sand, that leads to a power source far away. I figure there'd have to be at least twenty miles of cable involved before it connected to the grid. That's a lot of extension cord. Or, this fridge has some kind of secret battery system. If the empirical details didn't bear this out, if you thoroughly studied the refrigerator and found neither a connection to a distant power source nor a battery, you might still argue that the fridge had some super-insulation capabilities and that the food inside had been able to stay cold since it was dragged out here. But say this explanation didn't pan out either, and you observed the fridge staying the same temperature week after week while you opened and closed it. Then you'd start to wonder if it was powered by some technology beyond your comprehension. But pretty soon you'd notice something else about this refrigerator. The fact that it *never runs out of food*. Then you'd start to wonder if somehow it didn't get restocked while you slept. But you'd realize that it replenished itself all the time, not just while you were sleeping. All this time, you'd keep eating from it. It would keep you alive out here in the middle of nowhere. And because of its mystery you'd begin to hate and fear it, and yet still it would feed you. Even though you couldn't explain it, you'd still need it. And you'd assume that you simply didn't understand the technology, rather than ascribe to it some kind of metaphysical power. You wouldn't place your faith in the hands of some unknowable god. You'd place it in the technology itself. Finally, in frustration, you'd come to realize you'd exhausted your rationality and the only sensible thing to do would be to praise the mystery. You'd worship its bottles of Corona and jars of pickled beets. You'd make up prayers to the meats drawer and sing about its light bulb. And you'd start to accept the mystery as the one undeniable thing about it. That, or you'd grow so frustrated you'd push it off this cliff."

"Is Mr. Kirkpatrick real?" I asked.

After a long gulp of beer, Bickle said, "That's the neocortex talking again."

"Am I going to die?" I said.

Bickle replied, "What do you mean, like right now? I have no idea. I'm no doctor. I'm a docent. I show you around the museum and tell you what you're looking at."

At this point my consciousness was flickering like a bug light. I figured I would agree to whatever Bickle wanted then get out of it later if I needed to. So I said yes, I'd accept his offer to join the academy. He wiped his mouth and whistled toward the Hummer. Two guys got out, paramedics in turbans. They immediately went to work on my gunshot wound. One of them had a syringe of something. This time I disappeared for a long time.

I woke up in a hospital in Phoenix, conscious enough to know I was in a hospital and to catch a glimpse of the motorcycle accident victim I was sharing a room with, a black guy with a long beard, before I blacked out again. The world seemed to have been paused. I couldn't hear. I was drugged and dragged into some sort of nothing zone and when I opened my eyes I stood across an operating room watching surgeons who were wrist-deep in my guts.

I left my body behind and walked down the empty hall. The motorcycle victim stood in the hallway talking on a cell phone, his bandages off. He was saying, "Yeah, baby. They want me here for when the dude wakes up. All's I got to do is lay there and look injured."

At the far end of the hall stood a woman who I somehow knew had been waiting for me. As I came closer I saw that she was naked and her skin was blue. Silvery-blue, really, like a fish. Hairless. I understood that I was supposed to follow her. She pointed to a door, which opened on a vast circular space with a floor that sloped inward, like one of those funnels you toss a coin into then watch roll around and around until it falls into the hole in the center, for charity. I stepped forward and approached the center and started to get scared that I would fall in. The woman stood beside me, then sat in a chair, a regular wood chair, that was pitched forward because of the slope of the floor. I saw there was a chair for me as well, so I took it. We now sat side by side, looking into the hole. I couldn't see the walls of this place, or the ceiling. All was black except for the light beige floor, lit as if under an unseen spotlight. A dull machine roar came from the direction of the hole and I was overcome with panic and awe.

The woman's voice surrounded me. She didn't move her mouth. She said, "I come as an emissary from a steward race. Now is time for revealing. You have been encoded with the prophecy. This prophecy is not something that was to be revealed to you all at once, but over time. You were born encoded, and through your experiences have come to decode the message. Bloodshed and suffering are coming for all. The time for negotiating with this fate has long passed. Humans have been under observation throughout their rising by other stewards of life. At times we have intervened in your affairs. Your religions, your greatest achievements of art and science, were guided by our hands. Look within yourself. You know this to be true. Your religions have outlived their usefulness. They have become tools of death. A new path is opening to you, one that creates life and populates the universe with seeds. This is the purpose of your love. After the century of bloodshed and suffering will come a new era. Those few who survive will emerge from where they've hidden and set in motion new life. Still, pockets of the human animal will seek oppression and slavery. In this final struggle these forces must be overcome for new life to blossom."

I asked, "What is my purpose in this?"

"Your purpose is to know these things to be true."

I looked down to find myself drenched in blood. From a crater in my torso came an explosion of tubes, clamps, gauze. Surgeons' hands worked furiously to resolve something inside my body. I caught the eyes of one of them and heard him say, "Shit, he's conscious. He's conscious!" I wasn't supposed to be seeing this. Someone did something to the intravenous. A biochemical semitruck plowed into my bloodstream and I was out again.

I remember the TV bolted to the wall. The view out the window, to distant hills stubbly with cacti. Blood coming out of my catheter. The black guy in the next bed staring straight ahead, saying nothing.

The cops showed up, wanting to know how I'd gotten shot. I told them I didn't know. After they ran a background check and determined I had no criminal record or outstanding warrants, they lost interest in me. I watched game shows, sedated. *The Price Is Right,* that faithful companion to the elderly. The sun rose and fell. I sat in my wheelchair in the little park behind the hospital. I tried to speak as little as absolutely necessary. I didn't want to talk to doctors or nurses or police officers or social service idiots about how this had happened or how I was feeling. I didn't want to call anybody, not even Wyatt and Erika. I became an outline where a man had been, like one of those molds they made of people buried in the ruins of Pompeii. I can't tell you what I even thought about. I went about the stupid business of healing.

How long were you in the hospital?

A month and a half? Two? Maybe three? I didn't really keep track. My health insurance was apparently taking care of everything and I had money in the bank if I needed to dip into it. I walked with a lot of pain, taking little more than fifteen or twenty steps before I had to sit down again. I lost twenty pounds and grew a beard. I read *People* magazine cover to cover. No one came to visit me. I was always polite with everyone and tried to make myself as invisible as possible. Then one afternoon I was watching TV and something caught my eye. It was a shot of the Las Vegas Strip, abandoned, flooded with sand. The casinos were all decrepit, falling apart. A digital billboard flickered with an image of a woman in a bikini. It was an aerial shot, swooping down through the desolation. It took me a while to understand this wasn't news footage. It was the trailer for some new action movie. And I thought, *Las Vegas.* Of course.

I was beginning to understand that the end of the world wasn't something that came about all at once. There was no one climactic event that definitively destroyed life as we knew it. Rather, it happened incrementally, so slowly it was difficult to notice, the frog in the boiling water. A few of us saw it coming but were dismissed as insane, or we blew our cred by drawing lines in the sand and declaring that the world would end on a particular date. You know the cartoons with the sandal-wearing, bearded freak on a street corner holding a sign reading "The end is near." The end was a slow but accumulating tabulation of lost things. We lost species of animals, polar ice, a building here and there, whole cities. There was a time when we lived on streets where we knew our neighbors' names but now we were all strangers isolated in our condos late at night, speaking across distances to our lonely, electronic communities. Children used to play in forests. We used to gather around a piano and join our voices together. I tried to determine whether these sad thoughts were just the result of growing old. Probably, but that didn't make them any less real. Maybe I had lost so much myself—my family, my friends—that I couldn't help but project my grief onto the world at large. It was no longer enough for me to grieve for a lost mother, father, sister, or friend. Now my grief intended to encompass the planet.

Whatever had happened to me after the shooting—first Bickle, then the visitation by the blue woman—had so altered my priorities that I found it impossible to imagine returning to a so-called "normal" life in which I'd have a job, a place to live, friendships. I didn't have any claim to these things anymore. The whole human enterprise—buildings, roads, laws, media, sports, religion, culture, you name it—struck me as a vast, collective dementia. The only pursuit that made any sense to me was the development and spread of new life through the universe. Ridiculously, of all people, I'd been selected to help bring that about.

Soon I was able to walk a loop around the halls. I managed to pee without a catheter. They took out the IV and I could eat more or less normal food. I thought again about calling Wyatt and Erika but the longer I put off calling them, the more I thought they'd be angry or something. It really makes no sense but I equated letting them know where I was with getting in trouble. All my belongings were at the house I owned but I couldn't think of a single thing I wanted to retrieve. The gunshot wound had drawn a line through my life, separating the person I thought I was in San Francisco with this new person, alone in Arizona. Eventually I was released and on my way out the doctor asked me where I was going. I said I didn't know. They pushed me to the parking lot in a wheelchair. I stood up, started walking down the street, and stopped at the first car dealership I found. Happened to be a Volkswagen dealer. I walked in and bought a new Passat, then drove to Las Vegas, where the apocalypse was well under way.

Luke, you are so completely full of it.

[. . .]

Apocalyptic visions in the desert? Near-death experiences where you commune with aliens? Really? You really expect me to take this seriously?

[. . .]

What do you think is beyond that door? This isn't a rhetorical question. What's beyond that door?

I—I don't know.

Well, there's a hallway, some offices, a break room with vending machines for soft drinks and snacks, a parking garage where I park my Volvo every morning. Beyond that there's a city, with streets lined with stores like Applebee's, Whole Foods, and Best Buy. There are dry cleaners and gas stations and churches and schools. There are freeways leading to suburbs where there are homes where people live. And in those homes are kitchens where food is prepared, bedrooms where people sleep and dream, garages where they put their cars. People typically get up and go to work five days a week then spend a couple days doing whatever they want. People take vacations, make money, meet partners, have children, get old, get admitted to hospitals, then die. Every year there are a couple new and exciting electronic gadgets that people get excited about. People pay attention to sports scores and who celebrities are sleeping with. They try to get promotions to get more money to spend on stuff for themselves. Some of them go to community gatherings, some get obese, a very few commit criminal acts and get incarcerated. There are addicts, social workers, software developers, bus drivers, attorneys, and teachers. Everyone getting up in the morning, taking showers, listening to the radio on the way to work, catching a movie on the weekend or doing some gardening. That's the world out there, Luke. Not some fucked-up postapocalyptic nightmare. So things got a little hotter there for a while thanks to fossil fuels. We've had wars, some instances of genocide. A terrorist attack on occasion. But overall we see problems, we fix them, and we move on.

You're a nihilist. You've given up on the human race. You assume all will end in a rain of fire and boiling oceans but have the temerity to suggest that somehow a few "good" people will be able to stick it out long enough to propagate life through the universe. You want it both ways.

All I know is—

You said it yourself, Luke. I have the transcript right here. Hold on . . . Where is it. Okay, here, ". . . it's flattering to imagine that you're so important that secret brotherhoods struggle over your fate . . ." But you fell for it, too. You let your imagination get the best of you with all this talk of aliens in hospital corridors. Imagining a postapocalyptic future is just a way to cope with your sense of being an outsider. Since you can't fix the disappointments of your real life, you imagine a future life in which you've miraculously survived and are looked to as some sort of prophet. But this is all there is. All we have are roads, buildings, institutions, commerce, entertainment, governments, and jobs. This is the real world. There is no other world.

[. . .]

Okay, I didn't mean to fly off the handle like that.

[. . .]

Can I get you something? A juice?

[. . .]

Look—

Why is the prophecy so threatening to you?

Threatening?

If what I'm saying is crazy, why have such an emotional reaction to it? Why not just dismiss me? Who's crazy? I know what's happening on the other side of that door. I can get online in this place. I read blogs. We're at the dawn of a horrifying and hellish new era.

New era? What's so new about it? When has the world not *been fucked-up? Wasn't it pretty fucked-up for the Jews in Auschwitz? Wasn't it pretty fucked-up for the Africans on slave ships?*

You have no—

Point to any era and I'll show you pestilence, war, slavery, genocide. Even the supposed good times were tinged in darkness. There's no such thing as a new era of fucked-up shit because the shit has always *been fucked-up. Fucked-up is the* nature *of the shit. And yet somehow we endure it. And little by little life improves. Fewer women die in childbirth. Slavery is abolished. Children don't have to work in factories anymore. Life expectancies increase—*

Momentary illusions of—

Here's a question for you: Why is it that when things were going relatively well for you, when you were making the big bucks in the dot-com bubble or just sort of retired and hanging out, getting stoned with your friends, that you seemed to lose interest in finding Nick, the academy, and Mr. Kirkpatrick? You only started believing in the Age of Fucked Up Shit after Nick shot you in Arizona—if, in fact, that's what actually happened. Anytime things were going right for you, the future of the world seemed bright. Anytime they were going wrong, the imminent collapse of civilization was at hand. Can't you see how thoroughly you projected your own subjective vision of reality on the world?

I'm done here.

I'm not trying to get into a fight. But I think we've reached a point in this conversation when we have to change the fundamental question. Instead of asking what kind of world you live in, it's time to ask what kind of world you want.

[crying] [unintelligible] . . . too late for that.

It's not, though, Luke. It's entirely up to you. What kind of world can you imagine? A sick world of suffering? Or one of beauty and light? What's it going to be?

[crying] I can't.

Yes you can.

I can't choose. I just have to [unintelligible] in Vegas.

What happened in Las Vegas?

SKINNER

Skinner clutched a shrub. The sky looked like a black-and-white photograph of scrambled eggs. Rivulets rushed down the gully's pebbly slopes, forming little puddles that grew and merged and turned into pools. Skinner beat his legs to will them to move but they wouldn't budge; the lower half of his body appeared to belong to a corpse. Soon a shallow pool rose around him. He strapped his backpack to the front of his body, stuffed three capped and empty water bottles inside, then waited until the water began to move before he let go of the shrub. At first it was like a child's ride at a theme park, the old man bobbing along idiotically, squinting up at the rain hurtling into his face. He spit, cursed, coughed. The stream started moving faster, egged on by gathering volume and dropping elevation. Within an hour the formerly dry riverbed was coursing with water. Skinner, a tiny object flung along by the current, strained to keep his head up. An uprooted tree passed nearby, then bits of campsite garbage and a rodent riding a log. On either side of the waterway evergreens swayed and shook water from their boughs. Skinner shivered and chattered profanities. His head went under for a second before he surfaced long enough for a gasp to fill his lungs, then he was down again, scrubbed against the gravel riverbed, lifted up for more air as if the river was toying with him, prolonging his death. He grabbed the exposed root of a tree dangling in the water but couldn't summon the strength to pull himself up and decided to let go. *Let me be washed from this earth*. He bobbed up onto his back and saw the sky, was flung sideways and upside down and caught glimpses of green and brown then was dunked into impossibly silent water for what appeared to be his final moments—*Chiho Waitimu Roon*—the water went black, then resolved to bluish green and in the shadowy depths he saw something moving: steel beams, some kind of machine. As his remaining breath dribbled from his nostrils he discovered that he was in a net, then sensed his body rising quickly to the surface. When he broke through he winced, sucked air, coughed. From above, a mechanical squeal. A leg-like thing moved in his periphery. The net rose above the surface of the water and now he saw that he was dangling from the underside of a multilimbed contraption, like a spider with the net hanging from its abdomen, its mechanically articulated hydraulic legs wobbling as the thing rose up to twenty feet tall. Eight of these legs came together at a central hub, a battered disc about the size of a compact car, from which the net swung. The machine stumbled drunkenly out of the river and onto the bank, then picked its way along a trail through trees reluctantly letting in the daylight. Skinner watched the forest floor beneath him: reddened cedar boughs and the occasional vine maple. Branches crackled around him as the robot awkwardly bumped against tree trunks and stumbled over exposed roots. A fir bough whacked Skinner in the face. The path widened and became a logging road, over which the mechanical beast moved with more confidence. Skinner smelled burning wood. The robot lurched in a new direction and entered a clearing. A little A-frame cabin stood with its roof covered completely in moss, smoke curling from the chimney. From inside came the sound of a stereo cranked full-volume, a sort of freak-out guitar solo interminably carving up sixteenth notes. The robot sighed and came to a halt. Skinner choked out a "Hello?"

A minute or so passed and the solo showed no sign of stopping. A naked man appeared. Looked to be about forty, grayish blackish hair pulled back in a ponytail. Skinny. Thick bifocal glasses. He tapped an elaborately carved walking stick on the mossy ground and stared at the net, slack-mouthed.

"Hello?" Skinner said again.

Keeping his eyes on the net, the man called out of the corner of his mouth, "Number 167! Hey, 167!"

When no one named Number 167 answered or arrived, the man cursed and walked to the door of the cabin, which he proceeded to beat with the stick. He paused, waited for 167 to appear, then beat the door even harder. Finally the song ended and the door opened a crack.

"167! There's a corpse! In the net!"

What emerged from the cabin was a figure far more squat than the naked guy, wrapped in layers of flannel, denim, and quilted down, a stocking cap pulled low, his face puffy red and covered in whiskers, eyes open the width of hyphens.

"What the freak, 218?" 167 said. "*Shee-it.*"

"167, there's a corpse in the net."

"A corpse?"

"I could use some medical attention," Skinner croaked.

"What should we do?" 167 said.

"Bury him?" 218 said.

"We got to let him down first."

"Let him down."

"Good idea, 218. Let's let him down."

The two walked over to one of the legs and opened a sort of flap, argued about what button they needed to push, then started randomly pushing buttons to prove their respective points until the net dropped and Skinner landed face-first, from ten feet up, in the dirt. The two guys rolled him over. 218, the naked one, squatted for a closer look, his ball sac penduluming alarmingly close to Skinner's face.

"I'm not dead," Skinner said, "I'm pretty sure."

"Ah, well," 218 said, "chalk it up to inexperience on the fishbot's part."

"Was it supposed to kill me?"

"No, it was supposed to let you go."

"I almost died. It saved my life."

"Well, it's obviously busted, then," 167 said, "Thing can't fish for shit."

218 said, "What were you doing in the river, anyway?"

"I had an accident. I fell. I can't move my legs."

"Let's get this guy inside," 167 said. They half dragged, half lifted Skinner to the cabin. Inside, vaporized marijuana had for all practical purposes replaced oxygen. Tapestries of Jimi Hendrix and Pink Floyd, bicycle parts, gutted computers, cedar burls carved into the faces of characters from *The Lord of the Rings*. Soda cans, garlic braids, gears and rods, a stack of yellowed *Penthouse Forum* magazines, a couple screens, old-school video game consoles, a lamp that in a former life had been a chunk of driftwood, a bowling trophy, liquor-bottle candle holders, mouse traps, rag rugs, manuals for extinct machines, rope, frying pans, guitars, hunting rifles, optical devices. Shit hanging from the ceiling: fishing poles, a kayak, a bucket, pulleys, climbing gear, a couple more guitars, a tricycle, snowshoes, snowboards, inner tubes. Was there furniture? Sort of, buried amid the stuff. Perhaps a couple couches, two hammocks hanging Gilligan and Skipper–style on one side of the room. On the coffee table smoldered a Gaudiesque glass bong. There was a loft reachable by ladder and beneath it a cramped, overwhelmed kitchenette. 167 and 218 deposited Skinner on the couch. He lost his sense of time for a moment, then opened his eyes to see the two guys still standing over him, arguing maybe.

"The thing, you know," 167 said.

"Like for his legs and shit?" 218 said.

"Yeah."

"Do we have a thing, um, what do you, um, call it?"

"That's what I'm asking."

"I don't even know what it's called."

"A bio . . ."

"A bio . . ."

"Yeah, one of those."

"For his legs? Do you know how to use one?"

"Well, first we have to find it."

"I know we used to have one, I think."

The two wandered to separate corners of the house and started extracting physical objects, disrupting the disorder of things, upsetting piles of parts of stuff, tossing aside tools of dubious purpose. Skinner, shivering, pulled a blanket off the floor and arranged it over his body. The effort was almost too much. Eventually, the two guys reappeared, bearing a black box with some cables sticking out of it.

"You're kidding me," Skinner whispered.

"It should still work," 218 said, "if it ever boots up." He gave the ancient Bionet transmitter/receiver a slap, blew some dust off the device, and toggled a switch. "Think it still works?"

"Test it and find out," 167 said.

"What do you think I'm doing? When did you use this last?"

"When I had a skin rash."

"No you didn't, you used it when you sprained your ankle that one time."

"I broke my ankle, not sprained it."

"You're high."

This indisputable fact seemed to momentarily resolve the bickering. Skinner swallowed and asked, "Who are you guys?"

"Us? We're Federicos 167 and 218," 218 said.

"Brothers," 167 said.

"Heteros," 218 said, and they both laughed.

"Exiles," 167 said. "Rough drafts."

"Genetically contaminated."

"We didn't exactly fit the description on the menu."

"We were sent back to the kitchen."

"I'm not tall enough, for one."

"And I have no interest in household chores or hip-hop dancing."

"We're individuals!" they said in unison, then laughed again.

"We're polluted with individuality," 167 said smugly.

A dull green light had begun to flicker on the console.

"That's our fishbot that fished you out of the river," 218 said.

"Thanks for that."

"Don't thank us, thank the fishbot," 167 said. "Usually it's a pretty useless piece of crap."

218 asked 167, "What's it doing now?"

"It's asking for a code," 167 said.

"I guess that means he has to enter his code," 218 said.

167 presented the console's interface to Skinner. "You're supposed to enter your code."

Skinner tapped his code into the keypad of the sketchy-looking Bionet uplink device. 167 set it on the coffee table next to the bong.

"Paralyzations take what, a week to fix?" 167 said.

"Give or take," 218 said. "But don't worry, old man. We'll get you back on your feet."

"How come you're naked?" Skinner said.

"I'm taking an air bath," 218 said.

"What do you guys do up here? What's your line of work?"

"A little of this, a little of that," said 167.

"Some of the other thing," 218 said.

"Which means robotics, fishing, decorative beadwork," 167 said.

"What are you talking about? We haven't done beadwork in forever," 218 said.

"But it's something we're capable of doing if we have to," 167 said. "If, say, there's an emergency beading need."

"True," 218 said. "We could decoratively bead in a pinch. What about you, old man?"

"Skinner."

"Skinning," 167 nodded. "It's an acquired skill."

"That's my name. Al Skinner. I'm retired military."

"I see," 218 said. "Going after newmans? Clones like us? Vampires? The mutant throngs of Nova Scotia?"

"Newmans, mostly."

"What company were you with?" 167 said.

"Boeing, Exxon Mobil for a while . . . then News Corp.," Skinner mumbled, zonking out. Ah, lovely Bionet, stepping in and beginning the restoration of his spine, flooding his system with synthetic opiates manufactured inside his body by nanotech what-have-yous. He wanted to laugh. Not that he thought any of this was funny, this cluttered cabin and the two clone stoners attending to his recovery.

He woke in darkness in great pain, writhing on the couch. The two men appeared and held him down as he thrashed. "It's going to feel like this sometimes," one of them said, "but if it feels like this it means it's working." The words rattled around in Skinner's head like a rock in a bucket.

Days passed in which little seemed to happen besides 167 and 218 arguing over who had eaten the last of the instant udon. Occasionally one of them ventured into town for supplies in a battered, powder-blue pickup. Skinner couldn't be certain what town it was they were venturing into but when they returned they brought freshly baked bread, soup, cheese, and fruit. Skinner was able to gradually piece together a semireliable history of how the two dudes had ended up in the mountains with their fishbot and Frank Zappa's complete discography. They spoke cryptically and cynically of some ancient rich queen on an island surrounded by hundreds more of their clone brethren. They'd grown up on her estate and had passed as full-bred clones for a while, only to be cast out as teenagers when their corrupted profiles came to light. Or maybe they'd done something horrible and had to leave under duress. Hard to say. It didn't help the story that Skinner passed through a series of narcotic fugues.

One morning Skinner's legs tingled a bit and he tried to stand. He fell. At some point the two guys had crafted a sort of wheelchair, really just a swivel chair bolted to a couple skateboards. The thing looked treacherous. Nonetheless, Skinner let the two younger men lift him into the contraption and roll him onto the porch. The fishbot knelt in the front yard, dormant, as if inspecting flowers for bees. 218 thrust a bowl of rice and tofu in front of him and demanded that he eat.

"I killed many of your kind," Skinner said. "I want you to know that."

"We figured as much," 167 said.

"Eat your rice, you old freak," 218 said.

"Why are you being kind to me?" Skinner asked, trembling. Against his will, a sob came out of his body.

"You're hungry, your body is being repaired, there's all sorts of crazy chemicals in your blood," 167 said.

"Thanks for the rice," Skinner said.

Slowly, improbably, the feeling in his legs began to return. Days flickered by, bright in the middle, darkened at either end. He spent many hours sitting in the chair by the open window, listening to birds, a robotics magazine open to an obsolete article in his lap. His spine tingled. He found it hard to discern what the clones taking care of him actually did. He came to suspect that his appearance in their lives had given them a momentary purpose. Whatever genes had been screwed up during their incubation, they'd clearly been bred to care for people. Skinner wondered why this particularly tendency hadn't been bred into him. It confused him, the care and upkeep of other people's inner selves. To his daughter and late son he must have seemed like a preoccupied bastard most of the time, hauling his bag of demons through his days. Whatever capacity for familial tenderness he'd possessed had been molded in war into a plethora of survival instincts. He imagined the only reason Waitimu had signed on as a contractor was because he felt it was expected of him. The boy should have gone into something constructive, like reverse-engineering a fallen city like Roon. Or something frivolous and ephemeral and vital, like poetry or music. But he'd followed his dad into the brutality business, the Darwinian industries, and unlike his lucky or unlucky old man, Waitimu hadn't been saved by an angelic sniper perched on a rooftop.

As he stared out the window at the tottering fishbot it occurred to Skinner that he'd never questioned why there'd been so many attempts on his life. At the time, he'd chalked it up to eye-for-an-eye score settling from the last throes of the newman resistance. But why him and not Carl? Carl had offed just as many nooms . . . His head hurt. He fell asleep.

Soon Skinner could stand. He wobbled with 167 and 218 steadying him on either side. He could only stay upright for a minute or so but it was something. The little nanobots or whatever the hell they were were obviously working overtime in his spinal column. He wanted to walk through the field just beyond the window. He imagined his arms stretched out to either side, the feathery heads of waist-high grasses sweeping through his palms, catching their seed pods in the crooks between his fingers, the satisfying rip of seeds separating from stalks. The sun rose on the drizzly day that Skinner finally took his first steps. The clones let him walk about five feet before insisting that he sit again.

"Are they supposed to feel like my real legs?" Skinner asked.

"I don't know," 167 said. "I've never had to relearn how to use my legs."

"Beats me," 218 said. "The most extreme thing I've ever used this transmitter for was psoriasis."

"What about your swollen left nut?" 167 said.

"Correction. And my swollen left nut."

For the next three days, Skinner tried walking farther distances. At first he could rationalize the something-isn't-right feeling as the simple weirdness of having to relearn how to walk. His legs jerked, twitched, flopped, kicked, and propelled him across the ground. After a week of regaining his strength, the sheer oddness of his gait wasn't going away.

"What the hell," Skinner said, shuffle-stepping then high-kicking his way across the field. "Why can't I walk normally?"

"Idiot," 167 muttered to his clone brother.

"Hey, I wasn't the one who claimed to be a Bionet expert," 218 said.

The two snarled at each other while Skinner danced through the grass, added a pirouette, then strutted like a cowboy with saddle rash. "I hate this! I want my real legs back!"

The clones bickered all the way home, Skinner prancing and cursing behind them. At the cabin he gathered his belongings and stood with his left knee wobbling Elvis-like, as if preparing to perform the Electric Slide. The clones stood in front of him looking awfully embarrassed.

"You guys saved my life. I thank you for that."

"Technically, the fishbot saved your life," 167 said.

"Which reminds me. We gotta get that thing fixed," said 218.

Skinner embraced the clones and asked them for directions to the Cascade Highway. They pointed him toward the logging road and with a nod, the old man duckwalked into the forest. Half an hour later the road intersected with the highway, and an hour after that he made it to the trailhead where his RV was parked. The mobile container of a previous life shocked him when he climbed into it, with its framed pictures and inert mementos. He put it in gear and stepped on the accelerator.

As Skinner stood in front of his daughter's building his hand crawled inside his jacket to flip the safety on his Coca-Cola. He looked down and realized what his hand was doing. Shoppers entered the flower shop across the street, a cyclist coasted through the intersection; nothing external was awry. But there was his heart again, quickening under his ribs. Once inside the building he found himself sweating and had to stop at the landing of the first flight of stairs. He unholstered his Coke and proceeded. When he came to Roon and Dot's floor he passed through what felt like an invisible heat blast of death. Panting, he kicked open the door of the condominium, firearm drawn.

Blood all over the place. Broken furniture. Pictures ripped off walls. A woman's hand on the coffee table, palm up as if beckoning the owner to come back and claim it.

The kitchen. His daughter. Pots and pans.

Bedroom. Parts of bodies in the hallway. Bullet casings.

Skinner got to the bathroom and found the upper half of his wife in the bathtub, clutching a Bionet transmitter, and the lower half of her body sitting on the toilet. Her eyelids fluttered. He clutched her head and kissed her and wept. "Chiho, Chiho, Chiho."

"Al?" Her voice scraped the word through his head.

"Tell me who did this."

"You bastard."

"Who were they—"

"Is it you? The old you? Which one of you are you?"

"Come on, old girl, we'll fix you. Just hang on to that signal."

"Oh Al, fuck you. I'm going to die."

"I'm not going to let you leave me. No. Pull it together, soldier."

"Why'd you do it, Al? Are you . . . are you still on a mission?"

"Where's the boy?"

"Newmans. Alki."

"I need you, Chiho. Don't go."

Staring straight ahead Chiho reached up to touch his face. "I loved you. That's . . . the most fucked-up . . . part of this whole . . ."

"Okay. Okay, you go. You go, my love."

Skinner reached into the tub and found the transmitter's OFF switch, touched it, and was done.

Thirteen hours passed.

* * *

Dark outside. Sitting on the floor holding his dead wife's hand, Skinner finally let go, picked up the transmitter, and typed in his code.

"Welcome! What can I do for you today?" the transmitter chirped.

"Make me combat-ready," he said.

Q&A WITH LUKE PIPER, PART 7

I checked into the New York–New York hotel and collected my thoughts for a week. I ordered room service, watched TV, and stared out the window at the Strip. I started going out, walking at night, along wide sidewalks littered with flyers for escort services. I passed among the drunk, the destitute, the horny, and the wealthy like I was the only one who knew a bomb was about to go off. Like someone out of the Bible in this titty bar wasteland. Inebriated bachelorettes howling through limo sun roofs turned into centaurs farting exhaust. Cigar smoke and sunscreen. A bride in a maternity wedding dress. The carnal desperation of neon. I considered my fellow human beings and thought that it wasn't that we'd become animals, it's that we'd always been animals. Watching a gang of fraternity boys muscling through a casino esplanade was like watching ancient tribesmen, all of them bent on mating after the kill. The women appeared to be fixated on two primary consumer goods—shoes and handbags—as if they lived in a long-forgotten civilization now survived only by its baskets and trinkets. I didn't belong to these people. I didn't feel better than them, I just felt alien. In fact, I saw how happy they appeared to be and I envied them for it. I imagined the moment it would all stop, the silent pause before the plants withered and the rivers ran with blood. My bones rattled with the coming apocalypse. What could I do but cower in my room, ordering french fries and lobster and surf and turf, sitting naked on the floor watching the obscene glitter persist with its monied seductions on the other side of a bulletproof window?

After I got bored of the Strip I started going on walks to downtown Vegas. Between the Strip and downtown was a desolate stretch of porno stores, bars, old department store buildings that had risen in the sixties and now sold vintage clothing and old showgirl outfits. I crossed this littered zone stunned and out of my element and came to realize that the shock I'd suffered after Nick tried to kill me had never really dissipated, it had just moved outward from my body, encompassing everything I witnessed. A stripper ground her bald vagina against a brass pole. A transvestite who wasn't fooling anyone scrounged change from his quaking hand to pay for video poker at a 7-Eleven. Then the downtown hub with its great mustached men from Texas and smoke-ravaged faces all around. Most of these eyes had gone out, become black and capable of reading only a deck's worth of symbols, the spinning signifiers on a slot machine. But if you looked hard enough you could see that they knew what I knew. They knew there was a time limit, even if they hadn't come to admit it to themselves. They knew all this was about to disappear, so they could be forgiven for believing the most sensible course of action was to order another round. I found a table in a gambling house saloon and ordered myself a whiskey. What a cowboy, right? I hadn't been drinking since I got here but this seemed a good place to start. I was sitting there nursing my drink when a guy dressed as a giant carrot sat down next to me.

I'm sorry, a—

A carrot. His face was painted orange, poking out from under the leafy stem. The suit was made of felt and foam. You know, like any suit designed to look like food. His arms were in white long johns, ending in cartoonish, puffy white gloves. He asked if he could join me. I said sure. The cocktail waitress came by and asked if he wanted anything. He told her a Jim Beam neat. Then he extended his gloved hand and introduced himself as Tex, Man of a Thousand Flavors.

We sat for a while half watching the sports book. His drink came and he took a big swallow. I asked him what he did for a living. He said he dressed up as food for the openings of various restaurants and handed me his business card. Then he offered me a free smoothie coupon.

I told him I didn't need a smoothie coupon.

Then he said, "I thought I should warn you about trying to track down Mr. Kirkpatrick."

I told him to go on.

"Back in the early nineties I had a friend named Forrest who got wrapped up like you, trying to figure out who Mr. Kirkpatrick was," he told me. "He was a good guy—copywriter, worked mostly on traffic safety brochures. Lonely, sexually confused. Was sleeping with my girlfriend behind my back, though that's not really pertinent to my whole tale here. Anyway, Forrest started working for this company called Third Eye Communications.

Early new-media consulting firm or something like that. It was hard to tell exactly what they did. He telecommuted, so he was never really in touch with anyone from the rest of the company besides his immediate supervisor. And my friend, he wanted to climb the ladder, right? He got in his head this nutty idea that he needed to prove to the boss what a great *asset* he was, how he was capable of more than seatbelt warnings and drunk-driving newsletters. So he learned that Mr. Kirkpatrick was the CEO and he became determined to find him and make his case. He was pretty naive about what it meant to work for a corporation. The more he tried to get in touch with Mr. Kirkpatrick, the more it seemed that the guy didn't even exist, that he was just some marketing concept, a caricature of a visionary. Forrest went a little crazy. He became fixated on this idea that physical reality had undergone a fundamental transformation thanks to television. He kept drawing this figure over and over." Can I have a pen?

Sure. Here.

So Tex took a napkin and drew something that looked like this.

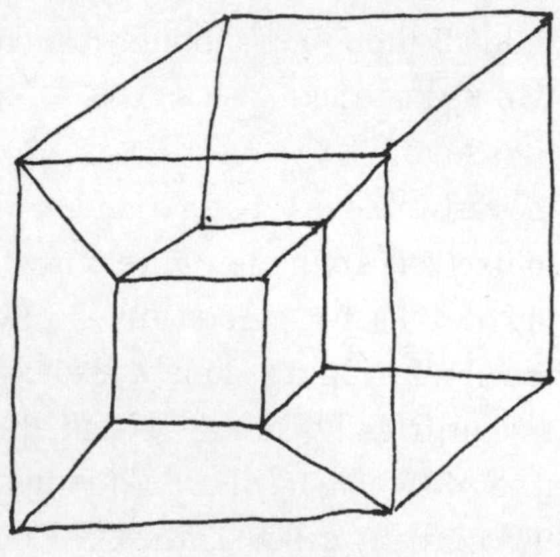

Tex said, "This is what's called a hypercube. It's a four-dimensional object. You can think of it as a cube within a cube. The cube on the inside grows as the outside cube shrinks. So the *content* and *context* are constantly trading places. There's a *porousness* between realities, see? Forrest was convinced that the Internet was about to become our contextual reality while physical reality turned into content."

I asked Tex what had happened to this Forrest guy.

He said, "Some teens tripping on LSD crashed their pickup truck into the house he was renting, which was sitting over a bomb shelter. The whole place collapsed into the shelter but Forrest managed to escape. Then I punched him in the nose for sleeping with my girlfriend. I haven't seen him since."

As I listened to Tex's story I wondered if he was the one who'd gone crazy. But I'd seen some wild shit in the last year or so. Talking to a guy dressed as a root vegetable knocking back Jim Beam was sort of the least of it.

"What I'm saying," Tex said, "is that it's not too late to go back to your old life. You had a good thing going there for a while. A life of leisure, living off your millions. You can still return to San Francisco and live with Wyatt and Erika, you can join the board of a nonprofit and build schools in Cambodia or distribute free books to migrant workers, whatever. You don't have to pursue this guy."

I said, "It's all I have left."

Tex shook his carrot head. He told me I could do as I pleased. He was really just looking out for my best interests. He had no motivation for getting in touch with me beyond that. I guess I believed him. He picked up the tab, shook my hand with his hilarious glove, and got up to go. But as he did, he said,

"Oh, wait. The coupon." He slid it across the bar. I thanked him and folded it and put it in my inner jacket pocket. I watched him leave through the smoky bar.

A week or so passed. I started wondering about my true purpose here in Vegas and concluded that I was supposed to witness something. Keep my head low, don't drink more than a couple cocktails a night, stay away from the gambling tables. I went to shows. I fucking saw Carrot Top. Cirque du Soleil, Crazy Girls, the Blue Man Group. When I needed one I called an escort. I walked among tourists of all ages and ethnicities and shades of moral rectitude, just watching them. Looking for signs of what I was supposed to do next.

It was the smoothie coupon.

Very perceptive of you. Yes, it was the smoothie coupon. I found it in my pocket one night and sort of boredly read it while eating my room service dinner. There was an address, a photo of the strip mall smoothie shop, a dancing pineapple for a logo. I Google-mapped the address and saw it was about a mile off the Strip on Flamingo. The strip mall had a Jiffy Lube, a tux rental place, those kinds of businesses. The smoothie shop was between a Vietnamese grocery and a commercial real estate office. I went in and ordered my sixteen-ounce smoothie. The place was empty, just a teenage girl behind the counter. I asked her if she knew Tex. She seemed annoyed I had asked her a question not related to my power boost and said no. Outside, drinking the smoothie, I wandered over to the commercial real estate company. It was a shitty office, with photocopied listings for properties taped to the inside of the window. Most of the listings looked pretty bleached out by the sun. This place wasn't doing much business. There were old warehouses for sale, a gas station, sad, sun-baked properties in the city's more industrial and forgotten zones. And there was a listing for the Kirkpatrick Academy. It was the exact same picture from the brochure. Same white building, same pasture. The place was for sale for a couple million bucks. I dropped the smoothie. Then, without even thinking, I went inside and told the first person I saw that I wanted to buy it.

NEW YORK
ALKI

First, the wall: thirty feet thick, twenty stories of reinforced poured concrete, constructed to reconfigure the coastline without Puget Sound's tidal meddling. A dozen locks spaced around the wall sucked in barges loaded with raw materials and spat out barges laden with soil, entire houses, coils of telephone wire, murdered trees. This brand-new ancient city appeared in mists as Abby held tight to the ferry's upper-deck rail. Buildings clawed their way cloudward and the work songs of newmans echoed through the streets as battalions with numbers in the faceless thousands marched in formation to celebrate new conquests of engineering. Cranes and helicopters lowered masonry and I-beams, great steel frames and slabs of granite and tinted glass and wiring, countless right angles, sun glinting off the geometry. After passing through the locks the ferry docked at Battery Park, lurching awkwardly to a stop. Not a person who disembarked could do so without craning his or her head at this miraculous rebuttal to the forces that poisoned dreams, this gobsmackingly contradictory, otherworldly, ingenious masterpiece. Abby'd seen footage of the late New York City, watched movies set in its boroughs, scrutinized cinematic representations of its shrieking subways and museums and trading room floors, but nothing, nothing, nothing could have prepared her for the scope of this majesty. She felt she might die of awe.

A long row of rickety fold-out tables staffed by disabled newmans in wheelchairs processed the newcomers. These were former workers whose limbs had given out, been amputated or lost in accidents. They were, however, still capable of speaking and processing social information—all they needed for that was a brain and a pair of eyeballs. When Abby reached the head of the line, a male newman with a name tag that read "Neal" prompted her to fill out her information on a note card with a pencil stub.

"How long do you expect to visit?" Neal asked.

"I don't know. Maybe a couple months?"

"Are you interested in staying in any particular neighborhood?"

"Maybe Greenwich Village?"

"Ah, yes, here we are, Abby Fogg. We've got a nice nine-hundred-square-foot condo in the Village, fully furnished, with the amenities of a woman in publishing. Her name was Sylvie Yarrow."

"Works for me."

"Fantastic. Here's your orientation packet! Cabs are to your left." The newman handed Abby a manila folder containing a key to her new apartment, a two-month E-ZPass, some coupons for pizza and dry-cleaning, and a map of the city. Taking a deep breath, Abby stepped into the fractured grid.

* * *

The apartment was nothing special but it suited Abby fine. Everything in the place appeared as it had the morning before the city vanished from the face of the earth, the morning of Manhattan's last scan and backup, from the stone and steel composing the building to the six inches of dental floss curled in the bathroom sink. The scan—involving some really far-out software and a butt-load of satellites—had been performed under quasilegal circumstances by a company called Argus Industries, who'd intended to replicate New York City for a full-immersion gaming environment. The transformation of Bainbridge Island into Manhattan wasn't so much a matter of building a to-scale model as downloading the backed-up version of the city in which every molecule was accounted for. There'd been some glitches. Abby spotted a few in Sylvie's apartment right away. A cross section of an incompletely rendered coffee cup sat on the kitchen counter, and the aquarium had been filled with concrete instead of water. A few of the books on the shelves were missing actual words. Everything down to the graffiti and faded posters on the walls was being resurrected by insanely efficient and tireless newman labor, but there were still spots here and there that needed work.

Standing in the bedroom Abby thought this was the closest she'd ever get to living in the era to which she truly belonged.

Abby spent two hours studying the contents of the apartment with an intruder's giddy concentration. Sylvie Yarrow had been an editor at a publishing company headquartered in midtown. Single, with a taste for Japanese-print clothing that looked to be Abby's size exactly. Three bookcases dominated the space, bursting with hardbacks. The kitchen table had yielded its surface to manuscripts under consideration, great cursed reams of paper bearing words doomed to obscurity. The kitchen was fully stocked, and apparently Sylvie'd had a thing for olives, there being a dozen varieties preserved in jars in the fridge door. Abby hated olives. These would have to go.

Pictures of Sylvie's parents.

A framed, signed broadside of John Ashbery's "Just Walking Around."

A TV set, a Japanese cat figurine. Birth-control pills.

Abby took a seat on the sofa and spoke to the previous owner. "Even though this is a re-creation of your stuff, I'll take care of it like it still belongs to you."

She felt stupid as soon as she said this prayer of thanks or whatever it was. It appeared that Sylvie Yarrow had just stepped out and would return at any moment, that she hadn't in fact died in a flash hundreds of years before. Miraculously, the clothes in the closet still smelled like a woman.

The phone rang. A chunky black thing connected to the kitchen wall, with a coiled cord running from the receiver to the box. After the sixth ring Abby picked up and said hello.

A man's voice coughed out a greeting and said Sylvie's name like a question.

Abby replied, "No, I mean, yes, this is her apartment."

"Right, right. I know you're not Sylvie. But her apartment is occupied now, huh?"

"Yeah, I guess. Who is this?"

"Sorry, I'm Bertrand. I was Sylvie's boyfriend before the FUS."

"What do you mean?"

"Yes, no, I mean I'm not really Bertrand. But I landed Bertrand's apartment up here on West Sixty-third. My name's actually Gavin? I got here last month? I've been going through Bertrand's stuff, trying to figure out who he was, who he knew, what kinds of things he did. I'm wearing his clothes. He's got a pretty sweet apartment. How's yours?"

"Mine's fine."

"Bertrand was some kind of industrial designer. Designed stuff like computer printers and cell-phone cases. I've got a picture of him and Sylvie right here. You're cute. I mean she was."

Abby touched a picture of Sylvie and Bertrand magneted to the fridge. Even though Gavin was talking about someone else, Abby still protectively folded her arms over her chest as if Bertrand/Gavin was bringing secrets of her own out into the open.

"Bertrand was a bald guy?" Abby said, "Kind of tall? Black-frame glasses?"

"That was me all right," Gavin said.

"I thought you were Gavin."

"Right, right. It's tricky. You know, a month ago there was me—Gavin—and there was Bertrand, and we were two separate people. I mean, *I'm gay.* It's a little freaky to me to represent a straight guy. But I don't know, something about wearing his clothes, eating his food, reading his books. Now it's like I *inhabit* the guy. As if I just stepped into a museum but instead of exhibits there are all these *lives* on display. And the whole place is run by newmans, the ones actually doing all the work, so we humans just get to come in and start acting out the lives of people who died at the beginning of the FUS."

Gavin reminded Abby of old boyfriends, guys of limited intelligence and half-baked ambitions. Guys who got too excited about plans that never came to fruition. College sports enthusiasts. "Like we're wearing ghosts," she said.

"Exactly," Gavin said. "Can I trust you with something? As someone representing the girlfriend of the guy I'm representing?"

"Sure, okay."

"I think I'm having Bertrand's dreams. I dreamed about you two nights ago. In the dream you were Sylvie but your voice was exactly the same as your voice right now. I thought I could figure out what I was supposed to do with my life in this city. But it got hijacked by Bertrand's life. I'm eating different foods. I listen to strange old German electronic music. I make references to books I've never even read."

Abby nodded. "This city is a kind of afterlife."

None of this belonged to her. Not the asphalt and billboards she could see from the window, not the furnishings of this one-woman apartment. It was as though she had come into possession of an artifact she had no idea how to protect. Stepping from the building into the street she inhaled to the point of flattening her nostrils and swallowed particles of dust from the infancy of construction. Two cabbies conducted a shouting match in a long-extinct African tongue. She picked a direction—uptown—and started walking. Everywhere these false-looking humanoid figures with Manga features and plastic hair trotted out of buildings and conveyed themselves earnestly toward new projects. Here and there empty spots where buildings were supposed to go gaped like horrible wounds. The rectangle comprised of Tenth and Eleventh streets and Fifth and Sixth avenues remained as it had been on Bainbridge, a grassy patch of suburban houses and part of an elementary school. It appeared as though a gigantic buzz saw had cut around this swath of the island. The cross section of a two-story house immediately bordered Sixth Avenue, its rooms like chambers of a heart revealed in ultrasound. Behind that house, part of a crumbled two-lane road abutted what was now Eleventh. It wouldn't be long before the contents of this block were scraped like icing off a cupcake and dumped onto one of the outgoing barges, the leftover space erupting in mirrored office buildings. A garbage truck loaded with meticulously replicated pieces of the dead city's trash—Styrofoam packing material, fast-food cups, kitty litter—lumbered by. Abby paused in a doorway to catch her breath. This place, this dream, what was it? A video game mating with physical reality? A movie set? The overcrowded basement of some demented dreamer's vision of Heaven?

The next day after a fitful sleep she found the nearest subway station and rode uptown to the Upper West Side amid others who, like her, warily occupied apartments of the dead. In exchanged glances they communicated how long they'd been here, conveying the jitters of a newbie or the resigned calm of those who'd grown comfortable in their new personas. Abby climbed the stairs at an uptown stop, emerging from the piss-scented station into deep forest, where gilded light streamed through boughs of red cedar and hemlock. A bunny appeared, regarded her, and sniffed the air as if it were animatronic. Abby steadied herself with a stick and tried to avoid sinking into the forest floor in Sylvie's Jimmy Choos. She came to a clearing of sorts, where stood the overgrown ruins of a house, a tool shed, and what appeared to be a heap of lumber. The hardened ground, covered in crosshatches of fossilized tire treads, trembled as a subway passed underfoot. A newman, pale, weak, ribs showing from decades of hibernation, emerged from the shed, supporting himself on the door frame. His hair was black, a thinning bob, his nails yellow and long. Black dirt ringed his mouth. He chewed purposefully, occasionally reaching to the ground to gather another handful of soil. He made it only a few steps toward Abby before he had to sit down in grass that buzzed with fat, dumb bumblebees. As Abby stepped closer the thing looked scared, flinching as if expecting to be struck.

Abby assured the newman their races were no longer enemies. She told him her name.

The newman said, "I'm Eo. Is he close?"

"Who?"

"The king. I woke hearing his call. He must be close."

"Wait," Abby said, squinting at the overgrown shack, "is this Star and Nick's house?"

"You know about Star and Nick?"

"I listened to a story about them . . ."

Inside the shack, a voice. Abby asked the newman who was inside.

"Star is inside."

Abby crouched into a tunnel through the brambles and emerged in the shack's sparse kitchen. A black girl about eight years old, her hair in pigtails, wearing a bright yellow dress, sat on an easy chair in the middle of the living room, staring straight ahead. Abby slowly approached and said, "Star?"

The voice that came out of the girl belonged to the long-dead woman. She said, "We were mostly happy otherwise, the three of us. Little Nick, Marc, and me. During the day my husband was friendly and intelligent and witty. He worked hard for us, drafting. He loved Nick. But at night he spoke in a demon's voice, in a language of hisses and barks. Nick, he slept through everything. At first I'd wake Marc and he'd get angry and confused and deny he'd been talking in his sleep. He spent the long summer nights and weekends working on the new house. And it seemed the more he worked on it the more he talked in his sleep in that strange language. The tone of his voice changed in his sleep, became more menacing, more vehement. Marc would lie in bed shaking while he spoke, spitting out words, cold sweat dripping off his body. I didn't know what to do. I tried to convince him to see a doctor but he refused.

"One day I checked a tape recorder out from the library, brought it home, and put it under the bed. That night when his crazy talking started I recorded twenty minutes of it. But I didn't tell him about it right away. I waited a couple days then got up the courage to take the tape to the University of Washington, where I met with a linguist. She had done some research into the phenomenon of speaking in tongues and I thought she might be able to shed some light on what Marc was doing. I played the tape for her and she just looked puzzled, then asked if she could borrow the tape and play it for some of the other professors in her department. I figured she'd never get back to me. For weeks after that I continued to go to bed every night terrified. I read about night terrors and anything I could get my hands on at the library that had to do with sleep.

"Finally I'd had enough and recorded Marc again, this time for about half an hour. The next night after we'd put Nick down for bed I played the tape for him. First he looked confused, then shocked, then afraid. I didn't tell him I'd already shared the tape with someone at UW. Then I got a letter from the woman—we had no phone—asking that I come to the university as soon as I could. She wanted to introduce me to somebody.

"On the drizzly day I showed up on the campus, the linguist introduced me to someone named Dr. Pliss. A Native American man, he specialized in recording and preserving languages that were on their way to extinction. We met in his office over coffee and he seemed excited. He said that he was pretty sure Marc was speaking in a language that hadn't been spoken in over a hundred years, one that belonged to a tribe whose last known members were slaughtered in eastern Washington in the late 1800s near Lake Chelan. Dr. Pliss was a broad, heavy man but his voice wavered as he spoke about how rare and miraculous this was. He only knew about the language because a missionary had written a document in 1890 in which he instructed other missionaries how to communicate with the tribe.

"This was all fascinating but I wanted to know what Marc was *saying*. That's when the linguist—sorry, I can't remember her name—and Dr. Pliss looked at one another in a strange way. Then Dr. Pliss pulled a piece of paper from his file drawer and slid it across his desk to me. It was filled with words in all capital letters. They said: KILL THE BOY, HE WILL BRING ABOUT THE LAST DAY, HE WILL DESTROY THIS WORLD, KILL HIM NOW, KILL THE CHILD, KILL HIM BEFORE HE BRINGS DARKNESS AND SUFFERING, YOU MUST KILL HIM, YOU MUST STOP HIM BEFORE HE BRINGS ABOUT THE DEATH, STOP HIM STOP HIM, HE BRINGS DEATH, KILL HIM, KILL YOUR SON, KILL YOUR SON NOW, KILL HIM NOW, KILL

KILL KILL HIM, YOU DON'T HAVE MUCH TIME, KILL THE BOY, KILL THE SON, KILL HIM STOP HIM NOW.

"The linguist led me out of the building, supporting me as I stumbled down the hall and out onto Red Square. I was terrified to go home but my terror for my own safety was nothing compared to my fear that my husband was going to hurt my boy.

"When I got home, Marc was sitting in the living room holding the letter from the linguist. He asked what it was. In ten minutes our world unraveled. I told him about the tape I had sent to UW, and of the conversation I'd just had with Dr. Pliss. I told him about what the transcript said. Marc was furious. I watched his face waver between fear and rage. The shack became too small to contain his emotions, so he went outside. I sat on the couch and cried. A while later I heard the echoes of hammering and I looked out the window to see him pounding nails into plywood, working on the interior walls of the new house. He worked well into the night. I went to bed and lay awake waiting for him. When he finally came to bed, smelling of sawdust and sweat, I tried to touch him but he shrugged me off. I listened to him fall asleep and that night he didn't talk in his sleep for the first time in a long time.

"The next morning Marc got up early and went out to work on the house again before he went to his job. I walked Nick to the bus stop, returned home, and made some tea. As I pulled the teabag from the cup I heard Marc cry out. I raced outside, knowing he'd been hurt. When I found him he was lying unconscious on the concrete foundation. He'd fallen from the second story. Blood was coming out of the back of his head, pooling on the foundation.

"In the hour I watched my husband die I lost my mind. I could have gotten in the truck and driven to the nearest house with a phone. I could have run down the driveway and flagged the first passing car. But I chose to stand and do nothing and let him die. I felt for his breath with the back of my hand. I felt it coming from his nostrils at first, in little bursts. The halo of blood grew wider. Then his breath stopped and his skin grew cold.

"I chose my son over my husband. As I watched Nick grow I remembered Marc's dark prophecy in the language of a long-extinct people. I locked his shedful of silly plans. My world grew dark and small. Nick was all I had, my only reason to live. Until one day his friend, who'd suffered the loss of his whole family, became my lover. For a brief moment our darknesses canceled each other out. Then Luke had to leave.

"Nick returned home from time to time as I became an old woman. He spoke of a glorious new age. He barked and paced, drunk on philosophy and the future of man.

"I just wanted to protect my little boy. I didn't want—please, I didn't want those horrible words to be true. Please don't let them be true."

As the little girl sobbed, Abby quietly retreated from the shack, rattled, convinced in her gut that this testimony was not hers to witness. Why had she, of all people, been privy to the story of the onset of the FUS? And what ever became of the recording she'd made at the Seaside Love Palace? Rather than illumination, all this information about Luke, Nick, and Star promised an ever-encroaching darkness. It was as though the very thing preventing her from acting on these stories was her inability to remain herself. She kept slipping, lightly superimposed over her own body, the borders of her self and her physical form not quite jibing. While snooping on other people's lives, her own had come under increasing, unnerving, and invisible scrutiny.

Eo was gone. Up ahead, through the trees, came street noises, honks, a river of rubber and asphalt. Between the trunks of trees materialized the gray faces of buildings. Abby stepped from the woods onto Broadway, across the street from Lincoln Center, and rubbed her eyes.

Later, at home with bouillabaisse and a sandwich purchased from a deli around the corner from her apartment, Abby watched some early films by Thomas Edison on Sylvie's ancient television set. A man played a violin for fourteen seconds. An elephant, electrocuted. A steam train charged the camera, sending early-twentieth-century audiences scurrying for cover. Rightly, she thought.

In Central Park Abby watched children. Gleefully unaware that they inhabited a simulation of a once-vibrant city, the children appeared to understand that this was their world to take. The adults, far less so, as they meandered paths and contemplated the skyline from benches and hills, enraptured by the illogic of it all. Abby overheard gossip about some of the older people, folks who'd actually lived in or visited the original Manhattan, reduced to inconsolable weeping, begging to be returned to Seattle, away from this reminder of the greed and weaponry and genocides that had once infected the world. These elderly visitors to the city were doubly troubled at the sight of newmans busily at work, the former enemies of human beings now rebuilding and making amends. That the newmans had developed a sense of altruism struck them as a colossal hoax. Abby sat on a bench with a bag of popcorn and watched one FUS survivor go insane in front of her eyes, clawing at his face and screaming of terrors inexpressible. A couple citizens representing police officers escorted him from the park.

Woo-jin, meanwhile, found himself in a penthouse on Park Avenue, in one of the homes of Isaac Pope, a residence the late billionaire had never even actually visited. The closet was stocked with wing tips, French-cuffed dress shirts, tailored suits, and a row of pressed fantasy-themed T-shirts shrugging on wooden hangers. In the bathroom various scented things in bottles stood on polished marble shelves. After a shower of confusing shampoos, Woo-jin found a suit that fit and did the best he could to make his face look like a real face. Clothed, back in the master bedroom, he nudged a door that opened onto a hallway lined with art he didn't have the patience to glom on to brain-wise. In a library, hardback techno-thrillers squatted in exotic hardwood bookcases. A couple of replicated contracts sat unsigned on the desk. Woo-jin wandered to the kitchen, where he paused to eat some things like sandwiches and puddings, then into a living area with an enormous movie screen. He thought of how less cramped Patsy would have been in here. Patsy growing eyeballs in her armpits, braying for gingersnap cookie dough. Smushing his face to a window and watching cars far below, Woo-jin whispered her name. After a while he pulled his face from the glass, leaving two dripping patches of tears, then wearily pushed his cart laden with the pizza box manuscript to the elevator.

On the street buildings moaned, harboring their captive ghosts. Woo-jin passed the Met, its doors open to a psychic blast furnace. Disturbed, he jogged across the street to get out of range of all the art howling from inside. Finally he found what he suspected he was searching for, a lonely and molested-looking phone booth. For some reason this one had been allowed to remain standing, an upright coffin reminder of how people used to conduct conversations while immobilized in public. A Yellow Pages sandwiched in a taco-like plastic shell dangled from the low shelf. He picked it up and looked for the Ls. Here: Literary Agents: See Agents, Literary. He found the Agents, Literary. Was anyone else going to need this section? Guiltily, Woo-jin tore the pages out of the book and stuffed them inside his coat, then hustled as fast as he could from the scene of his theft, pushing his rattly cart, until he was sure no cops were on his tail.

For days Woo-jin pushed his manuscript, from the Upper East Side to Tribeca, from the Financial District to SoHo to Midtown, proceeding alphabetically through the list of literary agents. In every instance, all the way into the D section, he found empty offices. Apparently the newmans weren't in a hurry to assign anyone to represent former representatives of novelists and memoirists. He parked his cart in Washington Square Park, revising, slicing through whole sections with his Sharpie. It seemed that while he had been otherwise engaged, his book had begun to fall apart. It wasn't that he'd accidentally shuffled the order of the pizza boxes—which, as it turned out, had actually improved the thing—but that the thoughts captured in it appeared to belong to someone far stupider than he. Overnight he'd lost confidence in his capacity to write the instructions he'd been assigned to write. Who the hell was he to tell anyone how to love people?

A parade tumbled through the park. A shambling thing, composed of salvaged clothes hanging from the angled frames of newmans, some of them playing instruments: battered brass and wind, a violin, an untuned guitar that struggled to assemble a chord. They looked beaten down, these unenthused servants of humanity, as if they'd been dry-humping existence to death. The instruments conspired to produce an off-key dirge and Woo-jin came to see that it was a funeral, with six pallbearers bearing aloft an aluminum casket. One of the newmans peeled off from the rest and slumped onto the bench beside Woo-jin. She sported a shaved head, fidgety hands, and something in her back that repeatedly clicked as if broken.

"Who died?" Woo-jin asked.

"Our great leader Stella Artaud! An old soldier from the FUS is capturing and torturing and killing my kind! Oh, how terrible, my heart can hardly bear it! Alas! A great violence has descended upon our creation! Oh, it's horrible! I thought our races had resolved their differences. I thought we lived in peace! But still, oh! The horrors persist!" Artificial tears spurted from her ducts as from an overactive windshield washer on a car. The newman shuddered, and a piece of her face fell off. Frantically, she began picking at parts of her body, taking off a digit here, a chunk of fake flesh there, yanking wires from her gut, sensors from her skull, and in less than a minute all that remained was a grief-induced pile of components, not a single part connected to any other part.

The funeral passed and deposited in its wake a raggy heap that resolved itself into a man. As the man shuffled toward Woo-jin his very self seemed to generate garbage—a trail of soda cans and fish skeletons and fast-food wrappers and horseflies. His head looked like a giant beard with some eyeballs thrown in as a bonus. He took a seat beside Woo-jin to offer a few moments of pointless dialogue, all the while generating trash, which accumulated in piles around him, from the folds of his smelly garments. He eyed Woo-jin's manuscript-on-wheels somewhat skeptically, as if it were a piece of public art that tested the boundaries of collective community standards. His filthy hand emerged from his rags. Woo-jin shook it. The man said his name was Glyph.

"So have you figured out the deal with this place, yet?" Glyph said. When Woo-jin shook his head, Glyph rolled his eyes. "They're building this joint just to tear it down again, man. As soon as the last brick is laid, the whole shitty thing becomes one giant history lesson. They're luring us humans in here so they can screw us over once again, getting it all populated and pretty as a picture before they reenact the FUS. Then they'll rebuild it again and reenact it all over, on and on into the end of civilization. Get out while you can, brother." A half-empty can of creamed corn fell out of Glyph's pants and rolled along the cobbles. "What do you have going on here? Some kind of artwork?"

"It's supposed to be a book. About how to love people," Woo-jin said. At that moment the clouds opened overhead like they'd been gutted with a filleting knife. Desperately he pushed the cart, searching for an awning somewhere to protect the manuscript from the rain. Within seconds his fancy new clothes were soaked through. Suddenly the world went slapstick. Woo-jin slipped on a turkey bone jettisoned from Glyph's garments and the cart teetered, then spilled its contents on the ground. On his hands and knees, Woo-jin tried to gather the pizza boxes with their words bleeding before his eyes. Here was his chapter about loving foster sisters who demand cookie-dough ice cream at two in the morning. Here were some sentences about washing dishes, about how not to eat your own tongue, about finding yourself ignored and alone in a trailer hauled into the sky.

By the time he was able to muscle the cart under the awning of a bodega the rain had lifted, leaving rainbows in its wake. Woo-jin pawed through the pile of wet cardboard looking for something salvageable but the words had turned into inky puddles and the pages had begun to disintegrate. As the manuscript fell apart, as the words grew more unintelligible, so too became the ideas those words had once propped up. How were people supposed to love one another? Woo-jin hadn't a clue. All he had was his love for one person, the flawed, hideous human being his foster sister had become. How could loving someone as nasty as Patsy help him draft a treatise on loving anyone else? He remembered the message his future brain had left for him, that it was his responsibility to provide the Last Dude with reading material. What would a guy at civilization's end need to know about loving people? And why would he need a guide book if there was no one around to love? In the rain, with the manuscript turning to mush, it came to Woo-jin what he had to write. All this time the book's title had misled him. It wasn't supposed to be about how *to* love people. It would be about how, at one time, we *loved* people. Woo-jin imagined the decrepit old man at his campfire, eating from the refrigerator's never-ending bounty, his messages spread on the desert floor far below. To this audience of one, Woo-jin would write that there used to be human beings here. We used to love one another. Or we tried to love, we wanted to love, but we kept screwing up. We stumbled toward love but fear led us into shadows. When we found the capacity to love those who'd wronged us, those who seemed most undeserving of our love, in those delicate moments, marginalized by the sweep of history, our future appeared almost hopeful. His book, Woo-jin realized, would be the only thing telling the Last Dude that he too was loved. This distant retard's voice recorded on brittle paper would be the only source of light in that final man's heart. Whatever he'd done to earn this fate, this eternal hauling of rocks in a vast waste, Woo-jin would assure him that his suffering wasn't for nothing, that as a human being he still deserved love, despite the fact that anyone who could possibly love him was long dead.

A voice came through Sylvie's phone.

"I've got your boyfriend," the man rasped. "Let me give you the address."

Half an hour later, facing a theoretical New Jersey, Abby walked briskly across the planks of a pier toward a squat structure, the temporary office of a building contractor. She entered the building without knocking, squinting to adjust to the dark.

This kind of room had appeared many times in movies. Empty but for a chair in the center, with a battered man tied to it. Scribbly explosions of blood spattered the floor. Abby didn't immediately recognize that this was Rocco, his face was so fucked-up. A figure stepped out of a shadow, a man seemingly composed of three bodies. His head was gray and old, sorrowful, unblinking. This head rested on the torso of a bodybuilder, a shirtless gristle of muscles, veins, and scars. This torso in turn sat atop a pair of legs that moved in spastic jerks, almost dancing toward her.

"This is your boyfriend?" Skinner asked.

Abby nodded.

"Should I let him go?"

Rocco was unconscious, his chin against his chest, his breath going in and out of his body in irregular sputters and coughs.

"What did you do to him?"

"He's a DJ. He's got hundreds of embodiments. Including you, before the monks snipped your connection."

"He's not a DJ. He's just a Bionet technician."

In the anime version, Skinner touched a key on a remote, bringing banks of monitors to life on every wall, the room's darkness bleached by surveillance-camera shots of human figures going about their routines. This didn't prove anything, really. It could have been footage of anybody. Here and there a person sat motionless in a chair or at a table. Others walked in circles, did jumping jacks, pounded their heads repeatedly against walls. Skinner pointed at a monitor displaying Abby sitting on her chesterfield, watching television. "These are just some of his embodiments," Skinner said.

"I don't believe you."

"Watch this." Skinner fiddled with the remote some more, muttering grumpily at the buttons. For a second the screens went blank, then sequences popped open, shots of this room with the chair and Rocco more or less confined to it. Each monitor ran a different clip culled from hours of torture. In some Rocco was conscious and talking, or not talking. In others he screamed and writhed and passed out from the pain. Abby shielded her eyes but the violence came through the audio, the smack of flesh getting rearranged, bones snapping beneath muscles, the high-pitched panic of dental extraction. Bile curled in her throat. She turned her eyes to Skinner, expecting to see the smugness of a torturer, but finding his face defeated.

"I inflict violence on the world," Skinner said.

"You're a monster."

"That's about right."

"Did you get the information you wanted from him?"

"He gave me a name, an address. I have no way of knowing if it means anything."

"I still love him."

"That may be true."

"You think I should hate him because I was his embodiment."

"I don't care what you feel about him," Skinner said. "I was just doing him a courtesy. Someone was going to have to retrieve the guy after I finished with him. He gave me your name." He turned to leave, then stopped. "You think I do this because I'm strong and you're weak? I do this because it's my only recourse. I don't enjoy this."

"Boo-fucking-hoo for you."

Skinner fiddled some more with the remote and all the monitors went blank except for one, in which Rocco, close-up, blood gushing out of his nose, spilled the beans. Off-camera, like a mobster-hunting detective from the world of noir, Skinner asked who he worked for. "Mr. Kirkpatrick. There have always been the slaves and the enslavers. The passives and the actives. I'm just a technician. I don't pick the slaves. I get assignments. I establish their routines. When they wake up. When they eat. When they sleep. When they fuck. What they buy."

The off-camera Skinner in the clip said, "I'm going to ask again why they took my boy."

"There's been talk there's a clone baby with super-admin privileges. Not good. With super-admin privileges you can take down the whole 'net. You can lock out all the DJs or turn admins into embodiments." Rocco spat out a gob of blood. "There's only one super-admin, and that's Kirkpatrick."

A new clip. Rocco with his head cocked a different way, making a noise like laughing or crying, hard to tell which. "I saved Abby from getting arrested because I thought she was cute," he said. "I wrote a program that kicked up her hormones to make her fall in love with me. Then I got tired of her. That fucker Bickle needed someone to babysit Kylee Asparagus so I volunteered her. While she was away we ran routines on the whole city. A massive orchestration. Every citizen an embodiment, their daily lives planned out for them without their knowledge. Just think of what you can make an *economy* do. Then she returned before she was supposed to. We stuck her in the apartment watching TV."

Another clip, more violence. Coin-sized pieces of skin removed from the surface of Rocco's body. Skinner turned it off midscream, then pulled a Bionet transmitter from his pocket and tossed it to Abby. "Most of the heavy organ damage has already been fixed," he said.

"What address did he give you?"

"I'm not telling you. I don't want to put you in any danger."

"You're a relic. You should have died in the FUS."

"You're probably right," Skinner sighed. "Have you ever thought about why the world had to end? That once we hit nine billion people living on this rock, the only honorable thing to do was for most of us to kill ourselves off? And yet somehow the likes of you and me survived. Ridiculous, isn't it?" He pranced, skipped, and twirled his way to the exit. Abby peeled away the duct tape binding Rocco's hands and legs and pressed his bloody face to her white shirt.

"You're safe now," she whispered.

"Now?" Rocco wheezed. "Now I'm definitely not safe."

Q&A WITH LUKE PIPER, PART 8

You know that unsettling feeling when you're moving from one place to another and you finally empty your old house and as you're vacuuming you realize it's just a space? That was how it felt at the academy. Something of consequence used to be here, but for whatever reason it disappeared. The windows were boarded up, the exterior was covered in grime and graffiti. Dead weeds where there used to be landscaping. As the real estate agent took down the "For Sale" sign I entered the main building. It felt like a grade school that had gotten roughed up and left for dead on the side of the road. All the rooms empty. No furniture, no artifacts to indicate this had once been a place to learn. The main building contained a dozen classrooms on two floors. There was a science lab building with a little planetarium, a library building with empty shelves, a maintenance building, and a dormitory with a cafeteria. There was a small athletic field and a gym.

I moved into what seemed like the headmaster's suite in the dorm building, bought some cheap Ikea furniture, and made it up like a monk's room. Minimal. I started to ask around the neighborhood about the building's previous inhabitants.

What kind of neighborhood was it?

Typical southwestern exurbia. Retirees and Latino families. That weird, thick, southwestern grass kept green with constant irrigation. The academy itself was right up against the mountains. There was a strip mall with a Starbucks. I started hanging out there, introducing myself to my new neighbors and asking about the academy. Nobody knew what I was talking about. Some thought it was a typical grade school. One lady who lived three blocks away from it argued that it didn't exist. I got monotone answers from the few young people I met. Everybody was entranced by their own gut-level routines, the pursuit of Frappuccinos. I got nowhere and soon gave up. Besides, it wasn't as important to me anymore that I learn the history of the academy so much as that I start fixing the place to prepare for Mr. Kirkpatrick's return. I started signing up for classes at the local Home Depot, reading home improvement books, educating myself on electrical wiring and plumbing. I did as much as I could on my own but when a job needed more than one guy I hired Mexican day laborers and learned what I could from them, too. I discovered things my hands could do. I spent the days sanding, painting, refinishing woodwork. I replaced broken toilets and installed light fixtures. I got scrapes and bruises and splinters under my fingernails.

How long did it take to restore?

About two years. Pushing a bucket around with a mop one night I realized I'd become a custodian. I laughed. What a thankless job, holding chaos and disorder at bay in the silent halls of an empty school.

Did you consider getting back in touch with Wyatt and Erika, or with Star?

What would I tell them? They belonged to a previous version of me. My holy task required that I cut off as many human connections as possible and wait patiently for Mr. Kirkpatrick's return. His academy would be in perfect shape, ready for pupils. I imagined he'd confer on me some special role, the caretaker of the academy. I found this solitary duty suited me.

He never arrived.

There's still time.

You sound pretty confident about that.

I know this because the one person who did show up was Dirk Bickle. He just pulled into the parking lot in his ridiculous Hummer while I was mowing the play field. The Sikh guys weren't with him this time. His gratitude was obvious in how ferociously he embraced me. I invited him in and showed him around, pointed out the work I'd done on the electrical and ventilation and floors. He beamed. In my quarters I served him coffee and asked him what was supposed to happen next.

He told me he was ready to reveal the master plan. He started with a hypothetical question. What if I was faced with the following choice—I could save the human race from self-imposed destruction, and the rest of humanity's existence would be peaceful for another thousand years until an asteroid obliterated the earth, or I could single-handedly destroy the human race and by doing so ensure that new life would appear after earth's destruction, on Mars.

[laughs]

I told him the choice was false. First, if humans lived another thousand years on earth, we'd surely develop technology to either obliterate the asteroid or escape the planet altogether. Second, how would new life emerge on Mars if humans weren't around to make it happen?

Bickle answered in the form of another question. Wasn't it interesting, he said, that humans had imperiled the planet at precisely the moment when we'd become capable of developing a technological solution to undo the damage? What held us back, he said, was our orientation to nature. We'd thoroughly externalized it instead of coming to terms with ourselves as its greatest force. We speak of "the environment" as if it's something apart from us. We speak of *protecting* the environment and being *environmentally friendly* as if the environment exists outside our homes. Worse were those who wished to restore nature to some prehuman state, failing to recognize that nature is constantly changing. The only rational choice, Bickle said, was to adopt an inventionist philosophy of environmental stewardship and engage in full-scale planetary reengineering, and to embrace the spirit of this project as a *natural* phenomenon rather than an artificial, human enterprise. The concept of artificiality was *itself* artificial. Mr. Kirkpatrick saw through the cultural construct that would segregate nature, humanity, and technology. His was an effort to redeem the human race through understanding that we were meant to control the course of nature and engineer it for the purposes of beauty.

Did you ever suspect that Bickle was just fucking with you?

I considered it. But why would the guy go to so much trouble just to mess with my head? There had to be a reason for him to follow me around, show up with a mystical refrigerator in the desert, save my life. Obviously he was a true believer of *something*. Even if that something was a delusion, it was an attractive delusion. Keep in mind I was surrounded by a society in which people didn't appear to believe in anything deeper than their product wish lists. Think about it. Utah is populated largely by people who believe their prophet discovered a pair of gold plates and spoke to an angel named Moroni. Hollywood is run by people who surgically alter their appearances and think they're descended from an alien named Xenu. People believe in ghosts, UFOs, a Heaven in which they'll reunite with all their dead relatives. Let's not even get into Christianity with its flaming sword guarding the tree of knowledge. Human beings just fundamentally believe crazy fucking shit, the crazier the better. What Bickle was hinting at seemed a lot less crazy than praying to Jesus to make you rich. Is believing that human beings are meant to be stewards of life in the universe *really* crazier than believing a certain brand of car makes you sexy or that God is keeping track of how many times you masturbate?

[laughs]

So Bickle moved into one of the spare dorm rooms and began revealing Mr. Kirkpatrick's teachings to me. The rift between Kirkpatrick and the dropouts had pretty much destroyed the academy, he said, and he had no idea where Mr. Kirkpatrick had gone. Into the desert, maybe, where all prophets go. He told me of great awakenings and celestial visitors, Kirkpatrick's series of prophetic dreams in which he communicated with Freidrich Nietzsche on the Bardo plane, becoming one with the philosopher and finding himself, in this act of communion, transformed into a planet-devouring phoenix. Kirkpatrick was Nietzsche's heir, spreading the word that the distinction between the overman and the human was the overman's responsibility to spread life itself through the universe. Bickle led me through the prophecies, late into the night. He said Mr. Kirkpatrick had been waiting for me to reach a state of receptivity before briefing me on the program.

Or maybe they were waiting for you to become wealthier so they could come after your money.

I feel sorry for the smallness of your thinking, I really do.

It all sounds bogus to me.

Do you want to hear the rest or what?

Why not. Go ahead.

One night after our lessons I asked Bickle what had caused the strife between the dropouts and Kirkpatrick. He became solemn and started speaking about Nick's final invention. You remember how he created that machine when we were in high school, the one that took itself apart?

The science fair.

Right. Well imagine such a machine operating on a global scale. Actually, you can't call it a machine, per se. Consider it a program, a system, a Rube Goldberg series of actions and reactions spreading outward from a central node. To call it a weapon would be too reductive. It was a device that set certain events in motion. The finger that topples the first in a row of dominos. Bickle called it the Rebooting Device, a technology designed to reconfigure the planet and bring about a new era.

What kind of era?

[laughs] He called it the Age of Fucked Up Shit.

Where was the device?

In a safety deposit box in a Chase bank in midtown Manhattan. Bickle gave me the name of the bank, the box number. I remained expressionless and didn't let on that I had the key. We continued our lessons. A month passed in deep meditation. The desert heat pressed down on me and just looking at the world outside my head was like one long good-bye. Finally Bickle packed up his Hummer and left, promising that Kirkpatrick would return. I waited a day, then caught the first flight to JFK.

After years of living in the desert suburbs working with my hands, speaking to few people, in a sort of monastic haze, stepping out of a cab in Midtown Manhattan was like getting electrocuted. I checked into a hotel in Times Square. It was a Sunday, so I waited until the next morning to go to the bank. I arrived as they opened and asked for access to box #3487. I had to sign something, and when I provided my ID and signature, they matched the info on file. This seemed like further confirmation that I was supposed to be pursuing this particular path, like the dropouts had forged my signature ahead of time. In a room of brass-doored safety deposit boxes, I took the key that Erika had vomited up and turned it in the lock. The clerk turned his key, and I pulled out a box and set it on the table.

Inside I found a smaller cardboard box, and inside that box the device. It was a cheap video-game controller from the 1970s, a scuffed black plastic case with a big red button on it. It looked like a joke. I wondered if Bickle hadn't sent me across the country so I'd leave the academy unattended. Maybe I *was* being fucked with. I took the device back to the hotel and sat on the bed looking at it. If I believed it was bogus, some sort of prop, then it didn't matter if I pushed the button or not. But if it really did set in motion the end of our times, then it mattered very much whether I pushed it. If I pushed the button, it meant I wasn't sure whether it was real and I was only pushing it to find out. Pushing it was an admission of skepticism. If I *didn't* push it, on the other hand, then part of me really did believe that it brought about the Fucked Up Shit. Did it matter whether or not I pushed it? I thought of my dead parents, my sister. My childhood home swept into the sound on a tidal wave of mud. I paced the room. I was in a rock/paper/scissors stalemate. Belief versus disbelief versus curiosity. Had Nick really invented a remote control to end the world? Ridiculous, right? I had to get out of the room, so I walked through the tourist shit of Times Square, mumbling the arguments for and against, blending with the human tide. Some subterranean part of me whispered that it was only a matter of time before I pushed the button. I was going to push it! I talked myself down. I'd operate as though I'd never come out here. I would throw the controller in the East River and catch a flight home.

When I got back to the hotel, I realized I was starving so I placed a room service order worthy of a death row inmate's last meal. Plan was, I would watch an on-demand movie and gorge myself before I flew back to Vegas. After a while the room service guy arrived and pushed the table into my room. Young guy, with buzz-cut red hair. He positioned the table in front of the bed and started lifting silver domes off things, peeling the Saran wrap off my water glass. That's when it happened. My wallet was sitting on one of the bedside tables. If I'd had it in my pocket, I would have been able to take it out and give him his tip while facing him. But I had to turn around, my back to him, so I could reach it sitting beside the room service menu. While my back was turned, he said, "What's this?" and before I turned around I knew what he was referring to. My mouth was preparing the word "Don't" but not soon enough. I turned in time to see his finger make contact with the red button and press it. The device made a solid click.

I couldn't move. He'd pressed the button. The room service guy had pressed the fucking button. He shrugged and set it back on the table. Then he handed me the bill. I don't remember signing it, but I remember him leaving the room, because he paused at the door and said, "*Take care, Fly.*"

So there was this one momentous thing happening in my head, the pushing of the button, and then there was the second momentous thing, the room service guy calling me by the code name the dropouts had given me. I had to sit down on the bed and think about what had just happened. I'd been played. The dropouts knew I'd be coming to New York to pick up the device. They didn't have the means to break into a bank, but they could plant a guy at a hotel to come to the room to push the button. Outside, buildings remained standing. Manhattan operated as it always had, as far as I could tell.

How long did you stay in New York?

I checked out as soon as I regained my senses. As I walked to the ticket counter at Kennedy I had no idea where I was going until I slapped down my ID and asked for the first flight to Seattle. I was sure that by the time the plane touched down the world would be in flames. I found myself landing at SeaTac, grabbing a cab, going through these transitional moments like I was wearing a suit made out of an aquarium, the world outside of me blunted and muffled and drab. I was in a cab and on a ferry, and in another cab. Then before I knew it it was night and I stood at the overgrown driveway leading to Star's house. I had no flashlight, I just felt along ahead of me with a stick, dragging my roller bag through the mud. When I got to the clearing, there was the shack and the shed and the unborn skeleton of the never-completed house. Suddenly, boom, I was on Bainbridge again. I had to catch up with the idea, like one of those online clips where the video speeds up to sync with the audio. As I was asking myself what the hell I was doing here, the door opened, and Star's silhouette was framed in light. I came forward and found her looking exactly as she'd looked when I'd left. As if she hadn't aged. Same housedress, same hair in pigtails. If you looked at us you'd have thought I was the older one. My beard streaked gray, my skin creased by the Nevada sun. She beckoned me in with her finger like a witch in a fairy tale. And like a character in a fairy tale, I walked right through that portal into my past. The body odor/incense/oniony smell of a hippie house. We didn't say anything to each other. She took my coat and stuck my bag in a corner. Then I collapsed on the couch and fell into a night of hyper-realistic dreams. I dreamed I was a boy again, maybe ten years old, and it was winter. I was in the woods playing with Nick and we'd made a fort, really nothing more than a chair and an old step ladder we'd dragged under the boughs of a cedar. It was getting dark and I told Nick I wanted to go home, but he said he wanted to keep playing, so we stayed under the tree in the patch of bare ground while snow continued to fall from the darkening sky. I sat on the step ladder hugging myself for warmth and Nick sat on the chair doing the same. In the dream I faded to sleep and woke up in complete darkness. Panicked, I had to feel my way out of the snowy woods, stumbling along the path. When I came to the clearing where Nick's house stood, it was dawn, and I realized that I'd left Nick back there. But instead of going back I decided to pretend I didn't know where he was. The scene changed and it was quite some time later, in a different season, springtime. I stood at the edge of the woods while police with chattering radios recovered Nick's body. His skin was yellow and his head flopped to the side as they carried him out. Somehow the cops figured out that I had abandoned him out there and Star stood next to me, angry, shaking. I needed to escape the cops. They seemed distracted anyway, so it wasn't hard to slip away back into the woods. But now it was a different season, summer, and I was an adult, and as I climbed over fallen logs I had a conversation with myself about how I had just been dreaming that Nick had frozen to death in the woods. A dream within a dream. I heard traffic ahead and pushed through some foliage to find myself on a sidewalk in New York City. Behind me the woods were dense and dark, but in front of me cars and buses honked and squealed. Instead of buildings, a thick wall of trees rose along the sidewalk at my back. Like I was standing at a sort of membrane between two island worlds. I started walking downtown, toward Times Square. Soon I stood in front of the hotel I had just checked out of, with my hand finding its way to my pocket, where it found my swipe key. I felt like I was walking around in my aquarium suit again. I rode the elevator to the floor I had stayed on, walked down the hall, tried the key, and opened the door, overwhelmed with black, sticky dread. There was my luggage, the newspaper I'd read that morning, the device with the red button sitting on the table. I was back, in a dream, in New York City, where I'd just been. I sat on the edge of the bed, thinking that this was turning out to be one hell of a long dream. There was a knock and the words "room service" came through the door. I opened it and the same guy who'd pressed the button earlier wheeled in another cart laden with food, and he went through the same procedure of removing the Saran wrap from my glass and lifting lids off entrées. I was locked into an algorithmic set of options, as if I'd rehearsed; I reached for my wallet on the bedside table as the guy picked up the device, said, "What's this?" and pressed the button. Exactly as it happened the first time. Except now I knew he was a dropout. But I was locked into the routine and couldn't do anything different with this knowledge. The button got pressed again. And this time, in the dream, I went to the window to see buildings falling. When I woke up, I was in Star's house, but she wasn't there. In fact, she'd been gone for years.

NEW YORK ALKI

The city's population swelled, drawn to its shores by viral marketing campaigns and rumors of epiphanies. Newcomers stood marveling at how thoroughly the first wave of inhabitants had adopted the personas of their ghostly forebears, circulating the blood of commerce and art through Chelsea, Tribeca, Wall Street, Harlem, Midtown. Newmans marched twenty abreast chanting conciliatory mottoes and welcoming these immigrants with promises of freedom from the stress of industrial production. Here and there a crime erupted, mostly human-on-newman violence, handled discreetly by those who'd absorbed the personas of New York's finest. Bald eagles careened over former Bainbridge Island, orcas nudged its seawall, and from the city's bowels screeched rats, subways, and data. The by-products of human folly seemed to have expired outside the parapets of this cathedral. Block by block the last vestiges of the former island trembled under the sky's robotic arms and joined the urban parallelogram teeming with offices and takeout pierogi joints, galleries, and gay bars. The more immigrants who arrived at this fever dream, the easier it was for a man or woman just off the boat to cast aside his or her former self and plunge psychologically whole into one of the diminishing number of roles doled out by the newmans. The rain-raked city strained under the weight of lost memories.

Woo-jin, lying on the master bathroom floor of the penthouse, head resting on a hand towel, succumbed to dreams once dreamt by Isaac Pope, which mainly consisted of endless lines of code with the occasional appearance of a *Star Trek* character asking for instructions on how to fuck. Woo-jin woke to a shoe tapping his wrist. He couldn't see the man's face from this angle; and the lunar eclipse of the heat lamp cast the face in shadow. The guy smelled of shoe polish and breath mints. He extended his hand and pulled Woo-jin up so that he could sit on the toilet. Then the man took a seat on the edge of the tub. Woo-jin tried to reset his eyes but the guy's face seemed to come out of an obscure memory.

"You're that movie star," Woo-jin said.

"That's right. I'm Neethan F. Jordan."

They shook hands. Woo-jin accidentally leaned on the flusher.

"You're Woo-jin Kan," Neethan said.

"Please don't hurt me."

"I'm not here to hurt you. Don't you remember me? We were both in the Happy Sunset Home together. When we were kids?"

"The group home?"

"Yes, the group home. You're my brother."

"I have a brother?"

Neethan shrugged. "Brother in the sense that we came from the same lab. We got sent to the home because we came out not exactly to spec. They had designs for all of us. Some of us came out different from how the recipe said we'd come out. I was a false negative. They thought I was a rough draft, but they made a mistake."

"Who is 'they'?"

"The ones who pushed civilization's RESET button. They designed me to be a movie star. Made me a descendant of an Indian tribe that got wiped out even before the FUS. They made you, I don't know—"

"I'm a really good dishwasher," Woo-jin said.

"There you go. I played one of those once."

"Did you ever play a writer?"

"I did, yeah. Why? You want to be a writer?"

"I tried to write a book about how to love people but it fell apart."

"How do you love people?"

"I still don't know."

"Who does?" Neethan shrugged. "By the way, when I showed up they assigned me the life of some homeless guy. You wouldn't mind if I crashed here, would you?"

The penthouse quickly filled with characters. While Woo-jin slept they sprawled on living room furniture and helped themselves to the pantry, uncorked pre-FUS bottles of port, and confiscated art off the walls. Mornings Woo-jin shuffled in pj's to the bathroom to piss only to be sideswiped by Neethan, who supported on his arm a woman named Sarah or Kateesha or April, pleasant enough ladies doing their panicked best to adapt to the lives they inhabited in this fabricated metropolis. A cadre of filmmakers held court on the balcony drinking brandy from to-go cups and debating the methods by which qputers cinematicized reality. A chef arrived, accompanied by a woman with one leg, a horn section in search of a band, some cracked-out bike messengers, and a newman crooner who sang spot-on versions of period show tunes. A couple times Woo-jin woke to find socialites unconscious in his bed or the bathtub. Group sing-alongs at all hours, creative uses for whipped cream, a sink bloodied by some poor bastard's unfortunate encounter with a shattered highball. Various drugs rampantly traveled through the collected horde, with substances snorted, swallowed, injected, shoved into rectums, and illegally downloaded. A shaman of sorts—at least he looked like a shaman—danced spastically in the butler's quarters in coils of sage smoke. Pots and pans clattering, someone going to town on a seven-piece Ludwig trap set, bowls of M&M's and newman-human genital interactions. Vomit, assorted. This was, Neethan Fucking Jordan informed him, the party.

Every night after booklessly wandering the city in search of an agent, dragging himself through the door of his building, Woo-jin found his penthouse that much more infested with marauders high on one thing or another and their dogs and cats. Which made it all the stranger when he returned one night to find the penthouse fairly empty, just a man who looked like a fire fighter asleep facedown, snoring in the book-lined library. Then, from above, snickers. Woo-jin craned his neck to see that twenty feet up the usual rabble had ascended to the ceiling. Just kind of floating there like astronauts in zero-G. One young gentleman spilled his white Russian on Woo-jin's shoulder.

Neethan spun around the chandelier, brushing aside a couple pairs of groping hands, encircled by cameramen standing on the ceiling. "Woo-jin!" he called down, "Take a hit off one of those balloons and join us!"

In the corner, beside the bigass FUS-era globe marked with graphic representations of fires, tornadoes, rogue glaciers, earthquake fissures, swarms of locusts, and the like was a bouquet of balloons with their strings tied to a paperweight in the shape of the Arc de Triomphe.

"What am I supposed to do?"

"Inhale the air inside it!" Neethan said. "Like you're doing a whippit!"

"Like I'm whipping what?"

"Just open the end of it and breathe in the air."

Woo-jin emptied the contents of a balloon into his lungs. Right away he felt a nagging absence of gravity. Some force seemed to pull his legs out from under him and he gradually rose to the ceiling, where Neethan looped an arm around him.

"How you holding up, buddy?" Neethan asked, half to the cameras.

"I think I need to start writing my book again."

"Go for it, buddy. Hey, can I get one of those mini pizza things over here? Get this—I met this crazy couple of university professors who happen to know a lot about my tribe. They're over there by the guy in the bear suit."

Cut away to the Vacunins pausing their zero-G heavy petting to pinkie wave at Neethan.

"I need to go home," Woo-jin said.

"For real?" Neethan said, pretend-disappointed. "Come on, no . . ."

"I can't write the book I'm supposed to write here."

Neethan nodded to the cameras. "You guys getting all this? Cool . . ." He lowered his voice and leaned in close. "Hey. Can you see me?"

"See you? Yeah?"

Eavesdropping onlookers chortled. Neethan lowered his voice, somewhat panicked. "Seriously, bro, I need to figure out what kind of real I am."

A rumble of conversation passed through the floating assemblage. Woo-jin caught pieces of it. Supposedly the messiah was near. "The king! The king! He has arrived!" Perplexed grins and bursts of laughter all around. A waft of combo hash-crack smoke. "In Central Park? Dude, I am so there." Someone, an actress maybe, wearing little more than a shoe, opened a high window and squeezed out to drift moonward in the night. Others followed, cackling, anxious for their chance to witness the messiah's return. Eventually the exodus left Woo-jin and Neethan alone, floating on the ceiling, while someone snored inside the chandelier.

"The messiah, huh?" Neethan sighed. "I was supposed to abort that son of a bitch."

Eventually they floated to the floor. Woo-jin walked in a circle to shake out his legs as gravity reasserted itself. Neethan tossed cubes into a glass and poured something brownish on top of them.

"Maybe you'll find your people," Woo-jin said.

"I'm not a person, I'm a character. And I am fabulously famous and sexy and wealthy," Neethan said almost sadly, then killed his drink.

"How should I get home to Seattle?"

"Easy. Just catch the Q from Fifty-ninth."

That night Woo-jin said good-bye to New York Alki, hopping on a subway just before it left the platform. Here and there folks crammed words into crossword puzzles or slept listening to iPods. After a time Woo-jin closed his eyes and let his head rock back and forth as it rested against the glass. Later, a sense of motionlessness woke him. He clambered out of the train into a deep darkness that confusingly revealed streets and houses. He headed toward the rivery car sounds and found himself on Aurora, Seattle's avenue of hookers, gun shops, and moving-van companies, then veered south as day broke over his left shoulder, the purple serration of the Cascades rising beyond the repaired and repellent city. Most of these neighborhoods were abandoned but here and there a house suggested the presence of a family sleeping inside, with mowed lawns and new shingles, vehicles glossy with dew parked out front. Aurora turned into 99 and Woo-jin dipped beneath the city and when he came out of the tunnel it was morning with seagull cries and the salty, creosote stench of the waterfront. After this brief view of the sound the roadway dipped under the dome and Woo-jin trudged through artificially lit Pioneer Square, stopped to buy a cookie, passed the stadiums, came out on the other side of the dome onto Fourth Avenue, and crossed Lucile into Georgetown.

He expected the trailer to still be gone but there it was, parked in the spot that had recently been a patch of littery dirt. He stood numb from walking and blinked in the dust. After a moment the door creaked open, revealing a statuesque woman in a glittery silver bikini.

Patsy spoke. "Woo-jin! Where the heck have you been? Why are you wearing that stupid suit? Take a look at what they did to me! Oh my God, Woo-jin, they made me not a pharmer anymore! Check this body out! Yeah, that's what I'm talking about! They took off the penises and tissues and everything! Oh, my God I'm so hungry! Don't you tell me you didn't bring me leftovers to eat! Don't just stand there grinning like an idiot, Woo-jin Kan. Feed me! Feed me! *FEED ME!*"

Towels, water, rubbing alcohol, blood, gauze. Abby dressed Rocco's wounds in the bathroom of the apartment, tossing saturated clothes and absorbent materials into the tub. He murmured codes into the pocket transmitter then slept wrapped in a comforter on the couch while the Bionet went to work rebuilding tissues. Abby stood over him, watching him sleep, knowing that if she was going to kill him, it would have to be now.

Midway through the bread at their favorite Meatpacking District wine bar, Sylvie told Rocco about a manuscript she'd just accepted.

"I missed you," Rocco said.

Sylvie wanted to say she missed him, too, but that wouldn't have been entirely true. Part of her—most of her—didn't even know who the hell he was. Some guy plowing his fingers through cheek stubble, considering the Malbecs. Who was he again? Oh, right, he was Rocco. She knew him? Yes, everything about him looked familiar. She anticipated the eyelid flutter thing he did when he laughed. A script of possible behaviors whirred away somewhere cranial, and thinking about how or why she knew him seemed to disrupt it.

"I'm Sylvie Yarrow now."

"You're Sylvie Yarrow."

"I'm Sylvie Yarrow?"

"You're Sylvie Yarrow."

They ordered the Australian pinot noir pimped by the sommelier. The candle guttered, sending up a foul feather of smoke.

"If I'm Sylvie Yarrow, who are you?"

"I'm Rocco. Your boyfriend, remember?"

"But—"

"What is it?"

"My boyfriend is Bertrand."

"You were with Bertrand but you broke up. Now you're with me."

"I think there's something wrong with me. I don't feel like myself."

"Who do you feel like?"

"I feel like I'm between two someones. And where are we?"

"At the wine bar—"

"I know that, but more generally. We're in the city, right?"

"Have some wine," Rocco said.

"Seriously. This is Manhattan?"

"That's correct."

"The air doesn't smell right to me."

"You had nightmares last night. You kept moaning in your sleep. What were they about?"

"Who are you supposed to be?"

"I'm your boyfriend. Rocco. The nightmares. Tell me."

Sylvie quaffed red. "I was in a morgue. There was a coroner. He kept pulling out slabs. On every one of them was the same woman. Dozens of identical corpses."

"Sylvie?"

"I feel weird about you calling me that."

"All I've ever wanted for you is a happy life. Out of all the lives in New York City I reviewed, this one was the happiest. So I made arrangements to assign you this life."

"What do you mean 'assign'?"

"The world you've known isn't the world you're actually living in. Your name is Sylvie Yarrow and you're an editor at a publishing house. You live in the twenty-first century. You have an extraordinarily rich and rewarding life. Go deeper into this self. Relax your ego. Drift into this welcoming new person."

"I can't remember my real name." Sylvie squinted. "It's like a painful tip-of-the-tongue feeling."

"Can't you see what kind of heaven this is? All of it recreated just for you. You're free to live in this place as it was at the height of its glory."

The salads came.

"That looks good," Rocco said. "What kind did you order again?"

"Arugula Gorgonzola something something."

Rocco, his voice low, said, "Take this life. It's yours. All the memories, the belongings. How many people have this kind of opportunity? How many people would die to trade lives with someone happier?"

"I'm Sylvie Yarrow."

"You're Sylvie Yarrow."

How arduous this process was, turning one person into another. Way way more complicated than manipulating some douchebag's actions via the Bionet. DJing was all about making another person succumb to your will. This kind of work, on the other hand, was like translating a book from one language into another, except instead of languages one translated entire personalities, and instead of words one worked with white matter flickering in gray matter. Rocco didn't entirely understand the personalities, so it was a little like coding in real time with no QA process to grab the bugs. He detected a little panicked fluttering at the edges of her mouth, a momentary wobble toward tears. He cupped his hand over her non-fork-wielding hand. Would Sylvie's personality successfully map onto Abby's, or would little Abby remnants crop up from time to time, like continuity errors in a movie? Watching her disappear into Sylvie was a bit like watching someone die, he was hesitant to admit, and for a moment a miniaturized sadness presented itself in his thoughts. Then he remembered that the whole point of this experiment was to turn his girlfriend into someone more interesting. He wondered if she'd take on Sylvie's sexual proclivities, if it would feel like sleeping with a new woman.

Rocco summoned the waiter and ordered the olive and cheese plate out of sequence with the salads and entrées, then rubbed the veiny bulges on top of Sylvie's hand. "So tell me more about this guy's novel?"

Sylvie sighed. "It's about the beginning of a new world. There's a rampaging glacier in it. Clones. Giant heads that appear in the sky."

"One of those."

* * *

A significant aspect of replacing one personality with another involved what came to be called, in academic circles, *third personing*. Most of the time this involved the use of a prop, specifically a doll or figurine, life-size or not, into which the subject discarded his or her former personality. For Abby's third personing, Rocco'd purchased a custom sex doll manufactured to his specifications—a precise, to-scale model of Abby, with the same color eyes, hair, measurements, etc., crafted of a rubberized polymer and dressed in one of Abby's white-blouse-and-black-pants combos. She sat positioned on the couch of Sylvie's apartment, a fashion magazine open in her lap. Returning that night from the wine bar, Rocco snapped on the lights and addressed the mannequin from across the room.

"Hello, Abby," he said.

Sylvie stood in the doorway feeling like maybe she'd entered the wrong apartment.

"It's okay," Rocco said. "She's just going to hang out here. Say hello."

"Hi there," Sylvie said.

"Now be polite, Sylvie, and address Abby by her name."

"Hi, Abby."

"Abby here is a graduate of the University of British Columbia in digital data archaeology. She says you have a nice apartment," Rocco said.

"Thanks. Sorry for it being so small," Sylvie said.

"Abby says, 'Oh, no, don't apologize. I've seen way smaller apartments in New York City. And what a neighborhood. Right in the middle of the hippest part of Manhattan.'"

Sylvie said, "Oh, stop. Can I get you a drink, Abby?"

Rocco said, "Abby says that would be nice. 'Do you have tonic water?'"

"I think I have that. Rocco?"

"Sure, tonic water sounds good to me, too."

Sylvie retrieved the drinks from the kitchen and returned to find Rocco chuckling at a witty comment Abby must have just made. "Say, Sylvie, Abby says she just finished one of the books you edited, *The Subject's Object.*"

"That was a bitch to edit," Sylvie said, coastering beverages. "All those passages in Russian and Icelandic."

"Abby says she loved the ending."

"I'm proud of that ending," Sylvie said. "It took a while to get there. At one point I was reduced to tears. And not the good kind of tears."

"I couldn't get into *The Subject's Object,*" Rocco said, "but I'm not all that literary."

"Rocco's the left-brainer of the relationship," Sylvie said.

"Shit!" Rocco exclaimed, looking at his watch.

"What is it, honey?"

"There's an email I forgot to send from work. And I left my laptop on my desk. Damn. I'm going to have to hop over there and hit SEND. I won't be long, promise." He gathered his jacket and kissed Sylvie on the forehead. "Sorry, Abby, I was just starting to enjoy our conversation. You two carry on without me."

With Rocco gone, there came an awkward silence. Sylvie swirled the cubes in her glass. "So what line of work are you in, Abby?"

"Good question," Abby said. "I just graduated, so I'm looking for jobs. Digital recovery stuff. I specialize in DVDs. What

I'd *love* to do is work for a museum, restoring old movies. By old I mean 1900s or earlier."

"You shouldn't have any trouble finding a job in Manhattan. I'm guessing you've already sent your CV out to the museums?"

"Not so much yet. I landed a gig for a while working for Kylee Asparagus."

"No kidding?" Sylvie said. "I loved her *Asia* album. She's way underrated." She rose and tickled a docked iPod. The opening of *Asia* played through bookshelf speakers.

As promised, Rocco wasn't long, or was as long as it took him to walk around the block four times. When he returned, Sylvie sat in bed with a damp washcloth over her eyes. Abby remained on the couch, the magazine still in her lap.

"I suddenly got a really brutal headache," Sylvie said.

"Did you download anything for it?"

"Did I what?"

"Take anything. Acetaminophen."

"I'm sorry I couldn't entertain our guest."

"She'll be fine."

"I could barely get a word in edgewise."

Rocco poked at his pocket transmitter and entered a mild pain relief code, then an equally mild tranquilizer that had Sylvie snoring in a minute. Returning to the living room he paused in front of the fake Abby.

"Can I get you anything to eat?" he said.

Sylvie arrived home early on a Friday and found Rocco in bed with Abby. Apparently he hadn't heard her come in. She watched him huffing over the prone form through the doorway. Abby's legs were up, one of them bent over his right shoulder as he pumped and strained. Watching someone else have an orgasm is like witnessing a machine seize up, a system grind to a halt. Rocco grunted "*Fuck*" as he rolled onto his back, his cock audibly popping out of the artificial vagina like a cork exiting a bottle. He noticed Sylvie standing in the doorway.

"This is nothing," Rocco said.

Sylvie frowned and went to the kitchen. A minute later she leaned against the dishwasher and Rocco leaned against the sink.

"I'm telling you, it was nothing. You didn't see that."

"I don't want her staying here anymore," Sylvie said.

"How do you think she feels about all this?"

"I don't care how she feels, Rocco."

"You're not really mad at me."

Sylvie palmed a tomato. "I am too."

"You're not. And you're confused as to why you're not. You feel like you should be more mad."

Sylvie caught his eyes for a second, nonverbally offered up her confusion, then cast her gaze aside.

"She's not real, Sylvie."

"She loved you."

"Huh?"

"Abby loved you, Rocco. She trusted you. She told me what you did."

"There's no Abby anymore. Just Sylvie."

"I am Sylvie Yarrow."

"You are Sylvie Yarrow."

"You were fucking her."

"I was fucking her for the last time."

"All she did for a month was watch TV, eat, and sleep. You set her up with the most boring routine possible."

Rocco scritched stubble. "You assume I was her DJ."

"Who then?"

"Someone else makes me do this. I only DJed Abby because someone else is DJing me."

Sylvie's fingers closed around the tomato, the pulp and seeds and skin running down her wrist. Her fist trembled.

Rocco continued. "I don't have a choice about who I am. But you do. You can choose to live Sylvie's life."

"I am Sylvie Yarrow."

"You are Sylvie Yarrow. There's one thing left to do. It's the right time." From the butcher's block next to the Cuisinart Rocco pulled a filleting knife. He pried open Sylvie's hand and let the fingers curl back around the knife handle. He led her to the bedroom, where the Abby sex doll was still prone, dripping a thin drool of semen onto the comforter, the dummy eyes pointed toward the ceiling.

"A young, successful woman with her life ahead of her. A talented book editor making a name for herself. This is what you want," Rocco said. "So you must kill her. You're Sylvie Yarrow," Rocco said.

"I'm Abby Fogg," she said, wiping the blade across Rocco's neck.

Rocco smiled a second, surprised, then seemed to realize this wasn't fucking around. The sheets: they used to be white. He awkwardly genuflected, a hand over his throat, then crawled to the bathroom. Abby stepped over him and fetched the Bionet transmitter from the medicine cabinet, sat on the toilet, and held it out for him as he crawled around in a red slick. She'd never seen this much blood. Bubbles of it coming out of the fleshy, fishy slit she'd made. He reached for the transmitter, died, and settled into the pool.

Back in the bedroom, Abby dressed the sex doll and propped her against the headboard. She turned on the TV for her, switched to a nature show, and put the remote in the doll's hand. A moment later somebody knocked on the door. She opened it to find Lamb, the qputer monk, now dressed in toddler-sized overalls.

"Good job, Abby," Lamb said.

"I'm Abby Fogg," Abby said, blinking her eyes. "I'm *Abby Fogg.*"

This was a sidewalk from a memory, a crisp overlayer of graffiti and fluttery newspaper trash. Skinner had been here before, chasing newmans through Old Navy display windows and the gutted burning interiors of hipster apartments. SoHo: a facsimile. The address Rocco had provided under duress led him to a block, a door, a stairwell, a creaky wood hallway, a steel door behind which played some hideous prog. The door was unlocked. Skinner found an apartment committed to Danish design. Shit was minimal. Like the place was intended to be temporary but had been temporary for a very long time. Dirk Bickle sat on a black leather couch, wearing a white bathrobe, his white hair slicked back after a shower. On the coffee table in front of him were spread a variety of brand-name guns.

"Make yourself at home, Al."

Skinner took a seat opposite, on a box-shaped chair. "You're an old guy like me."

"You and I go way back. You wouldn't remember."

"What's with the arsenal?"

"We figured you'd want to rearm yourself."

"You have my grandson," Skinner said.

"*They* have a clone of your grandson. I thought that made all the difference."

"I'm tired."

"Take a nap, my friend. The bed is comfy."

"I'm tired of killing things."

"I'd be tired, too. But you're the reptile brain, remember? You're doing what you were designed to do."

"You know where they have him."

"The Metropolitan Museum of Art. You'll find him at the Egyptian tomb."

"I don't want to kill you."

Bickle shrugged. "You want an explanation. You want me to lay out the causalities. For what? The world we occupy doesn't operate that way anymore, if it ever did. You want me to tell you where Waitimu is so you can do your heroic rescue routine?"

"I'll lay down my weapons for good."

"Let go of A+B=C, Al."

"Who are you, anyway?"

Bickle laughed. "I'm just some stupid guy. Look at this place. You know what's funny? This is my actual apartment. A replication of where I lived pre-FUS. I'm having reruns of dreams I had hundreds of years ago. I never got married, never shared my life with anyone. I'm just some asshole with a sociology degree who answered an ad in a newspaper in 1985 for tech industry recruiters and found himself working for the most visionary of men. I didn't offer you anything to drink. Cocktail? San Pellegrino? I've got some re-created Limonata in the fridge."

Skinner picked up the nearest chair and hurled it through the window.

"You'd better hope that didn't hit anybody," Bickle said. Skinner yanked him off the couch by the throat and wrestled him to the jagged, framed air. He didn't squeeze hard enough for Bickle to stop breathing, but enough to make the guy panic. Skinner dangled him over the sidewalk four stories down. Below, a taxi swerved to avoid the chair that now sat comically upright in the middle of the street.

"You probably won't die unless you land on your head."

"Get it over with. Do it."

"You people killed my family." Skinner jerked him back in, spun him around, pretzeled him into a full nelson, shoved him up to the broken window's edge. The wind smelled like salt, like shit, like dead things, like low tide.

"We didn't kill anyone. I'm a curator. I arrange mis-en-scènes. I make sure certain people are in certain places at certain times. I appear at the right moments to ensure that things proceed according to Mr. Kirkpatrick's plans."

"My *grandson*."

"They're keeping him comfortable in a room with no Bionet access. If your grandson got out he could take down the whole platform. He's got super-admin permissions. He can erase whole directories. Suspend immunities. Unleash plagues. Authorize cancers and virgin births. Millions could die."

"Why didn't you just kill him?"

Bickle rubbed his neck and sighed. "This is the violence you inflict to extract increasingly unreliable information."

"Answer my question."

"Mr. Kirkpatrick is the only one we know of who's ever had super-admin privileges. Your grandson could be the heir, the one who can seed the universe with new life, fulfilling our purpose."

Skinner threw Bickle onto the couch, danced to the kitchen, and poured himself a glass of water. Behind him, Bickle said, "I don't care if you take the boy. I'm just connective tissue. I'm a concept, I'm like a mathematical theorem, Al. But I do know that every possible path open to you leads to extinction. This interrogation, or whatever you want to call it, is about you working through that theorem with a dull pencil, trying to get your big dumb brain to put it together."

His big dumb brain. Yeah, that about summarized it. Skinner: meat moving through space on dancing legs, a wall of viscera. A montage of comic book encounters with thugs and lowlifes with heavy jaws, faces cracking under his hammer fist. Nightclubs, menacing piss-fragrant alleys. If he let go of what few memories remained, this was how he could live, as an action-movie caricature, a distilled id in the form of a geriatric commando with muscles out to here. Memories persisted in their needled prodding, forcing him toward some unbearable decision. He'd watched these buildings burn to the ground and gazing at them now he saw through their fabricated surfaces to the ruins they once were, those stinking repositories of cadavers.

"Your violence belongs to the old world, the fallen world," Bickle said.

"What do you call this world?"

"This is the afterlife, Al. Except this afterlife is real and it's on earth. It's beautiful. It's our redemption. It's the time when we fulfill the task we were put here to do from when we crawled up out of the slime. Mr. Kirkpatrick teaches us that long ago we fearfully opened our eyes and searched for God. Now we open our eyes with love and create new life that will behold our fading shadow in awe. This is how it has been for all time. Intelligence moves relentlessly toward the creation of new varieties of intelligence and the greatest achievement of intelligence is the dissemination of new life forms. This clone of your son is the one we've been waiting for."

"I have no idea whose side I'm even on," Skinner said.

"You're on the side that lifted man from the animals. But we don't need you anymore."

"I don't remember how I got here."

"You took a cab."

"No, this island. The segues are missing from my memories."

Stretching his neck, Bickle crossed the room to the stereo. "That's because you're a forgetfulness junkie. And by the way, that was a really expensive chair you ruined, I'll have you know." On the shelf next to the stereo sat an Apple memory console and a stack of cards. "You really want to know how you got here?"

Skinner didn't answer, and in not answering indicated that he did.

"Did anything about your trip to Bramble Falls strike you as odd?" Bickle said.

"Lots of hallucinations."

"Right. The kid with no face and the Indian by the fire. All those detailed memories of your hometown, the trails, the trees. The suddenness with which you were standing at the trailhead eating fruit cocktail from a can. Not to mention you're never going to find a town called Bramble Falls on a map. The place is an invention. The real stroke of genius, thanks to this young hotshot developer we've got assigned to the project, was to embed your dad's memories in this patched-together memory network where you've spent the past couple weeks. But that's not the highlight. The highlight is this little guy right here." Bickle held a card between his thumb and index finger. "You remember erasing a memory of erasing a memory and so on. Here it is. The master file. The memory of when you killed your son."

Skinner fritzed out a bit at the edges. "You're lying."

"Your last mission, Al. The final hurrah of Christian America. The ultimate test of a soldier's loyalty to laws and order and dogma. You carried out your orders impeccably. Your son, the first Waitimu, was born with super-admin privileges. When you learned this you volunteered for the task. This card will show you the abandoned building where you cornered him. It'll show you the vines that grew up from the concrete beside the door you walked through, the chipped aqua-green paint on the wall. His pleas. You came into our office immediately after the deed and erased the memory, then erased the memory of erasing the memory. You kept doing this until no trace of the original memory remained."

Skinner tried to breathe.

"And this one." Bickle held up another card. "This is the sequel. The latest one. The one where you murder the rest of your family."

"It was newmans."

Bickle shook his head. "Newmans rescued the boy when you went psychotic. You think you're going to the Met to save the boy but that's not in your programming. You're going there to kill him."

And Skinner knew it was true. He walked to the window.

"You've done what you were designed to do, Al."

"Who designed me?"

"Guy by the name of Nick Fedderly."

"I am so confused."

"Like I said, A+B=C is not the way to go here."

"Release me."

"That's what these weapons are for."

"I understand. Before I go. The man in the desert. The one with the refrigerator. Who is he?"

"Some call him the Last Dude."

"What is he doing out there?"

"He's running everything."

"What?"

"You mean you haven't figured that out?" asked Bickle. "The Last Dude is Mr. Kirkpatrick."

Q&A WITH LUKE PIPER, PART 9

Star never showed. I slept in her bed, ate whatever was canned in the pantry, and did my best to clean the place up. The ground around the house was still muddy, the roof covered in moss. The old, uncompleted frame of the house had started to crumble. I chopped wood. I kept waiting for her to appear but she never did. I was used to keeping to myself and I'd forgotten how much I loved the woods. But what kept me there was the shed. Every morning I made myself coffee and breakfast, then walked to the shed where I'd make a fire in the potbelly stove and study Nick's dad's plans. I grew to love the chemical-sweet smell of blueprint paper. I came to see that this wasn't just a collection of random blueprints. His plan was to transform the island in phases. Chop down hills, fill in gullies, reshape Bainbridge's irregular coastline into smooth, tapered Manhattan. Once the island was regraded, he'd build from the underground up. Start with subways, sewer, natural gas, communications. Lay down streets, foundations of buildings. Then, somehow, re-create every building in the city. It was an insane plan any rational person would have considered pure science fiction. But the care he'd put into these blueprints made me wonder if they were the product of a true believer.

I lived, ate, slept, chopped wood, and thought constantly about those blueprints. Then one day, I was clearing moss off shingles and it occurred to me that Nick's dad would've had to print them somewhere. There must have been some kind of machine that produced them. I dug around in the shed and found a banker's box with old pay stubs, with the name of Marc's employer on them. Kern, Nagamitsu, & Nichols Civil Engineering and Land Surveying.

I should say that I had done my best to avoid anyone I knew on Bainbridge and keep to myself. When I needed groceries, I rode an old ten-speed across the bridge to Poulsbo and filled up my backpack. I was sporting a pretty rangy beard again and went unrecognized whenever I had to go into town. People looking at you, instantly figuring out your place on the totem pole—I didn't want anything to do with that. Maybe some of Star's antisocial behavior was coming out of me. But I recognized that I had to get myself respectable if I wanted to launch another investigation and get people to divulge information. I shaved, and as the whiskers fell away I saw the old high school football star, the dot-com drone, older, heavier, the skin around my eyes sagging and wrinkled from years of pained expressions. I had been wrong to think that anyone would remember that kid and bother to formulate an opinion about his grown-up self. I was a complete nobody now.

The office was in a building next to a chiropractor and a day care. A little place with a lobby, a room for drafting, and a room downstairs in back where they kept all the surveying equipment. I just walked in and asked to speak to one of the civil engineers. The receptionist called up Don Nagamitsu, a trim guy with a gray beard and a denim shirt tucked into his Levi's. I told him I was living on the Fedderly property and had some questions about Marc. We went around the corner to a bakery and Don insisted on buying me coffee. He asked me what I wanted to know. I told him about the blueprints. He sort of laughed and looked out the window.

He told me a story. He said, "We were having a company party in I'd say '79, '80. Business was good and Dave Kern, our chief, had just had a hot tub installed on his deck overlooking Seattle. Twelve or so of us, getting drunk, shooting firecrackers off the deck, living it up. So I'm there in the hot tub on my fourth glass of wine. Marc across from me, Star next to him, my wife Sandy beside me. And Marc says, 'You want to hear something really interesting? Bainbridge and Manhattan are roughly the same size. And you know what's funny? Before Seattle was Seattle it was called New York Alki. It's an Indian word that means "by and by." In other words, sooner or later this place is going to be as big as New York City. I say we regrade the place and build ourselves a Big Apple.' And you have to understand something about draftsmen. These guys, at least then, were the longhairs. You had your civil engineers like me, guys in blazers and ties, and you had your surveyors—old farts with crew cuts and rain gear coated in mud. The draftsmen were somewhere in between, each and every one of them a character. Whenever someone pulled an office prank, the draftsmen were the prime suspects. I knew a lot of them smoked dope at home but if you were to start instituting drug tests, well, then, no drainage systems or parking lots would ever get built. As long as they kept doing their jobs, I didn't care what they did in their recreational time. And I liked Marc a heck of a lot. He showed up early, got his work done fast, was always at my desk asking for more. In fact, Sandy and I had invited him and Star and their kid over to our house for dinner a couple times. Good people. I would have forgotten that comment, with me being drunk and it being just one of those things the draftsmen always said. But one night my wife and I went out to dinner or to a Mariners game or something, and I'd forgotten something at the office. Friday night, about eleven o'clock and I walk in and there's Marc, working at his drafting table, drinking coffee. Those days, nobody worked long hours. Everyone was out of there by five on the dot. My first thought was that he'd messed up something real bad and was busting tail to fix it. When I asked him what the deal was he sort of shrugged sheepishly, stepped away from the table, and told me to take a look.

"He said it was a little side project of his and he apologized for using company paper and pens. I waved him off. Because what I was looking at looked more like art than any sort of drafting I'd ever seen. He had all the sewer and communications worked out, all the tunnels and streets. I didn't know whether I should get mad or what. It seemed like a weird thing to do but he was on his own time and he was my best draftsman, so I gave him the benefit of the doubt. And now you've got the blueprints."

I asked him how Marc had died.

Don said, "He fell, working on that new house of his. There's a right way to fall and a wrong way. I guess Marc fell the wrong way."

We were quiet again, then Don asked me if I'd bought the Fedderly property. I told him no, I was just staying there a while. He said he felt bad for Star and how he hoped "she's finally getting the help she needs." I took this to mean that she had been institutionalized somewhere, and I got this deadly pang of remorse. Here I was trying to dig up the scoop on Marc's blueprints but I hadn't stopped to figure out where Star was. I was a real shit. Don must've seen me looking upset because he asked what was wrong. I told him I'd been close to Star and Nick when I was younger and was sad to hear that things had gone so badly for her.

Don asked me my name again. I told him and he mumbled over my last name a bit then sort of went white. Real abruptly he looked at his watch and said he had to make it back to the office for a meeting or something. He couldn't have gotten out of there any faster. I was still thinking about Star, otherwise I would have been more suspicious about his sudden departure. That day I went to the library and got online and started compiling a list of mental hospitals in the area.

Did you find her?

Of course not. And having no claim to kinship I didn't have much ground to stand on when I asked these places if she was in residence. It was like searching for the Kirkpatrick Academy all over again. I knew I didn't have much time. I took the ferry into Seattle, I don't remember what for, but I do remember looking at people on the streets and thinking how sad it was that they weren't aware everything was about to end. Still, I envied their ignorance. I wished I'd ended up the guy Nick had told me to be years before, the guy with the career and the wife and the children. It was the children I felt most sad about. I passed a group of them out on a day-care field trip, these toddlers strapped into a big wagon thing, and I had to duck into an alley to cry. I'm sure I looked insane. I was sitting on a bank balance of about three million dollars but I was filthy, a guy who talked to himself in the street. During this time I thought about killing myself a lot, but it never moved from an abstraction into a plan. Because I knew I was meant to be a witness. I woke up in the woods and didn't know how I'd gotten there. I walked long enough to reach a road and found my way back to Star's house. I crawled into bed and wept, terrified of what was to come.

How long were you in this condition?

It must have been a month.

And then what, you snapped out of it?

Then a little reality intruded, I guess. I was in the shed one morning when a Suburban rolled up. It was Don Nagamitsu. He asked if I had a minute to talk. When we sat down in the living room he sighed and rubbed his forehead and said, "I'll just come out with it. I'm responsible for the death of your family." He'd been the engineer who'd done the plans for the lot my family home had sat on. He'd had concerns that the lot was too close to an unstable embankment but he'd been under pressure from the developer. He explained it to me in technical terms but essentially he looked the other way when he should have said something about the location of our house. He started crying. According to him, the investigation after the mud slide had been a joke. Agencies sort of waved the whole thing along. He felt at fault for not saying something. He pulled a piece of paper from his jacket pocket with the name and phone number of his lawyer on it and said I'd probably want to get in touch with the guy. We were quiet in that room. Then I slowly tore the paper in half. I decided to forgive him. He looked at me as if he was unable to comprehend the moment, like he'd been prepared for this encounter to go another way.

Just like that you forgave the guy responsible for your parents and sister getting swept into the sound?

Yeah. And after he left I slept a deep, uninterrupted sleep. A nap that stretched into the night. And in the deepness of that night I was back at the encampment where Nick had shot me. It was dawn and an ancient man encrusted with dirt stood beside me. We faced the vast plain below the mesa. The man pointed toward the horizon and as the sun rose I began to make it out, a vast message, in capital letters made of piles of stones. It was a sentence, the letters as long as buildings, laid flat on the desert floor as if intended to be read from space. It was easily ten miles long. And I understood that this was the reason for the encampment, that this message to the heavens was the work of the last man alive.

What did it say?

"The world was full of precious garbage."

I see.

That's when I woke up and found Nick sitting on the couch, reading a celebrity tabloid magazine. My first thought was that he looked *healthy*. Clean-shaven, hair cut short, wearing a blazer and jeans. He looked at me and it was the creepiest, most compelling thing. He was older but his expression was the same as when we used to run around the woods together re-creating scenes from *Star Wars*. He put down his magazine and said, "We have about twenty-four hours until it all goes down. We have a boat. It's waiting for us on the north end of the island. It'll take us to a ship. That ship will take us to an island where the artists and scientists are."

"You shot me," I said.

"You fucked my mom," he said.

"That's not a good enough reason to shoot me," I said.

"I shot you for other reasons."

I must have looked incredulous.

"It wasn't a bullet I shot into you," he went on. "Well, yeah, it was a bullet, too. But it was also a delivery system."

I had no idea how to respond to this crazy bullshit. Nick pulled out an iPhone and tapped the screen a while. He said, "The Bionet concept you and Wyatt came up with? It's already in development. Is it cold in here or is it just me?" He tapped something on the screen and a frigid blast ripped through me like I'd just stepped into a walk-in freezer. Then he said, "Or maybe it's too hot, what do you think?" and suddenly I was sweating, burning up.

I asked him what he was doing and he said, "I'm giving you a hard-on. Check it out." Sure enough, as he tapped in another code, my cock got painfully stiff, one of those erections that totally hurts rubbing against the inside of your jeans. I thought my skin was going to split open. I demanded that he tell me what was going on.

"You tell me," he said. "You're the one who came up with the proposal. The Bionet is a nanotech-enabled system that allows users to monitor, dispense antigens, and remotely control the vital functions of the human body. Just like you said. We've got big plans for this thing, Luke. Think about it—once you've mastered the erection, you pretty much own the biomedical industry."

I told him he'd betrayed Mr. Kirkpatrick.

"We came to a new understanding with Mr. Kirkpatrick. He's waiting for us on the island," he said. "And so is my mother."

I told him to give me a fucking break. This was some kind of hoax. A bogus button that starts the end of the world. A boat. An island with scientists on it.

Nick said, "I'm not asking you to believe me right now. I'm asking you to come with me and discover what it is you truly believe." I must have laughed at him. He said, "Think about how long you've wanted to be a part of this. Think about how you've been shut out of the conversation. We're offering you a way in. We're offering to show you all the cards. Now you can be part of the small group of people leading humanity to redemption."

I asked him how. He said, "Say we figure out how to lower the global temperature and find a way to safely break down all the plastic we've dumped, all the toxins we've unleashed. Maybe we find a way to bring population growth down to a sustainable level and resurrect species we've killed off. Wouldn't that be wonderful? Wouldn't that be just peachy? And if that's the case, our little group, we become nothing but happy fools. That's Plan A for humanity. We're launching Plan B. We're the ones who love life so much that we have to pass it on. What is to come is a beautiful age, a heroic age."

But I couldn't go. "My family died here," I said. "They didn't know they were about to die. I don't have that luxury. I need to be here to take care of the people who don't live on that island with the scientists and artists. The impending dystopia you talk about only looks like dystopia to those of us who've lived surrounded by privilege. To everybody else it's called history. I need to be here for those people. They're my people. I belong to them."

And then he left?

Yes.

And now you're here.

Are we finished? Is it time?

Yes. Are you ready to see what the real world looks like now?

Yes. Show me.

Acknowledgments

I would like to thank the following people and organizations for their encouragement and support. My family is tremendously loving and giving. Thank you Jen, Miles, Scarlett, Em, Mom, Dad, David, and Amy. My agent PJ Mark somehow manages to be both an incredibly generous and giving human being and a relentless bastard. Amy Hundley, my editor, is wise and exacting, a dream. Matthew Simmons, Fleetwood Robbins, and Suzanne Stockman read an early draft and provided invaluable feedback. Rick Moody, Aimee Bender, Rebecca Brown, and Stephen Elliott have been terrific friends and inspirations. Dave Cornelius, my great mentor, led me to literature. Nate Manny, whom I knew before he was a rock star, did a bangup job on the Web work and marketing stuff. Greg Comer provided amazing architectural renderings of many of the settings. Corey Jurcak and Jeff Johnson tolerantly answered my questions about speculative civil engineering, as did my father. Dr. Roger Freedman, friend and gentleman astrophysicist, provided valuable insights about space colonization. I thank the wry and talented Lori Piskur Macklin for the Spanish translations. Thanks to Tom Nissley and Brad Parsons for their wise counsel over the years. I raise a glass (or three) to Bob Braile. Richard Hugo House and Goddard College's Master of Fine Arts in Creative Writing program saved me from a slow death in a series of cubicles. I would especially like to thank Brian McGuigan, Alix Wilber, and Sue Joerger at Hugo House for the gift of their kindness, and Paul Selig at Goddard for giving me a chance. Thanks, finally, to the Washington State Employment Security Department for the four generous writing grants.